WILL DESTROY
THE GALAXY
FOR CASH

PRAISE FOR
YAHTZEE CROSHAW

"Hilariously insightful."
—Slashdot

"Yahtzee consistently makes me laugh, and even though I dig
computer and electronic games, he has cross-genre appeal to anyone
who enjoys a sharp wit, unique sense of humor and plenty of
originality—not purely gaming fans."
—The Future Buzz

"*Mogworld* is a triumph of storytelling and humor that just so
happens to be perfectly keyed in to the wild world of video games.
I cannot stress enough, however, that it can also be enjoyed by those
who have never logged in or picked up a controller in their life."
—Joystick Division

WILL DESTROY THE GALAXY FOR CASH

YAHTZEE CROSHAW

Dark Horse Books

Cover design by David Nestelle

Published by Dark Horse Books
A division of Dark Horse Comics LLC
10956 SE Main Street
Milwaukie, OR 97222
DarkHorse.com

First edition: November 2020

Library of Congress Cataloging-in-Publication Data

Names: Croshaw, Yahtzee, author.
Title: Will destroy the galaxy for cash / Yahtzee Croshaw.
Description: First edition. | Milwaukie, OR : Dark Horse Books, 2020. |
    Summary: "With the age of heroic star pilots and galactic villains
    completely killed by quantum teleportation, the ex-star pilot currently
    named Dashford Pierce is struggling to find his identity in a changing
    universe. Then, a face from his past returns and makes him an offer he
    can't refuse: take part in just one small, slightly illegal, heist, and
    not only will he have the means to start the new life he craves, but
    also save his childhood hero from certain death"-- Provided by
    publisher.
Identifiers: LCCN 2020027283 | ISBN 9781506715117 (trade paperback) | ISBN
    9781506721569 (epub)
Subjects: GSAFD: Science fiction. | Humorous fiction.
Classification: LCC PR9619.4.C735 W55 2020 | DDC 823/.92--dc23
LC record available at https://lccn.loc.gov/2020027283

Printed in the United States of America

10 9 8 7 6 5 4 3 2 1

CHAPTER I

IT WAS RAINING in Ritsuko City. Which is no small feat inside a gigantic plexiglass dome on the surface of Earth's moon.

The council had set off the citywide fire suppression system. They did this every now and again as a service to the hydroponic roof gardens. Also, if any star pilots were opting to sleep rough, it would wash them into the gutters, from which they could be gathered en masse.

I watched the water drool down the reception-room window and challenged myself to read the backward text aloud. "Oniris Venture Company," it began, but that much I already knew. "Personnel wanted for deep space research, colonization, and . . . recog . . . reconnaissance! Expeditions."

"Impressive," said Loretta, the Oniris representative who had just reentered reception. "We're looking for a slightly broader skill range, of course."

I leapt to my feet and casually gathered my hands behind my back. Loretta was only slightly younger than me and not unattractive at first glance, but I wondered how much of her would spill out of that excessively tight blue uniform the moment it was loosened. And the jaunty angle of her pillbox hat didn't go well with her sarcastic expression.

"If you'll follow me," she said in a bored monotone, gesturing halfheartedly behind her to the interview room. "We can discuss your application."

"Yes, ma'am." I followed her into the small office. There was a simple desk set up with a computer terminal and two chairs, and a single window with a scenic view of some dustbins and a brick wall, but it was the poster behind Loretta's chair that caught all my attention. A detailed schematic for an Oniris

Galileo-class galactic explorer, fully diagrammed and labeled. It might as well have been wearing lingerie and making a kissy face.

"So," Loretta said while briskly pecking at the keyboard a few times as if she were brushing something nasty off it. "Oniris Venture is conducting a series of long-term deep space expeditions to expand the edges of the known galaxy and stake a claim on any resources or discoveries that are made. We are constructing Galileo-class explorers at a rate of one per year for the next twenty years, each requiring a full complement of bridge and security officers, as well as science and engineering staff, to blaze the trail of courageous pioneers." She paused to stifle a little yawn. "And you would like to be added to the waiting list, Mr. . . ."

"Pierce. Dashford Pierce. Yes, I most definitely would."

Her eyes flicked to the screen and her eyelids began to droop as she droned the illuminated text aloud. "Do you understand that a position as an Oniris crew member will involve a long-term posting of a minimum of four years with Quantunnel access available only for emergencies, and as such you will be away from home and your loved ones for that period?"

Before answering, I stared out the rain-spattered window at one of the many alleyways of my home city. There was a half-eaten sushi sandwich in the gutter, spilling out of its cardboard container. A small patchy dog was carefully pooing on it.

"I think I could live with that," I said, turning back to Loretta.

"I had a feeling you could." She sighed.

I crossed my legs to stop them from jiggling, but it wasn't enough. My whole body was fizzing with excitement. I was still surprised that I hadn't thought of this sooner. No more money worries, no more tourists, no more adventuring. Just a nice long, quiet existence on the edge of known space, and all I had to do in return was move as far away as possible from everyone I'd ever known, as well as all the attached grudges and favors. Trac, that's a tough one. How many nanoseconds do I get to think about it?

"And how would you describe your personal skill set, Mr. Pierce?" Loretta propped her chin up on one hand.

"I'm fully qualified to fly any kind of spacegoing vessel."

"Of course you are." She rolled her eyes.

I coughed, reaching for the inside pocket of my flight jacket. "I don't have my diploma anymore, but I've got the electronic records from my old flight school . . ."

"Don't bother, I believe you," she said, typing something.

I pouted in disappointment. I'd spent the last four hours editing my digital diploma to convincingly display my new name, and I'd been rather hoping for some feedback. "That easy?"

She paused in her typing, fingers splayed out like spiders poised to strike, and her gaze did a complete circuit of the room before landing on me again. "You're a star pilot, aren't you?"

"No," I said immediately.

Her eyebrow shot up like the birth rate nine months after a prolonged power outage. "You're qualified to fly ships. You're wearing a flight jacket that looks like a patchwork quilt despite being nowhere near a spaceport. But you're telling me you're not a star pilot."

She was staring right at the bright-orange diamond-shaped patch on my breast pocket. The one that read "Star Pilots Do It with Only 24 Hours to Save the Galaxy" in flamboyant letters. I awkwardly folded my arms to cover it. "All right, I *was* a star pilot. But I'm between jobs right now, and I'm looking for a career change."

"I'm sure. The next step is to establish what onboard roles you are qualified for and place them in order of your preference. Can I take a wild stab in the dark and say your first choice would be on the bridge crew?"

"Uh, yep," I said, clasping my hands and bobbing in my chair. "Helm, navigation, I can fly anything with at least one wing."

"And on that note, your second choice?"

"Well, I flew my own ship solo for over a decade, and I had to do most of my own maintenance, so—"

"Second choice, engineering," droned Loretta, typing. It was at this point that I noticed that all the keys she was pressing had extremely weathered letters. "And I suppose next you're going to tell me that you're as good with your fists as you are with a wrench?"

My nagging sense of foreboding continued to grow, as those were the very words I had been preparing. "Y—"

"Third choice, security team." She spanked the Enter key several times decisively. "You will be added to the waiting list and we will be in touch when a suitable placement becomes available thank you very much goodbye." She had switched off her monitor, climbed out of her chair, and was holding the door open before she had reached the end of her sentence.

I didn't move from my seat. "So . . . how long do you think I'll have to wait?"

She checked her watch and tutted. "Mr. Pierce, I've had a long day and I just went off shift. Can I be honest with you?"

I nodded, confused.

She folded her arms primly, half rotated her chair, and angled her head toward the poster behind her. "How many individual bridge crew members would you say the Galileo class requires to function?"

"Including subs?"

"Oh, most definitely including sublieutenants."

I didn't even need to look at the poster. "Six."

"The current waiting list for the bridge crew is ninety-eight names long." She let that sink in for a moment. "We've had to staple two more pieces of paper to it."

"Oh." I started feeling rather hot and embarrassed in my pilot's cap. "What about engi—"

"There are twelve berths on the engineering team. Six teams of two. And before you ask, the security division has eight berths. Both also have a waiting list that's ninety-eight names long. The same ninety-eight names. All of them with bridge crew as first choice, engineering second, security third. Every single one."

I felt something inside me deflate, noisily buzzing around like an unsecured balloon before settling into my metaphorical breakfast cereal with a plop. "I'm . . . not the first st—er, former star pilot to have thought of this, am I?"

"No, as I think we've established, you're the ninety-ninth."

"Okay, well, six plus twelve plus eight, that's twenty-six to a ship, ninety-eight names, that'll fill three ships, so I'll just have to wait—"

"More like six ships," interrupted Loretta. "The company introduced a policy restricting star pilot representation to fifty percent per team. Apparently there have been recurring issues with bad language, crews voting to interfere with planetary wars and rescue captured alien princesses, that kind of thing. Would you like to offer me a bribe now?"

"Wasn't planning to."

Her eyebrow, which had only just gotten back down to horizontal, suddenly spiked back up. "This is usually when a star pilot would offer me a bribe. We've started calling it the 'bargaining stage.'"

"My cash flow isn't the healthiest right now," I admitted. In fact, at the time that I had first noticed the sign outside the Oniris office, I had been on my way back from the bank, where I had parted with a depressingly large sum to resolve a legal dispute. I'd been determined not to let it get me down, though. After all, it's not like it had been my money.

My shoulders drooped. Loretta must have thought I was dejected, because something approaching a sigh of pity escaped from her tight uniform. She settled back into the chair opposite. "Well, it's not like it would have helped," she said, conversationally. "None of our ships are going anywhere until we fill the science and medical teams. Twelve berths per crew, and a waiting list of four."

I glanced up. My great scheme had crashed on an unknown moon and attracted a horde of hostile locals, but it sounded like there was beer in the cargo hold. Maybe there was still a chance of turning a hopeless situation into a keg party. "You need scientists?"

"One head researcher, one chief medical officer, and enough associates and technicians to cover all the major sciences. My theory is that it's a pretty good time to be a scientist right now, quantum tunneling has opened up so many avenues of research . . ."

"Yeah, it's great, that quantum tunneling, isn't it," I muttered.

"So it's harder to find scientists in the right kind of mood to want to disappear from civilization for years. We've only got four names on the waiting list because some postgraduates at the university took it as punishment for releasing a piglet into the air filtration system."

"All right," I said, placing my hands flat and parallel on the desktop. "I've got a proposal for you."

She folded her arms, tightening up again. "And finally we reach the bargaining stage." But she didn't roll her eyes this time, just maintained expectant eye contact, which I took as encouragement.

"Could you bump me up to the shortlist for the next ship? If you wanted to?"

"Come on, Mr. Pierce. Why would I do that?"

"Because you owed me a favor. Could you do it?"

She gave a thoughtful little puff. "The company only wants to know that our waiting lists are full," she said. "They don't care if a few names have been swapped around. That's technically a yes. But why would I owe you a favor?"

"Because I'm going to get you a bunch of scientists for your next crew."

The eyebrow came up again with such violence that I thought it would knock the hat off her head. "I have to admit, this is a new one. You could do that?"

"Would it get me on that ship?"

"Mr. Pierce, if you really could do as you say, I could make you the captain."

I considered the idea for a moment, and just as quickly dismissed it with a wince. "Helm will be fine."

She leaned forward. "So, how soon can you get ahold of them?"

I'd been tapping my chin thoughtfully, staring out the window again. By now the little dog had finished pooing on the sushi sandwich but had evidently concluded that this needn't have affected its edibility. "Hm?"

"Your scientists. Where are they now?"

"Oh, I don't have any yet."

She frowned. "So how do you plan to get them?"

"I don't have a plan. But now I have a goal. The plan I just have to make up as I go along."

Loretta sighed and leaned back, rolling her eyes so hard I thought she might detach her retinas. "Of course. Why did I even get my hopes up? Imagine a star pilot being capable of foresight."

CHAPTER 2

I STALKED THE streets of Ritsuko like a ghost, listening to the rain drumming musically off my pilot's cap, letting my mind wander in time with my legs. There was a resting place for my troubled soul on the far end of an Oniris Venture Company deep space recon operation, and the only thing between me and it was the absence of some scientists.

I went over everything I knew about scientists from my years of experience as a galactic hero. I knew that they were socially awkward and had bad hair. And that they had an alarming tendency to try to take over the universe with doomsday machines. If not, then they would probably get kidnapped by someone who *did* want to take over the universe with a doomsday machine, in which case they could usually be relied upon to have a distressed daughter who might be up for postadventure hookups.

But none of the names that came to mind, villains and hot-daughter havers alike, were unattached, trustworthy, or sane enough for a mundane deep space recon job. Moot point, anyway. They'd all scattered to the four winds after the Golden Age of star piloting ended—when Quantunneling came along, making it possible to teleport across the galaxy instantly, removing all the danger and adventure from space travel in a stroke.

I awoke from my reverie when I felt the glow of familiar fluorescent lighting, and realized I had absent-mindedly wandered as far as the spaceport in Ritsuko's Arse. And that didn't make any sense, because it was only star pilots who hung around the spaceport all the time hoping to be hired by tourists. I was no longer a star pilot, and it would be nice if my plying subconscious could get onboard with this development.

I turned away, and saw another familiar light. It was the lit-up sign across the street that read KEN'S CAF, either because of a misspelling or because the last *E* kept winking out. Beneath that, there was a familiar awning with a transparent plastic tent draped over it in a slightly halfhearted effort to turn an outdoor dining area into an indoor one.

Of course. I must have unconsciously drifted here to get some inexpensive dinner at one of my favorite . . . well, most frequently attended, restaurants, which happened to be near the spaceport. That made perfect sense.

I parted the flap and headed straight to the counter, shaking the excess rain from my flight jacket. Most of the benches were packed, probably from the wet driving people in; some of them weren't even star pilots. They were easy to spot, the nonpilots, because they weren't hunched over their bowls like dogs trying to get their dinners scoffed down before a bigger dog came over.

Ken himself had risen to the occasion by putting on one of his cleaner singlets. He gave a little jolt of surprise at my presence, then a nod of acknowledgment, as he grabbed one of the bowls by his side and began filling it with rice and a lumpy brown substance that only the menu could attest was katsu curry.

"Try the salad tonight," said a familiar voice to my left. "I saw him get the lettuce out of a fresh bin bag."

I turned to see my old friend Flat-Earth Frobisher, waiting to pay for two bowls of curry on a tray. He was the same as always: shirtsleeves, trousers stained with fabric conditioner, paunchy figure, thinning hair, perpetual faint smile. It was a look that suited him so well, I could have sworn his waist had ballooned out like that the instant he first unstrapped his flight jacket.

Hardly surprising to find him here, two doors down from his launderette, but it was good to see him all the same. For one thing, he was smart: he'd gotten out of star piloting before most of the rest of us did, *and* he knew how to get grease stains out of silvery jumpsuits. That made him an ideal sounding board for my problem.

"Frobisher," I said in cheery greeting. "You got time to talk?"

"Sure. Come join our table." He eyeballed the bowl of slop that Ken was preparing. "Can I get this for you?"

"Oh, you don't have to . . ."

"It's fine, really. Least I can do."

"All right then, yes," I said quickly, having made the one refusal demanded by basic politeness.

He added my bowl to his tray, waved the back of his hand under Ken's chip scanner until it gave a watery electronic sigh to indicate a confirmed payment, then started leading me through the narrow rows between diners. "Where've you been, anyway?" he asked over his shoulder. "Thought you might've finally gone to Salvation."

I grimaced as the idea tossed around my head like a sourball in my mouth. "That's the place where star pilots go. I'm trying to break off from the whole star pilot thing."

"So now you hang around just outside the spaceport instead of inside it. Baby steps, is it?"

"I told you, I—"

I stopped dead as we passed into the deepest corner of the dining area, and my hands balled into fists. Not out of anticipation for dinner, but because of who I had just spotted seated at an otherwise empty table.

It was Electra Blue. Chief assassin of the Kraken Sector Triad.

"You!" I hissed, dropping into a quick-draw stance and batting my jacket aside to bring my blaster holster into reach.

Electra's eyes narrowed in recognition. She hadn't changed at all: the cool blue skin that glittered faintly in the dim fluorescent light, the snow white hair that clung tightly to her head, the slender limbs and angular features that seemed like they must have been carved from driftwood. "Zo, we meet again."

We stood frozen in a tense, silent standoff for a handful of seconds that seemed to stretch on and on like the moment between a torpedo's launch and its detonation, before Frobisher broke the spell by dropping the tray of bowls onto her table with a *clonk*. "Oh, give it a rest, you two," he said, without malice. "It was only funny the first few times."

Electra smirked as I took a seat opposite her. "Oh, it iz good to zee you again, though." The skin around her eyes crinkled in that papery way idiosyncratic of Kraken Sector humanoids. "Why haven't you been around lately?"

"Trying to break off from the whole star pilot thing, apparently," said Frobisher, passing out the bowls.

Frobisher wasn't the only former star pilot I knew who'd ended up marrying his archnemesis. After everyone stopped adventuring, it didn't take long for the nemeses to start pining for each other. It turned out that there are a lot of deep, soulful things you can only find out about a person by trying to kill them for years on end.

I'd messed around with Electra and her followers a few times, most seriously on the occasion they were hired to assassinate an ambassador I was transporting, but that was about as far as we ever got. We'd never reached the point of actively plotting revenge against each other—or "third base," as it was sometimes known—but there was still a warm regard between us.

"Oniriz Venture? Zeriouzly?" she said, after we'd been huddled around the little booth, tucking into reheated curry, and I had filled the Frobishers in on my plans. "Juzt to get away from ztar piloting?"

"What's so great about star piloting? You spend half your life star piloting, what do you get out of it? Nothing but unmarketable skills, and then Jacques McKeown rips your story off for one of his plying books."

"Is he still doing that?" asked Frobisher, holding his plastic fork aloft. "I thought that was why everyone was getting little secret gifts of money a while back. I heard he grew a conscience and decided to share the wealth."

"I heard he waz hunted down and killed," Electra said with obvious relish. "I heard the onez that did it zplit up the money over the ruinz of hiz corpze."

"Well, guess we'll never know," I said, hopefully not with too much obvious haste. "The point is, I'm done with it. I'm moving on."

"Doesn't mean you have to completely cut yourself off from everything to do with it." Frobisher gave a little smirk at his own thoughts. "This has always been your problem, hasn't it? You can't do anything in moderation."

I glanced from him to his wife uncertainly. "I just told you I've quit star piloting."

"Yeah, but most people would just quit. You can't even do moderation in moderation. Most people wouldn't move to the edge of the universe and change their identity. Most people aren't that dramatic." He made to put his fork to his mouth, but hesitated. "What's your new name, again? Captain Handsome?"

"Dashford Pierce," I muttered, accurately predicting Electra's reaction.

"Ha!" she barked with a spray of rice before covering her mouth apologetically. "That'z even better."

"Maybe we don't all trust ourselves not to give in to temptation." I lowered my gaze.

"You know what I think," said Electra, rocking playfully. "I think you need a zpecial zomeone." She fondly squeezed Frobisher's knife hand, and he gave me a confirmatory nod.

"Yes, well, we didn't all do the archnemesis thing."

"Mm, I remember." Electra pouted. "Could never commit for very long, could you. Alwayz holding out for zomething more interezting. If you'd taken the time to really get to know zomeone, maybe you wouldn't be zo unfocuzed now."

"There must have been one," wheedled Frobisher, raising a cheeky eyebrow. "There must have been one villain you'd always thwart first if there were a bunch of them needed thwarting."

I leaned away, letting the air blast out of my lungs as my back hit the bench. This wasn't a conversation I was at all in the mood for. "I dunno. I was never looking for anything serious."

"What about Mimi the Red?" Frobisher asked. "She was going on about you for days after the Caurus 9 job."

"Ugh, that little flirt. A new fazcination every other week."

"There was Terrorgorn," I said thoughtfully, eyeballing the ceiling. "I'd always notice when Terrorgorn was doing something."

"Everybody did," murmured Electra.

"Yeah, that's not really the kind of thing we're talking about," said Frobisher. "I don't picture Terrorgorn sitting with his feet up in quiet retirement. He's probably in a dungeon somewhere trying to chew his way out through the floor."

"With any luck," added Electra.

"I suppose there was Malcolm Sturb. I chased the Malmind off a few worlds."

Electra perked up. "Oh yez, dear Malcolm. Shame all thoze arrezt warrantz are keeping him out in the Black. What'z he up to now?"

I swallowed my mouthful of rice. "Last I knew, he was working with Salvation Station. Putting on shows for tourists."

"Oh, poor boy," said Electra, referring to the progenitor of the galactic cybernetic hive mind that once scourged a thousand worlds. "We uzed to catch up every now and again zo he could show me hiz new toyz, and hiz enthuziazm waz zo infectiouz . . ."

Quite a lot of things about the Malmind were infectious, but I'd never considered enthusiasm to be one of them. "So what were we talking about, again? You're suggesting I call up Malcolm Sturb and invite him out to a dinner dance?"

I noticed that they had both become distracted by something behind me, and that the hubbub of conversation in the entire restaurant had died down to a low conspiratorial rumble.

A man was moving through the diners, creating a bubble of silence around him everywhere he went. He was quite tall and wide in the paunch, and like many figures of authority in Ritsuko, he had a Japanese set to his features, with neatly trimmed black hair and a mustache as smooth and rectangular as a blackboard duster. It was someone I'd met before. The last time, he had been releasing me from a pair of handcuffs and advising me to stay out of trouble.

Inspector Honda of the Ritsuko City Police Department. I immediately took an even closer interest in my food, but he wasn't coming toward me. He was slowly and deliberately walking through the dining area like a school-exam officiant, and when he finally stopped, it was in a seemingly random position in more or less the middle of the room.

"Good, this seems private enough," he loudly announced, tottering sleep-ily. He addressed a uniformed officer who had just appeared behind him. "Now, give me that interesting report you gave me, again."

"Erm . . ." The officer looked at his tablet after a quick nervous glance around the restaurant. "It's about Salvation Station . . ."

"Salvation Station, that community of star pilots that live out in space and are connected to several less-than-legal acts of piracy!" bellowed Honda, deliberately lingering on every relevant word. "Sorry, that was for me, the old memory occasionally needs prompting. What about them?"

"There's a rumor that they're planning something," said the officer quietly, although he was clearly audible over the dead silence. "Something in this city."

"I think you said something that may involve the Henderson crime orga-nization, oh my goodness, how embarrassing, I of course meant to say family business," said Honda, in a flat, faintly slurred monotone. "Well, officer, just between you and me, if the star pilots are planning to do something silly in this city, then the police would take a pretty dim view of it, wouldn't we?"

"Yes, sir."

"And if anyone should happen to want to do their civic duty and share insider knowledge of such a thing, then our gratitude would manifest in all kinds of ways, wouldn't it, officer?"

"As you say, sir."

Honda made a prolonged sigh and slapped his buttocks. "Well, thank you for indulging me. Occasionally it helps my thought processes to loudly talk out a problem in a room full of star pilots. Let's get back to the station."

Every eyeball in the room stared fixedly at a point slightly to the left of Honda and his lackey as they shuffled awkwardly through the crowds and out of view, until a sudden increase in the volume of the conversation around me indicated that they had finally left the restaurant.

Frobisher leaned forward, still with one eye on the door. "Aren't you pretty close to that lady who runs Salvation now?"

A complicated rainbow of feelings arced across my mind as I mulled over my response. "We've, uh. We've worked together in the past."

Electra grinned impishly. "And do I detect zome feelingz for her?"

"Sure. Feelings of mutual dislike, antipathy, and the occasional night terror at the thought of ever running into her again. Can we change the subject?" I didn't like the knowing looks the Frobishers were giving each other. "I was hoping for some advice tonight."

"Right, this Oniris idea. What do you need advice about?" said Frobisher. Electra snorted tolerantly and pushed away her empty bowl.

"Where would you go if you needed to find scientists? The normal kind, not the ones that build doomsday machines."

Frobisher reeled slightly, heaving the air out of his lungs and staring at the ceiling in thought. "I suppose I'd go to the university."

Ritsuko City's only university was in the west side, roughly on the border between the Japanese and European quarters. I tried to remember what had been going on there on the very, very few occasions I'd had cause to go near it.

"But if you really want my advice," said Frobisher, suddenly serious, "I'd say, before you go hang around there in a sandwich board, hoping to draw in science graduates with no will to live, on top of the hope that Oniris are true to their word and actually will help you abandon everything and everyone you've ever known . . ." He took a deep breath. "Maybe instead you could have a good long, hard think and find another way to deal with whatever's making you unhappy."

I bit my lip, and let it slowly uncurl from under my teeth as I thought. "So what would you make the sandwich board out of?" I said.

CHAPTER 3

AS WAS MY habit, I spent the night in the forward luggage compartment of my ship, using the usual pile of unclaimed lost property as bedding. Empty suitcases for a mattress, an old dog carrier for a pillow, and my blanket was a gigantic flower-patterned muumuu that no member of one prior tour group would admit to owning.

Maintaining, and indeed living on, the *Neverdie* was not something I considered incongruous with my intention to stop being a star pilot. After all, I didn't intend to stop being *any* kind of pilot; it was my main skill set. There was always the chance of getting some nice sedate transporting jobs, assuming a highly contagious brain parasite went around at some point making everyone forget how quantum tunneling worked.

Besides, it wasn't like I had many alternatives. The rent on a parking space in the largely unused section of Ritsuko City Spaceport was a tracload cheaper than an apartment. The spaceport even came with manned security at no extra cost, even if they did occasionally mistake you for a tramp on your way back from the bathroom and truncheon you to the floor.

This also meant a free early-morning wake-up call, because there was usually some poor bracket whose parking permit had expired during the night getting turfed out by the security team at bang on six o'clock. I'd grown used to being stirred from sleep by a reassuring dawn chorus of truncheons hitting hull plating and angry swear words.

So when I was gently woken that morning by the shuttle-bay lights coming on for the day and bleeding through from the cockpit, I instantly knew that something was wrong. The spaceport was completely silent but for the distant hum of the Quantunnel section and the highly conspicuous sound of people trying too hard to be quiet.

I rolled over, scattering bags and holdalls, until my ear was pressed against the maintenance plate that led to the open landing-gear compartment. Sure enough, I could hear soft footfalls on the cement just outside. One person? No . . . two. Two people trying to very inconspicuously sneak past my landing leg.

"This is the one, right?" said one of them in a hushed tone.

"Red bay twelve," replied the other. "And keep your voice down. He might hear us through the landing-gear compartment."

Both the voices were male, and the first speaker sounded younger than the second, but that was all I was prepared to say with certainty. They probably weren't station security, because they were trying to go unnoticed. Security always tried to be as obvious as possible, as they had to pay for their own truncheons, and would sooner avoid needless wear and tear if intimidation could do the work.

I kept listening. The footfalls moved away, around toward the airlock entrance and out of earshot. I waited for developments, but all fell silent.

After a few minutes of consideration, I crawled out of the luggage compartment into the cockpit and peered down the central gangway to the airlock door. It remained closed and silent, but it was the kind of tense, expectant silence that two men waiting in ambush might create.

I weighed the possibilities. I was still paid up with the bay rental as far as I knew. Maybe security were coming to throw me out illegally? That might explain why they were being quiet. If word got around that they had tossed me out without cause, the uproar from the wider star pilot community would . . . not faze them in the slightest. No, that probably wasn't it.

As my mind raced, the mental fog of early morning began to clear and a memory of the previous night slammed home. I had been woken by my phone buzzing near my head, signaling the arrival of a new email. Instinctively I had checked it, and a single, devastating subject line had slowly swum into focus like a horde of invading barbarians appearing over a hill:

ATTENTION: JACQUES MCKEOWN

And upon seeing it, I had hurled my phone across the room as if it had transformed into a scorpion. By the time I had sunk back into sleep I had convinced myself that it had been a dream, but now that I was remembering this, I couldn't help noticing that my phone wasn't in its usual place.

I eventually found it at the foot of the "bed," in the pile of cheap stuffed toys that Luny Land put in their skill-tester machines and which parents had a regular tendency to "accidentally" lose in my passenger cabin. I brought up my list of recent emails.

The good news was that the subject line from last night wasn't there. The bad news was that it had been crowded out of view by several new ones.

RE: RE: ATTENTION: JACQUES MCKEOWN
RE: RE: RE: ATTENTION: JACQUES MCKEOWN
hey is this Jacques McKeown's address
HELLO JACK MCKEOWN
love your books
FAO: FAO: FAO: FAO: FAO: JACQUES MCKEOWN
checking to see if this is Jacques McKeowns address . . .
Paging Jacques McKeown
PLEASE LET ME PREVIEW NEXT BOOK. MY GRANDMOTHER HAS CANCER

I lowered the phone to my side and slapped the screen against my thigh. Someone had apparently been spreading around the old rumor that I was Jacques McKeown, renowned recluse and intergalactically famous author of star pilot fiction. This would be awkward, because an astonishing amount of people wanted Jacques McKeown dead. Half of them star pilots whose stories he had ripped off, the other half rabid fans who wanted to stuff and mount his corpse in their living rooms.

So the distinct possibility arose that this was connected to my visitors this morning. Word got around fast in the star pilot community, and since this wasn't the first time I'd been taken for McKeown, there were quite a few members of that community who would be quick to believe it. The men outside could have been assassins, here to strike me dead. And that wasn't even the most pessimistic scenario.

Unfortunately for them, they weren't dealing with some frightened, wide-eyed newcomer to death threats. I lifted the loose plate in the floor of the cockpit and recovered the secret items beneath.

Some years ago now, I had been walking past the security guards' locker room on my way through the spaceport, and had noticed that the door had been carelessly left open. So like a good citizen I had closed it for them. And as compensation for my civic-mindedness, I had taken one of the security uniform shirts that had been lying on a bench just inside the door. It had come in handy enough times since then that it was probably overdue for a wash, but it would pass inspection for now if I stayed downwind.

After I had doffed my flight jacket and put it on, I opened the hatch that had once led to the escape pod, back in a distant nostalgic age when the *Neverdie* could have passed a standard safety check. I lowered myself until I was hanging upside down from the emergency exit tube and could catch a glimpse of the men waiting outside my airlock door.

To my surprise, they were spaceport security guards, both in the standard brown uniform. They were poised either side of the *Neverdie*'s exit door, tensed up and ready to ambush at the slightest sign of movement, but didn't seem to be holding weapons.

So maybe I was being thrown out after all, but the way they were being stealthy still didn't sit right. Maybe some star pilots had paid them to assassinate me? An unlikely explanation, because it incorporated the words *star pilot* and *paid*. Maybe someone had made them an offer, and now they were coming to me to ask if I'd be prepared to make a higher bid.

I lowered myself from the escape tube to the floor of the parking bay, wincing slightly as my shoes clapped against the cement, but my visitors didn't seem to notice. I carefully kept the forward landing leg between me and them.

My first instinct was to sneak all the way out of the spaceport and get on with my day, check out the university, take a long lunch, amuse myself with thoughts of these guys waiting here, half-crouched in anticipation the entire time with leg cramps only getting worse.

But that wouldn't tell me who they were or what they wanted. Which was information I probably needed before I had to come back and confront two potential hostiles with shortened tempers and very painful legs.

I took a wide path around several other parked ships, slipping from cover to cover like a prowling tiger in a forest of landing gear, until I was behind the security men and could pretend that I had come from the spaceport entrance. I straightened my uniform shirt, gave both armpits a quick sniff, and effected a self-righteous air and an officious gait as I stomped forward.

"How's it going here?"

Both of the men immediately jumped a foot in the air, and landed in what they were probably hoping looked like casual poses. The older, more rugged-looking one with silver hair put one hand behind his head and glanced around, puffing out his cheeks. The younger, scrawnier one leaned against the hull of my ship and pretended to take an interest in an oil stain.

"Oh, hello," said the younger one, flamboyantly turning around and pretending to notice me for the first time. "Yes, it's going fine. Perfectly. How are you?"

"I'm fine. Do you need any help with this?"

"No," growled the older guard.

"No, no, I'm sure we can manage it," said the younger. "It's, you know, it's a tough job, but someone's got to do . . . it."

This wasn't getting me any closer to figuring out what "it" was. "Don't let me distract you from . . . it, then." I clasped my hands behind my back like a true official. "Carry on like I'm not here."

The younger guard nervously put his own hands behind his back as he attempted to blandly smile his way through the awkward moment. Shortly, the other was doing the same. All three of us stood surveying each other like that for a while, rocking gently on our heels. It was like being stuck in a dull conversation at a straitjacket party.

"Right, we'll get on with . . . it," said the younger, more verbose guard. His face was turning quite red, while his friend was directing a fixed scowl at me. "Um. Remind me, er . . . Johnson. What specific part of 'it' were we about to do?"

"Inspection," said Johnson, still glaring at me.

"Yes! Inspection. We're inspecting things." He looked the nearest landing leg up and down and rapped his knuckles against it. "That's a landing leg, all right. Metal, I see, which is a sturdy material, and therefore suitable for this purpose." He coughed. "Full marks for this one. Let's see if the other landing legs live up to this standard."

As he turned to look for more things to inspect, I noticed that the younger guard's uniform shirt must have been very ill fitting, as a large percentage of it was scrunched up and tucked into the back of his trousers. And as my attention was drawn in that direction, I noticed that his trousers were black jeans, which the dress code wouldn't usually allow.

"You're not spaceport security," I realized aloud, before I could stop myself.

The younger guard made a desperate scoffing noise and began to babble.

"Of course we're spaceport security! We're wearing the shirts, aren't we, Jefferson? Johnson? Whatever I said your name was?"

Johnson eyeballed his partner with naked contempt, then produced a Taser pistol, with which he promptly shot me.

It wasn't my first time being tased, but it's not the sort of thing you eventually take a liking to once you're used to it. The barb hit me in the gut, instantly penetrating the flimsy shirt fabric, and I felt a sensation like being slapped in the midsection with a metal tea tray. Every muscle in my body made a spirited attempt to cringe hard enough to powderize my bones, and I stood tottering for a few moments before something slammed painfully into my side. Something which, after a moment's reflection, I discovered to be the ground.

"Oh, what the plying hell did you do that for?" hissed the younger guard, clutching his temples.

"He saw through us," replied Johnson, although I was starting to seriously doubt that that was his name. "He would either have tried to stop us or alerted the rest of security. Therefore, the best option was to disable him."

"I could still have talked us out of it! You didn't have to tase him!"

"You tried to talk us out of it, and he saw through us anyway. There was no logical reason to assume that continuing to talk would have started to work. The only logical solution—"

"Look, will you stop with your logic trac? It's not helping."

"Maybe if you kept a level head, I wouldn't always have to take charge."

"Don't you do that. Don't you start twisting this around to somehow make it my fault, you bracket. You always do this."

Meanwhile, from my position on the floor in a little private ball of pain and disorientation, my addled mind was trying to connect a few important facts. The phony guard's use of Pilot Math had brought on a realization, and because being tased made it harder for me to learn from my recent mistakes, I voiced it aloud. "You're star pilots?"

The two men offered me matching affronted looks, then returned their attentions to each other. "And now he's figured that out. What does logic tell us to do now, Mr. Roboto?"

"It's telling me he might not have figured that out if you hadn't just confirmed it," said the older pilot, with infuriating condescension. "We need to take him with us."

"What? Why?"

"Scenario one: we leave him, he alerts the rest of security, they know we were here. Scenario two: we kill him, the other guards find the body, they check the security tapes and know we were here. Logically . . ."

"Oh, for plying out loud, fine. Let's go."

I slowly craned my neck to plaintively look my older tormentor in the eye. He met my gaze, displayed the merest flicker of sympathy, then shot me with the Taser again.

CHAPTER 4

I DRIFTED IN and out of consciousness like a shy wallflower passing in and out of their secret crush's personal space. I had a strange dream about lying in a hammock being held between two easily distracted gorillas, which probably meant the two men were carrying me by all four limbs. I'm fairly certain we passed through a Quantunnel at some point, because I felt the slightly nauseating sensation of the temperature and air pressure abruptly changing as we passed through a magic doorway to a completely different part of the universe.

When consciousness finally did tentatively return on what would hopefully be a semipermanent basis, I found myself in a sitting position with a black bag over my head. I twitched my aching limbs, and discovered to my utter lack of surprise that I was securely tied to the chair. My instincts told me that I was in a bare room with all the doors and windows closed, and the faint electronic hum on the edge of earshot sounded like an atmosphere cycler, which meant I was probably on a ship.

Again, this was not a wholly unfamiliar experience. When you were an adventuring space hero with a tendency to foil galactic supervillains, you did have to expect to get knocked out and tied to things a lot. As a rule, you usually weren't in danger until after the villain in question had had a chance to gloat at you and explain what they were up to. Until then, there wasn't much to do besides try to avoid cramping and practice the usual lines.

"You'll never get away with this," I muttered to myself, it being the best opener for general purposes. "Do you expect me to talk? You're insane." I exercised my cheek muscles and tried some different inflections. "*You're* insane. You're *insane!*"

I felt rather than heard footfalls in an adjoining room, and then the hydraulic *zuzzung* of a sliding door opening, letting new voices spill into the room.

I heard a woman's voice. ". . . You kidnapped a security guard, and now you expect me to clean this mess up for you, is that it?"

"You told us to make sure that no one saw us or knew we had been there," said a familiar condescending voice. "You didn't say anything about what to do if we failed. Logically, the course of action that made the most sense to us—"

"Yes, I see," snapped the woman.

"He's always doing this," said the slightly ingratiating voice of my younger kidnapper.

The woman sighed. "Your directive was to recover a man. Perhaps you needed me to be clearer. I meant a *specific* man."

"Well, I don't think the guy you wanted saw us or anything," said the younger man. "We can go right back and try again as soon as we've sorted this out."

"You mean, as soon as *I've* sorted this out."

I felt a hand fumbling with the bag on my head. I had decided I was going to go with "You'll never get away with this." Tired, sure, but a classic for a reason. It gave them a cue to start laying out the exposition and would allow me to retain my dignity at the same time. I cleared my throat.

The bag came off. "You . . . plying fat tracbag in a bracket case!"

Of course it was Warden. I hadn't recognized her voice at first, because she actually sounded relaxed, and while I had known her, she had been permanently wound tighter than a nervous sidewinder in an elastic band factory. But there was no mistaking that unhealthy Terran complexion, or that hair tied tightly back like a spool of high-tensile garrote wire. She was wearing a pale blue pantsuit that matched well with the cold metal bulkheads that surrounded us.

Her padded shoulders visibly dropped in relaxation when she took in my face. "Gentlemen, you can stand down. This *is* the specific man."

"Seriously?"

"But he's a security guard," said the logical one.

Warden examined my uniform shirt. "No, he's just wearing a security guard's clothing. Let me guess, you happen to have it on hand in case you need to con someone?"

I stayed quiet, but kept my scowl going.

"Guess he passed the audition," said the younger one, rubbing the back of his head.

"What audition?" I did a little hop in my chair to punctuate the question. "What the trac is this? Are we on Salvation Station?"

Salvation was the star pilot haven deep in the uncharted regions of space, one that I deliberately avoided largely because of its general administrator, who at that moment was standing in front of me, sighing and folding her arms. "On a cargo transporter a few light minutes from Salvation. For deniability."

"Well, that's lucky, because now you can use it to transport me right back to Ritsuko, plying sharpish."

"And the 'audition' was for a specialist," she continued, ignoring my statement. "A situation has transpired that calls for someone who can pass as someone he isn't."

"Okay, you seem to have gotten the wrong idea about me in a couple of areas. Firstly, that I'm some kind of first-rate con man just because I put on a security guard's uniform and tricked two complete plying morons who are stupid enough to work for you, and secondly, that I would ever consider working with you again before I'd drunk the contents of my cleaning-supply cabinet."

Warden arched an eyebrow. "Believe me, the second-rateness of your abilities is perfectly clear. But this situation calls for a person with the highly specialized quality of being able to pass as Jacques McKeown to some very specific people who already think he's Jacques McKeown."

I let a few seconds of pregnant silence pass as I considered the response that would best summarize my feelings. "Kiss my doints."

She chewed on her bottom lip, letting her jaw bob left and right like the head of a dancing cobra. Then she turned to her two lackeys, who had been seething together in the background ever since the "morons" comment. "Let me talk to him alone."

They left obediently, the older and crabbier of the two making sure to give me a threatening face just as the door slid shut. Then I was alone in a room with Penelope Warden. I'd often longed for a situation like this, although in my fantasies I hadn't been tied to a chair, and was usually holding a blunt object.

"This won't change anything," I said. "All you've done is increase the average amount of hatred I feel for all the people in this room."

She had produced her tablet computer from some dark recess of her outfit that no other human being would ever explore without mining equipment, and began tapping at the screen as she spoke, not looking at me. "Can we dispense with the melodrama? We should start from a clean slate. You could profit from this, if you'd be willing to look at it pragmatically."

"Dispense with the melodrama? Who's the one kidnapping people and tying them to chairs?" I attempted to turn my back on her, but the effort only made my neck hurt. "And as for pragmatism, the last time I pretended to be Jacques McKeown for you, I almost got killed, like, a hundred times." The memories came flooding back, and they washed up a compelling theory with them. "Oh, trac. It was you, wasn't it."

She glanced up from her work. "Hm?"

"You're the reason I got all those emails addressed to Jacques McKeown this morning. You changed my name on the population database again."

Her fingers paused in the act of tapping for a moment. "No. I'm sure you take a lot of comfort from your persecution complex, but I'll have to disappoint you. I only sent for you after I saw the post."

"What post?"

She switched her tablet to Project mode and a beam of light burst from the lens in the back. It drilled painfully into my retinas for a second before she aimed it at the bare wall in front of me, taking her position at my side. Once I had blinked the afterimages away, I saw what looked like a page from an online discussion forum.

"Hey, can someone confirm that this is Jacques McKeown's personal email? Trying to invite him to Jacques McCon," read the post at the top of the thread, apparently authored by an individual going by "DanDanMcKeownFan." Under that was an email address that looked heartbreakingly like mine.

"Who posted that?" I asked in a pained voice, suspecting that I could guess the answer.

"Daniel Henderson. The young man we fooled once before, and who still believes you to be Jacques McKeown. Son of Henderson the business magnate and crime lord."

I nodded. "Henderson, who was your old boss."

"Yes."

"Until you blew his leg off."

She did a very poor job of sounding unperturbed. "Indeed."

"Mm." I glanced around the room, popping my lips theatrically. "Well, consider me convinced. I mean, if I'm going to commit suicide, might as well do it in the most painful, drawn-out way possible, right? Shows commitment—"

"Robert Blaze is dying," interjected Warden, brutally casual.

Robert Blaze, the original star pilot, the hero to a generation, founder of Salvation Station and erstwhile leader of same, the only thing keeping the scheming general administrator before me from having total control of the station and all the star pilots therein. "Doints he is."

"Ever heard of the Ecru Death?"

"Of course." The Ecru Death was a manufactured virus that none other than Terrorgorn himself had unleashed upon the Fainkov system, on the fringes of the Black. It had almost wiped out the entire sentient population and would have spread even further if Robert Blaze himself hadn't synthesized a cure from the blood of one of Terrorgorn's immunized lackeys. I said, "The Ecru Death was wiped out. The antidote killed all the loose strains."

Warden touched her pad, and the projection on the wall changed. A molecular diagram of the Ecru virus on the left, and a photo on the right of what looked like the kind of sample bottle I'd used often when donating to the Ritsuko City sperm bank. "Blaze decided it would be wise to keep a very small quantity of it on hand for future study. He was keeping it in Salvation's medical lab, until one of the nurses knocked it off a shelf. The lab was quarantined, obviously, but Blaze volunteered to go in and seal it away again, exposing himself to infection."

I emitted a sigh that was about seven-tenths along the way toward being a growl. "Yeah. That's what a star pilot would do."

"Indeed. He had to fight off six other volunteers to get the job."

I shook my head. "So why hasn't he just taken the antidote?"

Warden smartly tapped her screen, and a new image appeared. It showed a large metal cylinder caked in bits of ice and frost, sealed in a glass cabinet on some kind of ornate plinth. "When the Ecru virus was assumed wiped out, the last remaining samples of the antidote were placed in a cryonic storage cylinder and frozen."

"I can't believe you actually made a slideshow," I muttered.

"After Jacques McKeown's typically self-aggrandizing novelization of the incident, the cylinder gained the status of a collector's item among fans of McKeown and McKeown memorabilia." She pronounced the last word with aloof distaste, like a nanny discussing a child's favorite mud puddle. "It is currently in the possession of the galaxy's most dedicated Jacques McKeown fan."

"Let me guess," I said. "Rhymes with Benderson."

She answered by switching to the next slide, which displayed a photo of a smiling Daniel Henderson, taken from a very long distance. He was standing outside the front entrance of what had once been the Ubatsu building in Ritsuko City, but was now named Henderson Tower. He was two years older than when I'd seen him last, seventeen now. He was largely unchanged, if somewhat more elongated, and his complexion had apparently surrendered in its battle with puberty.

"The younger Henderson is as desperately in need of a father figure as ever," droned Warden. "He mentioned Jacques McCon in his forum post. That's the fan convention he organizes and hosts at Henderson Tower, now in its second year. He intends to display his collection of memorabilia on the show floor. The antidote will be part of that."

"And you expect me to go in there by myself, sling it over my shoulder, and scarper?"

"Not by yourself. I have a plan in mind for its recovery, but it calls for an appropriate team of specialists, including an inside man. You are uniquely qualified for that position."

I made a token attempt to wriggle free from my bonds, just to make it clear that I wasn't coming around in the slightest. "Well. I'm sure it's a very well-thought-out plan and you're very proud of it. But I'm afraid I'm not buying this."

She switched off the projector and stood in front of me, hands on hips. "Buying what?"

"You expect me to believe that you're so invested in saving Robert Blaze that you'd risk getting back on the Hendersons' radar? If Blaze dies, you get to take over Salvation unchecked."

"If I were trying to kill Robert, I could just as easily not be arranging an effort to save him," she pointed out. "I could have used a method that wouldn't have potentially exposed the entire station to an incurable plague."

She made some valid points, but it was the unintentional one that made my eyebrows raise. "Robert?"

Her face colored noticeably as she shied back, breaking eye contact. "Blaze. Captain Blaze."

This was a surprising development. Surely she wasn't harboring anything as human as affection. Then again, she had been working under Blaze for a couple of years, and his charisma versus her attitude would have been an "unstoppable force, immovable object" scenario that would have had to resolve itself sooner or later.

And besides, I didn't actually believe she could run Salvation Station without Blaze as a figurehead. She was the lighthouse keeper, but he was the gigantic flashing bulb that drew the sailors in.

"Will you help me save him or not?" she demanded, returning to the subject like a drowning person to a flotation device.

"No," I summarized, staring fixedly at the corner of the room as the word tasted sour and vinegary in my mouth.

"That's all? You'll abandon your childhood hero to a highly unpleasant death?"

"I'm sure he understood the risks. You can't expect me to feel responsible every time Robert Blaze puts his life on the line. And besides. He's a hero to star pilots. And I'm not a star pilot anymore." The words felt like such a wrench to get out that I fancied my nose would start bleeding. Robert Blaze was more than a childhood hero; he was the inspiration for every star pilot in the sky. Most of us would do anything to save his life. If he needed a lung donated, virtually everyone I knew would get together to fight over the scalpel. But I couldn't give in to her. Not when she knew she was pushing my buttons.

"No, you really aren't," said Warden quietly, with an acid in her voice that could have stripped me to the bone. Her hands had ceased to fiddle with her tablet, and her foot was tapping with an anxious rhythm. "What would be your price?"

This I hadn't expected. "Seriously?"

"Tell me how much it would cost for you to overlook our history and take this as a contract job."

I stared at her for some time before answering. "Money isn't highly motivating right now," I confided. "I had money for a while. Nothing good came of it."

"Anything, then. What do you need?"

This was more like the Warden I remembered. Desperately trying to keep her expression fixed and her jitters hidden, clutching that plying tablet to her chest like she was hoping it would stop a bullet. "Maybe there is something," I said eventually, in spite of the part of me warning that I had reached the bargaining stage of the terminal illness that was Warden.

"Go on."

"I'm doing some recruitment work on the side for a company called Oniris," I said, choosing my words carefully so that it wouldn't sound stupid out loud. "They're having trouble finding scientists for their next project."

Her expression didn't change. "You're joining Oniris Venture."

"Yeah!" I snapped, angered by the blatant lack of a question mark on her statement. "Yeah, I plying am. So that's my price. You help me find some scientists who are willing to join a deep space recon mission, and I'll help you out. And after we're done, I'm going to retire to the edge of space, where I can be far away from plying you and plying Jacques McKeown and plying star piloting. Any questions?"

"What kind of scientists?"

"I don't know! The deep space recon kind!" I searched my memory for everything I actually knew about the kind of science they did on recon ships. Most of it came from a TV soap opera I used to watch about a medical team on an isolated scout ship who ended up plying each other in supply cupboards a lot. I said, "Doctors! Nurses! Biologists! Geneticists! Someone to tidy up the supply cupboard!"

"Very well." A suddenly much more relaxed Warden made a little note on her tablet. "I can help you with this. And in return, you work for me until the item has been recovered. Do we have a deal?"

I stared at her for a while, my mouth frozen in a skeptical sneer. "Don't trac me about. Where are you going to get them from?"

"You know that I still have contacts in the United Republic?"

I had a sinking feeling. The United Republic—or Earth, to give it its increasingly less popular name—was the nightmarish totalitarian society from which Warden and the Hendersons had been spawned. Any human being with any sense (or any money) had been glad to see the back of it the moment Ritsuko City had been founded on the moon.

"There are still people on Earth who manage to graduate in science, in spite of the education system," she said. "I suspect every single one of them dreams of defecting and taking a position on the scientific frontier. In fact, after they're smuggled off-world, they'll need to lie low for a while anyway.

The UR increased the off-world spying budget last year after they cut food stamps again."

Of course it made maddeningly perfect sense. I'd hoped it would have been such an obscure request that she'd have had no choice but to say her sarcastic farewells. Only now that she had laid out the details did I realize I'd priced my life and future safety at a cost she could have met with one afternoon and a phone. I hadn't even asked for expenses.

"Do I get expenses?" I asked in a monotone.

"Naturally. Do we have a deal?"

As the realization sank in that I had accidentally talked my way into agreeing to all this, my mind swiftly began to rationalize. I didn't have any other plan for getting hold of scientists, and these refugees she was talking about sounded like a match made in heaven. Maybe she was right. Maybe if I was so keen to move on from my star piloting life, it made sense to wipe the slate clean on my past relationships.

Besides, Daniel Henderson wasn't exactly an intellectual powerhouse. I'd fooled him once before, and more importantly, he was a spoiled little rich doint, and any piece of star piloting history that was in his possession should be taken off him on principle, whether or not Robert Blaze's life was on the line.

That was the moment. The moment I decided to join Warden's little crew, against all my instincts. That was the moment that would haunt me for the rest of my life. The one that would make me long for the invention of time travel so I could visit my younger self in that moment and stick one of the chair legs right through his plying skull.

CHAPTER 5

TWELVE HOURS LATER, I was back in Ritsuko City, looking up at the Henderson Tower's façade the way an overly complacent aristocrat might once have looked up the steps to the guillotine.

Warden had said, "The next step is for you to go to Daniel Henderson in person and tell him you'll be delighted to be guest of honor at Jacques McCon."

"I don't suppose it's worth suggesting that you could always just ask him to return the cylinder for Robert Blaze's sake," I had replied. "They seemed to be getting along all right the last time they met."

"Come on. You know how Daniel Henderson's father feels about Salvation Station."

"After you blew his leg off there."

"After I blew his leg off, quite. He may arrange to have the place nuked just because someone mentioned the name."

And so, after a brief stay on Salvation Station—very brief, as a large chunk of it was still sectioned off and under quarantine—I had made use of their one functioning Quantunnel to return to the spaceport in Ritsuko. My activities since then had consisted largely of using up every last excuse I could think of to put off doing what I was now doing.

With my hair freshly cut, my flight jacket dry-cleaned, and my teeth aching slightly from a thorough examination at the dentist, I stared up at Henderson Tower. The Hendersons hadn't done much redecorating; they'd only added the word HENDERSON above the door in sharp white lettering.

But it was enough to turn the once blandly welcoming front entrance of the Ubatsu building into a huge snarling mouth with a row of spiky fangs.

"You got business here, fumper?"

I stopped gawping upwards to take in the person who had moved between me and the door. They—for I wasn't ready to take a guess at their gender—were probably on the more physically threatening side of their teens, and were sporting a shaved head, multiple piercings, and an awful lot of ripped leather and denim. They were also sitting astride a ten-speed racing bicycle with a metal skull on the gears and spikes on the pedals.

It said something about Ritsuko City that even its biker gangs respected the unspoken rule that motor vehicles should be driven as little as possible. After all, to quote the slogan on the omnipresent Tend Your Rooftop Gardens posters, maintaining an atmosphere is everybody's problem. I was surprised to see a biker out in the open, and looking so well nourished; their numbers had been dwindling ever since Quantunneling had removed most of what reason there was to make use of the roads. They had also been getting somewhat resentful of the star pilot community, because they'd been trying different dialects of swear words for years and none of them had ever caught on.

"You gonna stand there staring all clotting day?" demanded the biker, gloved fingers drumming their handlebars.

"Sadly not, thanks. You with the Bell and Chain gang?"

"No," they sneered. "I'm the clotting doorman, aren't I, you fumping scranker."

"Just going in to see the boss," I tried, making obvious motions toward the door to signal my intention to end this conversation and move on with my life, forever enriched.

The biker rolled a couple of feet to block my path, and fixed me with a threatening glare as they rang their bell with ominous deliberation. "Boss doesn't see any scranker if he's not expecting 'em."

This was interesting. So Henderson was hiring bikers as security. I supposed that made sense. He had been some kind of terrible global crime lord back on Earth, but he was still a relative newcomer to Luna, and would probably have needed to employ local talent. The yakuza wouldn't touch Terran money with a hundred-foot dome-washing pole and the mobsters of the European quarter were too easygoing and almost always drunk, so that left the bikers.

A second biker rolled into the conversation, breaking off from the small cluster of them that was hanging around the main entrance. This one had paired his frightening beard and spiked leathers with a pink unicorn T-shirt as some kind of hilarious ironic counterpoint. "Who's the scong?"

"Some fumper off the street thinks he can just roll up and meet the boss," said the first biker, keeping me pinned in place through the combined use of a glare and their front wheel.

The second biker's eyes flashed with realization as they looked me up and down. "You McKeown?"

"Yeah," I said, feeling like it was the simplest answer to this extremely complex question.

"Leave it, Les. He can come in."

Les gave him a look like he'd scraped his earwax cleaning device off on their sleeve. "Clotting why? He's just some scranker."

"He comes in because he's Jacques Mc-yatching-Keown, you yatching scong, and the boss wants to see him as soon as he gets here, doesn't he. So get out of the wobblesplinking way."

Les did so, rolling backwards with a defeated ticking of spokes, not breaking their suspicious eye contact. I passed sheepishly between the two thugs and through the entrance, the automatic doors humming obligingly aside.

When I was satisfied that I was out of view of the hired toughs, I took out my phone and set the camera to take a picture every few seconds, just as Warden had instructed with characteristic condescension, and placed it in the breast pocket of my flight jacket with the flap propped up to expose the lens. Hopefully it would go unnoticed.

I put my hands behind my back and did a few slow, complete rotations, pretending to be drinking in the scenery. And then, having nothing better to do, I drank in the scenery for real.

The Ubatsu Building's intended function had been somewhat vague; I think the Ritsuko City Council had been sold more on its imposing size and presence than what it could actually be used for. It had ended up filled with generic, if fairly prestigious, rented apartments and offices, with a private spaceport on the roof and some convention space on the ground floor.

Not much had changed in the transition to Henderson Tower, except that the small convention space had been replaced with an extremely large and decadent one. The cathedral-sized reception hall gave way to two staircases wide enough to admit combine harvesters, and the whole place was decked out with black marble floors ingrained with thousands of glittering white specks, evoking what idiots think a deep space star field looks like.

Which was probably the intended effect, going by the centerpiece. On a raised platform between me and the reception desk, surrounded by lofty pillars that are interior design shorthand for "Please look at this," was a huge red fiberglass model of a spaceship. It didn't correspond to any ship design I was familiar with, but it slightly reminded me of the fat and clumsy Platinum God of Whale Sharks I had piloted for Henderson during our past acquaintance, just with some of its curves trimmed down and some more flashy fins added.

The reception desk was flanked on both sides by illuminated displays of star piloting memorabilia that brought all kinds of memories flooding back as I ambled toward them. Front and center was a mannequin wearing a sequined jumpsuit and high-collared flight jacket somewhat reminiscent of what Captain Blanche used to wear, or possibly a more flamboyant Dick Dynamite. The plaque in front of it, however, declared it to be "Jacques McKeown's outfit during his battle with the Pestilent Brotherhood."

That set the tone for the rest of the displays. They were all replicas of artifacts from a real-life star pilot or star pilot adventure, pushed through the filter of Jacques McKeown's writing. And then, because a sinking feeling was making me look for something like this, I noticed a plastic replica blaster in one of the cabinets that was slightly reminiscent of my own. The power dial had been replaced by a row of red LEDs that no actual gun would ever possess, as its only conceivable purpose would be to give your position away. "Jacques McKeown's blaster from *Jacques McKeown and the Malmind Menace*," read the adjoining plaque. I felt suddenly embarrassed and nauseous, like I was listening to a gushing, inaccurate eulogy at my own funeral.

I paused my slow advance to take another sweeping look around the room, confirming that there was nothing displayed here in the lobby but dodgy plastic replicas. Nothing along the lines of genuine star piloting memorabilia, like the cryonic cylinder that was the ultimate prize; I wasn't fortunate enough that any of the really valuable stuff would be in easy reach.

There was a rotating rack on the reception desk crammed with colorful Jacques McKeown paperbacks, as well as a few books from writers who'd tried to imitate his style after he got popular, colloquially known as Hack McKeowns. Which made me speculate for a moment on how traccy a writer must have to be, to be considered a poor man's Jacques McKeown.

"Sir?"

I'd now drifted into the detection range of the receptionist who was standing patiently behind the rack with her spine ramrod stiff. She was young, pretty, and smiling, but there was a slight pleading look in her eyes that tended to be a hallmark of people who worked for Henderson. She was wearing a dark blue waistcoat with the glittery star pattern that was fast becoming a recurring theme.

"Can I help you?" she asked predictably.

I buried my hands in my jacket pockets and took a step closer. "Here to see Daniel Henderson. I'm Jacques McKeown." I doubted that saying it would ever stop feeling weird.

Her eyebrows went up. "Really?"

"Yeah." I made a show of glancing around. "Take it you're pretty sick of hearing that name around here."

"No, not at all," she lied. "You're here to meet with Mr. Henderson?"

"Yes, I'm here to see *Daniel* Henderson."

"Of course. I'll inform Mr. Henderson right away." She reached for the reception console and adjusted her earpiece.

I coughed. "When you say Mr. Henderson, you are talking about Daniel Henderson, right? Not his father? I'm pretty sure Daniel Henderson is the contact."

She hadn't heard me, as she was still concluding a brief muttered conversation with someone on the other end of the phone line. "Someone will be with you very soon," she said to me when she was finished. Then the smile and welcoming posture disappeared in an instant to indicate that I was dealt with and she no longer cared whether I lived or died.

I took another look around the room, at the replica ship and the replica memorabilia. This time, I noticed a framed poster on the wall near the foot of one of the grand staircases. It depicted a ship not unlike the one behind me flying through space, in the style of Jacques McKeown's usual cover artist. The text at the bottom read JACQUES MCCON '75!—'75 being the current year—and just underneath that, WITH SPECIAL GUEST FOR REAL THIS TIME!

Something about all of this felt off. Nothing I was seeing gelled with my memories of Mr. Henderson as a person. I remembered him as a cheerful, upbeat embarrassing-dad type with a fondness for loud sweaters, who was also completely plying psychotic, ruthless, and sadistic. He wasn't a McKeown fanboy. Daniel was, and by all accounts had only gotten more so, but it was the senior Henderson who had to be footing the bill for all this. And this kind of expense went far beyond fatherly overindulgence.

A permanent Quantunnel archway set into the nearby wall slid open to reveal a hallway on the top floor of the building, this being an increasingly common arrangement in tall buildings, as the power expense was usually less than the cost of maintaining an elevator. A heavyset man in a black suit and dark glasses stepped through and gestured for me to follow. He must have been part of Henderson's inner circle, as he had the telltale orange skin tone of one who has spent too much time under the artificial sun reserved for Terran high society.

"You McKeown?" he asked brusquely after I had passed through the Quantunnel and shaken off the usual disorientation.

"That's me." This was the third time I'd told the big lie in as many minutes, and it wasn't getting easier. The sheer weight of it was heavier with every telling. If I was asked the question a fourth time today, I felt certain something would break inside me and I'd hurl myself through the nearest window.

"Mr. Henderson's waiting," growled my escort.

"Yeah, which Mr. Henderson are we going to see, again? No one's given me a straight answer on that yet."

"As I say, Mr. Henderson's waiting," he replied, not turning around.

"Right." I sighed and followed him down the hallway.

It would have been a very bad idea to throw myself through these windows. We were on the highest level of the building, and a wall of glass to my right looked out over Ritsuko City, sprawling out beneath its Perspex bubble like a reflection of a Christmas tree in a fishbowl. Above it, the motherly mass of the universe, gazing fondly down at us through its billions of burning eyes. I thought of my future life with Oniris, deep in the furthest darkness, and tried to feel encouraged.

The suited bodyguard stopped outside a plain, well-varnished door to what I assumed was one of the penthouse apartments. I had already pegged him for the kind of bracket who never gave much away, emotionally, but I could have sworn that he took a deep breath and steeled himself before he rapped upon the door with his large simian knuckles.

There was a conspicuous lack of noise on the other side of the door, until an amount of time had passed that would be roughly the amount needed for an excited fanboy to calm himself down to a socially acceptable level. Then there was a rush of incoming footsteps and the door flew open.

Daniel Henderson had had a growth spurt since I'd seen him last. He was taller and less dumpy, and his limbs dangled off him like loose cables from a detached air cycler, as if puberty had simply grabbed him by both ends and pulled until he was fit to ride all the roller coasters. Also, his complexion looked like he had imbibed a large quantity of ball bearings and they had attempted to burst out of his body through his face. He was wearing an imitation flight jacket of the type that I happened to know were sold predistressed from the expensive fashion boutiques near the spaceport, and an extremely weathered "I Found Elation on Salvation Station" T-shirt.

"Jacques!" he said, leaning on the door frame in a poor imitation of casualness and struggling to tone down his idiot grin. "Cool to see you again! Come in. We can talk about the con."

He stood aside, gesturing into the apartment with a little bow, and I slipped past him, feeling like a lamb being announced at the abattoir ball. He noticed the bodyguard who had escorted me here. "Oh, Mr. Heller. Now you can, er . . . you can clean the toilet again? I was just in there."

"Yes, Mr. Henderson," muttered Heller, stomping away toward the bathroom.

"Dad's people," whispered Daniel apologetically. "They keep asking me for things to do."

I was only half listening, as I was preoccupied with taking in the apartment. And there was a lot to take in. First of all, the inevitable ridiculous level of expensive luxury. The apartment was on two levels, with a gold-trimmed spiral staircase leading to the upper rooms. A set of windows taller than those of any cathedral you'd care to name watched over a set of bone-white leather sofas and an imitation fireplace.

The second thing I noticed was the small army of gangsters dotted around the place. Some were wearing the black suit and sunglasses of the Henderson inner circle, but most were bikers. All of them seemed to be engaged in a menial household task. Some were dusting, a few were polishing the windows, two had pulled rubber gloves over their jacket sleeves and were working away at a pile of washing-up in the fully outfitted kitchen. Every single one of them was wearing an expression somewhere on the spectrum between boredom and abject disgust.

But it was the third layer of discovery that finally made my jaw get around to the business of dropping. Every inch of space that wasn't taken up by expensive furniture or servants was crammed with a broad selection of artifacts related to the history of star piloting. A section of hull from the *Starplyer* was sitting on the coffee table, made unmistakable by visible traces of the thermoduric weed that had claimed it. The vaguely human shape carved from asteroidal rock propped up in the corner looked to me like Captain Blackbottom's figurehead. Tiffany Lurid's famous Zoobskin cloak was draped across the sideboard.

I was so occupied with taking all this in that it took thirty seconds of awkward silence for me to parse Daniel's previous statement. "Um, yeah, actually, where is your father?" I did another scan of my surroundings and didn't catch a single glimpse of colorful sweater.

"Oh, he's around," said Daniel, wobbling a hand. "Can I get you anything? A drink? Anything you want. I could tell someone to go out and get it if we don't have it here. They'd totally do it, too. It's so cool."

I caught the eye of the bodyguard who was doing the washing-up, and his completely frozen face was very telling. "I'm fine," I said.

Daniel shrugged, then words seemed to fail him for a moment. He merely stared at me ecstatically, jiggling up and down as if riding an invisible exercise bike, until words began to tumble out like cement from an unsecured mixer. "Sooo cool that you can do the con. Nobody believed me when I said I knew you. I tried to get you for our first one, last year, actually. But I never heard back, and everyone was really disappointed." He rubbed the back of his neck nervously. "Really disappointed, actually. Mr. Heller had to get onstage and apologize but everyone was still really, really disappointed. Some people died."

I boggled at him. "This was around this time last year, was it?"

"Yeah!"

I'd assumed that last year's citywide student riots had been about tuition fees, like they usually were. I took another in a long series of deep, steadying breaths. "I see."

"But we've got you this year. So cool." For a few more moments he continued staring at me the way a dog stares at a fist that it has been led to believe contains a biscuit, then he snapped out of it and turned to an open laptop on the kitchen counter. "Okay. So it's, like, a three-day convention, we'll have an exhibition floor for my Jacques McKeown collection, meeting rooms for people to talk about Jacques McKeown in, the competition for dressing up the most like Jacques McKeown, and . . . we'll have you!"

"And this is the collection?" I said, referring to the priceless antiques that were scattered around the floor like piles of used gift wrap after an overin-dulgent birthday party.

"Yeah!" Daniel beamed at me before returning to the database in front of him. "So the first day you'll probably want to take it easy a bit, so we'll just do a Q and A at nine a.m. And ten a.m. And eleven a.m. And twelve. And there'll be more people free at lunchtime, so we could do one at twelve thirty and one at one . . ." He pressed a few keys. "Oh, I forgot book signings. Do you think you could eat lunch and dinner at the same time?"

The phone in my pocket made a subtle clicking noise to signal another photo being taken, and I was reminded of my actual objective. "Is this your whole collection?"

"Not all of it," said Daniel cheerily, moving boxes around in his database. "Some of it's in my bedroom. Some of it's in the bath."

"What about a . . . cryonic cylinder?"

He looked up. "How did you know about that?"

There wasn't an ounce of suspicion in his voice. He was just thrilled that I seemed to have taken an interest. But I wasn't about to let anything slip. I flipped the imaginary switch in my head that I used when I needed to seriously commit to a role, and shifted my weight into what I thought would be an impressive stance. "I'm Jacques McKeown," I said, lowering my voice by half an octave. "If it's to do with star piloting, I know about it."

I heard a nearby biker give a brief grunt of undisguised contempt, but Daniel looked so impressed, I thought he might wet himself. "Oh, sure! Cool! Well, the tube can't just be lying around like the other stuff, it needs special care. I keep it in the fridge."

He pointed. The "fridge" was, in fact, a walk-in freezer, accessed by a steel door at the back of the kitchen preparation area. It was a heavy door, but I didn't see a lock. I angled the phone in my pocket toward it for the next snapshot, pretending to be scratching under my nipple.

"So you can stay in the other penthouse apartment during the show. Dad owns the whole building," continued Daniel. "It's exactly the same as this one and the balconies nearly touch, so if you need anything you can just stand outside and shout."

"That sounds . . . very useful, actually," I said. "I'll want to take a look at that before I go. And the whole collection is going to be exhibited down-stairs, is it?"

"Oh, sure. We'll bring it all down every morning and take it all back up each night. Safer that way."

This was getting harder and harder to believe. "You don't have a safe? Or a panic room? Does the bathroom at least have a lock on the door?"

He frowned with his eyebrows, but his excited grin didn't change. "No. But it's safe here. I've got people looking at them the whole time."

I glanced over at the bodyguard who was cleaning the window near Captain Blackbottom's figurehead. Sure enough, while his hands were busy rubbing cleaning fluid across the glass, his eyes were fixed upon the figurehead. By the looks of it, he had been maintaining his vigilance for long enough that his neck was in severe need of massage therapy.

"Except in the freezer," added Daniel. "Can't have someone in the freezer watching the cylinder, that'd be stupid. We'll just have to particularly hope that no one wants to steal it."

"Fingers crossed," I said distantly, staring at the freezer door. "Can I take a look at those balconies now?"

"Sure! Cool." He got onto his feet and led me along a weaving path through the scattered furniture and antiques. The laboring bodyguards all promptly slid out of his way with the grace of a choreographed dance routine. Every single one of them made sure to give me a very serious face as I passed by.

I followed Daniel up a hardwood staircase—whose varnish looked like it had seen a lot of careless foot traffic—to the upper level, where a secondary lounge area looked down upon the one below and a couple of plain doors led, presumably, to bedrooms.

"So . . . where did you get the cylinder from?" I asked, in the spirit of intelligence gathering.

"Oh, that was the first thing in my collection, actually. Dad got it for me. Just before he went into his . . ." He suddenly stopped, then spun with a haste that made me jump. "Do you want to say hi to Dad?"

Meeting Daniel Henderson's father was pretty high on the list of things I doubted I would ever want to do again, just above Scandinavian cuisine and getting exposed to hard vacuum without an EVA suit. But I couldn't help noticing a tangible change in the air the instant Henderson Sr. was invoked. One of the black-suited bodyguards paused in the act of polishing the doorknobs to watch my reaction.

"I . . . wouldn't want to bother him," I said, looking at the door Daniel was indicating the way an ant regards the burrow of a trapdoor spider.

"It's cool. Not much bothers him these days." I flinched as he hammered a fist on the door loud enough to rattle the wineglasses downstairs. "Daaad! We're coming in!"

The room beyond was straight out of a Christmas card for mental health professionals. The only source of light was a stone hearth with an open fire—a severe faux pas in a bubble city, but I doubted anyone had had the doints to say so—which cast flickering orange highlights across a grand four-poster bed and an array of moth-eaten hunting trophies from animals that had been extinct for generations. In front of the fire was an elaborately curving armchair whose backrest constituted about 70 percent of its total height.

Sitting in it was none other than Mr. Henderson himself, his elbows and knees at perfect right angles as he clutched the armrests and dug his single remaining foot into the bearskin rug. He was wearing a knitted cardigan with a picture of a yellow frowny face on the front. I stared at it for some time, as I was putting off having to look at his actual face.

I became aware of a rhythmic thudding noise, and saw that the fingers of his right hand were drumming against the armrest. It was a calm motion, with about a second's pause between each drum, but I also noticed that the upholstery under his fingertips had been almost completely worn away, exposing the wood.

"Dad?" said Daniel, standing between his father and the fire. "Dad, I need more money for the convention. The band wants to be paid upfront."

No response came, but Daniel didn't seem to be expecting one. He produced a tablet that was displaying some kind of banking application, and with careful timing, slid it under Mr. Henderson's hand as his fingers were upraised in the act of drumming. The fingerprint lock made a cheerful chime, and a ridiculous amount of money was transferred.

"ThankyouDad," said Daniel, all as one obligatory word.

That was when I finally looked at Mr. Henderson's face, and immediately regretted doing so. I was reminded of a piece of advice my old instructor at Speedstar Academy had given me: If you have to dash under a starship's launch jets, and you should never *have* to do that, then at least don't look up. Because there's something hypnotic about the way your gaze will travel along the lines of the exhaust funnel's black spiral to the distant spark of the ignition light, and the deep subconscious knowledge that a single unheralded test fire of the engine will instantly reduce you to a splatter of wet granules on the floor.

Mr. Henderson's orange tan had shifted slightly to a permanent shade of sunset pink. His lips were pressed tightly together like a fully compressed accordion. His eyes stared into the fireplace with such intensity that I wondered if his gaze was what had started the fire in the first place. His head was motionless, but an extruding vein on his temple was quivering like an earthworm in an owl habitat.

"Yeah, he's been like that for over a year now," said Daniel cheerfully. "The doctor said it was something like, he got so angry about something that his body entered a state approaching rigor mortis. That's why I had to take over telling everyone what to do."

I took a careful step back to ensure that Daniel was between me and him. "Is it about . . . what happened last time?" I whispered.

"Oh, you mean when that docking ramp shut too fast and cut his leg off?" said Daniel, a little too loudly. "No, he got over that pretty fast. He was talking about getting a new leg that could run super fast and, you know, shoot lasers and things. But something went wrong with the prototype, and I guess he changed his mind. Hey, Dad, you remember Jacques McKeown?"

The invoking of the name caused an astonishing reaction from Mr. Henderson, made no less so by the fact that all he did was swivel his eyes. As he turned his glare to me, I felt myself pinned to the spot by two red-hot spikes. Then, ever so slowly, his eyes narrowed, making his hatred pour out even harder, as water does from the pinched end of a hose.

"He says hi," translated Daniel helpfully.

CHAPTER 6

WHEN I RETURNED to the spaceport hangar and caught sight of my parked ship, I instantly knew she had been broken into.

I'd stepped out of the Henderson building in a stupor, escorted by Mr. Heller, now smelling faintly of pine-scented toilet cleaner. He had done nothing during the walk back through the Quantunnel to the lobby but show me his advancing back with no apparent concern for whether or not I was following, and between that and the sudden onrush of relief from getting away from Mr. Henderson, I had felt the urge to be chummy.

"Can I ask you something?" I had said as we were passing by the fiberglass spaceship.

He replied by continuing to stride across the lobby, but didn't specifically tell me to be quiet.

"How do you guys feel about the way things have been going here?"

Heller visibly shuddered, but quickly composed himself. "Things've changed," he admitted, from the corner of his mouth.

I shot an uncomfortable glance at the fiberglass centerpiece. "I gathered that. So why stick around?"

"Mr. Henderson might get better."

"So what?"

He stopped, as we were close to the exit, and this was apparently his chosen interpretation of "seeing me out." He turned around neatly and folded his arms, pointing a thumb toward the large entrance doors. "So then, things change back."

He was a terse bracket, but I picked up on his subtext. Things would change back, and then Mr. Henderson would have something to say about anyone who had abandoned him in his hour of need, or failed to keep his son happy. Probably something along the lines of "Ready, aim, fire."

So, having been put in something of a daze by the whole encounter, I had flipped to my default setting and wandered back to Ritsuko's Arse, to get back onboard my comfort zone and have some time to myself. And as I entered the parking bay and approached the *Neverdie*, my step faltered when I realized that someone else had been inside.

The *Neverdie* had been my special lady for a very long time, and in the course of a relationship like that, one develops certain instincts. Who knows what tiny details my subconscious had picked up on—a stirring in the layers of dust, the protective cover over the access panel left at an angle slightly unlike the one I preferred—but the effect was stark. A cold, sinking sensation, like I'd come home early from work to find my wife sitting flustered in her negligee, innocently glancing around at everything but the wardrobe in the corner.

I drew my blaster and took up position to one side of the inner airlock door. If some drunken bum had stumbled into my ship looking for shelter, then it wouldn't be the first time, but I preferred the drunken bum to be me. I smashed the opening mechanism with my fist, waited for the door to slide aside, then leapt into the doorway, attempting to simultaneously point my gun at every part of the ship's interior.

The central hallway and steps were clear, all the way up to the open cockpit hatch, and it didn't look from here like there was anyone at the helm, or that any of the consoles had been turned on. But I was more certain than ever that someone had been in the *Neverdie*. At the very least, someone had been monkeying with the airlock access panel, because the familiar, reassuring pattern of grime around the housing had changed.

There was still the luggage compartment, passenger cabin, and engine level to check. It was probably safe to rule out that last one. A thief would find nothing worth stealing there, and someone looking for shelter would hopefully know better than to stow away in a place that might become superheated or flooded with toxic fumes if I needed to start the engine in a hurry.

My train of thought came to an unscheduled stop when I heard a sound from the passenger cabin. A short ringing clink of what I guessed to be porcelain against porcelain.

It was probably too late to get the drop on whoever it was; the noisy airlock doors weren't designed for subtlety. But as the owner and resident of the ship, I could actually threaten to call security with a straight face for once. I strode boldly toward the sliding door to the passenger cabin, hauled it to one side, and jabbed my gun at the first person I saw.

That person turned out to be a man sitting on the cushioned bench in front of the main viewing window with his feet up on the lower shutter. He was older than me, probably in his fifties, with brushes of gray hair at his temples and a slim, wiry build that he had emphasized with the trousers, shirt, waistcoat, and tie from a formal, well-tailored suit. One of his hands was missing: his arm terminated at the wrist in a circular metal bracelet. His one remaining hand was holding a delicate china teacup with a tasteful flower pattern matching that of the saucer in his lap.

My gaze followed the line of his slim legs to the little metal table in the center of the cabin, on which a miniature picnic set had been arranged. There was a square of gingham cloth with a few other pieces of china and a plastic box containing what looked like scones.

He seemed to be completely unrattled by my presence, or my gun. "Ah, you must be the proprietor," he said. His voice was placid, educated, and as smooth as a silk undergarment sliding down a recently shaved leg.

I didn't lower the gun. "Did you break in here, you giant bracket?"

He rolled his eyes. "Spare me your gutter dialect. No, I did not *break in* like a common lout. I have *infiltrated* your disappointing little yacht. Nothing has been broken or tarnished in any way. Many would argue that my presence has only increased its value."

He lifted the circular cover from the device on the end of his arm to reveal a butter knife extruding from his wrist like a straightened pirate hook. He used it to begin buttering one of the scones in front of him.

"Okay," I said, reasonably. "And what kind of asking price would we be looking at after I've liquefied your doints and smeared them across that wall?"

He stared down the barrel of my gun, unimpressed. Then he carefully returned his scone to the table and held up his greasy butter knife until it caught the light. "You are not in a favorable position to make threats, sir."

I nodded to his knife. "What're you gonna do, open letters at me?"

He scowled, retracted the butter knife, and replaced the cover. Then he blinked precisely once and let the cover fall open again.

This time, instead of a piece of cutlery, a chainsaw blade extruded from his arm, roaring like a ferocious beast and spurting puffs of petrol smoke. It extended a full two feet and only stopped when the end was an uncomfortably small distance from my crotch.

"Hello?" came Warden's voice from down the hallway, breaking the frozen, confrontational silence that followed. "The door was open. Are you in, McKeown?"

The bracket in the sharp suit made a little scoffing noise, then withdrew the giant chainsaw blade and replaced the cover. I boggled at it. From the way his elbow bent, I could have sworn the arm was flesh and blood, aside from the device at the end, but it had just leisurely sucked in two straight feet of buzzing lumberjack equipment like a diner sucking in spaghetti.

"Warden?" I called back, not looking away. "Is this bracket yours?"

I felt her presence just behind me, at my shoulder. I could tell from the sound of her tolerant sigh that she was rolling her eyes. "Mr. Derby. I did ask you to wait outside."

"Like a pedestrian awaiting public transport?" He waved his one hand as if physically brushing the idea away. "Davisham Derby is not kept waiting. The universe waits for Davisham Derby."

"He should have kept it waiting longer," I said. "Could either of you divs explain why Davisham Derby is on my plying ship?"

"Mr. Derby is another specialist I've hired for this operation. He's a professional thief."

"Thief? Please," said Derby, with the merest hint of reproach. "I am the finest and most accomplished burglar, infiltrator, and acquirer of specialist items in the known universe."

"Never heard of you," I said flatly.

He smirked. "That's how good I am."

I could tell he intended it to be a clever retort to put me in my place, but I wasn't going to let him have it. "So you have the same qualifications as a liar."

"Mr. Derby's qualifications have been made fully clear to me," said Warden, primly taking a seat at the end of the cabin. "We can save the proper introductions until the last member of our team arrives."

I had stopped pointing my blaster at people, but I wasn't quite ready to reholster it in case some brackets around here started getting too comfortable, so I let it dangle from my hand as I talked. "And who said you could start organizing meetings on my plying ship?"

She gave a small but nonetheless infuriating tut. "We need a meeting place in the city that's in a convenient location for mobility."

"You didn't even ask!"

"I had no way of knowing how long your meeting with the Hendersons would go on. Would you have preferred me to call while you were still in the building? Made my name light up on your phone as visibly as possible?"

"Pathetic, isn't it," said Derby, with the air of a teacher's pet. "Star pilots with their ships. They're like teenage boys with their first girlfriends. Look at him clinging to the doorway like he's got an arm around her shoulder. No one's the least bit interested in stealing her away, sir. She's old and clapped out and symbolic of an embarrassing age of human development that only you are determined to cling to."

I hadn't even realized I'd been gripping the door frame with my free hand. I snatched it away, suppressing the urge to stroke the nearby bulkhead apologetically. "Fair enough. Maybe I'll cling to your throat instead."

He shifted position, idly letting his shortened arm point toward me as it settled. I gave an involuntary little flinch.

"Yes, yes, I'm extremely impressed by you both," said Warden as she busied herself with her tablet. "If you wish to continue this urinating contest, I would request that you exchange contact details and arrange a more formal get-together in your own time."

Derby and I threw her matching scowls, then he returned to his scones. I sat down, after a brief pause to make it clear that I was doing so of my own free will, spreading comfortably across the nearer bench with one leg hooked over the armrest. "So who's the last guy?" I asked.

"The technology expert. We have the getaway vehicle, the infiltrator, and the acquisitions expert. Tech is the remaining factor."

A little nagging thought that had been idly bumming around my mind for some time suddenly sprang to life at her use of the phrase "getaway vehicle."

"Is this a heist?"

She glanced up. "I beg your pardon?"

"This little enterprise we're planning here. Is it a heist?"

She and Derby exchanged an odd look. "I thought you were clear on this, McKeown. I said in our previous meeting that we plan to steal the cylinder. And you just spent most of the afternoon casing the joint."

"I know!" I snapped. "It's just . . ."

"Oh, let me guess," said Derby witheringly. "You're a star pilot, so you're a 'good guy.'" He made highly emphatic finger quotes with his one remaining hand. "And heists are things that 'bad guys' do. And for no better reason, you're getting cold feet because there is no room for moral pragmatism in your mind, it having ceased developing at the age of twelve."

"Mr. Derby," said Warden warningly. "You have not been hired to cast aspersions on my other specialists."

"Hmph." He backed down.

"Besides, as I'm sure Mr. McKeown will be quick to remind you, he is no longer a star pilot."

"Yeah," I said. I was developing a tendency to forget this important fact.

"I see," said Derby, bored. "I note you still dress like a star pilot and live on a spacecraft with several hygiene and safety concerns, but I'll assume you're going through a slow weaning process."

There was a tap of knuckles against the outer hull, near the airlock. Evidently the fourth member of the crew was polite enough not to barge in through an open door. All in all, they sounded like the kind of company I would rather be in right now, so I stood up. "I'll get it."

The person waiting just outside the airlock door was a man, slightly shorter than me, and slightly overweight, dressed like an elderly woman. *Dressed* may be too generous a word, as the amount of effort that had gone into the disguise seemed low. He was wearing a gray wig that was only barely lined up with his actual hairline, as well as a cheap pink dress that was baggy enough to reveal a man's polo shirt and trousers underneath. He had created fake breasts by shoving two empty noodle cups down the front of his dress.

"Hello, young man, please offer me shelter," he said in a ridiculous high-pitched wheedle straight out of a pantomime rehearsal. "I am but a poor bent old woman."

I let my fingers drum on the doorway for a few moments as I considered this. "I don't believe you."

"Sorry," the man said in his natural voice, which was breathy and nasal. "This wasn't my idea."

Warden materialized at my shoulder again. "I wasn't prepared to let you walk around in the open undisguised. Not with all those warrants out for you."

"Another one?" I barked, rounding on Warden as the newcomer apologetically slipped past me into the passenger cabin. "How many career criminals are you going to let on my plying ship today, Warden?"

"They're all going to be career criminals, McKeown, this is a heist."

"All right! Yes! I know that! I'm coming around to that. It's just . . . all coming on a bit fast today."

"If it's any consolation, the percentage of people onboard your ship who are criminals hasn't changed. It's gone from one hundred to one hundred."

"I'm not a criminal!" I blurted out, knowing almost immediately what she would say.

"Going by amount stolen without facing repercussions, you're probably one of the top ten criminals in the universe," she said, before turning about with the merest hint of a sassy hip shake and going back to the cabin to join the rest of the "crew."

She was of course referring to the fact that I had personally stolen Jacques McKeown's royalties and distributed them among the star pilots whose stories he had ripped off, including myself. I didn't think it fair to count that, as most of my share had been eaten up by unrelated legal costs.

I took a moment to take stock, and felt a change of mood in the air. The *Neverdie* no longer had the vibe of a cheating housewife being surprised in the bedroom. Now, in my mind's eye, she was a quietly angry housewife standing in the doorway, patting her open palm with a rolling pin as her husband staggered drunkenly up the garden path with a number of unseemly friends in tow. I gave her a half smile and a guilty wince, then dug my hands in my pockets and followed Warden.

"All right then, make the introductions." I sighed as I trudged back into the den of thieves.

"I didn't think I'd have to," said Warden.

I looked to the newcomer, who had now removed his wig and dress to reveal a man in his thirties, younger than me, with thinning hair and rectangular spectacles, who wouldn't have looked out of place behind the help desk at a popular electronics retailer. But what made me freeze where I stood was his face. I recognized it. It wouldn't have looked out of place on a wanted poster, or behind an army of enslaved cyborg drones.

As he lay his dress across one of the unoccupied benches, he seemed to sense the increase in tension, and turned to notice me staring. He straightened up with a bright smile. "Captain! Can I just say, it's very nice to see you again. I'm looking forward to working with you on something productive."

I kept staring at him for a moment. Then I strode smartly across the room, grabbed Warden by the arm without slowing, and pulled her out into the hallway, slamming the cabin door closed behind us as she did a stumbling pirouette into the head.

"Stop that!" she demanded, pulling her arm away. "McKeown—"

"Tell me that's not who I think it is," I growled.

She brushed down the creases in her suit jacket and sniffled. "Who do you think it is?"

"I think it's Malcolm Sturb."

"You'd be thinking along the right lines, then."

I clutched my temples and paced back and forth a few times, although with the lack of space, it was more like turning around on the spot. "Okay. That's my limit. I've had enough. You and your little evil plying bracket support group can meet somewhere else. I'm not working with Malcolm plying Sturb."

"So Derby was right," she said, firing the words from her mouth like bullets to my most sensitive parts. "I believed you when you said you were trying to move on from the star pilot lifestyle, but you're still clinging to the childish hero-villain narrative . . ."

I pointed a finger in her face. "I can tell when you're trying to do the plying clever-clogs manipulation thing. It's not going to work this time. Malcolm Sturb is dangerous."

She stared contemptuously at my finger for a moment, then looked away. "Malcolm Sturb has come a long way since he disbanded the Malmind. You saw it yourself, back on Cantrabargid. He had released most of his cybercollective and begun play-acting a version of himself for tourists."

"'Cos he had to," I pointed out. "After Quantunneling killed space adventuring. Not out of the goodness of his heart. Don't tell me he wouldn't go right back to slapping slave crowns on everyone he met the instant it became financially viable again."

"Look, I've been working closely with Malcolm ever since I started at Salvation Station. He's been instrumental in getting the tech infrastructure in place."

I let my head slowly cock to one side as my brain did some quick calculating. "And was he doing this around the time Robert Blaze was exposed to Ecru Death, by any chance?"

She spat out a couple of gasping sighs as her hands wobbled in front of her. She was starting to look as exasperated as me, which was slightly gratifying. "No, he wasn't, as it happens. He hasn't shown the slightest inclination to enslave anyone in all the time I've known him. I happen to genuinely believe that he's reformed."

"Oh, how convincing. A character reference for Hitler. From Satan."

She fixed me with her glare again. "And need I remind you that this isn't for me or Malcolm Sturb. It's for Robert."

"Robert?"

"Blaze." She flushed.

I treated myself to an impish smile, followed by a defeated sigh. I was kidding myself by pretending I wasn't already committed to this, between wanting to save Blaze, meeting my scientist quota, and having signed up for the convention. "All right. Fine. But if he so much as puts his wristwatch within clamping range of my brain, then we're done."

"Of course." She stood up and marched huffily away before I could decide if the conversation was officially over or not.

Back in the passenger cabin, where Malcolm Sturb and Davisham Derby were engaged in a fiercely awkward silence, Warden straightened one of the shutters until it provided a decent-enough surface to project onto, then glanced around. I could tell she was trying to decide if it was worth dimming the lights; my batteries were well overdue for replacing, so probably not.

"Gentlemen," she said, projecting a blank screen onto the shutter to draw everyone's attention. "This will be the official briefing for this venture. Some of you may already know each other." She gave me a pointed look as she emphasized the word *some*. "But for clarity's sake, let me make introductions. Davisham Derby is our acquisitions specialist, in charge of the actual physical recovery and movement of the object we seek. He is a highly experienced professional thief."

"Burglar," corrected Derby, hoisting his nose in the air for a mighty sniff. "Cat burglar. I sometimes prefer 'cracksman,' but I am no mere pincher of rubbishes."

Malcolm Sturb, who was sitting in the middle of a bench with hands clasped interestedly in his lap, caught my eye with a conspiratorial look and a brief grin of amusement. I replied with a scowl.

"Malcolm Sturb is our tech specialist," continued Warden. "His role will be managing the equipment we use, and finding a way around the Henderson Tower security system."

"And he can do that, can he?" I interjected.

"Artificial intelligences were the first thing I learned to control, actually," said Sturb, with a sudden nervous glee that made words start spilling out of him like turds from a sewage outflow pipe. "Much easier than the organic ones. Principles are actually surprisingly similar. See, it all comes down to isolating the nodes involved in decision making and applying some kind of staple to certain pathways, and actually you probably aren't that interested right now." I had been giving him another warning look.

"Lastly, Dashford Pierce." Warden pronounced my new name with obvious distaste. "The inside man. Jacques McKeown impersonator and, if necessary, getaway pilot."

"Once! I impersonated Jacques McKeown once. I do not consider myself a 'Jacques McKeown impersonator.' "

"I hardly expect you to put it on your business cards," said Warden dryly. "But I doubt anyone else could lay claim to the title."

"This plan is foolhardy," piped up Derby, who clearly felt he had gone without attention for long enough. "We could insert someone as an attendee or member of staff if we need an insider. None will be under greater scrutiny than the guest of honor."

"Well, yes, that is a good point," said Sturb diplomatically. "But on the other hand, no one else would have complete run of the place." Warden pressed a few buttons on her tablet, and the display was filled with rows of thumbnails. "And no one else would have access to the penthouse level. No one else would have had the chance he had today to take these reconnaissance pictures."

I squirmed a little in my seat when I noticed that about one-third of every picture was devoted to a blurry green smear that I assumed was the flap on my flight jacket breast pocket.

"Incomplete at best," groused Derby. "Incomplete views of the exterior. Nothing of the show floor, nothing of the maintenance infrastructure . . . it would only be adequate if we were planning a raid of your jacket pocket."

"Come on, Mr. Derby, be fair," said Sturb. "You have to remember, not everyone is a professional thief."

"Yeah, really," I said, before realizing who I was agreeing with and reestablishing my threatening stare. "Some of us managed to get through life with honest careers."

"And what a shining advertisement for the lifestyle you are," sneered Derby, doodling in the dust on his nearest armrest. Warden sensed a gap in the conversation into which she could lever some relevance. "No matter, we have enough to formulate a plan. During the night, the object is stored in the unlocked meat freezer of the northern penthouse apartment, and Jacques McKeown is being granted use of the southern apartment for the duration of the show. He can let Derby in, and Henderson's apartment can be accessed from the balcony."

"Pfuh," pfuhed Derby. "This is beginning to sound unstimulating in its simplicity."

"Security will almost certainly be light in the southern apartment if McKeown requests privacy." Warden pointed out the pictures I'd taken of the apartment in question, which was virtually identically furnished to Henderson's, minus the star pilot artifacts and omnipresent bodyguards. "The difficulty will be in getting through the northern apartment unnoticed by guards."

"Just leave that to me," said Derby. "I know the object. I know the location of the object. It is practically already in my grasp."

"Having it in your grasp is one thing," countered Warden, "bringing it to Salvation Station is another. Mr. Sturb has a solution in mind for that."

"I've been playing around with a portable Quantunnel kit." Sturb sounded modest, but his excitement was building again. "It's made from a simple light alloy and I can put a gate together in just under ten minutes. If I can get the parts into the freezer, I can assemble the gate there, and we can theoretically transport the cylinder anywhere in the city via Quantunnel."

"What?" I piped up. "Can you do that? I thought Quantunnels had to be fixed in place?"

"Do you star pilots actively try to live behind the times, or does it come naturally?" Derby smugly looked around at the others for agreement.

"Mobile Quantunnels are perfectly possible," said Warden. "They are, however, illegal."

"Because someone might do what we're doing," added Sturb, smiling.

"Which, of course, is of no concern for those of us who live unhampered by the laws of the small minded." Derby flashed me a devilish grin, and held up his shortened arm, the one with the strange device on the end. "How did you think *this* worked?"

Despite myself, I was momentarily impressed. "You've got a little Quantunnel on the end of your arm."

He let the cover fall open, and this time, no tool emerged. Instead, the circle at the end of his arm stump was a window looking into a dimly lit storage room with a number of metal shelving units. "I have an assistant prepared to supply me with any tool I might require," he boasted.

"Hi, everyone," said a female voice from deep within his arm stump. A slim hand came into view on the other side of the Quantunnel and waved in greeting.

Derby quickly clapped the cover shut again. "A far more intelligent solution than lugging everything about my person." He self-consciously smoothed his suit. "I simply request tools as required with a system of non-verbal signals."

"Right, I'm with you. Wiggle your nose for a screwdriver, clench your bum cheeks for a wrench, that sort of thing." I frowned. "Doesn't the city council monitor all Quantunnel activity?"

"Well, that's where it gets really interesting." Sturb pointed to Derby's hand. "Tunnels only show up on monitoring at the moment they're opened, and that one's continuously open. Not to mention too small for most standard scans to pick up."

"And the one we intend to use during the heist?" said Warden. "The cylinder is large enough to require at least a human-sized Quantunnel."

Sturb nodded. "That's going to be trickier. If we use the Quantunnel to transport the cylinder to anywhere outside Ritsuko City, it'll light up on monitoring like a Christmas tree. They don't want you using them to bypass immigration. Now, theoretically, there's not a lot the police can do about it. They can send units to where the signal is detected, but we could always make a run for it before they arrive. But I've been hearing rumors about the new range of top-line Quantunnel detectors that can actually redirect a tunnel as it's activated, and I'd rather not risk it. Especially if Henderson Tower is paying for additional private Quantunnel security, which they almost certainly are."

"So what are we going to do?" I said.

"The tunnel will get harder for any monitoring system to notice the smaller the distance between the two points it connects." Sturb made excited hand gestures like a sign language expert speaking in tongues. "If the exit tunnel is roughly directly above or below the entrance tunnel, physically, they should barely notice it at all, because of the way the standard detection system works. Anyone investigating the theft later could probably trace it, but I should think we'll be long gone by then."

"Indeed," said Warden. "Here's my proposal. Our inside man can park his ship on the building's rooftop spaceport. There are no end of plausible reasons why Jacques McKeown might request such a thing. If we place the exit tunnel onboard the ship, we can move the cylinder, fly it away, and be halfway to Salvation by the time anyone notices the theft."

"Yes, *I* could fly it away," I pressed.

Warden swiped across to reveal a poster very much like the one I'd seen in the Henderson Tower lobby. "The convention begins this weekend. It will last for three days, starting on Friday. McKeown will touch down with Derby and Sturb stowing away, to be let out on the night of the theft. That will be Sunday night . . ."

I stiffened myself out of my defeated slump. "No, it plying won't."

She blinked. "What is it now?"

"I'm not gonna survive three plying days of a plying meetup for McKeown's creepy fans," I said, folding my arms. "I'll be choking someone to death by Saturday lunchtime. Probably myself. Why can't we do it on Friday night?"

"You will be expected to leave on Sunday," said Warden, with her usual patient condescension. "If you disappear before then, suspicion will be raised a lot sooner."

"Then I'll just fly us very, very fast," I said through clenched teeth. I'd given a lot of ground on this whole venture, but I was determined to dig my feet into the last square foot of sod she had left me with.

"Much as I hate to admit it, I agree with the pilot." Derby smacked his lips to dispel the bitter taste of the words. "Davisham Derby will not skulk in this flying plague pit for two whole nights. All the storage units in the universe couldn't contain enough hand sanitizer."

Warden looked to Sturb for support. "Actually, I agree with them."

"Oh, for plying out loud!" I barked. "Will you stop all this being-reasonable and agreeing-with-me bulltrac? Nobody's plying fooled!"

Sturb stared at me like a kicked dog, his smile quivering and his eyes like twin distress beacons. "Sorry. I just agree. The convention's gonna be full of hardcore Jacques McKeown fans who know his work inside and out. One of them's bound to figure you out eventually if you hang around for too long."

"Oh yeah!" I turned to Warden. "That as well."

"Fine," sighed Warden, defeatedly moving some boxes around on her tablet with a motion similar to flicking a bogey. "Friday. Mr. Sturb will construct the first half of the portable Quantunnel somewhere within this ship. At midnight, Mr. Pierce will escort the others from the ship to his apartment.

Mr. Derby will jump from the balcony to the Hendersons', then use his own discretion to neutralize any resistance and secure the apartment. He will then escort Mr. Sturb to the meat freezer and keep watch while he constructs the second half of the Quantunnel. Meanwhile, Mr. Pierce will return to his ship on foot and prepare to take off and fly to the Black as soon as Mr. Sturb and Mr. Derby have brought the cylinder onboard through the Quantunnel. Is everyone clear?"

"It sounds, to use the common man's parlance, like a plan," said Derby, idly buffing his wrist device with his sleeve. "I can only pray that I can stay awake long enough to see it concluded."

I couldn't help noticing that Warden's contribution to the plan was mainly sitting on her arse eating sticky buns while we did all the work, but I didn't raise the issue, as I knew what she would say, and I'd had quite enough of being made to look stupid in front of everyone. If anything could bring Henderson out of his catatonia, her physical presence would. Either that or cause him to angrily explode with enough force to level the building. "Right. What could go wrong?" I said.

Malcolm Sturb frowned in thought, then fumbled at his top pocket for his smartphone, which he held to his face. "Jimi, what could go wrong?"

"Running simulations," said a placid, gender-neutral voice in reply. "Identified fifty-seven distinct elements that could go wrong. Sorting in ascending order of likelihood. One. Invasion of the surface by hitherto un-discovered race of underground dwellers. Two . . ."

"I wasn't actually asking," I said.

CHAPTER 7

FRIDAY MORNING SAW me in the cockpit of the *Neverdie*, sitting cross-legged in the pilot's chair with the detachable keyboard from the computer terminal in my lap.

Frobisher. After I send this, I have to pretend to be Jacques McKeown. There's probably going to be some talk about how I am him, maybe even something in the news, so I'm sending you this to let you know that I'm totally, totally not really Jacques McKeown, and I'm just pretending to be to get one over on some of his stupid bracket fans.

"What are you doing?" said Warden, right behind me.

"Not making the same mistake a second time." I gave her a dirty look before returning to the screen.

It'll all be over by Monday, so until then, I need you to make sure that any brackets who talk about coming after me for being Jacques McKeown know what the score is. Just keep it a secret within the star pilot community for the weekend at least. Thanks. Love to the missus.

"Are you sure you want to do that?" said Warden, perching on the radar scanner and folding her arms casually.

I looked over the draft. "Do what? Ensure we don't get hunted across space by warrior star pilots with big grudges who just live for the days when they have an excuse to fight something?"

"We were hunted across space by more than just those people last time," she pointed out.

"Granted, but I'd sooner fight two Xagraboran mammoths than three." I slapped the Enter key, and a festive little animation of a spaceship zooming into an open mailbox informed me that the mail had been delivered.

Warden clicked her tongue. "You may have burned a bridge there. This will get outside star pilot circles within days, and then the game is over. You may one day have a need to impersonate Jacques McKeown again."

"Yeah?" I boggled at her sarcastically. "Well, if that day comes, I'll have to think of some other way to get myself killed, won't I. Any reason you're still here?"

She held out a tiny plastic baggie that I thought was empty at first glance, but a closer look revealed that it contained two tiny flecks of matter—one white, one black. "Place the white one in your ear. The black one clips onto the inside of your teeth. Miniature transmitters. So the four of us can be in constant contact. Don't lose them, they cost a lot of money."

I held the baggie in front of my eye, turning it over and over. One might easily have mistaken the contents for a grain of rice and a dead spider. "What will they think of next."

"Quantum tunneling is a miraculous technology," she said, knowing full well that it would irk me. "I'll be monitoring the three of you from Salvation Station."

"Well, try not to get a stomach ulcer worrying about us," I muttered, settling in my chair in an "I would like you to leave now" sort of way. "Hate to think you were being plying inconvenienced at all."

Again, I could tell without looking that she was rolling her eyes. "Feel free to take off as soon as Derby and Sturb come aboard. I take it you won't want to fraternize for long."

"Great," I said, clutching the joysticks. "Just wait until the two supervillains get onboard, then proceed with the crimes. Got it. Maybe I'll make them some plying tea and biscuits while they figure out how they're going to destroy the galaxy with their share of the fee."

She didn't seem to be in any hurry to leave. She stopped at the cockpit hatch. "You know, this hero-villain thing is a sign of intellectual laziness. I suspect it comes of wanting to live an adventure story. What is 'good'? What is 'bad'?"

"It'd be 'good' if you plied off."

"You were a star pilot for years," she continued, regardless. "Saving lives, helping to build spacegoing society. Then Quantunneling comes out and you're left practically destitute. Was that 'good'? Was that just?"

I heaved a sigh and surrendered to this inescapable conversation. "You didn't do it 'cos you were expecting a reward. The villains were trying to hurt the innocent or take over the galaxy and you stopped them because no one else would."

"And how are all these 'innocents' you mentioned now? Now that star pilots are no longer around to solve their problems for them?"

I spun my chair around and peered at her from under my cap. "Don't you have to be back on Salvation? Making sure Blaze has enough hot lemon drinks?"

It took me a few moments to figure out what she was doing with her face, because I could have sworn she looked guilty, and that would have been absurd. "I just think it's a waste that you find this kind of work so unconscionable. I remember how you worked the president of the United Republic. You have a natural gift for confidence trickery."

I cocked my head. "What is this? You don't have to butter me up anymore. I'm already doing your plying stupid heist that's going to get us all killed. You just make sure those scientists are ready."

She was staring at her shoes. "For the record, I am sorry. I wouldn't have enlisted you for this if I hadn't thought it was completely necessary."

"You're serious. You're actually trying to make amends." I spun my chair back around. "Don't bother. The best thing you can do for that is go forth and multiply."

"Goodbye, McKeown," she spat, offended.

I listened to her sensible shoes clang-clanging down the gangway and out the airlock, and when silence finally fell, I felt a twinge of guilt. That had probably been the exact opposite of "being the bigger man." As she would no doubt be happy to patiently explain with her usual infuriatingly superior tone of voice, there really wasn't any specific reason to be mad at her about any of this. Blaze needed the antidote, and the arrangement had been completely upfront, if you didn't count the whole "illegal heist" thing. Blowing her off wasn't helping any. Plying satisfying as it was.

Sturb arrived well on time, knocking politely on the airlock wall. "Hello? Anyone in?"

"Set up in the passenger cabin," I called down the gangway. "We go as soon as Derby gets here."

"Hello again, Captain, looking forward to working with you," said Sturb. I heard him stomp clumsily up the steps and pass through the hatch into the cabin. A moment later, he poked his head back out into the gangway. "Captain?"

"What now?"

"Derby's already in here."

"Indeed," came Derby's voice from the cabin. "Let us not prolong this grubby little venture any further than is needed."

"You—" I began yelling down the hall before I remembered there was a perfectly good intercom for this. I thumbed the speaker button and tried to keep my voice level reasonable. "You could have told me you'd arrived."

"Davisham Derby is a master of stealth." There was a brief pause and a clinking of porcelain as he paused for a casual sip of tea. "Can Davisham Derby be blamed if his instincts unconsciously—"

I released the button to shut him up, then began preparations to fly, mentally running down the preflight safety checklist and disregarding the usual eight or nine items. I sent spaceport ground control a permission-for-takeoff request, and since this was the least effective way to get the brackets to notice you, I also noisily fired my hover jets.

The roof of the spaceport hastily split apart and the *Neverdie* took off into the glittering sky above Ritsuko City, bouncing jauntily on her vertical jets. The city council had this weird objection to ships attempting to move between buildings, so I would have to ascend to just below dome altitude and then descend to the roof of the Henderson Tower.

The jets were probably overdue for service, so the climb would take a while. I held the Jet Sustain lever down with my foot, made myself comfortable, and flicked on the local news station.

". . . cycle traffic is fully backed up on downtown Ritsuko's Leg, extending to Left Elbow, Collarbone, and Right Elbow," said the traffic reporter from the city-observation platform at the apex of the dome. "There's also significant slowdown on Shoulder, Armpit, and around both Nipples. So do expect delays if you're trying to get to Paizuri Pass tonight for the market."

"And this is all due to the crowd that has formed in the city center?" asked the newsreader in the studio.

"Yes, I assumed that was obvious," came the testy reply. The observation platform was a long way from the city's heating coils, and it was a rare traffic reporter that didn't start harboring resentment about it. "The crowds are still packed shoulder to shoulder around Henderson Tower."

"Chock-a-block, Steve?"

"Yes, that's another way it could be described," said Steve. "Tell you what, why don't you come up here and we can sit around thinking of all kinds of ways to say the same damn thing."

"Okay, Steve, talk to you later."

My ears had prickled at the mention of Henderson Tower, and that prickle had now spread to all my body's most uncomfortable crevices. Jacques McKeown couldn't possibly have a following *that* big. The convention was probably catering to a couple of fan bases. Hell, going by how freely Daniel was spending his father's money, maybe he was just drawing a crowd by chucking handfuls of euroyen off the balcony.

"If you're just joining us, the only news anyone is talking about is that Jacques McKeown, the megapopular author who has never given interviews and whose true identity is a complete mystery, is making his first-ever appearance at Jacques McCon today," said the radio presenter professionally.

"Mm, could be one of the most significant cultural events in modern history, Linda," said the other presenter. "Over the years Jacques McKeown has been rumored to be dead, alive, lost somewhere in the depths of space, the daughter of the Terran president, and everything in between, so interest in this is huge. Some have decried him as a hack who stole all his best stories from struggling star pilots, and who writes for fat nerds with arrested development, but if those crowds out there are telling us anything, it's that today it's chic to be geek."

"It sure is," said Linda, her voice dripping with self-disgust.

I swallowed hard. I'd been hoping for a somewhat lower profile than this. Suddenly that email I had sent to Frobisher was starting to feel uncomfortably premature.

A spark flew off the socket where the altitude warning light was supposed to be, so I cut off the vertical jets and set a course toward the roof of the Henderson Tower.

"This just in," said Linda, interrupting some completely vapid speculation on what the well-dressed star pilots were wearing this season. "We've just heard reports that a spaceship is coming toward the roof of the convention center now. Steve?"

"Yes, I'm still here," said Steve the traffic reporter spitefully. "It's a red ship, exactly the kind of thing you'd expect a star pilot to fly. I think we've got it on the Dome Cam now, so you can see for yourself."

I peered up through my cockpit viewers at the upside-down tower that hung from the center of Ritsuko City's dome like a rectangular stalactite. The viewing platform at the very bottom was clearly angled toward me, and I suddenly felt naked.

"Now, what do you make of that, Linda?" asked the second studio presenter.

"Well, if that is Jacques McKeown's ship, then obviously he places a lot of importance on authenticity," replied Linda. "You've got to think, someone with his kind of money and popularity would be able to afford a ship that isn't so—"

I swiftly reached out and snapped the radio off, because I'd decided I didn't want to know how that sentence was going to end, and neither did the *Neverdie*. Lord knows I was in the doghouse enough already.

Another thought occurred, one that I hadn't thought in some time, but which for a while had been making me wake up with a start each morning and fumble for my gun: this might be exactly the kind of thing that the real Jacques McKeown would notice. After I stole his royalties, and while I'd been dishing it out to the deserving star pilots, I'd spent the whole time peering over my shoulder like a nervous meerkat, but no one had come forward to try to stop me. It came to the point that I was approaching every blind alley and closed door hoping he'd finally jump out with a knife and put an end to all the plying anticipation.

Eventually, after a sufficient amount of nothing had happened, I'd decided he didn't know about what I was doing with his money. After all, he'd never cared about collecting it, because apparently he lived under a rock with all the other small wriggling life forms. But he'd have to be living under Olympus plying Mons not to notice this.

Suddenly, I remembered the miniature transmitter that Warden had given me, and fumbled with the baggie. The speaker very nearly fell right down the back of my seat cushion, to be lost amid the discarded grains of rice from countless sushi-sandwich lunches, but I caught it just in time and stuffed it down my ear.

". . . must be thousands of them," came the voice of Malcolm Sturb, as clear as if he were in the room.

"Huh," said Derby, reluctantly impressed. "I must learn not to underestimate the credulity of the masses. Little boys no longer grow up, it seems, they merely expand."

I clipped the microphone onto my tooth, very nearly spearing myself through the gum in the process. "Ow."

"Are you reading us, McKeown?" asked Warden, from some no doubt extremely comfortable chair back on Salvation.

"Loud and clear."

"I was just saying, Captain," said Sturb. "It was a good idea of yours to bring the heist forward to tonight. There must be thousands of Jacques McKeown fans down there. One of them would almost certainly figure you out before Sunday."

"Hmph," bristled Warden. "They may yet figure it out before tonight, looking at these numbers."

"So what do you suggest we do about that?" I asked archly. "Bit late to turn around and pretend we were never here. They've noticed the ship now."

And as the *Neverdie* drew closer to the rooftop landing pad on Henderson Tower, I could see that quite a crowd had formed to notice the ship. Some of them were holding up signs that were still too far away to read, but more than enough meaning was conveyed from the prevalence of hearts drawn with the careful curves and diligent shading of the truly psychotic.

The landing pad was clear, though not because of any self-restraint on the part of the fans; bikers surrounded the perimeter of the landing ring, looking like slightly overdressed professional wrestlers as they stood in alert poses, aggressively shoving back anyone who tried to get closer. Safety didn't seem to be their main concern, however, as Daniel Henderson himself was in the middle, staring adoringly up at me. He was standing in the perfect spot to be "accidentally" decapitated by the emerging claws of a descending landing leg.

I won't deny that the thought crossed my mind, as did the one about ditching the whole caper and speeding away. But despite everything, I still didn't have it in me to wish death on Daniel Henderson. He just wanted to be liked and hang out with space heroes. It wasn't his fault that his dad had been too busy slitting throats to learn how to be a proper father.

"Captain? I've had a little brain wave, if you'll indulge me," said Sturb. "We could help you out, if you want. I've got Jimi with me. If you need any help with their questions, we can feed you information on Jacques McKeown's books through your earpiece."

"Tha-a-anks." I sarcastically extended the word until it was fully three syllables long. "But don't worry, Sturb. No star pilot needs help with the details of Jacques McKeown's traccy books. He ripped them all off from people I know." A moment passed. "Ex. Ex–star pilot. You know what I meant."

"Are you sure?"

"You just stay on the ship and stay quiet. So I don't have to worry about you mind slaving people on top of everything else."

"Okay, if that's what you want." Sturb sounded slightly hurt. I was getting more and more annoyed with him. He'd shown much more commitment back when I was saving planets from his cyborg collective, but I felt like I was the only one still putting the effort into our mutual hatred.

"Of course he won't accept," said Derby. "Have you forgotten? He's a dashing space hero, and we are foul villains, and he can't be seen associating with us, because he may never again be allowed to join the other dashing heroes when they have a great big bubble bath together and pat each other's backs for being such paragons of do-gooding."

I allowed the conversation to dribble away into seething silence and concentrated on landing. The ship was directly above the landing pad now, and I could no longer see Daniel Henderson, so I'd just have to finish the descent and hope he wasn't so starstruck that he wouldn't get out of the way when the landing legs came out.

I could still see part of the crowd, though, bubbling away at the bottom of my view like the vat of boiling oil into which I was willingly lowering myself. They seemed to have stopped trying to force their way closer and were now mostly staring in wonder at the *Neverdie*, some with their mouths hanging open, the rest coughing up exhaust fumes.

The landing legs thumped down onto the tarmac, and I felt the ship creak and rattle as it settled, accompanied by the backing vocals of the deactivating jets.

As I gripped the armrests of my chair to stand, it suddenly struck me that this was the very last point of no return. I could still conceivably stay where I was, reactivate the jets, and speed off to somewhere nice and quiet to hide, preferably somewhere with a soft floor into which I could bury the corpses of Derby and Sturb after I had shot them both in the head.

I chewed on my upper lip for a second, listening to the crowd's halted, expectant murmur. Then I stood up and made my way to the airlock.

If I ever did acquire the ability to travel back in time and kick myself in the doints, and the moment I'd first agreed to the heist was fully booked up by other future versions of myself, then this moment would have been my second choice.

CHAPTER 8

AS I OPENED the *Neverdie's* external airlock door, everything descended into chaos. The roar of the crowd was a tidal wave washing away all other sound. A fusillade of camera flashes popped and snapped at me from every angle. All I could do was stand there dumbly in the middle of this assault of light and noise, like a weather balloon in a fireworks display.

A large black shape that smelled like Mr. Heller appeared to my left, and something meaty and powerful clamped around my arm like the jaws of a playful hippo. Then I was hurried past a heaving mass of fans that a row of bikers was just barely keeping back, and bundled into a narrow maintenance hallway.

Heller was joined by a second bodyguard who took my other arm, and my feet barely touched the floor as I was propelled along a concrete passage like an urgently needed kidney through the corridors of a hospital. Finally, I was brought to a door with a handmade sign reading Green Room and practically hurled inside.

The green room also had much of a hospital about it—a hospital just behind the frontlines of a bitter, prolonged trench war. The soft couches and coffee tables that had been set up for my benefit were virtually all being occupied by moaning patients with a variety of blunt-impact and crush injuries. About half were bikers, and the rest I assumed were convention staff; they were younger, wearing T-shirts adorned with the logos I'd seen on the convention posters, and many of them seemed to be suffering from their pimples having traumatically burst.

"All right!" said Daniel Henderson, who had apparently been hustled along directly behind me. He was drenched in sweat, and his grin had acquired the merest hint of mania. "Great turnout this year, guys. Whew. Oh, Mr. Heller, hey, I left my tablet on the helipad, could you get it?"

Heller, who had been leaning against a wall trying to get his breathing under control, turned the color of a slightly used shroud. "Yes . . . sir," he quavered, taking shaking steps toward the maintenance door we'd entered by.

"Okay," said Daniel brightly. "Jacques's here. Cool. I'm gonna see if the hall is ready for the first signing sesh." He glanced nervously at the other door, the much grander one that led out to the convention area proper. "Jacques, why don't you . . . hang out with the other guest and stuff, Jacques? Cool. Jacques." Then he was gone.

It didn't take long to figure out who the other guest was. There was only one other person who wasn't among the wounded or a member of convention staff slapping multicolored Band-Aids on anyone who was still oozing something. She was a middle-aged woman in a dark sweater, jeans, and sporty ponytail, sitting with arms folded and legs crossed to avoid having to touch the biker lying full length on the couch next to her, who was suffering from having had one of his facial safety pins shoved halfway up his nose.

"So you're Jacques McKeown, are you?" asked the woman, as I made to sit on one of the more vacant couches. She had an educated voice that could have cut plexiglass.

"Maintain cover at all times," said Warden, unheard to all but me.

"I know!" I hissed.

"And don't acknowledge me!"

"I—" I cut myself off in time. I smiled tightly at the woman, whose suspicious expression hadn't changed in the slightest, then gingerly completed the task of sitting down. "I mean, yes. I'm Jacques McKeown."

"Geranium Pleasant," she said.

The bikers and staff had started tactfully giving the two of us a wide berth, and I found myself alone with the woman in the peaceful eye of the human storm. I looked around. "Where?"

She frowned. "What? I'm Geranium Pleasant."

"Oh. Sorry." I rubbed the back of my neck. "I thought you were complaining about the decor, or something."

She looked confused for a moment, then shook herself, making the foot on her crossed leg jiggle limply. "Perhaps you've heard my name before?" she asked with a just barely detectable ounce of sarcasm.

I stared at her with bit lip, because now that she mentioned it, I had heard that name before. I couldn't quite put my finger on where, although for some reason it felt like a name that should have been written down in very severe serifed letters.

"It . . . rings a bell," I admitted.

She gave me a broad, squinty-eyed smile that had all the sincerity of a heart-shaped chocolate box with a turd inside it. "I rather thought it would. I wrote a little book called *Flowers Dying in Electric Lights*, have you heard of it?"

"Y-yeah," I said, to my own surprise. It had been a novel about a struggling star pilot in the immediate aftermath of Quantunneling taking off. I'd read it along with a lot of other star pilots at the time it had come out, because we were all feeling starved of sympathy. I hadn't liked it; nothing much happened, not even a moderately interesting laser battle, and the main character tended to stare out of the window and think for tens of pages at a time, with about an average of twelve trips to the dictionary per page. None of which felt like anything worth mentioning.

"It was first published about eight years ago," said Geranium Pleasant. "Critically acclaimed. *Ritsuko Review* called it the progenitor of the star pilot fiction genre."

"Good . . ."

"In one short paragraph," she continued, straightening her back even further. "As part of a twelve-page article about you. Remind me when your first book was published?"

I hadn't the first plying idea. "Erm . . ."

"Seven and a half years ago." Her stare bore into me like an asteroid-mining laser. "What a very strange coincidence that it came out so shortly after my book. *Flowers* was only a modest success, did you hear that?"

All I knew was that it can't have made much money among star pilots, because we'd all been lending around the same four or five copies. I'd borrowed mine from Jabril the Mad, and had ended up passing it on to Kid Donny as partial payment for him sweeping my airlock.

"No," I summarized.

"Do you do much research when you set out to write a book, Mr. McKeown?" Her tone had shifted from flat and accusatory to somewhat lilting and interested.

"Well, I, you know, a bit." I rocked my buttocks left and right on the seat as embarrassment started prickling me. "I talk to star pilots—"

"I suspect you do," interjected Geranium, dropping right back down to flat and accusatory. "I suspect there was one specific book you researched for your first novel. Or maybe you'd like to tell me that it's complete co-incidence how, not three and a half months after I publish a book about a star pilot named Jack, you publish your book about a star pilot named Jacques?"

It was impossible to be intimidated, as she was quite small and tightening her muscles so hard with tension that she was only making herself smaller. "That does sound like a complete coincidence," I said in a neutral tone.

She made several incredulous gasping noises as she started rummaging around in her purse. "Ach! Gach!" She produced a copy of Jacques McKeown's very first book, *Space Hero Jacques McKeown, Hero of Space*. Her incredibly weathered copy was so stuffed with Post-it notes that it seemed to have double the correct number of pages. "So this was all a co-incidence as well, was it?" She turned to the first Post-it note. "Item one. Jacques McKeown visits a planet called Mulkus 3. At the start of *Flowers*, Jack Quirinus is living on Manson Street. This not only starts with an *M* but also has the same number of letters. Item two . . ."

I pointed awkwardly at the indicated passage. "I think that one definitely is a coincidence."

"Are you serious?!" she snapped, thrusting her jaw toward me like a vicious ferret. Then she examined her Post-its again. "Well. Maybe that one is. But what about your second book?" She produced a second volume, almost as stuffed with yellow notes as the first one.

"What was that one again?"

I had been leaning over to get a look at the cover, but when she saw me doing so, she tilted it out of my view, raising her eyebrows at me. "You don't know the name of your own second book?"

"Sure I do," I said hastily, realizing an instant later that there was a precisely 100 percent chance of her asking the question she then asked.

"So what's it called?" She eyeballed the cover I couldn't see.

I took a long, slow drink from a nearby water bottle as I went over the possibilities in my head. I was pretty sure they hadn't started the *Jacques McKeown and the* —— naming scheme until the third book. The second one had had something really plying uncreative, I remembered, but that didn't narrow it down. It might have been *Jacques McKeown Returns*. Or *Reloaded* or *Regurgitates* or some other plying *Re* word.

The bottle was empty now and my bladder had started to register complaints, so I was going to have to say something. "It's the . . . the one," I tried. "The one with the thing. The star pilot thing." I made the mistake of meeting her gaze. Her face was cold and disapproving, but there was a slight cock to her hips giving away how much she was enjoying watching me squirm.

"You don't know," she said flatly.

I folded my arms. "I've written loads of books. So, you know, I've probably forgotten some little details."

Her mouth opened and closed a few times in silence, before she slowly leaned back in her chair, shocked. "Well, well," she chanted, when she finally found her words again. "I've figured it out. You're a fraud."

My mind raced. My blaster was still hanging off my belt, and while I was well behind on quick-draw practice, I was confident I could explode her head before she got another word out. A slightly less hysterical inner voice then took over and pointed out that a stun shot would probably suffice. Assuming I got the shot off while nobody in the room was looking, I'd then have to explain to them that she had suddenly contracted the kind of airborne narcolepsy that makes plasma burns appear on your skin and clothing . . .

"I know exactly what kind of writer you are now," said Geranium Pleasant after I had gaped in silence for a good few seconds. "The kind who hammers books out with so little thought or care that he can't even remember writing them."

"Yes!" I said, nodding. "I mean, how dare you."

"So you just hack them out? Like cattle passing through a mincing machine? How many drafts do you write?" She thumped her own chest. "My books are my children. I would sooner bring my child to a fast-food restaurant than submit a work before the fifteenth draft."

"Well, everyone's got what works for them," I mumbled, failing to penetrate her rant.

"There are young persons out there who obsess over your books." She threw an arm toward the main doors, from which the sounds of the war zone outside were still thundering. "They've taken you into their hearts and you clearly don't even care. Well." She stood dramatically. "I'm going to expose you, Jacques McKeown. We're going to find out exactly how little you know about your own business."

She marched away, her ponytail bobbing with suppressed rage as she walked, and took up position beside the door with her back to the room and arms folded.

After a few moments, I heard Malcolm Sturb coughing in my ear. "So are you sure you don't need us to—"

"*Yes*," I hissed.

CHAPTER 9

THE MAIN THING I had long wondered about Jacques McKeown—besides when, precisely, he was planning to jump out from a side street and pin my doints to the ground with a nail gun—was why he had never come forward and identified himself, even to his own publisher. True, a lot of star pilots had marked him for death, but that was after they figured out he was ripping off our stories. In fact, right after he got really famous, some star pilots were broadly in favor of him.

I thought it was particularly strange that he had never even tried to claim any fame or riches. But after one hour of living the lifestyle in store for him, I was gaining a much deeper understanding of the thieving divbasket. If I had to deal with a near riot every time I left the house, and the company of people like Geranium Pleasant, I'd probably end up wanting to live under a rock, too.

A member of the convention staff, with one hand clutching a clipboard and the other holding a piece of raw steak to his eye, arrived at the green room after a few minutes to inform us that the meet-and-greet tables in the lobby were ready for the first session. Geranium Pleasant went ahead, on the reasonable assumption that she didn't have quite so many psychotic fans to worry about, while I had to wait for a suitable protective detail to assemble.

Shortly, I was surrounded by a ring of four of Henderson's trusted black-suited bodyguards, all wearing the tight lips and steely faraway looks of loyal military men about to rise from the trenches and go out into no man's land. Around them, a platoon of colorful bikers formed a larger circle, whose job was apparently to clear the path for us through the strategic use of massive blunt trauma.

Once the two circles were fully formed, the staff member with the clipboard subtly crossed himself, then flung the doors wide open. I was moved out into the adjoining hall in the center of my personal wheel of destruction.

Surrounded by heavyset bodies in black silk, I was spared the sight of the crowd (and, as was presumably the point, they were spared the sight of me); but I was aware of them, in the way one is aware of the crowd of murderous cyberserkers trying to peel the armor off your protective bunker. Even behind two layers of human protection, I could feel the mob on all sides, jostling for room to move. It was like being a cat trapped in the center of an overloaded tumble dryer.

The floor abruptly changed into a descending staircase, and I would have fallen catastrophically if it weren't for the tightly packed inner circle giving me no choice but to remain upright. Gradually I became aware that we were descending into the grand lobby of the building; it had been hard to recognize at first with every last square foot of space filled with human traffic. It was like a churning ocean unfolding below me, clad in hundreds of flight jackets and jumpsuits that had none of the frays or coolant stains to suggest they had ever been within a light minute of an actual starship's engine.

Looking down at the lobby from the staircase, I could see our destination: a couple of covered tables that had been set up alongside the main reception desk. One was surrounded by signs and cutouts of imagery from Jacques McKeown books, and marked the beginning of the disorderly queue that accounted for most of the people in the room, and the second had a name written on a single piece of folded printer paper. Geranium Pleasant was already sitting behind that one, hands clasped tightly in front of her like a little knobbly grenade.

The first thirty feet of the queue for Jacques McKeown's table was kept in line by a rather overoptimistic velvet rope, and once it ran out, the queue snaked wildly around the entire lobby, weaving around every piece of furniture and exhibit like a tapeworm in a particularly unhealthy small intestine. I was hurried past it toward my seat, through an atmosphere of hushed anticipation that thickened more and more as the conventiongoers noticed my presence.

From the table, with my back to the wall, I had an enviable view of the queue as it stretched away into infinity. It was like being a condemned man whose execution was going to take place in a room with mirrors on all the walls. I clasped my hands in front of me on the wobbly table that was to be my gibbet.

"Okay, cool," said Daniel, appearing in front of us. He was still physically intact, although I noticed his own bodyguards a few feet away were all nursing black eyes. "This is just gonna be a, like, signing and meeting and greeting thing. Obviously it's, you know, a big turnout, so maybe we'll keep it to one signing and one question per visitor . . ."

A groan went up that did a few circuits of the room like a stadium wave. Several people started disappointedly picking through the vast sacks full of books they had brought.

"Ready?" said Daniel.

"*I* am," said Geranium Pleasant, straightening her back and briefly stabbing me with a look. I gave Daniel the nod.

I didn't know when they'd let people start queuing for this, but the first fifty or so individuals had a haggard look about them, and one person was hurriedly packing away what looked like a small collapsible tent.

The first two were deceptively easy; they were clearly feeling intimidated by me, the omnipresent security, and the flashing cameras of the journalists, so they hurried up, faces red, and got their books signed so quickly that I didn't have time to commit their appearances to memory. I invented a signature for Jacques McKeown on the spur of the moment, going for what I hoped was a convincing amount of self-important twirly bits, but they didn't even look at it before they tottered away.

The third one was where the difficulties began. He was a robust young man who had set his sights on growing a beard, but the result was to a full, luxurious beard what a dirty frying pan is to a complete breakfast. He handed me a copy of *Jacques McKeown and the Slatterns from Saturn* to sign.

"So, I just want to ask, ha ha," he said, in a distinctly wet voice, "in *Jacques McKeown and the Terror of Terrorgorn*, it says that your first ship was a Nairo Cruiser, but then in *Jacques McKeown and the Bogon Encounter*, you have to steal a Nairo Cruiser and it says you aren't used to how it handles, and my friend says that you were saying you'd only been a crew member on the Nairo Cruiser and hadn't actually flown it, but he's an idiot, ha ha, and I think you were just saying that Nairo Cruisers take a really long time to get used to, so was it that?"

"Yes, I'd like to know that myself," said Geranium Pleasant, who hadn't signed anything yet and had little else to do but watch me undergo my trials.

Time seemed to slow and the bustle faded away as I fixed my gaze on the sweating grin of this fat doint and considered my next move. The temptation was to just say yes, but I had lost track of whatever the hell he had been banging on about halfway through his question, and now the cameras were closing in and I didn't know if saying yes was going to contradict three other books and refute ninety-seven fan theories.

I felt a metaphorical finger hovering over the switch in my head, but putting myself in automatic banter mode could have unpredictable results if I didn't have a strategy worked out. Still, the silence was drawing on and my instincts were usually reliable. I closed my eyes, hit the switch, and Jacques McKeown spoke.

"Do you honestly care?" I heard myself say the instant my eyes flicked open.

He seemed thrown by the question. He barked out an unconvincing laugh, a fresh bead of sweat navigating the slalom of his chin tufts. "Uh. No. Ha ha. I was just wondering . . ."

"You care enough to queue for three days and waste your one question with Jacques McKeown on it," I said, lazily signing the book with some extra-big curves. "There are people starving to death on old Earth because they voted for the wrong party, and this is what's most bothering you?"

"Ha ha, I know that it's stupid, but . . ."

"If you really knew it was stupid, you wouldn't have asked, would you." I held out the book for him to take, maintaining withering eye contact. "Take your book, kid, and multiply."

He stumbled off, mouth set into the kind of philosophical smile one adopts when trying not to cry, and just like that, my strategy was clear. My instincts had come through.

All I had to do was get through one day, and I could do it by blowing everyone off as obnoxiously as possible. After all, I was the big celebrity guest; if I was tired and didn't feel like answering their stupid questions, everyone was just going to have to deal. It was exactly the kind of attitude I'd expect from the kind of bracket who'd try to get rich stealing other people's stories.

Plus, it couldn't hurt to ruin his reputation in the eyes of his public. Maybe they'd stop buying his plying books if they knew what a divbiscuit he was in real life. With any luck, the universe at large would know after this weekend that Jacques McKeown was a massive doint who had contempt for his fans. And who stole extremely valuable cryonic cylinders from his host.

I settled into character and waved a hand to keep the line moving. Numerous visitors went by, most of them uncannily similar to the first one, appearancewise, with mild variations in beard growth and acne patterns, and I ensured that every single one went away feeling like trac.

"So what advice would you give to someone wanting to start out in writing?" asked one.

"Forget it," I replied. "Don't need the competition."

"I love your books, I've read them all, like, fifty times," said another.

"Good on you," I said as I signed the book. "Keep at it. With any luck, you won't have time to breed."

"So where do you get your ideas?" asked several people.

"I get inspired every time someone asks me a question that makes me want to stick their head in an exhaust pipe," I said, each time.

Halfway through the day, I took a moment's downtime to examine the remaining queue. The end still wasn't in sight, but I'd worked my way through the ones who had camped overnight, and the remaining attendees looked more bored than psychotic. Most were dressed in cringeworthy interpretations of star pilot attire, but a few were in costume as other, non–star pilot figures from Jacques McKeown's canon. There was a rather convincing Malcolm Sturb costume about twenty people down the line. The wearer must have decided to play to their strengths, since they had the perfect build for Sturb, and now that I was looking closely, an uncannily similar face . . .

The penny dropped with a thunk. I put my hand over my mouth and spoke quietly enough so that only my tooth microphone could hear. "Sturb. Is that you?"

I saw the Sturb standing in the queue put his hand over his mouth just as I was doing. "Oh. Yeah. How's it going?"

"You're supposed to be staying on the ship," I whispered.

"Yes, sorry, I know I said I would. I just want to get one book signed." He stirred the dirt on the floor around with one toe. "And then I need to pick up something to eat for Derby and me. I can definitely say I'll be back before midnight."

"Indeed," confirmed Derby. "And remember, if Derby must taint his palate with mediocre Lunarian wine, I will only tolerate a Watanabe red. The '54 for preference."

I still didn't know what Sturb's angle was in all this, but there was nothing I could do about him while I was stuck at the table, and I'm sure he knew that damn well. "Someone might see you," I tried.

"Yeah, like six people have asked for selfies already! It's great, this. I can tell people I'm the real Malcolm Sturb all day and they just love it more and more."

"Anyway, why do you want a signing?" I asked, as another of the many issues jostling for attention in my mind rose to the surface. "You know I'm not the real McKeown."

"Yes, but my thinking was, if this heist becomes famous, your signatures are going to be collector's items anyway. Besides . . ." With the tooth microphone, even his shamefaced mumbling was clear as a bell. "I did want to attend the con. I've been looking forward to it."

"Seriously?"

"I heard last year was pretty good. Even without McKeown, it was a lot more fun than Galaxpo. Shame about the riots."

I shook my head, and inadvertently glanced at Geranium Pleasant's table. She was receiving one of her extremely small number of visitors with a genuine warmth and grace that had been entirely absent from her dealings with me, leaning forward and clasping their hand to shake. She caught me watching after the attendee left, and gave me a look that could have punched holes in the wrapping on a microwave dinner.

"It must be such a burden to you," she said, sarcasm gushing from every syllable. "To be so popular, having so many people wanting to make your work part of their lives. Perhaps that's why you can't help treating them with such contempt."

It was hard to hold anything against her for her attitude, since she thought she was dealing with the real Jacques McKeown, and in her position I'd have already leapt across the table wielding a broken bottle. But I was committed to the character now. "No need to be jealous, lady."

"Jealous?!" She flushed. "Some of us aren't in this for money or fame, you know."

"Right," I said, nodding. "And I can tell you're not in it for the sex, either."

Her face, already the color of a red dwarf, looked like it was threatening to go supernova. Her jaw flapped up and down for a while before her throat came up with some words to go with it. "H–how dare you? You can't just treat people like . . ." She looked ahead at the queue, and her expression softened rapidly.

I followed her gaze. There were two people approaching, one on foot, one in a wheelchair. The latter was the size of a child, but with the hollow look and sunken features of the prematurely aged. Her head was shaved, and the cheap flower-patterned dress she was wearing was the only indication that she was female.

The adult with her was pushing the wheelchair with the apologetic sensitivity of a devoted parent. She was a tall woman with a face that looked like I had caught it in a brief window between streams of crestfallen tears.

"Hello, Mr. McKeown," said the adult, in a heartbreakingly meek tone of voice. "This is Kelly. She's a big fan of your stories. We both are, aren't we, Kelly?"

Kelly nodded weakly, jostling the various tubes that connected her to a suite of life-support equipment on the backrest of her wheelchair.

"I used to read them to her because her eyes don't work terribly well," continued Kelly's mother. "That was until the house burnt down, of course. That's why we haven't got any books for you to sign." Kelly's life-support equipment gave a little pneumatic hiss to punctuate the statement.

"I'm . . . sorry?" I said, instinctively, which scarcely felt like enough. I kept my eyes on the mother, because I could sense Geranium Pleasant watching my reaction with keen interest.

"Kelly just wanted to thank you for making her life a little bit happier," said the mother, dropping her gaze as emotion began to build a quaver in her voice. "And we were in the middle of *Jacques McKeown and the Doomtrac Tournament* when the fire happened, so we were wondering if you could tell us how it ended?"

"Yes, how did that one end, Jacques?" asked Geranium with unconvincing interest.

The thought occurred that blowing off this particular attendee would be a spectacular black mark against Jacques McKeown in his future endeavors. This was the stuff of social media boycott campaigns.

This thought was swiftly drowned out by the occurrence of another, significantly louder, thought, one that had been nagging at the back of my mind all day: *What the plying hell am I doing?* I'm genuinely thinking about tearing down a burn-victim cancer kid out of spite for someone I've never even met. In the middle of a heist. A heist to crush the dreams of a not-that-much-older kid whose only crime was being slightly annoying.

Ten years ago I'd been a space hero, damn it. Back then, if a villain had offered me a chance to rule the galaxy alongside them, I'd have beaten them up on pure principle and left them for the authorities. Now, I was apparently more likely to haggle my price and request an expense account. This was Warden's doing. She'd successfully brought me down to her level.

"Mr. McKeown?" prompted Kelly's mother, after I had been blinking stupidly at her for a good thirty seconds. "*Doomtrac Tournament?*"

"How it ended," I said, mostly to myself.

"Don't worry," said Geranium Pleasant, in her most grandmotherly voice. "It sometimes takes a while for something to sink in when you have an imagination as vivid and creative as Mr. McKeown's, but he'll be able to tell you soon. After all, what kind of writer can't remember the endings to his own books?"

There was only one course of action I could take that would save my self-respect. Stand up, admit everything, abandon the heist, and walk out of the building with my head held high. And my arms held even higher for when the crowd started throwing things.

I blinked a few more times. They blinked right back. "I . . ."

"If I may?" said a hushed voice in my ear.

"Er . . ."

"He wins the final battle against Mungnash by inciting the mole people to dig underneath his feet and knock him over," said Malcolm Sturb. I glanced at him, and saw that he had a hand in front of his face as if pretending to pick his nose. "Then the special request he makes as his prize is to end mole-people oppression."

I let my mouth hang open for a few moments, then pushed the words out. "The mole people help him defeat Mungnash," I conveyed.

"Oh, we knew Jacques McKeown would win out in the end," said Kelly's mother, clapping her hands in relief. "Kelly's been so worried about what might have happened, I'm sure when I get her home, she'll just be bouncing off the walls."

My brain immediately conjured an absolutely inexcusable witticism along the lines that Kelly looked like someone who'd been bounced off more than enough walls for one lifetime, but this time I didn't even entertain the notion of voicing it aloud. I merely watched the mother and daughter roll back off into the convention proper, and bathed in the unimpressed scowl of Geranium Pleasant.

Sturb offered me a cheery thumbs-up, and I put on a scowl of my own that made all my cheek muscles burn. Warden had successfully made me sink to another low: accepting help from Malcolm plying Sturb.

After that, I went sulkily back into maximum trac-head mode for the remainder of the queue, until by the end of the day, I was signing each book with little more than a squiggle and answering each question by blowing a dismissive raspberry. The line finally dissipated two hours after the convention was supposed to have ended for the day, presumably because the convention staff had gone from polite requests to threatening to break out hoses and tear gas.

Even having used as little energy as possible, my signing hand was curled into a stiff claw of constant ache. I was blowing on my wrist when I saw Daniel Henderson emerge from the usual cloud of bruised bodyguards. Mercifully, Geranium Pleasant had already left, her fans having dried up at around dinnertime.

"Cool, okay," he said, shifting his weight back and forth, either from nervous excitement or a pressing need to use the bathroom. "Uh. Shame we didn't get around to any of the panels, slightly bigger queue for the meet and greet than we thought, but it's all cool. We'll do some tomorrow."

"Yes, tomorrow," I said, relishing the word. "There'll be plenty of time for everything tomorrow."

For a moment I had thought happily of repairing to my extremely luxurious penthouse suite and collapsing onto a bed the size of an apartment in a low-income neighborhood, until I remembered that I had a daring heist on this evening, and that the Henderson organization and the police were going to be hunting me across space pretty soon, so I wasn't looking at turning in until about three a.m. at the very earliest.

"I'm going to bed," I said bitterly, getting up.

"Okay, cool," said Daniel, hovering around the edges of my personal space. "You can just, you know, get on up and walk around the table and go up to the apartment, like that, cool. We're all really, really grateful to you."

"I know." I buried my hands in the pockets of my flight jacket. "You keep saying that."

"I know, I know, cool," repeated Daniel. "Just can't say thank you enough for all this. And to Ms. Warden."

"Great." Two steps later, I stiffened, my forward heel down and my toe hanging in the air. Then I carefully rotated myself 180 degrees by shuffling with my back foot. "Why would you thank Ms. Warden?"

"'Cos she gave me your email address," said Daniel, still beaming.

I felt a multitude of emotions, mostly hatred, mostly directed at myself, but the one thing I did not feel was surprise. "Did she, now."

"Yeah! She said she knew you'd be onboard for this but you need her to give you a little push sometimes. So are you going out with her now?"

CHAPTER 10

I WALKED ALL the way to the Quantunnel, through it to the penthouse level, along the magnificent hallways, and up the access stairway to the spaceport without untensing a single muscle in my upper body. I walked with my teeth bared, my shoulders squared, my fists clenched, and my elbows out like I was carrying two invisible carpets under my armpits.

I was running on automatic at that point, as most of my conscious mind was occupied with words like *kill* and *death* swimming around in multiple sizes and colors like tropical fish in an overcrowded aquarium. I could just about spare enough reasoning ability to recall the way to the rooftop landing pad where the *Neverdie* was parked.

A small amount of relief washed over me at the familiar sight of her, although in these strange surroundings, she looked like I'd left her waiting at the bar in a shady establishment. Not entirely to my surprise, she was guarded. A bored biker was leaning on a six-foot cube of concrete.

"Just grabbing my overnight bag," I said as I approached, gesturing toward the *Neverdie*'s airlock steps.

"I ain't fumping stopping ya," growled the biker, not looking away from their phone. They looked and sounded similar to the first biker I had encountered, Les, and might even have been them, but frankly all bikers look the same to me once they go past a certain number of facial piercings.

I took a single step toward the ship, then froze, because it was at this point that a couple of relevant details sank fully into my conscious mind. The first was that the six-foot cube of concrete that the biker was leaning on was an anchor block, the kind of thing spaceports keep around when a ship needs to be kept where it is. The second was the enormous steel cable as thick as a gorilla's bicep that led from the top of the block to one of the *Neverdie*'s landing legs, where it was attached by a locking mechanism the size of a small fridge.

"My ship's on an anchor," I said aloud, instinctively.

"Yeah," said the biker, not looking up. "And you'd better clotting appreciate it 'cos three guys got hernias dragging that thing up here."

"Why?"

"I dunno. Lack of clotting exercise or something, you'd have to ask them."

"No, I mean . . . why anchor my ship?"

"Boss man ordered it. Thousands of scrankers at this convention, any one of 'em might get drunk and want a joy ride."

"But what if I need to fly somewhere?"

Finally they looked up, their lips pulled back in a harassed grimace. "What for?"

"Um." A number of possible answers surfaced and were swiftly rejected. Medical emergency? A call to adventure from distant stars? If I foresaw an urgent need to get somewhere quickly, then there was no reason to use a ship, not with Quantunnels all over the building. "I might need to air the engine out."

"Air the engine out."

I detected a note of incredulity in their voice. "Y-yeah," I said, trying to feign confidence in my own words. "These old models get a lot of particle buildup. Especially in a bubble atmosphere. It's best to at least turn the parts over once a day or so."

They looked up at the extremely heavy cable with exasperation. "It'll take, like, four guys to get the clotting clamp thing open again. Pretty sure it'll survive till Sunday."

I had officially run out of energy for this conversation. It wasn't like there was a pressing need to take off right now, and if there was a way to talk this doint into releasing the anchor, then it would work just as well in an hour or so. I simply let my shoulders sag, then stomped off and let myself into my ship without a word.

"All right, Warden," I growled the instant the airlock door had closed behind me and formed a nice tight, soundproof seal. "I know you're still plying listening to me. Is it true?"

A brief tense silence, then an annoyed click of the tongue. "Is what true?"

"Your giving my email to the Doint Emperor."

"Yes, it's true."

"So you lied."

"Not at all. You asked if I was the reason you had started receiving emails from Jacques McKeown fans, and I was not. I gave Daniel Henderson your email last year, when he was trying to contact you for the first convention. He only posted it publicly in the last few weeks as he began seeking you out for this one."

I was pacing around the airlock like a tiger in a photo booth, one finger stuck in my ear. I didn't remember getting an email from Daniel last year, but at the time, I'd avoided checking my emails much, as they were usually just more bad news from the lawyers. "Why did you let him have it in the first place?!"

"He asked for it. I saw no reason not to give it."

"Oh, didn't you, now." I stomped into the passenger cabin.

Sturb and Derby were waiting on the benches, and Sturb hadn't mind slaved any helpless convention attendees as far as I could see, so that at least was a mercy. A forest of Sushi Station takeout boxes was arranged on the coffee table, some on a delicate silk tablecloth that Derby must have provided.

"Hello, Captain! Do you want some takeout?" said Sturb. "We saved you some takeout."

"Stick it. Heist's off."

"Why?" asked Derby, recrossing his legs comfortably.

"Warden's played me like a spoon," I ranted, only partly certain I knew what the hell I meant by that. "She's the one who told Daniel Henderson how to contact me in the first place!"

"Yes, we . . . overheard," said Derby, tapping his ear. "My question stands. Why is the heist off?"

"Because! She suckered me into it!"

"Ah, stop me if I've read the situation completely wrong here," said Sturb. "But aren't we all here to get an antidote for Robert Blaze?"

"Yes!" I was still using my loud, ranty voice but beginning to lose confidence. I nodded sarcastically in an effort to stall. "But! I've been, you know, manipulated!"

Warden piped up. "So, if you'd known this from the start, you wouldn't have wanted to save Robert Blaze?"

I waggled a dynamic finger at nothing in particular. "You might well ask that."

"I am not going to let you jeopardize the payout I have in store," promised Davisham Derby, brandishing his wrist device. "A deal was made, and I'll see you sit in that pilot's chair even if I must saw off your legs for it to be so."

I had been halfway to slumping, defeated, on the nearest bench before I remembered the other thing, and rose triumphantly back to my full height. "Actually! It's all academic. The spaceport guards have put an anchor block on the ship."

"Oh. Really?" said Sturb, looking to the closed shutters. "We did wonder what all that noise and screaming was about. Sounded like three people getting hernias at once."

"Pft, have you forgotten?" Derby held up his shortened arm and let the cover fall from his miniature Quantunnel.

Sturb and I exchanged a glance. "Forgotten what?" I asked.

Davisham peered down his arm, affronted. "Eighteen F!" Moments later, his shortened forearm was significantly extended by a diamond-tipped cutting drill on the end of an angled metal limb. He only just moved his head out of the way in time.

"Sorry, Uncle Dav," came the muffled voice of Derby's assistant. "I had my dinner in my lap, so I couldn't get up right away."

"Yes, well. My point is, whatever is holding the ship in place, I have something that can cut through it. Davisham Derby has the tool for every task. I would have said that more emphatically, but I fear the moment was lost."

"I said I was sorry," added the assistant, slightly ruefully.

"Great, so everything's sorted out." Sturb rubbed his hands together keenly, then gestured to the other side of the cabin. A rectangular metal frame, about three feet wide by five high, was leaning against the wall. It was attached to a nearby tablet computer by a single cable. "I've already got the exit Quantunnel set up on this end, and I've got all the pieces for the entrance gate ready to go." He hefted a small jangling kit bag. "Are we all set to get cracking?"

I was offended by the way everyone had entirely brushed off my compelling reasons to abandon the heist. I jerked a thumb in the vague direction of outside. "What about that guard on the landing pad? We can't just wander out and let them see you two coming off the ship."

"Leave them to me," said Davisham Derby, the cutting tool withdrawing back into his arm as he closed the cover with a snap. "You shall have the enormous privilege of witnessing the elite skills of Davisham Derby in action."

CHAPTER II

A FEW MINUTES later, the three of us were on the landing pad, standing around the unconscious body of the biker guard.

"You tased them," I said flatly.

Derby was still winding the Taser's thin wires back into the miniature launcher sticking out of his arm hole. "Your point?"

"That's elite skill?" I opened my flight jacket to reveal my blaster in its holster. "I've got a stun gun, too. I could've done that."

Derby leveled a severe look at me. "The skill lies not in owning the tool, but in knowing when to use it."

I folded my arms. "So far, I know that *you're* a complete tool. And you aren't any use at all. So that must mean I've got elite skills, too."

"Gentlemen, they will not be out cold forever," said Warden through our earpieces. "You must proceed with the plan. Even more hastily, now."

I sighed. I was very much aware that whatever small chance I had of getting everyone to call off the heist had disappeared. Wanting to bring my ship, refusing to answer any questions, all of that could be easily excused as conventional Jacques McKeown dointery, but tasing the staff went a bit beyond the territory of celebrity mood swings. One way or another, we were all in this to the end. But that didn't mean I couldn't be grumpy about it.

"Yeah, obviously. Follow me. *At a distance*," I added hastily, as they began to shift their weight. "I'll scout ahead. Maybe I can talk us past the other guards without anyone else needing to be tased."

"Right you are, Captain," said Sturb brightly. "Can I just say, I was very impressed by your performance as Jacques McKeown at the con. I think you fooled everyone."

Derby scoffed. "A star pilot can imitate another star pilot. Shocking. Put on a cap and a jacket and refuse to grow up, and you could pass for any one of them."

It was probably too late to run ahead and scream for the guards to help save me from these Taser-wielding madmen, so I just consoled myself with a little thought experiment on the nature of Quantunnel physics, and if it would be theoretically possible to take Derby's arm thing and get him to ply himself.

I advanced from the stairwell to the main corridor of the penthouse level, trying to keep my gait somewhere between sneaky and not so sneaky that a surprise guard would be made instantly suspicious. But luck was on my side—or at least, keen to see how we would ply this up next—and we ran into no more guards on the way to the apartment. All the ones currently awake on this level must have been in the Hendersons' apartment, fiercely staring at priceless star piloting artifacts.

I reached the door to the other apartment and casually held it open, staring upwards as if momentarily fascinated by the pattern of the ceiling tiles, and pretended not to notice Derby and Sturb slip in. I felt like the good boy finally succumbing to the pressure to let his two naughty friends into the tuck shop after closing.

Even in the darkness, the luxury of the apartment was obvious. I could feel the siren call of the soft bed above me, and the fully stocked bar under the kitchen counter ahead. But in the context of being midheist, the high ceiling and tall windows were more judgmental than alluring.

Derby, of course, was loving the new surroundings. "And why, pray, were we not waiting out the day in here?" He stood in the center of the living space with his one remaining hand on hip. "Instead of huddling in that miserable man-child cave. It'll take days to wash the smell of failure from my clothes."

"If we could silence the unnecessary chatter," requested Warden, her disembodied voice cut with the stern diplomacy of a playground monitor.

"So is this the balcony through here?" asked Sturb.

"Through the balcony doors, yeah," I snarked. "The doors to the balcony."

The balcony doors were integrated so well into the large windows that they were difficult to spot until you noticed the tiny rectangular latch, but once I was out in the still night air, I could see why that had to be the case. The view of the city was so breathtaking that putting anything in the way of it should have been a capital crime. At least, rich people probably thought so. As a pilot and former space adventurer, I'd put it near the bottom of my top twenty views, probably just below the view of the basalt plains of Yuctha from the top of Karfung the Tall's burial mound.

It also meant that the other apartment had an equally good view and equally big windows, and as such, it would be virtually impossible to get onto its balcony without being instantly spotted. Going by the moving shadows in the shafts of bright light that spilled from the windows, the Hendersons' lounge must have been fully manned by the night-shift security team.

I whispered all of this to my companions. Derby listened to my concerns, nodding politely, then patted my upper arm with the back of his hand until I stepped to one side. Then he leapt across the gap.

I was less impressed by the leap—the balconies were only about a foot and a half apart, so a single stride could've done the job—as I was by the follow-up. His sensible shoes landed precisely on the opposite balcony's railing with the merest whisper of a sound, and then he remained balanced there, standing fully upright with only his hand keeping him steady on the nearby wall. There, he was still out of view. "Sturb," he muttered, audible only to those of us with earpieces. "If you wish to make yourself useful in the manner we discussed, now is the time."

"I'm on that right now. Jimi, can you access the household computer network?"

I checked over my shoulder and saw that he had his phone out.

"Searching," said the little computer voice. Sturb waved his phone around his head, looking for the signal. "Accessing most likely wireless network. Assessing Henderson organization. Entering network password most likely to be correct. Network accessed."

Again, I was grudgingly impressed by my coworker's tech; my own phone could just barely run *Joogie Bounce*, and even that seemed to crash every time I was about to beat my high score.

"All right, now—" began Sturb.

"I have assessed the situation and have concluded that you are conducting a heist," said Jimi the phone voice. "Displaying security camera feeds and household convenience functions."

"That's very perceptive of you, Jimi, well done." Sturb made some stall-ing noises along the lines of "bumble bumble bumble hum" as he swiped through a number of displays. "Mr. Derby? I can confidently state there's one guard patrolling the ground level, he's just passing by the windows now. Three more in the lounge area, playing . . ." He peered closer to the screen. "Scrabble, I'm prepared to say. Two are looking at the game, the other one's staring out the window. Looks very bored."

"Yes, we knew it would be guarded," said Derby impatiently. "Can you do anything about the lights?"

"Just let me get the home console up. There we go. I can turn out the lights, open the balcony doors, play something over the speakers . . . there's a thought. I've got some really disorienting Finnish black metal on here somewhere, maybe . . ."

"Let's try to keep quiet," I suggested, thinking of Henderson sitting in the adjoining room, harboring a fury that could have burned through the floor.

"On my mark, turn off all the lights and open the balcony door a crack," said Derby. He popped the cover off his wrist device, and plucked a small metal cylinder out of his mini Quantunnel. I caught a glimpse of skinny fingers passing it to him from within his secret hideout. "Around six inches will do. Three. Two. One. Mark."

Sturb made a decisive finger movement, and the lights that bathed the opposite balcony winked out, prompting a cry of irritation from someone inside. There was a moment's tense silence that lasted just long enough for us to collectively wonder if some kind of massive doints-up was on the cards, then the glass that separated the balcony from the apartment slid a few inches aside with a thud.

Derby had already plucked the cap from his handheld device, the way one pulls the ring on a tin of microwave dinner. He smartly tossed it through the gap with impressive accuracy, and a few white tufts floated into the night air to indicate that the apartment was flooding with blinding smoke. Derby crouched to spring, and then I blinked, and by the time I had finished blinking, he was gone.

"What's going on in there?" I asked Sturb, turning on my heel. I stared at the screen over his shoulder, and saw only a bright rectangle of grainy night-vision green, with the occasional glimpse of thrashing limb.

We both looked up when we heard a thump of flesh against glass, and then one of the black-suited bodyguards staggered out of the swirling white fog, coughing and half collapsing onto the balcony railing. He took a moment to recover, then looked up. Directly at me.

His brow furrowed. "W—"

Suddenly his body spasmed, his back arched, and his clenching teeth cut off whatever he'd been about to say. Then he collapsed, unconscious, and I could see two narrow black wires leading from his back to the open balcony door.

"Report," said Warden testily. "Ground team, report." Derby peered through the gap while winding the wires of his Taser back into his arm device. He had been wearing a pair of thermal goggles that were now pushed up onto his forehead. "All hostiles neutralized. The way is clear."

Sturb nodded, took a deep breath, and jumped over the tiny gap to the other balcony, landing in a crouch and clutching his chest as the unfamiliar sensation of physical exercise took the wind right out of him. I followed, stepping nonchalantly across the eighty-story drop. A lifetime of space travel is excellent for overcoming vertigo.

"Your task in the freezer awaits," said Derby, brushing imaginary dust from his lapel. He slid aside to let Sturb into the Hendersons' apartment, then promptly slid back to block the way as I made to follow. "You're no longer needed, pilot. Why don't you go keep your engine warm while we take care of the important business. You'll be informed when we're ready to leave."

I jerked a thumb behind me. "And what am I supposed to do about that anchor block?"

"You'll have some time. I'm sure you're equal to the task."

"The cable is as thick as my plying leg. What am I supposed to do? We don't all keep superdrills up our magic holes."

Sturb stopped and turned halfway to the kitchen. "Actually, didn't you say you would cut it, Mr. Derby? You said you have a tool for every occasion. It was a whole bit you were doing. Why don't you go back to the ship, and the captain can come with me?"

Derby's smug look vanished like an inconvenient corpse in a junkyard. "What?"

"You can get to work on cutting the cable now and we won't have to worry about it later. You've already done a wonderful job neutralizing the guards, and I'm sure Mr. Pierce and his blaster are quite up to the task of assisting me. Plus, he'll be able to return directly to the ship through our Quantunnel and get on with the business of piloting."

"Yes, fine, whatever," said Warden. "Just get the job done."

I gave Derby a completely reasonable look, and his nostrils flared as he analyzed Sturb's logic. "And if I am discovered by guards on the way back?"

Sturb shrugged. "Tase them?"

Derby scowled at him, then me, before gathering his dignity and stepping back across the gap with considerably less aplomb than before.

"He can be a bit much, can't he," said Sturb in a hushed tone, when it was just me and him, creeping through the darkened apartment toward the meat freezer.

I noted the coffee table in the lounge. Two of the guards were slumped unconscious over the Scrabble board. Judging by the large number of four-letter words, it hadn't exactly been a clash of the mental titans. "A bit much," I repeated, before giving him a stern look. "I dunno. I haven't seen him enslave people's minds and turn them into cyberserkers against their will, but maybe we've all got different definitions of 'a bit much.' "

Sturb stopped dead right outside the door to the freezer. His egg-shaped torso heaved with a deep sigh, and he turned fully around to address me. "I understand why you're wary of me."

"Do you."

"But I want to give you my complete assurance that I really have moved on from mind slaving people. My priorities are completely different now."

"Oh. You've moved on." I irritably kicked the snoozing form of a muscular biker out of the way. "As long as you've 'moved on.' Wish I'd thought of saying that at my last court summons. 'I know I sold that tourist's luggage to a pirate, but hey, maybe we should all just move on.' "

He pouted sadly as he turned his attention to the handle on the freezer door, but paused in the act of turning it to eyeball me again. "Forgive me, but . . . I thought you were a star pilot?"

"I am! Was!"

"But you were selling luggage to pirates?"

I waggled a finger at him aggressively, trying to think of the no doubt extremely good and obvious counterargument that, for some reason, was escaping me for the moment. "Things changed," I said eventually, letting my hand drop. "And it was nothing like your supervillain trac."

He gave a conciliatory sort of half shrug, then finally pulled open the meat freezer's door, releasing a hiss and a waft of cold air.

The space inside was roomy for a refrigerator, but still a little uncomfortably poky with two adult males inside it, along with a shelving unit covered in prepackaged frozen cheeseburgers and the cryonic cylinder that we had come here to steal.

It was larger than I had expected, as tall as a man and about two feet wide, constructed from highly reflective stainless steel that was caked with frost. Some of the urgent stenciled lettering on the side had rubbed off in places, but it didn't take a genius to infer what WARNING: HA ARDOUS BIO ATTER was supposed to mean. In keeping with the way Daniel had treated his other priceless artifacts, there was no further protection or housing; the cylinder had simply been leant against the wall, with nothing but a packet of fish fingers to keep it from falling over.

Sturb went straight to the far corner—to use the word *far* generously, as it was still only about three feet away—and knelt to start work on the Quantunnel. I pulled the freezer door shut behind us. If any of those guards outside woke up, with any luck they wouldn't think we'd be stupid enough to still be around, trapped in the fridge.

Sturb slid one piece of the Quantunnel frame into another and clapped his hands together with glee when it stood up on the floor without falling over. "The funny thing is, I never actually intended to become a supervillain." Sturb was standing with self-satisfied hands on hips. "I just started messing around with some human-machine interface systems, then one thing led to another; I wanted to see how far I could take it before someone tried to stop me, and no one did. Well, they did, but by that point there were cyberserkers to fight them off." His tone was more remorseful than nostalgic.

"Oh, now that you've explained, it all sounds perfectly understandable." I was barely paying attention to him as I listened at the door for the slightest noise. "Could you get on with what you're supposed to be doing, please?"

"Right, good idea," said Sturb, with his ever infuriating reasonableness. He added another piece to the developing tunnel frame, sliding it into place with a solid click, then stepped back to survey it. "Need to concentrate. Has to be perfect. You know how close it has to be to the size of the other tunnel?"

"Yeah, it's, like, point three of a millimeter, or something." A few nagging thoughts coalesced. "Hang on. You said the cops might be able to redirect an illegal Quantunnel if they detect it?"

"Just a rumor I've heard, but it wouldn't surprise me, the amount of money that's gone into Quantunnel-security research since they were invented," said Sturb, pausing in his work again with infuriating nonchalance after he had inserted one more piece. "It'd certainly be a deterrent, if the police could just drop you into a prison cell when they detect you coming in."

"Wouldn't they need a Quantunnel in the prison cell exactly the same size as this one?"

Sturb had been reaching for his tool bag, but aborted this to make some illustrative gestures as he spoke. "Ah. Very good question. This is the interesting thing. It's not that the tunnels have to be the same size or it won't turn on. They'll still turn on. But it becomes a lot more dangerous to pass through them."

"Why?"

With another piece of frame attached, it was getting close to around person height. "You might come out the wrong shape," he explained. "If you're lucky, the universe figures out its mistake and you pop back to normal, which can be pretty traumatic in itself. If you're unlucky . . ." He huffed in mock concern. "I know someone who ended up looking like one of those forced-perspective drawings being looked at from the wrong angle. The point-three-millimeter thing is just the threshold where that's never happened."

"Okay . . ."

"So far."

"Okay!" I barked, suddenly conscious that I was getting dangerously close to having a casual conversation with Malcolm Sturb. "Just get it done. Quickly. Stop pausing to talk to me." I thought I heard a faint bump from somewhere in the apartment, so I listened against the freezer door. Nothing but silence, and now my earlobe was getting frostbite.

The top bar clipped on, connecting the sides and completing the six-foot Quantunnel entrance. Sturb spooled a cable out of his phone as if it were dental floss and plugged it into a port at the base of the frame. "Jimi, how are we looking? How close are the proportions to the exit gate?"

"Deviation of two point four millimeters," said Jimi the phone voice. "Highlighting maximum deviance points." A number of lasers burst forth from the projector on the back of the phone, illuminating some of the joints in the frame. Sturb took up a handheld electric wrench and tightened one of the highlighted screws with a brief whir.

I heard another bump. This time, I was pretty certain it was coming from the second floor of the apartment, but before I could continue my analysis, Derby's voice flooded my earpiece. "I have returned to the ship," he reported in a sulk. "Davisham Derby is ready to begin cutting a cable like a glorified handyman—"

"Shh!" I hissed, with such urgency that even he shut up. "Sturb! You saw the cameras. Was there anyone upstairs?"

Sturb was still correcting the screws, unconcerned. "No, I can't say there was. Besides that catatonic fellow."

Another sound. Definitely from upstairs, and definitely the sound of a door opening.

"What about Daniel?" I asked.

Sturb put his wrench down and talked over his shoulder. "No, I don't remember seeing him anywhere. It's the big first night of the con, I assumed he'd be at some kind of after party."

That made sense, but it was difficult to imagine Daniel having enough actual friends to populate a party. Still, the con had been crowded enough that he had probably gathered a few opportunistic people who were prepared to pretend in return for some free cake and fizzy pop.

"Jimi, how about now?" asked Sturb of his phone.

"Deviation of one point eight millimeters."

Sturb clicked his tongue, and started incrementally turning the screws with brief attacks of the wrench, seeking the perfect spot for each one.

Upstairs, I heard the sound of a foot on the top step. It was swiftly joined by a solid clunk, the kind of thing that might be made by a walking stick held by someone who had trouble walking because one of their legs had a nasty case of absence. Surely something as everyday and harmless as a daring midnight heist of his expensive possessions couldn't have been the thing to finally rouse Mr. Henderson from his stupor.

"You need to hurry this up," I informed Sturb.

"Don't worry, Captain. I already said I've been getting these done in under ten minutes."

"Zero point nine millimeters," reported his phone.

The stomp–clunk sounds of foot and walking stick were descending the stairs. Ten minutes was a long time in the world of daring heists. More than enough time to, say, catch two idiots in your freezer and bring down the entire wrath of your criminal empire upon them.

"Zero point six millimeters."

"Is that close enough?!" I asked, trying to focus on Sturb and listen at the door at the same time.

"Mm, hard to say." Sturb rested his wrench on his shoulder and talked with maddening slowness as he thought. "Most of the time you can probably get away with point four. Point three's just the maximum allowed by safety regulations. Actually, the really interesting thing is—"

"I don't care! Get it done!"

The footsteps were now moving around the apartment, presumably inspecting the new decor themed around unconscious bodyguards. I heard a faint fleshy thump that a moment's thought identified as the sound of a walking stick prodding a human torso.

"Zero point four millimeters," said Jimi.

"That'll do! Start it up!" I yelled slightly louder than I'd intended. My hand instinctively slapped across my mouth when I heard the footsteps outside suddenly halt.

Sturb poised his hand over a button on his touchscreen dramatically. "Mr. Pierce, don't look this way. Quantunnels don't open while anyone's watching."

I knew that, and it was a pointless request anyway: all my attention was devoted to the freezer door. The footfalls, now softer and more cautious, were getting closer.

"One. Two. Three," said Sturb.

As always, the effect of opening a Quantunnel was rather underwhelming. I heard the sound of rattling metal, a slightly uncomfortably loud snap, and then a persistent hum that sounded like the thrumming of an atmospheric cycler in dire need of a clean.

I turned. With the completed Quantunnel frame propped against the wall, the meat freezer appeared to have acquired a brand-new door, which led directly into the passenger compartment of the *Neverdie*. Sturb gingerly prodded the edges of the doorway. "I think we did it."

I hurried over to the cryonic cylinder. Sturb was already standing on tiptoe, struggling to tip it toward the new door. I put a hand under the other end and lifted until my back took the weight.

"It's rather heavy," said Sturb, in response to my surprised grunt. "Why do you think that is? Does this antidote stuff need a lot of padding around it?"

I was about to reply—probably with some kind of clever putdown relating to Sturb's weight—when I heard someone rattling the freezer's door handle outside, and all my words were replaced by a frightened high-pitched squawk. The two of us hurriedly took the strain and carried the cylinder across the threshold before we could spare a thought for the icy sensation scything painfully through our hands.

In unspoken agreement, we dumped the cylinder horizontally on the nearest bench, then simultaneously snatched our hands up and shook them vigorously to restore sensation to our fingers. "Cylinder's on the ship," reported Sturb. "Derby, get ready to close the building's Quantunnel on three." He threw his arm over his eyes, and I did the same. "One. Two. Three."

A few seconds of silence passed, and cold air continued to waft from the meat locker into the passenger cabin, along with the faint hum of the refrigeration system.

"Did it close?" I asked.

"I . . . don't think it did," said Sturb in the quiet voice of someone experiencing an ongoing sequence of sinking feelings.

"I don't think it did either." I heard the fleshy sound of Sturb's thumb patting the touchscreen on his phone over and over again, but I didn't dare open my eyes. "Is it because we can still feel the cold? We have to stop sensing it, not just stop looking at it?"

"Maybe, but . . ."

He trailed off in such a way that I felt moved to uncover my eyes. He was boggling at his homemade Quantunnel with his mouth hanging open wide enough to admit a Silusian belchwasp.

I followed his gaze. The Quantunnel was, as expected, still open into the Hendersons' meat freezer, facing the heavy steel door. That door was now open, and Mr. Henderson was standing on the threshold, leaning comfortably on a pair of crutches.

"Jacques McKeown, as I live and breathe," said Mr. Henderson calmly.

CHAPTER 12

"THIS ISN'T WHAT it looks like," I said, on instinct. It probably wasn't my worst ever attempt at improvisation, but no other candidates sprung to mind at that very moment.

Henderson remained in the doorway of his apartment's freezer, staring at us through the Quantunnel as he blinked rapidly and swayed dreamily, drunk on either the effects of prolonged catatonia or the heady prospect of revenge. He waved a limp hand at the carnage in the apartment behind him. "Did you knock all these guys out?"

"I can't close the tunnel while he's looking at it," muttered Sturb out of the corner of his mouth.

"Yes, I knocked them out," I said loudly. "Especially that one." I pointed behind Henderson. He frowned, then smiled, but didn't turn.

"I think I'm going to keep an eye on you," said Henderson sluggishly, digging his phone out of a pocket of his cardigan. "I think I'm going to call some guys and then I was thinking I might tell them to kill you." He held the phone to his ear.

I shot him. I'd already drawn my blaster out of nervous habit and had clicked the dial to the Stun setting, so all I had to do then was go with my instinct to pull the trigger. A sprawling cluster of plasma bolts riddled his chest and he swiftly went down, his back arching uncomfortably over the freezer door threshold and an expression of pain and overpowering rage fixed on his face.

Sturb had reflexively put his hands up, and now gawped at me in unconvincing pretense that the man who'd enslaved half the Black at one time or another was thrown by a little violence. "O-okay."

I turned to him. I'd only meant to point, but forgot that I was holding a gun in my pointing hand, so he flinched and put his hands up even higher. "Get this plying tunnel shut," I spat. Then I bolted for the door. The real one.

I climbed the steps three at a time until I was in the cockpit, and flung myself into my chair with such force that one of the bolts that kept it attached to the floor popped out and pinged away. Muscle memory took over, and my hands flew about the controls, activating the ship's systems in the order that usually succeeded in making the engine start. I was only half-aware of the sweat dripping down my face; firing the gun had triggered something in me, and my brain was producing adrenaline like a lawn sprinkler.

"Derby, you onboard yet?" I barked.

"No," said Derby contemptuously, as if I were supposed to know that. "At present, I am still on the landing platform, addressing the anchor-block situation."

I made a frustrated noise and slapped the steering column. "You haven't cut that thing off yet?! We need to get in the air, like, ten seconds ago. We've been made! And we've got however long it takes to recover from a stun-blaster shot before Henderson's goons are on us."

"Oh," he said loftily. "If only, say, some kind of stealth expert and master thief had been assigned to the task of recovering the cylinder."

"DERBY, YOU TRAC-HEAD—"

"Calm yourself, Captain, the grownups are on the case." An earsplitting high-pitched whine started up, making me snatch at my ear in surprise. "I'm switching to my most powerful saw. Rest assured that this infernal cable will not trouble it for long."

I wasn't reassured. I activated the external view monitor that would theoretically show me the view from the belly camera on the underside of the hull, but of course, it didn't work. I hadn't used it in years; it was more of a training tool for when you're still learning how to land or parallel park, and my instincts had taken over for it long ago.

Sturb crashed clumsily into the cockpit behind me, patting his ear to dispel the noise of Derby's sawing. "Do you know how long Mr. Derby's going to be doing that?"

"You're the plying tech guy." I thumped the buttons under the monitor, and caused it to flash to life for precisely one quarter of a second. "Make this plying camera work and then maybe we'll know."

"Right. I can do that, actually." Sturb brought his phone out with suspicious speed. "Where should I plug in?"

An alarm bell rang through the haze of my energized mood as I stared at the vicious little teeth on the end of his dongle. "What're you planning to do with that?"

"Oh, sorry. I need to install a link for Jimi. They can diagnose and find the most efficient way to bypass the malfunctioning systems. You see, Jimi uses a sort of modular coding system that can theoretically emulate any—"

"Yeah," I interrupted. "But then what? You turn my own ship against me? Fly out to the Black to start enslaving planets again?"

"Well, I really wasn't thinking of doing that, but . . . Jimi, could you assess this system's processor potential for mind slaving?" He held his phone toward the main computer housing by my leg.

"Assessing," said the phone, projecting holographic lines across the nearest panel. "Local computer system has sufficient processing power to maintain a slave colony consisting of . . . one . . . severely mentally disabled . . . domesticated animal."

"So you see, there's nothing to worry about," said Sturb, waving his phone. His face was going red and sweaty with tech excitement again. "I can only run Jimi on my phone because I've customized the ansible system to give it the equivalent processing power of three naval-fleet strategic mainframes."

I pursed my lips. In other circumstances I might have stuck to a hard line stance on keeping Sturb's weird supertech trac out of my ship's computer, but we were pressed for time and the whining noise in my ear was grating across my nerves like a carpenter's file across a recently drilled tooth. I gave him the nod.

Sturb reeled the cable out of his phone and shoved it rudely into the universal input slot. A moment later, he started swiping through windows on his touchscreen. I felt slightly insulted by the way his expression turned aghast at the sight of my archaic systems, which I think had been updated around the time of Halley's comet's last visit. Eventually he found what he was looking for and turned the screen for me to see: the feed from the *Neverdie*'s keel camera.

There was the anchor block, still connected to the front landing leg; the cable extruding from its top led windingly to the underside of the image and out of sight. Derby was standing on top of the block with one foot upon the large iron ring in a suitably dramatic pose, attacking the cable with a thin chainsaw-like device extruding from his wrist. Blinding sparks were flying off the spot where it connected, making it impossible to see how much of the cable he had gotten through.

"Derby, how much longer?!" I demanded.

He stopped sawing for a moment to put one finger to his ear. "No faster for having to incessantly reassure you. You just keep your engine running and be ready to take off."

My eye flicked to the readouts on the main console. "It is running. It's warmed up. We're waiting on you."

Now that he had stopped sawing for a moment, I could see that he was barely a third of the way through the tether's six-inch thickness of wound steel. I could also see a few background details, including the biker Derby had left lying unconscious on the tarmac. I noticed them straightaway, because they were acting a lot less unconscious than would have been preferred.

They were sitting up, apparently making a groggy attempt to pat their head and rub their tummy as they made up their mind which part of them they wanted to clutch first. They glanced around, confused, then noticed Derby.

"Derby, the guard!" I yelled, informatively.

He paused to click his tongue and roll his eyes just as he was about to resume cutting. "The guard will be out for more than enough time, fret not. Trust in the expert, star pilot. Your micromanaging is getting tiresome."

"The guard is—" My sentence was drowned out when his saw reactivated and he touched it to the cut, filling the view with sparks and our ears with the sound of pigs being slaughtered in fast motion. I had to scream Derby's name three times before he turned it off again.

"What now?"

"The—oh. Well, I was going to let you know that the guard behind you was awake, but that's become plying moot, hasn't it."

Derby finally looked behind him, and saw, as I had, that the biker had run away. They must have weighed up the potential results of attempting a sneak attack, and had decided that discretion was the better part of valor.

Gratifyingly, Derby was momentarily lost for words as he examined the spot where the biker had been lying. When he turned, I could see that he was sweating profusely even with the camera's incredibly low resolution.

"I don't . . . that probably couldn't have been avoided," he eventually said.

"Keep cutting," I suggested through my teeth, clutching the joysticks as if they were a pair of skinny throats.

"Um, the thought occurs, sorry to interrupt, they've probably run off to fetch more guards," said Sturb, clutching the back of my headrest urgently.

"If Henderson wasn't already getting on that," I said. "I guess this might speed things up since they know exactly where we are now."

"On balance, I think we're all still doing a very good job under the circumstances," said Sturb, eyes bulging wildly.

I checked the monitor. Derby was still cutting, the steel glowing red hot under his arm-mounted saw. Sparks were flowing from the cut in spectacular floods, but the ship wasn't getting less tethered to the anchor block any faster.

There was a brief lull in the sparks as Derby repositioned himself, and I caught another glimpse of the scene behind him. The door that led into the building was being held open, and two indistinct blobs peering around the door frame could conceivably have been the faces of concerned guards.

"Are those guards?" I asked.

Derby stopped sawing and sighed extremely audibly. "Would you please let me get on with this? I'd be done by now if you didn't keep . . ." He finally looked behind him, and his voice trailed off. "Erm. Yes, I was talking to you two. Let me get on with this. It's important."

The guards barked something at him that we couldn't quite hear, but it was safe to assume it wasn't friendly.

"How intimidating." Derby rose to his full height and placed his hand on his hip. "Perhaps you gentlemen don't understand that you're dealing with Davisham Der—"

A shot rang out. Derby hopped down from his perch, clinging to the edge of the anchor block to keep it between him and the shooter. He slowly raised his head to see what they were doing, and swiftly dropped back down when a second shot hit the top of the block, sprinkling him in concrete dust.

"Doints to it!" I gunned the takeoff thrusters.

The *Neverdie* ascended gracefully for all of two yards before all the slack went out of the tether and she stopped with a lurch, rocking sickeningly back and forth. I felt Sturb grab my backrest before he could be thrown off his feet.

"What are you doing, man?!" hissed Derby.

"I'm the getaway driver," I replied, pushing the takeoff thrust up to maximum. "So I'm getting us away."

The tether cable was creaking so loudly that I could hear it through Derby's microphone. I could see on the monitor that the cut he had made had expanded into a triangular notch about three inches wide, and getting wider.

Then the creaking was drowned out by the growing roar of the thrusters. If either of those guards had tried to run toward the ship at this point, the engine exhaust would probably have reduced their entire bodies to the consistency of barbecue sauce.

"You're going to kill us all!" cried Derby, just about sheltered enough by the block to avoid getting much worse than a sunburn.

"It's going to snap," I said, with strained confidence. "Sooner or later it'll have to either snap, or—"

Sturb lurched forward again when the ship suddenly shifted, then just as suddenly stopped. I could see on the monitor that the tether cable was still in one piece, but the anchor block was definitely sitting at a slightly different angle to where it had been before.

Slowly, ever so slowly, the *Neverdie* inched upwards, as the anchor block tilted onto one edge. Then it crashed down onto its side with an almighty thump, halting the ship's progress with another stomach-turning lurch. Derby narrowly avoided being pancaked by scrambling up onto what had until recently been the side of the block, like a tarantula navigating a person's hands.

"Or, this might happen," I conceded.

I kept the thrusters running at maximum heat until the tether was back at full strain, then hit the auxiliary thrust. This was a system that activated a short burst of additional power, which was supposed to be used for slight course corrections, but in this situation, it succeeded in getting us and the anchor block a good eight or nine inches off the tarmac. We bobbed gracefully up and then back down again like a magpie trying to carry a brick.

But now we had momentum working for us, and a moment later we were off the ground again, dragging the block along with surprising grace, our horizontal speed increasing rapidly. I tried to block out the constant sound of Derby's terrified gibbering and focus on the notch in the tether. It had definitely grown by another couple of inches. If I could keep this up . . .

"Careful, we're about to—" began Sturb, before we ran out of landing pad and his warning became moot. The anchor block dropped off Henderson Tower like a stone, appropriately enough. One nanosecond later, so did the *Neverdie*.

Sturb clung even more tightly to my backrest as the windows on the side of Henderson Tower streaked vertically past the view screen, occasionally featuring the astonished faces of onlookers. Any chance of ending this heist by vanishing undetected into the night was officially in the bin, but surviving the next thirty seconds was the bigger concern.

Smashing the anchor block into the sturdy foundations of Ritsuko City was conceivably a way out of this problem—it'd shatter like a watermelon with a hard-enough impact. The snag in that plan was preventing the ship from pancaking on top of it a fraction of a second later, on flat, unyielding ground newly strewn with painful lumps of jagged rock.

Not worth the risk. I put everything the *Neverdie* had into slowing our descent. The thrusters screamed. I was hitting the auxiliary thrust like it was a malfunctioning drum machine. I activated the emergency parachute without even knowing if it was even still there, as I seemed to recall using it to carry a load of laundry to Frobisher's a few months ago. I emptied my lungs on the off chance that the extra air was making us heavier.

Somehow, between all of my efforts, I was able to slow the fall just enough that the anchor block landed in the middle of the street with only a mildly ear-shattering boom. The *Neverdie*'s descent slowed and stopped with two feet between her underbelly and solid concrete, narrowly saving Derby from becoming the filling of a jam sandwich.

I saw from the monitor that an encouragingly large chunk had broken off the block. "All right!" I said, suddenly buoyed. "Derby, you can finish cutting. That cable's got to be weak as trac by now."

Derby didn't respond. I noticed that he was hugging the section of cable directly above the anchor block with all four limbs, his face buried in his own armpit for comfort.

"He's frozen up."

"Well, he did just fall off a building," suggested Sturb, who was still slowly picking himself up from the floor.

"We all just fell off a building, you don't see me complaining. Derby! Come on!" I was feeling the warm, prickly sensation of adrenaline come-down. I was still energized, but I could already tell that before the end of the evening, I was going to crash like an inexperienced asteroid racer with an outdated autopilot.

Derby's one fully intact arm detached from around the cable and began dangling loosely toward the cracked asphalt. He must have passed out. Part of me relished having something like this to hold over him later, but a less manic and rational part knew that this wasn't going to get us off the ground any quicker.

I quickly set the ship into hover mode. "I'm going out there," I announced, getting up.

"What?!" Sturb rapidly glanced between me and my newly vacated chair. "But you're the pilot!"

I nodded toward the gantry steps that led down to the main airlock. "You want to go out there?"

"No," admitted Sturb instantly.

"Didn't think so. I'm just going to pop out, cut the cable, grab Derby, and pop back in. We might have bought enough time, taking the express route to the ground floor."

I headed to the airlock, my shoes rattling down the gantry steps like an impromptu glockenspiel performance. Technically, standard safety regulations prohibited opening the external airlock door while the ship was in flight or in motion, but I'd always considered "safety" to be a highly interpretive concept.

The pleasant coolness of Ritsuko's night air hit me as the exit door slid aside. There wasn't much traffic at this time of night—thankfully we hadn't landed on a late-night cyclist—but a commotion was developing in the street. A ring of onlookers, composed mainly of cyclists and a few convention attendees who had been trying to keep the party going, was forming around the edges of the shallow crater we had made in the tarmac.

I tried to focus on the situation. The anchor block was directly below me, and Derby's unconscious body was still slumped around the cable; it looked like he'd hastily attached himself to it with the straps of a concealed harness he had on under his suit.

I stepped out of the airlock and dropped the six or seven feet onto the anchor block, which rocked a little as I landed, because about a quarter of it had broken off in a big, pyramid-shaped clump lying nearby. I turned my attention to the cable, and saw that the cut was only holding together with an inch-thick strand surrounded by frayed steel threads.

It didn't seem ready to snap from the two cautious prods I made with my finger, so I took a searching look around, pretending not to notice the boggling eyes of the crowd. Eventually, my thoughts turned to the inactive saw that was still on the end of Derby's false arm.

I picked up his limp wrist. It was a vicious-looking tool, the slightly cracked edge sparkling with diamond dust, but I couldn't see any visible way of turning it on. I was about to try rubbing it against the remaining strand like a hacksaw when I heard the muffled voice.

"Hello?" It was young, female, and coming from where the tool met the Quantunnel ring on Derby's stubby arm. "Uncle Dav?"

"Hello?" I put my mouth close to the crack. "You're Derby's assistant?"

"Yeah, hi," she said, concern overpowering the process of formal introductions. "Is Uncle Dav all right?"

I saw no reason to lie. "He's passed out and strapped to a concrete block dangling off a ship in flight."

She clicked her tongue. "Any idea how I'm going to explain this to Auntie Pru?"

"You won't have to," I said, "if you can turn this saw on from where you are."

"Erm, why are you talking to that man's wrist?"

I looked down and saw that the gathering crowd had nominated a spokesperson, in the form of a slightly tubby, dark-haired woman wearing the fluorescent vest of the Ritsuko Traffic Police. Her hand was poised near the stun gun on her hip, but for now she was only indecisively tapping the hilt with her thumb.

"This your ship, sir?" she asked, eyes wide and with one corner of her mouth curling up in a grimace of confusion.

I performed a double take as if I'd only just noticed the battered red ship hanging over the street like a giant proactive vulture. "Yes. Sorry. Emergency landing. I was having some engine trouble."

"What kind of engine trouble?"

I glanced around again, then gestured toward the giant cracked anchor block I was still standing on. "Erm. This." I cautiously flicked the switch in my head, blinked hugely, then offered her a pained smile. "I know what you're going to say. If I didn't keep skimping on maintenance, the little problems wouldn't build into big ones. But I'll be out of everyone's way just as soon as I've gotten this sorted out. Would that be all right?"

Her eyes flicked all around. I could sense her trying to mentally catalog what crimes I could potentially be charged with at this point. "I . . . suppose."

On cue, the electric saw on Derby's arm came to life and began to whine like a dog anxious to get back to chewing on its favorite toy. I grabbed

Derby's elbow and held the whirring blade to the frayed section of cable, recommencing the flow of flying sparks. I offered the policewoman a reassuring smile and a nod, in what I hoped would be enough body language to communicate the phrase "please plying go away."

"Right," she said. Her foot stirred a couple of shards of concrete as she backed uncertainly away. "Wait a minute. What are you planning to do with this block?"

"Erm, I hadn't quite decided," I said casually over the cutting noise.

"Well, you can't just leave it here," said the policewoman, squaring her shoulders. "This is a no-littering zone."

I drew the blade back and was about to answer when a small explosion on the edge of the anchor block spat up shards of concrete, and I was interrupted by my own flinch.

Several bikers were emerging from the ramp that led to the Henderson Tower's underground car park, waving handguns and ringing their bells menacingly. They streamed from the building in a disorderly queue that didn't seem to be showing any signs of stopping when another gunshot rang overhead and I was forced to take cover behind the block, yanking the cable down with me to bring Derby into at least relative safety.

More shots hit the anchor block, then stopped, although the incoming sound of bells and rattling chains continued. Presumably they were waiting for a clearer shot before using up any more ammo, and it wouldn't be long before they would have me fully flanked. I clung to the covered side of the block with three limbs like a climbing monkey, soon to become like a sitting duck.

I wasn't entirely surprised to see that I had unconsciously drawn my blaster again with my one free hand, but it wasn't immediately helpful. Even if my aim was on point, I didn't have nearly enough ammunition to do more than dent—and subsequently infuriate—the biker horde.

Instead, I brought the gun up to my face, turned the dial as far as it could go with my teeth, then aimed for the weakened part of the tether cable and fired.

A jolt of recoil added another few years of crippling arthritis to the end of my life, and a massive fireball went up, splashing plasma about the cable like a roaring sea around a lighthouse. When it cleared, the cable was glowing red hot, but still defiantly intact.

In retrospect, a more concentrated shot might have been smarter, but now my repeated pulls of the trigger were producing nothing but the dismal clicks and occasional sparks of dry fire. The cable was specifically designed to hold together like grim death, and somewhere behind all my screaming terror I was gaining a grudging respect for the manufacturing quality.

"Without wishing to interrupt, don't we need to get moving now?" asked Sturb in my ear.

"It would be nice, wouldn't it!" I yelled.

"So just so I've got this clear, you agree that we need to move?"

"TRAC, YES!" The sound of encroaching bicycles was like the clashing of an army of supermarket trolleys in my mind.

"And if we get moving you'll forgive whatever needed to be done for it to happen, even if it was something that'd normally put you out?"

I frowned, but the hostile ringing of bells was making it hard to divine what he was getting at. "Yes! Anything!"

"Right. That was all I needed to know. Hold on."

I was about to make some snap sarcasm along the lines of having few other plans at present when the block moved. I looked up and saw the *Neverdie's* maneuvering thrusters glowing, then roaring into life.

"Oh, trac. Sturb! Not that!"

My words were swiftly drowned out by the grinding of the anchor block against the road as it began to move. Enough of it had broken off after the fall that we could build up a decent horizontal speed, but there still wasn't much chance of gaining altitude.

It took all of my strength to keep clinging to the concrete as it vibrated violently, occasionally making little skips and hitting the ground again with jarring impact.

"Sorry," said Sturb after a particularly violent one. "I'm sorry about that. Jimi's managed to key into the road database that the driverless cars use, so we can keep moving without hitting any buildings. Is that okay? Say the word and I can put a stop to it."

The ship curved widely around the intersection of Ritsuko's Knee and Ritsuko's Tailbone, making the anchor block swing around nauseatingly and smash the top half of a light pole. Impressive as it was that Jimi had jury-rigged an autodrive system for my temporarily grounded ship within seconds, it was abundantly clear that the driverless-car road database operated on the assumption that the vehicle fit inside one lane, and didn't have a large piece of jagged rock dangling from it like an inconveniently huge dointsack.

Sadly, I wasn't articulate enough to express all of this in my present frame of mind, so I compromised by just inventing new swear words at full volume, like "GYARGHTRACMURDER."

Another gunshot hit the top of the block, inches from my white knuckles. I summoned some energy to my arms and pulled myself up, feet scrabbling at the concrete for purchase, until I could see over.

We were still trailing a war party of bikers, although the ship was keeping up a decent-enough pace that we had weeded out the less athletic ones. The remainder, a universally burly lot, were cycling their pedals like a platoon of furious organ grinders on steroids. I could see blue and red lights behind them and just about hear the hum of electric police scooters, but if the bikers had any doubt about the legality of their actions, they weren't letting it slow them down. Working for Henderson must have been a plying lucrative gig.

As I watched, another stray gunshot hit the anchor block and detached a fist-sized chunk that had been umming and aahing about breaking off for several minutes. It bounced in front of one of the lead bikers and almost made them go into a fatal skid before they wrestled their handlebars back under control.

Inspired, I waited for another break in the fire, then hauled myself back up on top of the block and started kicking away at the crumbling concrete, which by now was looking like a scale model of a highly accident-prone asteroid. Another big fragment came away and smashed gratifyingly into the chest of the nearest biker, sending them and their mount spinning catastrophically away.

This effectively reduced the bikers' pursuing numbers from tracloads to still tracloads. I was forced to duck behind the block again as a fresh volley of blaster fire peppered the air above me.

My endeavors, combined with the continued impacts with the ground, caused another few lumps of concrete to break off, skittering away into the darkened street behind us. "Sturb! Try pulling up!" I called. "We might've lost enough weight!"

He replied only with an excited gasp and a grunt of effort, and then the ruined block made a particularly high leap as the *Neverdie* began to gain altitude. I hung on for dear life as the block swung forward on the end of its tether, and this time, we were already high enough that the block didn't touch the ground at all. I couldn't help letting out an invigorated whoop as the pursuing bikers grew smaller and smaller and we swung back and forth like a theme-park pirate-ship ride.

And then, the tether snapped.

It was probably my fault for getting optimistic, but I made sure to portion out plenty of blame for Sturb, Derby, the local steel industry, and God, too. The block plunged back toward the road, still traveling forwards with alarming speed, and I was almost jarred right off it the first time it bounced off the ground.

Instinctively I was clinging to the six feet of tether that was still attached to the top, and the six feet of Derby still harnessed to it, so it and the pair of us trailed after the jagged chunk of concrete like the ponytail on the head of an angry teenage boy with a bad complexion. It was only sheer dumb luck that we weren't smashed against the ground as the block rolled end over end with each impact.

The block finally came to rest, thanks to the road curving suddenly and a row of parked bicycles that was swiftly pulped into a single jingling mass between the block and the nearby wall. With an enormous amount of conscious effort, I managed to persuade my white-knuckled hands to separate from the tether.

"Urgh." Derby groaned as our sudden lack of movement signaled to his danger senses that it was safe to regain consciousness. He looked around blearily. "Never fear. The uncanny skills of Davisham Derby will . . . do whatever it is we're doing."

I looked up. We had stopped mere feet away from utterly destroying the ground floor lobby of the nearest building, but more importantly, Sturb had flown out of view in my plying ship. It was entirely possible that he would notice our absence and come back for us, but that would be the sort of thing one would expect of a human being, rather than a criminal tech-genius monster superficially resembling one.

I looked back. The boost of speed provided by our temporary ascent had put some distance between us and the biker horde, but they were closing in fast. They had spread out across the entire road to cut off our escape and, possibly, to indicate how little trac they gave about traffic laws at this moment. I could see their handheld chains whirling around their heads with the painful clarity of a near-death experience.

"Sturb has abandoned us, I take it," said Derby, slightly muffled from the concrete his face was resting on.

"Yeah, what a shame." I carefully moved behind the pile of concrete and gripped my blaster, in the hope that taking a combat position might persuade the gun's power cell to be slightly less depleted. "Would be nice if someone could mind slave these brackets and get them to pedal somewhere else."

"Oh, I'm given to understand the process is more complicated than that," he said groggily as he rose to his feet and brushed concrete dust from his sleeves, very nearly disemboweling himself with the unpowered saw on his wrist. "I suppose it falls now to Davisham Derby to save the day?"

"Yeah, sure," I said, eyes wide, the act of talking using up most of what little energy I had left. "Get out there and save the day. As visibly as possible."

"Naturally." He stepped in front of the wrecked anchor block, facing down the front row of the incoming biker kill squad, and shook his arms free of his sleeves.

I was still trying to figure out precisely how he signaled for his assistant to shove new tools into his arm Quantunnel. He didn't seem to do anything with his hand, and we would have heard any spoken commands through his tooth mic. Whatever it was, he was apparently doing it now.

The electric saw rattled awkwardly back into its housing. There were a few moments of faint clattering noises and adolescent swearing, then a new tool came out, locking into place with a clunk.

It was tubular, like a cannon, with two attachments along its length that could have been triggers. Derby pointed it far to the left, entirely away from any of the targets, and pulled the trigger closest to the barrel's mouth.

His elbow jerked with recoil, and a fist-sized object vaguely resembling a beetle with its legs splayed out fired from the cannon, trailing a black wire that was so thin it was barely visible. It embedded itself in the side of a bus shelter, creating a spider web of cracks in the plexiglass protecting a poster for Jacques McCon.

Without skipping a beat, Derby swiveled on his heel, pointed his cannon at the other side of the road, and pulled the other trigger. A second grabbing device fired, trailing the other end of the wire, and lodged in the building opposite.

There was a subtle whirring noise as the two grappling hooks pulled the wire taut between them, followed by a considerably more catastrophic noise when the first bikers hit it. The bikes stopped instantly and tilted up onto their front tires, bucking the riders off like angry mules. The bikers coming in just behind tightened their brakes far too late and skidded into the new pile of abandoned bicycles, getting each other's limbs caught in the chains they had been swinging around.

"Lesson one," said Derby grandly as he surveyed the carnage. "A vehicle can be a useful thing, but in battle it does little more than make your movements predictable."

"Does lesson two cover what to do about angry bikers you've just made slightly angrier?" I asked, still behind cover.

He put one hand on his hip to consider my point. While a lot of the bikers were struggling to get out of the pile of metal and limbs just behind the tripwire, the ones that had been unseated first and thrown forward had only been brought closer to us faster. The closest one, a bald man with enough chains dangling from his piercings to imprison a rhinoceros, was already up on his elbows, showing skinned flesh through the holes in his outfit and looking at Derby the way a sumo wrestler looks at a new opponent provocatively waving a sandwich.

A barely perceptible increase of tension in Derby's muscles indicated his sudden drop in confidence. "We may have . . . lost the element of surprise."

Two, three, four more bikers were getting to their feet, all looking upset and two already holding guns. The nearest one steadied his aim, drawing a bead on Derby's center mass.

There was an earsplitting bang, and a streak of energy arced across the street, showering sparks and sending the nearest bikers diving reflexively for cover. I clutched the sides of my head in despair. "Plying hell!"

Derby, unharmed, uncoiled himself from his defensive flinch. "What was that?"

"That was my last plying countermeasure!" I looked up. The *Neverdie* was hovering just above us, the port missile tube still emitting heat haze from the launch. "Sturb, you bracket! I was gonna pawn that to pay for Christmas dinner!"

"Sorry," came Sturb's voice. "Did you know the labels have worn off most of your buttons?" The ship descended further. The other half of the anchor cable was still attached to the landing leg, and the frayed end of it was already low enough to grab.

I wound my arm around it and scowled. "Don't touch anything else, you doint, I've got those set up exactly how I like them." I jumped and began to climb with just my arms, the effort driving all the air from my lungs until I had climbed high enough to bring my legs into the equation.

Derby, meanwhile, had ditched his double grappling hook launcher for a smaller, more conventional one with a standard winch, which he used to draw himself into the open airlock. I made a brief hand gesture as he flew past in an attempt to let him know that I would be checking very carefully for any marks the grappler left in the hull.

By the time I had clambered off the landing leg into the airlock, the *Neverdie* was ascending again. I stood in the external door, surveying the carnage below me, and the damage our actions had caused to the streets of Ritsuko. I winced, mentally cataloging the new set of bills I was going to have to avoid paying.

CHAPTER 13

BY THE TIME I reached the *Neverdie's* cockpit, the ship was already above the buildings and heading for the upper airlock in Ritsuko's bubble. It sounded like Sturb was talking to the air traffic control lads.

"All right, yes, to be perfectly honest, this is his ship. Very observant of you, quite impressive actually. But I assure you he is onboard. I realize how it must look, but I'm sure he'll be up here in a . . ."

He looked around and saw me enter. There was something gratifying about the way he snatched the headset off and leapt to his feet like the pilot's chair had acquired a nest of Koberian rattlers, but I maintained my scowl as I grabbed the headset from his hand.

"Now I see why you came back for us," I growled before sitting down and donning the gear. "Who's on shift tonight? Shinji? Adelaide?"

"*There* you are," said the voice of Shinji the air traffic controller. "Who was that doint? Tried to make us think we don't recognize your ship when we see it . . ."

The star pilot community had always been close to Ritsuko's air and ground control personnel, and it'd only gotten chummier after Quantunneling, when we started constantly running into each other in bars and soup kitchens. "It's a long story. We're heading out."

"No prob." I heard the tapping of the heavy, outdated switches in Shinji's booth, and the airlock in the plexiglass directly above us began the typical cycle. "This long story got anything to do with that big fuss going on downtown at the moment?"

"Frobisher's sex life," I said.

"Gotcha. Tower out."

Sturb was still standing awkwardly to my left, toying apologetically with his fingers. "Frobisher's what?"

I glared at him for a second, then returned my focus to controlling the ship. "It's star pilot code. It means, you're better off knowing as little about this as possible."

"Oh, I see," he said, smiling desperately.

The airlock completed its cycle, and the *Neverdie* popped out of Ritsuko City's bubble like a champagne cork, heading for open space and putting more and more distance between us and the mess we had left behind. I plotted a course for the solar system's trebuchet gate. It was a fairly obvious escape route, but hopefully the ISS—the peacekeepers of the protected territory around the solar system—wouldn't have time to mobilize anything to intercept us. A lot of their fleet had gone into mothballs since their last budget cut.

I pointed the *Neverdie's* nose cone directly at the tiny pinprick of light that represented the trebuchet gate's guiding beacon and set the autopilot. Hopefully, moving forwards along a perfectly straight path wouldn't tax the old thing, but I made sure the cooling vents were uncovered anyway.

That left me with nothing to do but bask in the company of Malcolm Sturb. "Can I just say, I thought you did a very impressive job down there. I think we can all be proud of this heist, but you in particular demonstrated some very keen problem-solving skills under pressure."

"Thanks," I said, talking out of the sides of my mouth.

"Sorry Jimi had to take control of the autopilot. Actually, we may have done you a favor. Did you know how much spyware your mainframe had running in the background? Jimi had to create a sort of direct backdoor—"

I couldn't hear the rest of what he said, because I had slipped my headset back on and tuned into Ritsuko City's newscasting station, which for the moment was still in range.

". . . watched his ship head up to the city airlock and off into space," came the voice of Steve the traffic reporter. "Certainly couldn't blame him for wanting to get away. Looks like it's still quite a mess down there. Police have closed off the damaged streets, so traffic's rock solid all the way to the Hips. Must be a terrible time to be down on ground level, right now." There was more than a hint of satisfaction in his tone.

"Ye-es, quite," said Linda in the studio. "If you're just joining us, the breaking news is that the already historic occasion of Jacques McKeown's appearance at Jacques McCon this weekend has suddenly become even more so. We are getting reports that Jacques McKeown himself appears to have masterminded a daring heist and kidnapping, targeting the Henderson company, which was hosting the convention. Moments ago, he fled the scene in his ship, pursued by police and convention security in a spectacular high-speed chase, and appears to have successfully escaped from Ritsuko City's jurisdiction."

"Already, this seems to have only added to the legend of Jacques McKeown," said the other presenter. "Sales of his books have tripled and the day's trading hasn't officially begun. We called the office of Blasé Books for a statement, but when they picked up the phone all we could hear was the sound of people singing and champagne corks popping."

"Well, the thought of driving home tonight isn't something that I'm in the mood to celebrate, I can tell you that," said Linda.

"Mm, I imagine," said Steve in the observation tower. "I'd make room for you all up here but, you know, you'd probably find it a bit chilly. Which is a problem I'm sure the people in the business district are wishing they had right now. Looks like the rioters have lit another fire."

I flicked the radio off and pulled my headset down around my neck with a sigh. This hadn't exactly been the ideal outcome. McKeown was getting free publicity and the collateral damage was going to take some serious blowing over. I'd probably have to dig into my box of fake mustaches when it came time to bring my scientists to Oniris. But something was nagging at me. "Kidnapping?"

"Mm?" said Sturb, who had been idly examining a nearby readout with a hand to his chin.

"The news said this was a heist and kidnapping." My thoughtful stare focused into an accusing one when I remembered who I was talking to. "What did you plying do down there, Sturb?"

"Nothing! Captain, I swear I didn't do anything. I just got some things signed and bought some collectibles." He grabbed a white plastic bag from the corner by the door and held out a pathetic little action figure. It was a scantily clad female warrior bearing a slight resemblance to Mrs. Frobisher.

Without taking my eyes off him, I leaned over and locked the controls. I had no doubt that an amoral tech genius like Sturb could do whatever he plying wanted with my ship, but the gesture was more about letting him see the blaster I was still wearing under my jacket. "I'm gonna check over the ship." I backed toward the door. "Stay here. Don't touch anything. If I find anyone in slave crowns, we're going to have a long, enlightening conversation about boundaries."

He kept his hands up, hanging his head defeatedly, until I was far enough through the door to lose sight of him. I descended the steps backwards, keeping one hand under my jacket, ready to draw at the first sign of hostile nerd.

When I had retreated as far as the cabin door, I stopped when I heard voices. Not from the cabin—from the sturdy hatch opposite that led to the head. It was slightly ajar, and I could hear Derby arguing with someone. Probably his assistant, assuming he didn't have an ongoing beef with something he'd eaten today.

"... could hardly cut through that cable," said Derby. "It really did come close to ruining everything."

I moved my ear a little closer to the door. It was undoubtedly Derby's voice, but there was something different about it. It was still condescending, but in a whiny, petulant way, with a hint of disappointment. He sounded like a weak-willed father trying to tactfully confront his teenage son about the magazines he'd found under his bed.

"Sorry, Uncle Dav," said his young assistant. I tried to peer through the crack in the door, and saw Derby's shadow upon the wall. He was sitting on the toilet, leaning over his knees and talking into his arm stump.

"And I don't want you to feel like this was your fault, but if you'd just been a little more alert and provided me with the G32 like I signaled for, then . . ." He left his sentence hanging.

His assistant made the kind of quiet little sigh one makes when about to launch into a statement you've been mentally preparing for the last couple of hours. "Uncle Dav, you signaled for a G16. That's why I gave you the G16."

Derby hesitated for just a moment. "Now, come on, Nelly, we have been doing this for quite a while now, I don't think I would have signaled for a G16 when I needed a G32, would I."

"I know we've been doing this for a while, but I'm telling you, you made the G16 signal."

Derby sighed tolerantly. "Nelly, I am one hundred percent certain I did not. I did left wink, look up, blink."

"Yes, and that's for the G16," Nelly insisted. "The G32 is two blinks."

A pause. "Is it?"

"I've got the cheat sheet right here. Hang on." I heard a very faint rustle of paper. "Here, look. Definitely. One blink for the G16, two blinks for the G32, and three blinks for the G32 pushed out already running and at maximum speed because you're trying to impress someone. Look."

"No, no, it's . . . it's all right, I believe you." From the movements of his shadow, it looked like he was leaning further forward and pinching his eyes with his real hand.

"Okay." A note of concern entered Nelly's voice. "You holding up okay, Uncle Dav? It sounded like things got pretty intense back there."

Derby suddenly switched to his normal voice. "Nothing is too intense for Davisham Derby," he crowed, before straightening up a little too hard and hitting his head against the empty paper-towel dispenser above the bowl.

"It's just, I got another email from Uncle Ted this afternoon."

He stiffened. I know, because he hit his head on the towel dispenser a little harder this time.

"He said to tell you that they can't keep the job open at the fish shop for another year. So if you were serious about taking it, then they need to know if you're coming home soon."

Derby's fingers drummed on the underside of the toilet bowl. "Is that all he said?"

"Well, he asked if you're planning to stop . . . doing the things that we're doing."

"I take it that wasn't exactly how he worded it."

My limbs were starting to ache from standing still for too long, so I shifted my weight slightly, and accidentally kicked a spent power cell I'd left lying on the floor. It rattled down a couple of metal steps with sphincter-tightening obviousness.

"Davisham Derby is the greatest thief that ever roamed the galaxy," said Derby, back to using his confident voice at a much higher volume. "I can no more resist the call to adventure than I can the siren's song."

"Okay, well, he said if you don't show up to Auntie Maggie's birthday—"

Derby silenced her by promptly slapping the lid shut on his arm Quantunnel, then rose to his feet. I pretended to be very thoroughly checking the airlock seal as he emerged from the head.

"Ah, you," he said, like an aristocrat addressing the new shoeshine boy. "How long until we are returned to Salvation Station?"

I put on a skeptical face, idly flicking the little tear in the worn black rubber that ran around the internal airlock door. "About an hour to the trebuchet gate. Couple more hours to get to Salvation, depending on how accurate the gate feels like being today."

Derby made a scoff that blasted out of his nostrils like a round of flak. "What a wonderful, efficient experience space travel is. One wonders how Quantunneling ever managed to make it completely redundant."

He didn't wait for a reply, but strode right across the hall and pushed his way into the passenger cabin, shoving the door aside as if it were a beggar on a train platform. I was about to start searching the engine deck for Sturb's new cyberslaves when Derby's head suddenly reappeared in the doorway.

"Pilot," he said, brow furrowed. "Remind me how many individuals our mutual friend employed for this heist?"

"Me, you, and Sturb," I said, as slowly and clearly as I could. "Three."

"I thought as much." He pushed the door open wide to invite me in. "We seem to have picked up a stowaway."

I looked past him. There was the cabin, there was the cryonic cylinder we'd stolen, there was the Quantunnel exit Sturb had put together, and there was Mr. Henderson lying unconscious on the floor.

CHAPTER 14

"HELLO?" WARDEN WAS saying. "Ground team, report. McKeown, what's happening?"

"*Shhhhhhh,*" I replied, pausing in the act of tying Henderson securely to a folding chair with some spare extension cables. "Sorry, Warden, we're getting some interfer-*shhhhhhkrkkk.*" I dug my tongue into my teeth to switch the microphone off, and signaled for the others to do the same.

"Okay," said Sturb. "Good news. I think I've figured out how this happened."

"Great," I prompted, glaring. "'Cos, the last time I saw him, he was on the far side of a Quantunnel. And unconscious. I remember that very clearly, because it's just about the only time he and I have gotten on."

"I think he might have been a little bit not unconscious. I think that after you shot him with your stun blaster"—he emphasized the word *you* slightly, possibly on the off chance that Henderson could hear—"I think he might still have been just aware enough to keep the Quantunnel from closing. But I didn't realize that. I was thinking back to that theory you put forward that it wouldn't close because we were still sensing the cold coming from it." There was that emphatic use of *you* again.

"So?"

"So, I told Jimi to keep attempting the close function until it worked, and then I left." He looked at Henderson, who sat slumped with head deeply bowed. "He must have been conscious enough to crawl in through the tunnel and then pass out."

"This is why they were calling this a kidnapping," I thought aloud, nervously rapping a knuckle against the nearby bulkhead. "What the hell do we do now?"

"What, exactly, is your concern?" asked Derby, sitting comfortably on one of the benches with legs outstretched and ankles crossed.

"My concern," I said, in a perfectly reasonable tone as my hands clenched and unclenched around imaginary doints, "is that we are now holding one of the most ruthless and wealthiest crime lords in the solar system. Who commands a personal army of loyal killers who will do anything to stay on his good side."

Derby's eyes rotated all the way around as he internalized this information. "So what I'm hearing is, we need to issue a ransom demand."

"NO!"

"Can I just say that this doesn't have to be our problem alone," said Sturb. "I'm actually still wondering why you insisted on cutting Penelope out of this discussion."

"Because I don't trust her! I don't trust that she won't do something crazy over this. She has a history of going a bit psycho where Henderson is concerned." I gestured both hands at Henderson's leg stump.

"If you say so," said Sturb skeptically. "But let me just say, I've worked with Penelope for some time at Salvation Station, and I really think she's come a long way since her time as Henderson's protégé."

"Besides," said an unconcerned Derby. "She must honor our deal."

Okay, so now Hitler was vouching for Satan. And the Boston Strangler had declared his neutrality. I tapped my foot uncertainly. Part of me wanted to inform Warden, if only because it didn't seem fair for her to be sitting on Salvation Station blissfully scoffing fig rolls while we were left to panic amongst ourselves.

"Look, if nothing else," said Sturb as my thoughtful silence drew on, "she's got to be the person who knows the most about him. How best to handle him."

My gaze flew to Henderson's leg stump again, but I had to concede the point. After all, shooting it off had undeniably handled him. I tongued my mic again. "Fine. For the record, I was against this. Warden, come in. Warden?"

Henderson snapped awake instantly, glaring daggers at me so hard that I flinched from the imagined stab wound. "Warden!" he barked like a dog that had been amusingly trained to say a single word. "Warden, Warden, Warden."

His body slowly untensed as he repeated the name, then he seemed to actually wake up. He looked down, tested the strength of his bonds, then looked back at me. A pleased smile spread across his face.

"Ah yes, Jacques McKeown," he said brightly. "That makes sense, if Penny's behind this. Glad to see you two tied the knot at last. I don't remember getting an invitation?"

"Hello?" said Warden in my ear. "Status, McKeown?"

"We have a problem." I pressed one finger to my ear and turned to face the wall.

"What kind of problem?"

Henderson hummed happily in thought. "Really, this was quite clever. You've done a super job with this heist, you should all be proud of yourselves. It'll add some lovely spice to the news story after they find whatever's left of your corpses."

"I'd classify it as 'miscellaneous,' " I replied, trying to talk over him. "We've got the cylinder, but Henderson followed us through the Quantunnel. We've tied him to a chair and we're en route to the trebuchet gate."

"Henderson . . . is with you?"

"Yep."

Warden hesitated significantly. "Make the trebuchet jump. Hold your position when you get to the Black. I'll send someone."

I glanced at Henderson. He met my gaze and renewed his friendly smile, wrinkling his nose encouragingly. I turned away again. "You expect us to just sit around in the Black like lemons waiting for him to . . ." The rest of the sentence failed me.

"To do what, McKeown? You tied him up, yes? And you took away his phone?"

I tongued my mic off. "Did we take his phone away?"

"Good idea, I'll do it now," muttered Sturb, cautiously moving up behind Henderson's chair.

I nodded and tongued my mic back on. "Yeah, obviously we took his phone away. We're not idiots."

"He's tied up, he's cut off from his men and out of his center of power," summarized Warden. "What are you afraid he'll do?"

"First one of you three to kill the other two, I'll pay you ten times whatever she's offering," said Henderson, in a bored, extremely loud voice.

A rather tellingly long silence followed. I'm sure Warden picked up on the sudden rise of tension in the room even from across the galaxy.

"He might do that," I said quietly.

"He might do that, granted." There was an edge to Warden's voice. "Make the trebuchet jump. Hold position. Try to keep the situation stable."

Easier said than done, I thought, as I looked about the cabin. The way the three of us had taken up position around the room, all now in alert, poised stances, trying to keep eyes on both of the other two at once, the atmosphere had taken on the quality of a Mexican standoff. No guns were out, but Derby was idly holding his wrist device, and my shoulder holster was starting to make my armpit itch.

"Kill, knock out and tie up, I'm not that bothered." Henderson inspected his shoes. "Anything along the lines of betrayal is what I'm after. Then help me ambush Warden. For something along the lines of revenge."

"All right, well, let's get on with the, er, the jump," said Sturb, swinging his arms pointedly toward the door but not moving his feet. "I'm sure I speak for us all when I say that none of us are even going to consider an offer like that."

"Not at all." Derby's eyes darted from side to side. "A deal was struck, and Davisham Derby is a man of his word." He was standing as straight as he could and trying just a bit too hard to maintain eye contact.

"Anyway, Henderson can't be trusted," I said. "We broke into his home, shot him, and took his stuff. He's going to want revenge on us, too. Revenge is a big thing with him."

"Well, granted." Henderson nodded reasonably. "If you hadn't kidnapped me, I'd send the most violent and depraved scum in the universe to hunt you down and turn all your testicles into one of those little executive toys that knock back and forth. But you have me in a bind, no pun intended, and you know that I can be pragmatic when I need to be, don't you, Jacques?"

The smile he directed at me filled the room. "Uh . . ."

"Look, everyone, we're this close to completing this job, as a team," said Sturb, moving with heavy, deliberate sidesteps until he was right in front of Henderson. "We can't listen to him. He's just trying to drive us apart."

There was a long pause. Derby and I exchanged a glance just long enough for Sturb to notice.

"Oh no," he said, letting his shoulders sag. "No, no, no. You're not actually thinking about it."

"No, I'm not!" I protested. "I don't care what Henderson's offering. I'm here to save Robert Blaze." And to get my scientists, I thought to myself;

even if Henderson could do as he said and provide ten times as many, there was such a thing as overkill.

"Indeed," said Derby, although some of the self-assuredness had drained from his voice. "Derby has given his word. And even if he did consider it, as would be perfectly rational to do so, in the larger process of weighing up pros and cons on a moment-to-moment basis—"

"You are not going to think about it!" Sturb's programmer pallor was turning hot pink as he stepped warningly toward Derby. This was a side of him I hadn't seen, at least not lately; he used to work up the odd head of steam back in the day, usually after I'd foiled one of his master plans and was speeding off into the sunset.

"Well, suit yourselves." Henderson was enjoying himself to an infuriating degree. "You want to miss out on an opportunity and mark yourselves for highly unpleasant deaths, it's no skin off my nose. After all, I'm sure I don't know Warden as well as you three. I'm sure she's changed a lot since I saw her last and would absolutely sacrifice herself for any of you if the circumstances were reversed."

Sturb spun around so fast that Henderson genuinely flinched. Then he took off one of his shoes, hopping awkwardly as he worried it off, and removed a black sock patterned with computer code, which he promptly tied around Henderson's mouth. Henderson tried to keep up his self-satisfied expression, but then he made the mistake of inhaling through his nose.

Sturb turned to face us again, visibly trembling. "We're not listening to him and that's final! Because Penelope's my friend and this isn't what friends do!"

The deep red complexion and furious spittle at the corners of Sturb's mouth would have been difficult to fake, especially for a complete emotional cripple. Maybe he really had reformed. Either that or Warden had sealed him nice and manageably into a custom-designed friend zone.

"Okay," I said, keeping my tone calm and my hands visible. "I'd better get back to the cockpit."

Sturb turned his furious gaze on me, love handles jiggling as he stepped into my personal space. "Why?!"

I blinked a few times before replying. "To . . . guide us into the trebuchet gate." I gestured toward the stairs. "So we can make the jump into the Black. Like we need to do. For the job."

"I'll come with you."

I let a sigh out through my teeth. "Why?"

"Just . . . in case."

"In case I secretly conspire with Henderson?" I started throwing my hands around as if distributing invisible custard pies. "From three rooms away? While there's a sock in his mouth?"

"Just in case," he repeated firmly, shadowing me as I moved toward the steps.

I nodded toward Derby, who was standing on the far side of the room with his hands behind his back. "You gonna leave him alone in here, then?"

Sturb stared at him for a few moments, reflecting on how badly he did not want to do that very thing. "Derby, you're going to come with us, too."

"Have I not made it clear enough that Davisham Derby is a man of his word?" He didn't move from his spot. "I have no intention of colluding with the hostage."

"Well then, you won't have any objection to coming and joining us in the cockpit, will you?" I said patiently.

His eyes rested on Henderson for the merest fraction of a second before his gaze flinched away as if from a hot stove, and he tried to make it look like he was flamboyantly rolling his eyes in contempt. "Of course not. Lead the way."

"You first," growled Sturb.

"Follow the way, then."

CHAPTER 15

THE RIDE THROUGH the trebuchet gate was even bumpier than usual. It'd only been getting worse ever since they'd built that Quantunnel on Salvation Station and removed a large chunk of whatever reason remained to use the trebuchet network for FTL travel. I wasn't even sure who was supposed to be maintaining the trebuchet gates. Last I checked, the company that had originally built them had largely shifted to manufacturing electric scooters.

They were, at the very least, still functioning, although we arrived in the Black spinning wildly on three axes and I had to burn the side thrusters for a full minute to get us to stop.

"Jump complete," I said afterwards, when I finally permitted myself to breathe. I punched up a few readouts. "Looks like we're near the Biskot system. That's about a thirty-minute flight to Salvation. You get that, Warden?" I transmitted our precise coordinates to the station, then flicked off the engines and let the persistent background hum fade into silence.

"Got it," she said in a low voice.

Maybe the bumpiness of the trebuchet jump had been augmented somewhat by the presence of Derby and Sturb in the cockpit, which was designed at best to hold one pilot's chair, one console, and a small amount of space in which to fling discarded fast-food wrappers. During the jump, I'd taken a jarring hit to the shoulder from Derby's arm device, and there was a greasy dent on one of the overhead vent panels that corresponded to the contours of Sturb's forehead.

"So, we are resigned to simply sit here?" Derby was trying to tug the creases out of his clothes. "Could we not meet them halfway?"

"It's the Black," I said. "Still a lot of Zoobs and non-Salvation pirates roaming around. Best not to draw attention to yourself if you can avoid it."

"I was just thinking," said Sturb, "that I'm more worried about the dangers in here than out there."

Derby made an offended scoff. "Does a gentleman's word mean nothing anymore?"

"Look, there's no need for us to fall out over this, we just need to watch each other until Penelope decides what to do with Mr. Henderson," insisted Sturb, peering down from the imaginary moral high ground. "I'd say that's perfectly reasonable. All we have to do is . . . stay calm."

I coughed. "Someone should probably check on him."

"Why do you say that?!" exploded Sturb, flicking a few droplets of sweat in my direction as his face snapped around.

"He may have smashed his head open in the jump." Henderson's death in our custody might not have been the worst possible outcome, and would certainly solve a few of our immediate problems, but it was easy to imagine some negative consequences in the long term. Besides, killing a defenseless prisoner didn't sit well with the old hero instincts, testicle executive toys aside.

"Or he may have smashed the chair and is plotting the takeover of this vessel as we speak," contributed Derby.

Sturb knuckled the sweat from his eyes and stared us both up and down as if assessing us for the first time. "In that case. We can all go check on him."

"You two go," I said. "I have to stay at the controls in case something finds us." I tapped a few buttons that had no effect, but which I kept around to randomly tap when I wanted to emphasize a point.

Sturb didn't move. His gaze swept over my controls, and I could practically hear the cogwheels turn as he thought about all the terrible things I could make the ship do unsupervised. "N-nooo. You have to come with us, too."

"Look—"

But Sturb would never find out in what precise way I wanted him to look, for at that point the proximity monitor gave an urgent triple blip, swiftly followed by a second.

"Two ships entering sensor range," I reported, leaning over the scanner to check the readout, booting the scanning unit in the vent until the twelve black holes it was mistakenly reporting disappeared and were replaced by two small, fast-moving dots.

Sturb inspected the display. "Penelope's people?"

"I'm assuming as much." The two lines were undoubtedly moving toward us, so either they were two of Warden's pet star pilots from Salvation who knew to look for us here or they were pirates with a profoundly good nose for booty.

Shortly, the approaching ships entered visual range. They looked like the usual star pilot fare—small, maneuverable, curved like a beach beauty reaching for her suntan lotion—with none of the cosmetic spikes or tattoos that signified career pirates. Then again, they could have been new recruits. The line between pirates and star pilots tended to be blurry in the Black, since each were routinely turning into the other.

I wriggled my headset back on and opened a direct channel. "*Neverdie* to approaching ships," I said to get the formalities out of the way. "You from Salvation?" I transmitted Salvation's designated friend signal, just in case.

The ships continued approaching in silence. They were definitely within listening range, and my headphones were receiving the telltale static of a connected line with someone on the other end hovering their finger over the button, ready to answer.

I added a hint of gruff impatience to my tone. "Approaching ships, please respond."

Another few seconds of wordless hissing in my ears, then an abrupt clunk, a few words too staticky to even determine the gender of the person speaking, then another clunk. "*Neverdie*, stand by." I got the impression that a discussion was taking place between the two ships, and possibly also Salvation, if that was where they were from.

"What are they doing?" asked Derby. The ships were close enough now to be visible through the forward view screen. They slowed and stopped around eighty yards ahead, outside the range of umbilicals but well within the range for weapons.

"Something's wrong," I whispered uneasily.

"Oh, come on, guys," said Sturb with slightly strangled joviality as he mopped sweat from his face again. "Look, I know we all got a little bit paranoid back there, but these are Penelope's people, and we're all equally keen to get this antidote to Robert Blaze. They're probably doing a systems check. The interesting thing about the systems in early-model SST-grade ships like those is—"

The two ships opened fire.

Luckily, my constant annoyance with Sturb had been keeping me good and tense. My hands had been irritably clamped around the control sticks and I was able to instinctively twist them the instant I saw the first volley of white plasma burst from the ships' frontal cannons. The *Neverdie* pitched left, and the two streams of death sped by, above and below us.

I yanked the sticks back and to the side and kicked the reverse thrust lever to build up a bit of distance before their guns could cool down for another round. The more alert of the two ships broke off from its tiny formation and tried to get its sights back on me, and soon we were spinning around each other in the classic ballet of the circle strafe.

"Warden! Call them off!" I yelled into my mic. There was no response, but somewhere amid the clatter of controls and the warning bleeps, I imagined I heard the scratching sound of a mic being deactivated.

"Stand down! We're carrying antidote for Robert Blaze!" cried Sturb, butting his head against mine to yell into my mic. "The cryonic cylinder is onboard! Stop attacking!"

If anything, that only spurred them on. Another plasma lance scythed through space and glanced off the *Neverdie*'s protruding underbelly, leaving a black mark that would be hell to clean off. The second ship was a bulkier model, too slow to keep up with me like its partner could, so it was holding position and rotating in place, trying to line up a shot.

"Assassins!" declared Derby.

"You don't know that!" said Sturb. After the firing had started he had none-too-subtly taken a defensive position crouched behind my chair. "It must be Henderson's people. Did you call them here?"

"When could I have done that, you idiot?! We've been in the same room!"

"I wasn't directly looking at you the whole time!"

I gave the artificial gravity unit a kick, throwing my two nonseated passengers to the floor. "I don't have time to destupid this entire cockpit right now. Shut up and let me concentrate."

I focused my attention on the slower ship. I wasn't sure offhand how much of my ammunition I'd pawned since I'd last been in a dogfight, so I started with a burst of Gatling fire that my target easily saw coming and lazily dodged, but at least it got them on their toes. If I could keep the pressure up, avoid giving them time to adapt, I'd roll them over quick.

But then I sensed the other, faster, ship sneakily slipping out of my field of vision on the left edge of the view screen. On instinct, I fired the vertical jets, and the *Neverdie* bounced upwards just in time to let another lance of plasma pass by underneath. I turned my attention back to the faster ship and strafed toward rather than away from it, just as a shot from the slower ship passed through an area where one might assume a less experienced pilot would have moved to.

So they knew how to work together tactically, which confirmed that we were dealing with actual star pilots, or rather discounted the possibility of them being mercenary thugs or sophisticated Zoobs. I didn't think they could have been on Henderson's payroll, but why would star pilots be trying to sabotage the Robert Blaze rescue effort?

Maybe it was Warden trying some incredibly convoluted backstab. But that didn't make sense, appealing as it would have been to build a case against her; if she'd meant for Blaze to die, she could easily have *not* organized the heist. Was she so desperate to rid herself of Henderson that she'd sacrifice everything, just as the heist she'd planned so carefully was about to pay off? It didn't feel right.

The fast ship and I had been circling each other for several seconds now, with the slower ship making little circles of its own nearby, so it was about time someone made another play. I seized the initiative first and swung back toward the slow ship, hitting the boost to cross the distance quicker, making them back away defensively like an awkward partygoer getting their personal space invaded.

But I kept boosting even when we were close to collision, forcing them to get out of the way to let me fly straight past, neatly placing the slow ship between me and the fast ship and ensuring that the latter couldn't fire on me without hitting his friend. In a single moment, slapping two buttons at once like an overexcited pianist, I sent one of my last precious torpedoes toward the slow ship and sped off in the opposite direction.

I didn't think for a moment that the torpedo would actually hit. The guidance system was horrendously out of date and the occupants of the target ship could have thrown it off by chucking a fridge magnet out their airlock. But it would give them something to think about for a few moments while I considered my next move.

The torpedo impacted the hull of the slower ship just where the port nacelle met the main body, and the fireball tore through to the engineering decks. I knew this for certain, because a moment later their main reactor went up, consuming the entire ship in a sphere of white-hot conflagration, leaving nothing but a blackened skeleton that had once been a star pilot's pride and joy.

My hands came away from the joysticks damply as my arms went limp. I boggled, jaw slack, at the scorched wreckage that was drifting apart before my eyes. The other ship hung back, apparently as shocked as I was. "I killed them," I heard myself say.

"Ye-es," said Derby uncertainly. "Are you waiting for us to blow party squeakers?"

"You don't shoot to kill!" I barked at him, showing him my shaking hands. "Star pilots don't shoot to kill! Not against other star pilots!"

"They were shooting to kill," he replied. "They were using plasma."

I gave him an aghast look. "Obviously you use live ammo! You just don't shoot to kill! You're supposed to dodge! Make it interesting! A five-year-old could've dodged that! They . . . it wasn't . . ."

"I think we're losing him," said Derby to Sturb dryly.

Sturb leaned in close to my ear. "Er, Captain, you're doing a really good job at flying, well done; don't you think you should take the controls again and get us away from the other one?"

"Unless you feel up to killing them as well," said Derby reasonably.

"I didn't kill them!" I spun around on my chair and made gestures of protestation to no one in particular. "I barely even fired! It was more like littering with missiles! They just didn't dodge! It's not my fault!"

"Jimi, could you scan the near vicinity and determine our best escape strategy," whispered Sturb tactfully into his phone.

"Of course it wasn't your fault," said Derby, with a slightly sarcastic attempt at a soothing tone. "All you did was take your torpedo out for a walk. How can you be blamed if someone should trip over it?"

"Shut up, Derby! You've stolen plying loads of things. That's worse than killing someone. Probably. If you put it all together."

"Debris field located in the orbital path of the third moon of Biskot 2," chirped Jimi. "Density and average object size suggests multiple opportunities for concealment."

"Captain," said Sturb timidly. "Jimi says there's a debris field located in—"

"And you!" I turned to him. "You're Malcolm Sturb. You enslave people's minds. I'm still the least worst person in the room."

He emitted a pained little sigh. "Yes, you're absolutely right. But I think it's fair to say that if you don't get us into that debris field soon, you are going to be indirectly responsible for at least four more deaths."

I checked the proximity scanner. The other ship was still hanging back, the destruction of its friend having given it pause for thought, but the way it was edging back toward the *Neverdie*'s flank suggested that it had paused for long enough. And that it wasn't thinking that the best approach was for everyone to shake hands and part ways with good sportsmanship.

I pulled up the navigation map. Jimi hadn't led us astray—the debris field added a pretty halo of orange glitter around the circle representing Biskot 2. The moon itself was visible through the view screen, close enough to be a bright blue beach ball among the thousands of grains of sand that was the star field.

"R-right," I said, shuffling forward in my chair and shaking the cobwebs out of my head.

A burst of the rear thrusters and we were underway toward the debris field. That was enough to snap our opponent out of it, and they began their pursuit.

They fired more plasma, but the advantage of hightailing it away from a fight is that the projectiles are only moving slightly faster than you, relatively speaking, and they're a lot easier to dodge. I only had to leisurely shift left, right, up, and down to step out of the way of incoming fire.

The attacker was maintaining pace with the *Neverdie*, so we must have been equally matched, speedwise. Either that or they weren't willing to push their engines to full power, which changed nothing, because I wasn't, either. My coolant reserves were partially depleted, because I'd made Krohar of Belj drink some of it. His species had the ability to do so without ill effects, and this was something I tended to find amusing when drunk.

When we were halfway to the debris field, the pursuing ship stopped firing and slowed a little, allowing the distance between us to grow.

"It looks like they're backing off," said Sturb, watching the rear view.

"Doubt it," I said.

The other ship changed course, moving upwards in an arc that would take him right over the strip of debris that followed the moon like a comet's tail, which was more or less what I'd expected. He was going to position himself where he could better cover the debris field. He'd be able to see if I popped out of the other side of it, and if I didn't, he'd be in a good spot to watch for the moment we did decide to break cover.

I was all but certain at this point that I was dealing with another star pilot who knew all the same star pilot tricks. Fortunately, I was an ex–star pilot, and as of recently a heist participant, so my trick repertoire was slightly more expansive. At least, I had to hope so.

The debris field consisted largely of intact drifting ships and discarded modules from larger vessels and stations. There were no small broken fragments or plasma scarring to indicate battle damage. This wasn't the debris of war; this was the monumentally more tragic debris of abandonment.

The Biskot system was smack bang on the halfway point between the solar system and the Spanish colony in the Mateo system, so the Speedstar Corporation had constructed a space station in Biskot to act as a rest stop for star pilots making the grueling trip to Mateo. And after a couple of minor galactic wars broke out in the Mateo area and used up most of the natural resources, suddenly there were rather a lot of star pilots making the trip.

The rest stop in Biskot swiftly expanded into a whole network of space stations and grew into a major hub for travelers, with a trading post, repair and refueling facilities, hotels, restaurants, entertainment centers, shooting ranges, anything the weary star pilot might need. Local business owners began hiring Biskot's indigenous population to help run the place. The founder of Ritsuko City and father of off-world development, Kaito Ayakama, had pledged that humanity would never interfere with the development of lesser races, but profit was on the line, and the courts ruled that it was less a law than a piece of somewhat solid advice.

Biskot's downfall was, of course, quantum tunneling. After the construction of Quantunnel gates in all of Mateo's spaceports, star pilots were no longer the only practical choice for transporting supplies. And as much as we all enjoyed stopping at Biskot Central, it wasn't worth a trip by itself. Especially when work dried up and the fuel costs amounted to three weeks' worth of blood donations.

Biskot Central was among the first of Speedstar's many branches to snap off as the company's prolonged downsizing began. The locals returned to their home planets to resume pushing dirt around their farms or whatever, and all that remained of the system's former glory was the dense cloud of

discarded technology that now surrounded the *Neverdie*. All the stuff whose
resale value couldn't have made up for the cost of towing it away.

I swiftly found a piece of debris bigger than my ship: a drifting residence
module that had once clipped together with several of its fellows to form
a mobile, flexible hotel. I positioned the *Neverdie* flat against its underside
and oriented the stabilizers so that the ship would automatically match its
rotation.

After that, I cut the power and switched to emergency reserves, plunging
the cockpit into red twilight. The constant electric hum stopped and silence
settled upon my senses like a fat, tired dog.

Derby looked around, interested, at the sinister atmosphere the ship's
interior had suddenly acquired. "So, what is the plan, *mon capitaine*?" he said,
with sarcastic deference. "Wait until they go away? Assume their resources
will run out before ours do?"

"We're buying time"—I drummed my fingers on the arms of my
chair—"until I can figure out the next move."

"Then prepare to marvel, for I have figured it out with no time at all. We
resume the battle."

"No."

He clucked. "There's only one ship left. I thought things were going
rather well."

I raised a warning finger. "A, that wasn't even a fluke, that was an accident.
B, I have nowhere near the ammo for a proper dogfight. And C, I do not kill
star pilots. Not on purpose."

"So?"

"So, we wait, and you, me, and Sturb stay together and away from
Henderson, all right?" I spun around in my chair. "Where the plying hell
is Sturb?"

Derby followed my gaze and inspected the Sturb-shaped hole in the
scenery. "Hm."

I leapt out of my chair hard enough to keep it spinning for a good minute, at least, and hurried down the steps, the metal thundering and rattling
underfoot. I grabbed the edge of the doorway into the passenger cabin as
soon as it was within arm's reach and swung around it, dropping into what
I hoped was a close approximation of a martial arts stance.

Henderson was still where we had left him, tied to a chair with a sock
in his mouth, the fury that had been perpetually burning in his eyes now

reduced to a mild simmer. Sturb, turning in surprise at my appearance, was on the opposite end of the cabin, apparently engaged in dismantling the mobile Quantunnel gate.

"What are you doing?!"

"Oh, I'm glad you're here," said Sturb rapidly, holding some bits of Quantunnel gate in front of his torso as if to protect himself. "As you can see, I've checked on the hostage and everything looks secure. I was going to come back straightaway, of course, but then the thought occurred, maybe I should dismantle the portable Quantunnel in case—"

"Sit down," I commanded. Sturb's knees twitched immediately, but he managed to get in front of one of the seats before he obediently dropped.

I sat down in a seat next to his, then gestured to the seat on his other side. "Derby. Sit down."

Derby, who had been waiting at the door, spat out a contemptuous sigh, but then crossed the room with long exaggerated strides and plopped himself down where I had indicated.

"Okay," I said, in measured tones. "Now. We're all going to sit still, here, together, and we're going to quietly wait, and that way we can all be sure that none of us can betray the other two." I gave Henderson a dirty look, and he responded with a cheerful wink.

"Unless they've already betrayed the other two," said Derby quietly.

I passed my dirty look around for everyone to enjoy. "Then we can all make sure none of us try to kill the other two."

"Could I just ask . . . what we're waiting for, exactly?" said Sturb, clutching his knees.

"For the other ship to give up and go away. It might be strongly motivated by the fact that we killed their friend, but they can't stay out there forever."

"And how will we know they've gone away?" asked Derby.

I took a deep, calming breath and counted to ten before replying. "We'll just wait long enough that we can assume."

"Jimi could monitor nearby space, if you like." Sturb shuffled in his seat as he made to dig his phone out. "All they'd have to do is put out what we call a remote surveillance—"

"No, no, no," I interrupted. "There is a little thing you might not have heard of called 'silent running' which is the thing we're trying to plying do. We don't know what kind of scanning capability they have. What kind of signals we produce that they might be able to detect. That's why we're also going to turn our mics off and not send any help requests to Warden."

"Oh," said Sturb, hanging his head. "I might have already done that."

I counted to ten again. "Then we're not going to send any *more* help requests to Warden."

I was sitting hunched forward, hands clasped, and keeping a close eye on Henderson. Sturb was sitting back but with shoulders slouched, and Derby was sitting straight backed with arms tightly folded. Sitting side by side, we were creating a sort of three-level effect.

"*I* suggested we should resume the battle," said Derby, after a minute of awkward silence.

"And I told you to go forth and multiply," I added in precisely the same tone of voice.

"I agree," said Sturb. "About the not-battling thing, not about him going and multiplying. It seems to me that, if there's an option with some guaranteed risk, and there's an option with a chance of no risk, then no risk is the obvious, smarter way to go."

"Quite," I muttered. I was increasingly of the opinion that Sturb only agreed with me because he knew it ticked me off.

"Ugh," said Derby. "The bold space hero and the galactic scourge, agreeing to sit quietly on the settee together. Lord knows how the Golden Age ended."

"Well, if you feel like sticking a plying cricket bat out of your arm thing and going out to challenge them to a duel, there are plenty of EVA suits."

Another tense couple of minutes passed. Henderson began tossing his head from side to side, loudly humming a melody that sounded vaguely like the anthem of the Terran military. His eyes widened and he gave me a significant look each time he got to the bit of the chorus about "crushing the noses of the enemies of freedom neath our proud boots."

"How much air do we have?" asked Derby eventually, looking around at the darkened cabin.

"The air cyclers don't turn off during emergency power, they just get turned down a bit. We'd only need to worry about that if we had about six more people onboard."

"What about the electrical outlets in the walls?" asked Sturb, in the quiet tones of someone beginning to realize something horrible that everyone else is going to be upset about.

"No, they're depowered. What? You need to charge your phone?"

"No, but I did plug the cryopod into one of them."

Mr. Henderson suddenly stopped humming. He stopped tossing his head. For a moment I could have sworn his eyes were reflecting the same sudden fear that Sturb was displaying before he willed his expression into a more neutral one.

"Okay," I said slowly, not looking away from Henderson. "Let's move it down to the engine deck. Carefully. And then we can plug it directly into the backup generator."

Sturb and I moved over to the cryonic cylinder that was taking up all the seats on the furthest bench. It was still caked in frost, but was starting to glisten moistly. Sturb took up position on the far end, grabbed it with both hands, and began to lift.

A layer of frost came away instantly and the cylinder slipped out of his grasp, rattling back down onto the hard bench. I distinctly heard Henderson make a little squeak of fright through the sock in his mouth, and turned my head to see that all of his muscles had tensed up, increasing his seated height by three or four inches.

When I turned back around, Sturb was doing something similar, standing frozen with his back arched and his hands halfway to picking up his end of the cylinder again. Sweat glistened on his brow, mirroring the condensation that beaded on the stainless steel cylinder between us. His eyes looked like they were about to plop right out of his head.

I followed his gaze. The frost had almost entirely melted away from the plexiglass window in the cylinder's upper portion, and through it, I could now clearly see the cylinder's contents.

"Oh cal-cu-lus." I pronounced each syllable slowly in time with the pieces falling into place inside my head. My body went as tense as Sturb's and Henderson's.

"Oh, what is it now?" asked Derby, getting up and looking around at the three sudden cases of petrification. "Did someone start freeze tag and forget to tell me I'm it?"

I met his gaze and tried to say something, but my jaw could only shudder in abject fear. His sarcastic manner vanished, and he frowned.

"What?" He looked down through the thick plexiglass in the viewing window. "Huh. That doesn't look much like a set of antidote containers."

"No," I managed to croak.

"That looks more like a person."

It was a small person, of whom all we could see were their shoulders and the lower part of their face, but it was enough. There was no mistaking that skinny build, the unnaturally pink complexion the color of a first-degree burn, the cruel angles of the jaw, and the mouth so crammed with oversized teeth that the paper-thin lips could only just touch.

The face of the worst, most relentless evil that had ever blighted the galaxy. The face of terror.

Terrorgorn.

CHAPTER 16

I'D BEEN HOLDING up pretty well, trapped in a debris field by a hostile ship, in a small room with a career criminal, a murderous crime lord, and the infamous progenitor of the galaxy's most persistent cyberscourge, but this new fact that I was also sharing that room with the cryonically preserved body of Terrorgorn was taking just a little bit too much piss.

I was the first to move. I shoved Sturb against a wall. He was sweating so hard that liquid flew off him like I was wringing out a sponge. "You knew about this?!" I demanded.

He shook his head rapidly, showering me further like a lawn sprinkler. "No! I . . . I wouldn't have agreed to this if I'd known it was Terrorgorn in there, I swear to God!"

His argument checked out. Evil tech genius, yes, but not an evil lunatic, which is what one would need to be to want to be anywhere near Terrorgorn, even if he was imprisoned in a thick cylinder of stainless steel.

Still pushing Sturb into the wall, I dropped my head and stared at my shoes. I was only half-aware of my own babbling voice. "There's nothing wrong with Blaze. Trac. Warden said I couldn't see him for myself because of the quarantine. It made sense at the time."

I looked to Derby, who put up his "hands" in innocent protest. "Don't look at me. I had the same understanding you had. And why are we all soiling ourselves over this person? I could saw off their head with my plasma cutter with nary a stir to their slumber."

I shook my head. "Terrorgorn can't die. He can regenerate from any wound. No one's ever found a way to kill him."

"Suspended animation's the best you can do," said Sturb. "Extreme low temperatures actually halt the regeneration cycle in his cells, as I understand. I'd heard he was cryopreserved somewhere, but the last I heard he was being passed around the, you know, stupidly rich collectors . . . but anyway, I don't . . . why would Penelope want us to recover Terrorgorn?"

Henderson emitted two hums, the second an octave lower than the first. With the sharp clarity of thought that tends to come in a crisis situation, I understood that he was saying "I know" in a singsong voice.

I stepped over to him and pulled the now extremely moist sock away from his mouth. "What?"

Henderson spat a few times and blew out his cheeks to dispel the last few traces of sock, then offered me a friendly smile. "I said, I know why she had you steal it. And I'll be relaxed enough to be forthcoming about it as soon as you blow that damn thing back into space." He was trying to maintain his trademark deceptively cheerful manner, but his current state of mortal terror reduced the effect somewhat. Henderson wasn't big on star pilot history, but even the layman knew to fear Terrorgorn. He was to space villains what Robert Blaze was to space heroes: the one everyone knows even if they know ply-all else about it.

"We're not shooting it into space," said Sturb firmly, trying to control his breathing.

"Agreed," muttered Derby.

"Right," I said. "Except . . . why not?"

"At least plug it in first if you're going to have a debate!" cried Henderson through gritted teeth. "Little professional advice from the hostage!"

I wasn't prepared to risk waiting however long it took to get the cylinder below decks to the emergency generator. I took a quick look around. The air cycler relay unit and the emergency bulb in the ceiling were still powered, so I went for the former, on the grounds that there were enough relays throughout the ship to keep the atmosphere breathable and I still needed to see what I was plying doing.

After I had yanked the power cable out of the relay unit and plugged it into the universal inlet at the base of the cryocylinder, and the reassuring hum informed us that the refrigeration cycle had restarted, I turned to Henderson. "Well?"

"Story time." Henderson sighed. "Danny found out about it from one of those delightful freaks he talks to on the computer. I decided to buy it because I saw an opportunity. I put a discreet feeler out to Mr. Blaze's people, offering to give them Terrorgorn for safekeeping in return for a certain loose end I've been inclined to tie up."

"Warden," I deduced aloud.

"That might have worked, actually," said Sturb. "No one knowing where Terrorgorn is has always been a loose end that Captain Blaze worries about."

"Except Warden *is* Blaze's people," I said. "So she must've intercepted Henderson's offer. And I'm guessing she thought she had to get the cylinder away from you before anyone else at Salvation got wind of it."

"That's my guess," said Henderson. "Oh, wait. I don't need to guess. She started bribing one of my security men. He made sure to make everything very clear to me when he came around to inject me with paralytic drugs every Friday night." He gave a weirdly broad smile and stared into the middle distance as he pictured all the wonderful, horrible things he was now capable of doing to that person. "Until today, when you obligingly knocked him out before my weekly jab."

"Friday night," said Derby, a thoughtful hand flying dramatically to his chin. "Remember how she was so insistent that we do it on Sunday? She was afraid we'd mess with the injection schedule."

"Spot on," said Henderson. "And now I'd just bet she's sent those star pilots out there to get rid of me, and Terrorgorn, and all the witnesses in one stroke."

"She's cutting her losses," I thought aloud. "If it'd just been Terrorgorn's cylinder she might have been able to keep it under control, but with Henderson onboard as well, she must have decided the risk had become too great."

"Mmm," agreed Henderson with relish. "Don't you all feel silly now, knowing we were practically on the same side all along? It's certainly going to suck some of the fun out of my testicle executive toy. Now, would you kindly get back to shooting this thing into space?"

"We're not shooting it into space!" yelled Sturb.

"A deal was struck." Derby brandished his wristlet deliberately. "I am owed a considerable sum for this object, regardless of its contents."

"And it won't stay powered in space!" said Sturb, clutching at his fully reddened face. "He might thaw out! Someone might find him! Then Terrorgorn will be loose! And we'll be the ones who set him loose!"

Henderson rolled his eyes so hard it seemed to make his chair rock back and forth a little. "And what is the good captain's view? It is, after all, his airlock."

All eyes turned to me. I'd been lost in thought, clenching my fists tightly and staring at the floor, and it took me a moment to realize that I was being prompted. When I did, I opened my mouth, wrangled the churning thoughts that swam around my head, and began to laugh.

It was a strange laugh, partly because I was doing it while absolutely nothing was the slightest bit funny, but partly because it seemed to be coming from an unfamiliar part of me. Deep down in the guts where all my bile swam around, bubbling up through my torso and emerging from my mouth in low, humorless barks. I looked up at Sturb, and the expression on his face made me laugh even harder. He had the nervous expression of a dog that urgently needed to be let out.

"Was it like this for you?" I asked him, my smile and my eyes just a little too wide.

"Was what?" asked Sturb.

"When you were doing your thing, you know, sitting on your big plying throne, kidnapping people, slapping slave crowns on them to make them do your bidding, getting beaten up by every star pilot that came by, was there ever a moment when you thought to yourself, *Hey, I've just realized I'm a supervillain?*"

"Captain . . . are you all right?"

"What are you getting at, man?" asked Derby.

I tottered a little, as if drunk, and my voice seemed to come from far away. "It's suddenly so clear to me. I just blew a star pilot out of the sky. While buddying around with my pal Malcolm plying Sturb. And Henderson. And Terrorgorn."

"And Davisham Derby," said Davisham Derby, bridling.

"Yeah, let's plying add that on. Davisham plying Derby, galactic div. After we'd finished stealing Terrorgorn from Daniel Henderson and insulting a load of innocent fanboy doints and wrecking up half of Ritsuko City on the way." I stared at my hands, and another little laugh escaped from my throat. "I've been in complete denial ever since this all started."

"About what?" asked Sturb warily.

"I am a baddie." I paused for a few seconds, ignoring the sudden blast of laughter from Henderson. "I'm a bad guy. A villain. I'm a murdering, stealing space pirate and the enemy of everything star piloting is about."

"Erm, Captain," stammered Sturb. "I think you might be—"

"Silence, dog!" I screamed, making him flinch. I bobbed on my heels in delight. "That was fun, actually. I'm starting to see the appeal of all this. What do we do now? Should I shave my head? Turn my collar up?"

"If you could put a halt on this epiphany of yours for a moment," said Derby, bored, "what are we going to do now?"

"Oh, I know." I straightened up. "Let's go kill that other ship. Those so-called star pilots will rue the day they crossed the dread pirate Dashford Pierce!"

I marched out and trotted up the stairs to the cockpit with Sturb following at my heels, leaving Derby and Henderson to exchange mutually contemp-tuous glances. I had already reactivated the main power and booted up the flight systems before my posterior had touched the pilot seat.

"Captain, if you don't mind me saying . . ." began Sturb.

"Would you shut up if I said I did?"

He would, as it turned out, but only for two seconds. "I just wanted to say, I really think you might be having some kind of breakdown."

The scanner pinged the nearby surroundings after being persuaded with a sharp kick, and the dot representing our adversary lit up. As I'd suspected, they were some distance above us, monitoring as much of the debris field as they could.

I pulled down my headset and set it to broadcast locally. "Attention, med-dling fool," I announced. "Your ill-mannered attempt to bring an end to my glory will be your destruction. Leave now and you will not share the fate of the other fool." I pulled the headset down again. "Am I saying *fool* too much? I feel like I should mix it up. Should I grow a beard?"

"What?"

"I've got this stubble thing going on but I'm thinking I might let it grow out, that'd be more villain-y, wouldn't it. I could shave it into a triangle, but something tells me that would be overdoing it. I don't want to seem like I'm trying too hard."

"Captain . . ."

"Whoops, they're on the move." I grabbed the joysticks.

The enemy ship, which had stayed still up until now as its pilot processed my statement, suddenly darted sideways. They strafed the section of debris field we were, for want of a better word, "hiding" in. The residence module we were clinging to shielded us, thudding like an umbrella in a violent storm.

Something broke away from the module. It looked like part of a bulkhead and some ceiling, followed closely by an extremely modern toilet that must have known the bottoms of hundreds of sleepy travelers back in the heyday of Biskot Central. But more importantly it had created enough new moving objects that I could execute the next stage of my plan. The *Neverdie* flew alongside the broken chunks, spinning as it went, as I did my best impression of a piece of floating debris.

It worked, for the moment. They maintained plasma fire upon the module, hoping to keep burrowing through it to the prey hiding behind, ignoring the bits that came off it. All they needed to do was look at their scanner and the deception would be revealed, but I'd bought myself some seconds to act.

In the meantime, my tactical systems had had time to compensate for their movement speed, and a new reticle appeared on the view screen, helpfully indicating where I should be aiming my Gatling cannon.

"Aha," I crowed. "You have made your fatal mistake now, star pilot fools."

I thumbed the red buttons on the joysticks without hesitation, and the floor shook as bullets rattled from the rotating cannons with blinding speed. Good old-fashioned lead was practically invisible against the blackness of space, and the enemy ship remained oblivious until it strafed right into the bullet stream like a cyclist speeding into a cloud of stinging hornets.

The bullets weren't much use against armored hull—they were more useful for deflecting missiles—but there was a decent hope of getting some lucky hits in on the joints, engines, or windows. The ship halted when the bullets hit, turning up its nose to let the underbelly take the brunt. Clearly we were dealing with keen instincts.

Their nose leveled out, then turned directly toward me. They'd spotted us. And now there was nothing between us but vacuum.

"Captain, I would like to state for the record that I really do seriously think that maybe you should calm down," said Sturb, back stiff and fists clenching and unclenching as he said his piece.

"Fair enough." I lined up the other ship in as close to the center of my view as I could. With loving slowness, I folded my hand tightly around the forward thrust lever. "I won't do a laugh. I'll work on a really good villain laugh in my spare time. Just imagine it for now."

I slammed the lever down. The *Neverdie* screamed toward the other ship. With the artificial gravity, Sturb shouldn't, technically, have felt any physical pull, but he dropped into a crouch anyway. My thumbs found the cannon controls again and I sent a hailstorm of hot lead ahead of us like a violent calling card.

The other ship's engines fired and the game of chicken began. It spun in a barrel roll as it lined its crosshairs up with me, and I felt my lips part and my mouth spread into a wide grin not entirely on the right side of sanity.

"All right, I didn't want to do this," said Sturb. He was fiddling with his phone again. "But you will thank me later."

Suddenly, there was a loud *clonk* and the joysticks shuddered in my hands. I tried to yank them, but they refused to move. "What did you do?!"

"I'm making Jimi lock your controls out." He raised his chin with proud self-righteousness.

"How dare you, you sniveling worm!" I cried, really getting into the swing of things now. "Give me that phone!"

"No!" He held his arm up fully, keeping it out of my reach. "You don't want to kill them! I'm stopping you from making a mistake!"

I reached fruitlessly for his hand. "The mistake was your mum going off birth control!"

"Now that was unnecessary . . ."

I jumped off my chair at him. The cockpit hadn't gotten any bigger, so my legs became entangled with the chair, but I dragged him to the floor with me and pinned him into the corner. He was still holding the phone out of reach, but I was able to grasp his elbow and smash his forearm against the nearest panel again and again.

Derby appeared at the door. "What on earth are you doing?!"

"This plier won't let me blow up that ship!" I yelled over my shoulder.

"What ship?"

I thrust a hand toward the view screen, but my pointed finger faltered when I saw that my opponent was no longer there. In his place was something smaller, faster, and torpedo shaped.

As the missile smashed into the *Neverdie* just below the engine decks and exploded, sending the ship spinning into a death dive and sparking a hundred warning lights to life that bathed the cockpit in blood red, I realized that I'd forgotten one fairly major aspect of doing things the villainous way: traditionally, you're expected to lose.

CHAPTER 17

CONSCIOUSNESS RETURNED GINGERLY, like a cautious hippo breaching the surface of a muddy pond, but I kept my eyes closed. It was a habit I'd gotten into; one tends to get knocked out a lot in the life of a space adventurer, and it pays to be able to check if you're waking up with the appropriate dramatic timing.

I used subtle twitches of my whole body to feel my surroundings. I was in the cockpit, lying on the floor beside the pilot's chair. The texture of sandwich crumbs and flicked bogeys was a dead giveaway. I didn't fully remember how I'd gotten there, but the pains all down my side indicated that I hadn't gently laid myself down for a snooze. I let my eyelids slowly crack apart, and discovered that the cockpit was in almost complete darkness. The lights were off, even the emergency strips, and all the screens and readouts were dead.

I remembered the duel. I remembered the torpedo impact. If it had knocked out the reactor, then the ship would have lost power. That would also have killed life support, and sure enough, I couldn't hear the constant reassuring hum of the air cyclers.

And yet, I had no trouble breathing. Perhaps I had already died, and was now a ghost, doomed to haunt the ruins of my ship forevermore. I swiftly dismissed this notion, because if I was a ghost, then the old footlocker on the cockpit floor would be passing through me, rather than uncomfortably shoving my head to one side.

So life support was off but I could still breathe. Either I hadn't been lying here unconscious long enough for the air to run out—which the level of stiffness in my joints gave me reason to doubt—or I'd crash-landed on a planet with a breathable atmosphere, and a hull breach was letting it in.

That made me finally sit up. The last I knew, Biskot 2 lacked an atmosphere, and so did the moon we had been orbiting. Biskot 4 was the nearest planet with breathable air, and that wasn't anywhere near close enough for an emergency landing. I happened to know it was on the complete opposite side of the star, enjoying its decadelong summer.

I peered through the central viewing window, and saw that the *Neverdie* was lying in a crumpled heap on a standard Speedstar landing platform. One with a design consistent with the prefab spaceport module that Speedstar used to ship out wherever they needed to construct new facilities in a hurry. There must have been about fifty or sixty such modules scattered throughout Biskot Central.

I hauled myself upright with the help of whatever components and levers came into grabbing range, and saw what was beyond the landing pad. The first thing that caught my attention was a large illuminated sign advertising authentic Ritsuko-style sushi sandwiches, complete with an animated image of a fish happily leaping between two pieces of bread and submitting to a hand wielding an enormous cleaver. It was old enough that most of its colors had faded into a shade of institutional blue, but it was lit up nonetheless.

There were other adverts around, all extremely old and out of date, but still powered and apparently well maintained. Beneath them, I saw the familiar boxy enclosures, shops, and walkways of a hastily constructed Speedstar rest stop station. Above, there was only the void of space, the shadowy arc of Biskot 2's third moon, and the occasional blue-white shimmer indicating an active force field. Probably of the type designed to let solid objects through but keep air inside, as evidenced by my nonasphyxiated status.

Force field bubbles were a cheap and quick way to maintain a station's atmosphere, much more so than a plexiglass dome, although you did have to come to terms with the fact that everyone on the station would instantly die if there was ever a major power outage. They were normally only used when the station was still under construction and a more permanent solution was in the works, or (in the case of Biskot Central) when the executives were planning to cash out and retire before it became an issue.

Presumably the force fields around Biskot's various trade hubs and entertainment centers had winked out one by one after the Golden Age ended and neglect settled in, which made it all the more difficult to explain why this one was still online, along with all the signs and electric lighting below. Could there really have been enough travelers still coming through Biskot to sustain one of the stations, after the Quantunnels were built? Hard to see how one budgets around a customer base of zero.

This probably wasn't as important as the fact that there was a grand total of four unaccounted-for galactic criminals onboard (five, including me), so I put our current whereabouts aside and turned to checking over the ship.

Sturb was accounted for first. He was lying unconscious across the gantry steps that led down from the bridge, one leg in the air with his foot propped up against the door frame. I pushed it down, rubbed at a little mark his sneaker had made on the wall, then checked him for a pulse.

Satisfied that he wasn't in immediate danger of much beyond waking up with very sore joints, I continued past him down to the cabin level. The mystery of the hull breach was solved in that both the airlock doors were wide open—either jarred open by the impact, or one of us was already out looking for someone to sell out the rest of us to. I closed the external door, for want of keeping the ship's current population consistent, then went to the passenger cabin.

The furniture was still bolted down and precisely where I had left it, but I was infinitely more concerned about Terrorgorn's cryonic cylinder, which was now angled upside down over the backrest of the far bench. That brought a lot of memories urgently back to the forefront of my mind. The cylinder didn't seem to be open or damaged from where I was standing, but the new number one priority was getting it attached to a power source of some kind. I took a step forward.

I heard a footfall directly behind me, and a hand seized one of my wrists, yanking me back. A sharp point pressed coldly against the side of my throat. It was a sensation I'd felt before.

"Henderson?" I hazarded, trying to speak without moving the flesh of my throat too much.

"The same," he said cheerfully, his voice right next to my ear. "You're getting sloppy, McKeown. Before you enter a room, check the corners. Same principle as cleaning out a litterbox. You remember the ring I was wearing at our first little get-together?"

"The one with the cassowary talon."

"You remember what I told you about cassowaries?"

My brain had clouded over, and speaking was only getting more difficult.

"Slit, glurgle glurgle glurgle." I mimed various stringy objects falling out of my midsection.

"Glurgle glurgle glurgle, exactly. Now, I think there's going to be some changes to the dynamics of this situation. Here's the good news: you can fly this thing, so you get to live. I might cut some of your fingers off, I haven't decided. Let's round up your chums and see how I feel."

Both of us flinched when the cryocylinder made a sharp cracking noise, and a cloud of condensation puffed out of a vent in the cylinder's upper half. I felt Henderson's hand tense up, squeezing my arm painfully, but the talon came away from my neck.

"What was that?" he hissed.

I swallowed. "If we're lucky, it was the cryopod making some kind of compensation for the loss of power," I said carefully.

The pod was face down, with the part that folded out like a lid blocked by the bench and the floor. It made another crack, followed by another blast of vapor, and then wobbled left and right.

"What was that?" repeated Henderson.

"That . . . was us not being lucky."

The cryopod wobbled again, then slid right off the bench onto the floor with a sharp clang. It rolled back and forth until it had built up enough momentum to turn itself right side up.

"Stop it," suggested Henderson. I could feel the sweat gathering in his palm.

"How?!"

With a final, apocalyptic crack, like the detaching of a glacier above an orphanage, the cryopod opened. Its entire front half split apart and folded aside like the engine hood of a flashy space yacht. A massive belch of condensation mushroomed out, instantly reducing the temperature of the cabin by several degrees.

Terrorgorn sat up, shaking off his lengthy frozen sleep the way anyone else would shake themselves out of a daydream. He was a deceptively small humanoid, skinny with sharp joints and pointed fingers, with a skin tone on the slightly unnatural side of Pepto-Bismol pink. His hairless head tapered down and transitioned into a neck without the merest hint of a chin, and his tiny jet-black eyes were buried in crinkled folds of flesh.

He looked at the pair of us, and his fanged mouth opened briefly in curiosity, before he dropped his gaze and reproachfully examined the cylinder, as if he were sitting in a bathtub that had lost its bubbles. Eventually, reluctantly, he stood, his knife-like legs unfolding like a pair of bloodstained scissors, and stepped out of the cryopod.

Henderson took a step back, jerking me along with him. "Terrorgorn!" he said. He gave another little jolt when Terrorgorn's black eyes turned on him. "I bring you an offering of a star pilot. One of your hated enemies. You can do what you like to him. Just remember that the Henderson organization wants to be your friend and ally!"

Terrorgorn blinked, scrutinizing me. I could feel rivulets of sweat running into my collar. There were barely two meters of space between me and Terror-plying-gorn. If only it were three meters, I might live an additional fraction of a nanosecond.

After a tense moment that seemed to extend into infinity, he lowered his gaze. "Nah, I'm fine," muttered Terrorgorn, in a voice like granite blocks being rubbed together.

Several seconds of silence passed, and Terrorgorn glanced around with mild interest, apparently considering the conversation suspended. I could sense Henderson's puzzlement, but his grip on my arm didn't weaken in the slightest. I noticed that Terrorgorn was standing with his bony hands gathered just under his belly, covering his crotch, so I made a rather high-pitched throat-clearing noise. "Ahm, Terrorgorn," I said. "Perhaps you'd like me to find you some clothing?"

Terrorgorn regarded his own nakedness for a painful few seconds. "Yeah, okay."

"Trousers, shirt?" I prompted. "Shoes as well?"

"Okay." He stepped over the backrest of the nearest bench and sat down demurely, keeping his knees together.

I pushed back against Henderson to signal to him that we needed to leave. "Terrorgorn wants clothes," I said through my teeth. "I need to check around and see what I have." I carefully pulled my wrist out of his grip and ducked out of the way of his cassowary talon, and he didn't fight me.

He followed me out into the passage. "What the hell was that?" he demanded before I could take more than two steps toward the luggage compartment.

"Terrorgorn wants clothes," I said again, more emphatically. "That means I need to go and get him some."

"Oh, I'm sorry, it seems I didn't make it clear enough who's in charge."

Henderson stepped into my personal space and brandished his talon ring again. He was red in the face and flustered, and his attempt at a confident tone faltered. He could probably tell from the look in my eye that there was no plying way he was going to intimidate me more than Terrorgorn could.

"Do you even know what it is that we're dealing with in there?" I hissed, thumbing toward the cabin door.

"I know it's one of your . . . space villains. I know he's supposed to be the worst. I'm not seeing why. He's just sitting there."

"Exactly! He's already plying sitting there! Trac knows what he'll do next!" I gave a little gasp of exasperation in response to Henderson's confused look, letting a few flecks of spit fly from my mouth like popcorn. "Look, I don't have time to fill in all the background for you. I've got clothes to find."

"Are you serious?"

From the passenger cabin, I heard a prolonged, deliberate sigh of mild irritation. To me, then, it was like standing under a rocket engine one believes to be depowered and hearing the sound of a pilot light clicking. "Terrorgorn!" I called, heart pounding. "Did you want us to leave you alone?"

"No, it's fine," droned Terrorgorn, barely audible.

"You'll have to stay with him," I muttered to Henderson.

"What?!"

"He doesn't want to be left alone."

Henderson staggered back and clutched at his head in a "had quite enough of this trac" kind of way. He puffed himself up and tried to get in my space again, but he was still the least frightening part of the whole equation, and his colorful jumper didn't help his case. "Did you forget already that I'm in charge now?"

"All right," I said over my shoulder. "I'll get the clothes; you go back in there and explain to Terrorgorn that you're in charge. See where it gets you."

I headed to the luggage compartment behind the cockpit and clawed a few handfuls of lost property out into the light. There were a couple of child-sized coats that looked like they might fit Terrorgorn, but I didn't run the kind of ship where children and small people tended to lose their trousers, so that was about it. I decided to bring a pile of medium-sized garments and let him choose for himself. After a moment's thought, I also picked up the large muumuu I used as bedding, on the basis that it might fold up into a toga, or something.

I found Sturb sitting up on the gantry steps by the time I was ready to head back down. "What happened?" he slurred.

"Terrorgorn's awake," I said quietly, deciding it probably wasn't worth sugarcoating. "He's awake and he's in the passenger cabin with Henderson."

"Terrorgorn's awake?"

"Yeah."

He looked down the steps at the cabin door, rubbing his head, then peered up at me, confused. "So . . . why are we alive?"

"I don't know, but I'm not questioning it. He wants clothes."

"Where's Mr. Derby?"

"I don't think he's onboard. If he's alive, I think he went outside to figure out where we are." I paused to mull over my own words. "We should probably figure out where we are."

Sturb pushed his tongue into his lower lip, and the crackle of the speaker in my inner ear made my hair stand on end. "Mr. Derby? Can you still hear us?"

I'd completely forgotten about the communicators. I jammed my little finger in my ear and twisted it around until the crackling turned into something that sounded like Derby's voice, but I couldn't make out any words. He was moaning, but not in pain or sorrow; it sounded more like anger. Like he was trying to insult us but something was holding his tongue in place.

"I think . . ." began Sturb, before having to pause as Derby let fly a parting salvo of incoherent abuse. "I think he might have gotten into some trouble."

I stared at the airlock door at the base of the stairs as if I could somehow see through it. "Out there."

"Erm. Possibly." Sturb blinked. "Do you know what is out there? Are we on a planet?"

"Looks like a rest stop station," I said, taking a little pause before I dropped the really interesting part. "Still powered and functioning."

"At Biskot?" His head tossed as he weighed this up. "Could pirates have taken it over?"

"That's one possibility," I conceded. But my thoughts instantly returned to those lit-up electric signs I'd seen in the concourse just below our landing pad. They must be pretty significant power hogs, and it felt unlikely that pirates would be running unnecessary systems, not with the frugal life the Black demanded these days. Then again, the Black was a scary place; maybe they needed a night-light.

"Do you think they've got Mr. Derby?" asked Sturb.

I made up my mind. "I'm going out there." I pushed my armload of clothing into Sturb's arms. "You go down and give these to Terrorgorn."

His slightly groggy expression disappeared in an instant as his eyes boggled and fresh beads of sweat visibly popped into existence on his brow. His jaw waggled like the hind leg of an excited dog for a few moments before he found words. "You—Terror—me—gorn—tell you what, how about I go looking for Mr. Derby instead? It's no trouble."

"I need to check around the ship, too." I was already most of the way down the steps. "Make sure we can actually take off once we're ready."

"I could do that if you want!" said Sturb in a very high-pitched voice. "I know quite a lot about technology, remember? I used to make cyborgs!"

I already had the airlock open. I stood in the doorway and looked back at him. Even with him silhouetted against the meager light coming through the cockpit, I could see the moisture glimmering in his terrified eyes. "Look, it'll be fine," I said. "You've got stuff in common. Just talk about, I dunno, your favorite murders." I turned and left before he could add anything and closed the airlock door behind me.

CHAPTER 18

I FELT A lurch as I stepped down, which a moment later I attributed to the airlock step being considerably closer to the landing pad than it was supposed to be. The *Neverdie* wasn't beyond repair, but the landing had been heavy enough to flatten the underbelly, like the ship was a soft clay model that had been dropped on the floor. The landing legs were bent and the takeoff thruster was askew. If I got the reactor back online and tried to take off, the ship would corkscrew horizontally off the landing pad and smash into one of those perplexing signs on the concourse below.

The repairs were well within my ability. A few hours with a sledgehammer and a welding gun would probably suffice. The problem was that I needed the ship to be raised off the ground to do it, and foolishly I had neglected to bring a giant twenty-foot novelty jack.

The more realistic option would be another ship, hovering overhead and suspending the *Neverdie* from tow cables. The *Neverdie* being a light, maneuverable star pilot model meant that virtually any passing vessel could do the job. That just left the issue of the Biskot system being in the middle of nowhere and how there wouldn't be any passing vessels for decades.

There had to be at least one pilot who owed me enough favors to cover this. I dug my phone out, only to find it refusing to respond to my thumb jabs. The battery had run out, or it had been damaged in the crash. Either way, there wasn't going to be any wireless recharging with the reactor shut down.

I looked around the spaceport. It was very basically laid out, as was typical of these modular Speedstar stations. A couple of elevated landing platforms on pillars, sticking out of the perfectly square shopping concourse like forest mushrooms on stalks. If it followed the usual Speedstar template, then underneath that would be a small labyrinth of private sleeping areas and miscellaneous infrastructure.

There were the lit-up signs I had noticed earlier, advertising the services of the shops below. Strangely, all the electric lights that were actually there to help people see—the light strips on the walls and the four-sided light posts on the concourse floor—were turned off. Only the signs were powered, as well as . . .

This was odd. The landing pad we were "parked" on was lacking the usual guiding lights, but a string of what looked like multicolored Christmas lights had been wound around the perimeter safety rail. They were unnaturally bright, probably with more power running through them than specifications demanded. Probably enough to make them burn out in a matter of days, but every single bulb that I could see was intact and functional. Someone was maintaining them lovingly.

Inadvertently my gaze slipped from the string of lights to the landing pad floor, and I tottered back a few steps in surprise. The words LANDING PAD had been stenciled across it in the usual urgent six-foot letters, but the original paint was little more than scattered wisps of light gray. In its place, someone had filled in the shapes of the letters with dense, swirling patterns and spirals, drawn in paint, chalk, and correctional fluid by finger painting from multiple small hands.

The patterns continued outside the letters in a variety of different colors, circling and swirling all the way to the edges of the landing pad, breaking off into all kinds of different imagery: flowers, bubbles, and strange triangular blue things that reminded me of star pilot ships, albeit drawn by someone who'd only ever had them verbally described to them by an inarticulate person.

I headed for the metal spiral staircase that wound down around the pillar to the concourse floor. The moment my head descended below the landing pad, a powerful stench of rot hit me like a shovel across the bridge of the nose. I came close to toppling right off the steps but managed to cling to the handrail as I staggered, and my foot squished messily into a cake.

As far as I could tell from what hadn't been destroyed by my foot, the cake had at one point been white, with blue icing on the top in a shape that reminded me of that ill-informed spaceship cartoon I'd seen earlier. Age had changed the blue-on-white icing to an ugly rotten brown on snot green, and the sponge that was now clinging to the tread of my shoe was practically in a liquid state. I covered my nose and mouth with my sleeve.

On further examination, virtually every step of the spiral staircase was adorned with some kind of food item. Not cast thoughtlessly aside like rubbish or leftovers, but full plated meals lovingly crafted and arranged. Many of them were on trays, some were accompanied with glasses of drink or small floral arrangements, but all were completely uneaten and had been left here rotting for a very long time. It was easily one of the worst smells I'd ever encountered, and I'd once been paid to clear out bodies after a sulfur-mine disaster.

I descended the stairs, carefully planting my feet around the plates, trying to grind my shoe on the rough metal with each step to dislodge the rotting cake. I noticed that the food was getting fresher the further down I went. At more or less the halfway point, I was seeing plates of chicken wings and fried potato that I might conceivably have considered eating, were I in a particularly hung-over state, and at the very bottom, the food was virtually fresh cooked. The smell of it immediately made my stomach complain about how long it had been since my last meal.

It wasn't just the steps. Food and flowers had been reverently laid on the floor in a wide radius around the landing pad's pillar, and more multicolored Christmas lights were scattered around to draw attention to it all.

Now that I was on the concourse level, I could see that most of the shops and stalls were closed, abandoned, and dark. Only the signs advertising their services were lit, along with the menu screens at the fast-food outlets. Curious, I walked over to the nearest one, my slightly cake-softened footfalls filling the huge empty space with echoes.

It was a fried-chicken restaurant, and the mouthwatering smell indicated that it had seen very recent use, in stark contrast to its neighbors. I hopped over the counter and peered through the serving window into the kitchen, squinting to see by the mediocre light offered by the signs outside.

I could just make out a few fryers and worktops that were glistening with grease and wet sauce stains, so someone must have been using the kitchen as recently as today, probably to create more dishes to add to that minefield of assorted dinners in the concourse. But the serving counter behind me was covered in a thick layer of undisturbed dust, including the cash register.

This was getting weirder by the second. Clearly someone was living on the station, but I was losing more and more faith in the theory of it being pirate squatters. Maybe a group like that might waste some food and power frivolously in the first few elated days after finding this place, but even pirates would quickly settle down, find a broom, and start thinking about long-term survival. Someone had been placing meals on and around the landing pad stairway for years.

I headed back out into the deserted concourse, and quickly found what I was looking for: a sheltered area with an illuminated sign above it showing an icon of a staircase. The floor around it was as dusty as everywhere else, but the dust had been kicked around and streaked by countless feet, far too many to identify individual prints. I headed down the steps.

The stairs were lit with bare functionality by white fluorescent strips, and on the first landing I saw a shiny, gold-colored object that had been kicked into a corner. It immediately struck me as familiar, and it took me a few moments to remember that I'd usually seen it on the end of a doint in a sharp suit. It was Derby's arm device.

I picked it up, brushing off the dust. The side that his arm stump normally fit into was a stiff cloth tube, and there was a leather strap made from a cheap belt that was presumably what held it on.

"Hello?" came a muffled voice from under the metal lid. "Uncle Dav? Is that you?"

The lid was held shut with a brass clasp that looked like it had come from an antique jewelry box. I flipped it aside and opened the lid, to be greeted by an unflattering view of the underside of a young woman's chin. Derby's assistant appeared to be holding her end of the Quantunnel tube between her knees.

"Uncle Dav?" she said, looking down. The appearance of my face immediately snuffed out the gleam of hope in her eyes. She was of around college age, as near as I could tell with her face silhouetted against a ceiling light. Her hair was tied back in a ponytail, and she was wearing huge spectacles and an ash-gray hoodie. "Oh. Captain. Is Unc—is Davisham Derby there?"

I checked around, just in case there was an unconscious well-dressed tosser lying in a nearby corner that I'd missed at first glance. "No. Just his arm thing. Do you know what happened?"

"They took off his wristlet?!" She looked up, staring urgently into the middle distance for a moment, and I was subjected to the sight of her chin wobbling with concern. "Can you save him?"

I shifted my weight and let out a sigh. This was by no means the first time I'd been entreated to rescue someone at the behest of their distraught female relative, but it wasn't exactly consistent with my recent career change. I mulled it over, and decided that rescuing Derby would mean that I could turn my ear speaker back on without having to listen to him complain. Yes, that was exactly the sort of calculating approach us supervillains would take. "Did you see anything?"

"No, I couldn't see past the Taser."

"What Taser?"

"I heard voices," she remembered aloud. "Lots of voices. Uncle Dav was doing his, you know, his . . ." She puffed out her chest and spoke with Derby's dramatic voice. " 'I'm Davisham Derby, unhand me, knave,' thing. Then the voices got louder, that's when he gave the signal for a Taser, so I stuck one in. Then I didn't hear anything else because the Taser was in the way. It activated, like, three times." She was starting to babble. "It went quiet for a while, so I pulled it out and all I saw was floor. So I waited another while, but then there was just more floor. Then there was a spider, then floor again. You've got to go after him, Captain. I don't know what's happened, but he might be in trouble."

I peered down the stairs ahead of me that led into the darkened residential area below. It was quiet enough for the silence to be audible, a sort of deep, sepulchral yawn that bristled the hairs on the inside of my ears. I drew my blaster—it was still out of ammunition, I was pretty sure, but it made me feel slightly better and it might make potential attackers feel slightly worse—and continued descending, one step at a time.

"Oh! And," said Derby's assistant, whose name, I seemed to recall, was Nelly, "when you rescue Uncle Dav, could you not make a big thing out of it?"

I turned Derby's wristlet around again to show her my confused expression. It was like having a conversation with a shaving mirror. "What?"

"Just, you know, don't lord it over him that he needed to be rescued, or anything like that." She bit her lip worriedly. "He doesn't like it when he thinks people are trying to make him feel inferior. He does silly things." Her voice lowered. "Silly things like running off to become a master criminal."

I took another step down, peered fruitlessly into the darkness, then decided I wasn't quite ready to end the conversation. I brought her up to my face again. "How long have you two been doing this master criminal thing?"

"Er . . . eight or nine months." Her gaze darted around as she avoided eye contact. "I was the only person he knew who knew anything about computers. I told him that working as a TA for the Introduction to IT professor didn't count for much, but he said it couldn't be that difficult."

"I see," I said.

"B-but things have been going pretty well since he came up with the micro-Quantunnel idea," she added quickly. "He hasn't been caught or had any more hands cut off . . . have you found him yet?"

"You wouldn't happen to have a flashlight or something, would you?"

"Oh, sure." Her face disappeared and I heard a clattering of items on metal shelving units. "Flashlight, that's . . . one blink and a complete eye rotation, that's . . . over here. How bright did you want it?"

"Bright enough to see by, but not bright enough to alert every doint on this level."

"Roger. Try this."

I held the wristlet outwards, toward the darkness, and it began to judder in my hand as something was slotted into place, instantly doubling its weight. A moment later, there was a click, and the room ahead was bathed in a gentle green glow.

It was the reception area for the motel portion of the spaceport, which was still in line with my experience of modular Speedstar rest stops: the good-looking commercial stuff at the very top, then the residential level under that, then administration, then finally engineering at the bottom, the least photogenic layer of the increasingly disappointing trifle. I was in a circular room decorated with wall panels advertising the wonderful sights of the Biskot system, and three connecting passages presumably led to the bedrooms. A ring-shaped desk was in the middle of the lobby, which would allow staff to instantly serve incoming customers as well as the ones coming out of the rooms to complain about the toilets.

I stepped onto the carpet, and immediately had to look at it, because it felt like I had stepped onto a sheet of greaseproof paper. Just as on the stairs, the carpet had been heavily worn down by innumerable footprints. It might have happened during the Golden Age, when hundreds of star pilots would have been passing through Biskot every day, but Speedstar would usually have been replacing the carpets every few months or so.

The desk was polished and impeccably clean, and some flower petals had been scattered around it, but none of the electronics were functioning. The

hover module for the check-in computer was clearly broken, as the fastidi-
ously polished screen was neatly lying on top of it.

This wasn't getting me anywhere. I fingered my ear to turn the speaker
back on. "Derby, can you hear me? Make any kind of noise if you can."

"*Rrrngle!*" said Derby loudly. That was good, because it meant he was alive,
and he wasn't somewhere where he felt the need to be quiet.

"One *rrrngle* for yes, two for no. Are you on the residential level?"

"*Brfk!*"

"You are?"

"*Grwnph!*"

"You're saying yes, right, you're not just complaining at me?"

"*Bwgl. Brmp,*" said Derby sarcastically.

Tragically, this was about the closest Derby and I had ever come to making
an emotional connection. I cast another look around. "I'm in the lobby with
my back to the stairs, and I see three corridors. From left to right, one, two,
three. Are you down corridor number one?"

"*Nhngn. Nhngn.*"

"Are you saying no, or do you mean you're down corridor number two?"

I heard a hissing sound that I assumed must have been Derby sighing
lengthily through his nose. "*Nhngn. Nhngn. Nhngn.*"

There was only one possible meaning for that. I headed for the third
hallway.

As I moved along the hall, waving what I was beginning to think of as my
magic amulet left and right to sweep the green glow around, it all looked
how I would have expected. Plain corridors broken up by the occasional
seam where the modules had been slotted together, with a placid color
scheme and calming design for when drunk star pilots are having trouble
finding their rooms at three in the morning.

"Okay," I said quietly. "Do you know what door number you're in?"

Derby heaved another long sigh and I had to pause to concentrate on
counting the long series of moans he patiently emitted.

"Room twelve?" I concluded.

"*Ygfn.*"

Right at the end of the hall, then. A growing sense of foreboding crept
over me as I made my way, step after cautious step. It wasn't like the sensation of being watched; more like that of being a mouse passing through a
roomful of sleeping cats. The silence wasn't the oppressive silence of being

totally alone in an empty place, it was the prickly silence made by multitudes of sleeping things. I wasn't about to start randomly trying doors.

It seemed like it took an age to quietly creep all the way down the corridor. When I was faced with the bedroom door with the number 12 painted on it in Speedstar's trademark font, I tried the handle and found it locked, to my complete lack of surprise.

Suddenly the glow stick was yanked back inside my magic amulet, and I was plunged into darkness. "Have you found Uncle Dav?!" asked Nelly, quite loudly.

I snapped the wristlet's lid closed and cringed as her words echoed through the silent corridor behind me. After it faded, and no doors were flung open to disgorge platoons of crazed survivalist pirates bent on stripping me for parts, I let my shoulders sag and opened the amulet again by the tiniest crack. "Shhh."

"Sorry," whispered Nelly. "Have you found Uncle Dav?"

"I think he's behind this door," I said, my lips practically touching the amulet's rim. "Do you have anything that can pick a lock?"

"Yeah. Dude, yeah." I couldn't see her, but I could tell from the vibrato in her voice that she was nodding rapidly. "Like, ninety percent of the stuff here."

"Do you have anything that can pick a lock, and that can be used by someone who doesn't know anything about lock picking?"

"Ah. That narrows it down. Yeah, hang on." I slapped the lid closed again as the amulet started making loud rattling noises from Nelly hurriedly sorting through her inventory. It sounded like a ferret loose in a cutlery drawer. "Try this. It's a sort of experimental intelligent-plastic thing. Just stick it in the lock and it'll do the rest—"

Her voice was cut off as a tool was shoved into place. It resembled a flexible white cylinder mounted on the end of a sophisticated-looking piece of electronics. Dutifully, I placed the end of the cylinder at the mouth of the lock and smartly rammed it home, feeling slightly indecent as I did so.

There were a few moments of churning sounds, and then the device made a short confirmatory beep, loud enough to make me cringe again before falling silent. I rotated it, and the lock turned. When I withdrew the device, the white plastic part maintained the shape of a key for a second before it popped back into its default shape.

The room beyond was a residence module originally designed to be nothing more than a place where one person could sleep between legs of a journey, typically containing one bed about the size of a low-rent coffin and a combination shower-toilet sectioned off by a curtain about half as thick as the toilet paper.

After Nelly restored the glow stick, I discovered that some remodeling had taken place. The bed was missing, and the indentation in the floor where it had belonged was now filled with garbage. There was a plate of stale food similar to the ones I had seen on the concourse, some wrapped chocolate bars, a couple of pamphlets advertising other services offered by nearby out-posts, and a collection of brightly colored toys that looked like the kind of thing Speedstar used to put in the claw machines in the amusement arcades.

Looming over the items was a full-sized cardboard cutout of a star pilot, propped up against the far wall. Judging by his improbably muscular physique and dramatic pose, it had likely been cut out from an advertising display for a Jacques McKeown book. The colors were faded with age, making the character's square-jawed face look like it had come down with a bad case of space scurvy.

I was then treated to the sensation of hearing Derby moaning in stereo, the sound coming simultaneously from my earpiece and from the shower area to my left. I shone my light toward it, and discovered what had happened to the bed. The mattress was nowhere to be seen, but the metal lattice on which it would have sat was propped up in front of the shower cubicle as a makeshift gate, held in place with a couple of iron bars.

Derby was sitting on the toilet with his one intact arm tied behind his back and his mouth gagged with a Speedstar-branded tie that at one point would have been on sale in the souvenir shop. He didn't seem to be badly hurt, besides his missing wristlet and a lurid bruise under one madly staring eye.

The bars across the shower gate were each sitting across a pair of what looked like metal coat hooks that I suspected had been glued into place with industrial adhesive. I lifted off the bars, pulled the gate aside, and fingered the gag out of Derby's mouth.

"Well," he said pompously, "I was going to warn you about the alien behind you, but one suspects the point has become moot."

CHAPTER 19

IN THE TIME it took to spin on my heel, I drew my blaster and pointed it ahead at full arm's length. I let Derby's wrist amulet fall from my grasp and clatter into the corner, the glow stick throwing crazy shadows around the room as it settled. All in all, probably one of my most impressive quick draws, and once again I'd neglected to set a plying timer.

And in the end, it was wasted. The alien didn't look hostile, or even remotely dangerous. They were humanoid, but about half the size of a human, with skinny limbs and skin the color of weak custard. They were probably female, although I was going more from the flowers woven into their long brown hair than their body type, which was mostly concealed by a baggy white garment. On a full-sized human it would have been a tank top, but on her it was a nightdress.

She was staring up at me with dark, glimmering eyes and her tiny mouth hanging open. She gave off the general vibe of a sleepy toddler wandering into their parents' room late at night and witnessing something inappropriate.

One pregnant pause later, she smiled joyously, clasped her hands together beneath her chin, and leapt a foot into the air, as if hoisted by the sudden upward movement of her cheek muscles. "Oh, joyous day!" she exclaimed, in a high, fragile voice like air being passed through a wooden flute. "The Day of Return has come! Father! Oh, Father, our prayers are answered!" She spun around as she hopped into the air again, tank top twirling, before skipping back into the darkened corridor, kicking her feet high in effervescent joy.

I looked to Derby, who was making a concerted effort to avoid eye contact. "What was that all about?"

"Nothing," he spat, rising from the toilet and hopping out of the cubicle. I noticed that his knees were tied together with duct tape. "We need to get out of here before they return. These people are lunatics."

I was more interested in the fact that there were people here at all, but I wasn't about to argue. I untied his arm and stepped back to let him untape the rest of himself.

Before we could formulate the next part of the escape plan, the female creature returned excitedly, dragging another member of her species by the hand. "Father, Father!" she babbled. "You must see! It's so wonderful!"

Her father was roughly the same height as his daughter, but about twice the width. He was older and saggier, resembling several handfuls of lemon pudding slapped together into a humanoid figure, and was wearing an extremely old and frayed souvenir T-shirt that reached down to his knees.

"What has made you so excited this early in the morning, little one?" he asked, stumbling sleepily after the girl. His voice was slightly deeper than his daughter's, in that it sounded like the voice of a human boy about half an hour into puberty.

"It's as I said, Father! The visitor was not an enemy at all, but a herald of the Ancients!" She practically shoved him toward us, smiling so wide I thought her cheek muscles might burst out through the skin.

The older creature squinted at me, trying to make out my features in the meager light offered by the glow stick in the corner. His gaze traveled from my face to my cap, then to my flight jacket, then to the Jacques McKeown cutout behind me, his eyes and mouth widening further at each stage of the trip.

"B–by all the writings," he breathed, hands beginning to shake. "It's true! An Ancient walks among us!"

"I'll rouse the others!" The daughter barely got the words out before she darted back into the hall to start making a strange hooting sound through her hands.

"F–forgive me, O Ancient," stammered the father, cringing so low that he was practically bent double. "It has been so long . . . I am neglecting my proper vestments. Spare us your most justified retribution for one moment while I prepare."

He darted out just as the female one darted back in, as if they had some kind of tag team arrangement. "O Ancient, do not punish the unbelievers too harshly for the treatment of your herald," she entreated, bowing even lower than her father had. "The ages have been long and the corruption of faithlessness has taken its toll on our people."

I had been keeping quiet so far because, as a career star pilot with a number of rescued primitive planets under my belt, being deified wasn't entirely new to me. It was always embarrassing and frequently dangerous, but it was never productive to antagonize your new followers by denying your godhood, as long as they didn't take it too far. The point to start reining it in was when they began throwing around words like *unbeliever*, because heresy trials and stoning couldn't be far behind. It's hard to add a primitive planet to your scorecard when the people you saved ended up sacrificing the entire year's harvest to your glory.

"Um, your devotion does you credit." I held my arms out for the all-purpose vague messianic look. "But I fear I am an unworthy recipient . . ."

"You're worthy! You're worthy!" said Derby, hanging back somewhere behind me as he struggled to strap his wristlet back on without help. "Just play along, for Christ's sake. They're insane."

"I don't tell you how to get captured by natives, don't tell me how to rescue you from them," I hissed.

The girl's father reappeared, striding nobly into the room this time like a Cub Scout carrying the flag at the troop parade. He was wearing a child-sized version of the pink polo shirt Speedstar used to make all its employees wear until they lost their last shred of dignity. On his head was an empty cardboard container for french fries, which he was wearing like a papal crown.

"You've ar-rived at Bis-kot Cen-tral," he intoned like a Gregorian chant, holding his arms aloft in worship. "The Speed-star Cor-po-ra-tion wel-comes you."

"Would you like to hear a-bout to-day's spe-cials," added the girl, head fully bowed into her clasped hands as she reverently voiced the holy syllables.

And that made rather a lot of pieces fall into place. These were the natives indigenous to Biskot's planets, the local talent that Speedstar had hired cheaply to beef up Biskot Central's staff in a not entirely ethical kind of way. But surely Speedstar had returned them to their home planets before they had withdrawn from the system?

On reflection, I couldn't remember anyone from Speedstar specifically mentioning that they had done so. I'd just assumed they had, and the relevant regulatory bodies apparently had as well, because it was something that a corporation with the tiniest amount of shame would have done without saying.

"How . . . long have you all been waiting here?" I asked.

The smiles didn't leave their faces, but the girl and her father exchanged confused glances, firstly with each other and secondly with the growing number of Biskotti-sized figures in the darkness behind them, emerging from motel rooms to see what was making all the noise. "Our people have waited since the Before Time," said the father helpfully.

"And how long has that been?"

"Eons," breathed the girl. "Many generations have passed since the time of the Ancients."

"But Speedstar . . . I mean, the Ancients would have been here less than ten years ago."

"Indeed," said the father sadly, a nostalgic shine in his eye. "My great-great-great-grandfather was the last of my line to see the Ancients with his own eyes. Perhaps it was their blessing that caused him to lead such a long life. He almost reached the age of nineteen months."

That filled in the rest of the picture. The cherry on the top of this already reprehensible sundae: the unusually short lives of Biskottis, thanks to their fast-moving planets.

"O Ancient," said the father, voice quavering. "We exist to serve. Speak that which you desire, and you shall have it." His voice switched to the weird staccato chant again. "Co-zy beds. Sump-tu-ous food. Twen-ty-four-hour en-ter-tain-ment. What-ev-er you need to make your stay Speed-star spe-cial."

My jaw was hanging open. This was monstrous. Speedstar had exploited and abandoned these people and left them totally alienated from their home environment and culture for generations, until the last instructions they had been given had mutated into some plied-up religious dogma. They needed help. They needed to be taken back to where they belonged to begin the slow process of overcoming lifetimes of brainwashing.

That was what a star pilot would have done.

"Actually, what I could really use is a phone-charging station," I said.

CHAPTER 20

THE PHONE-CHARGING STATION I was directed to was barely visible through a thick layer of painted artworks depicting ancient star pilots drawing down heavenly nectar with long drinking straws. The connection ports were stuffed with dead flowers, but the wireless recharge was functional enough.

It was located in a booth on the spaceport concourse between a couple of food stands, in an area that the Biskottis seemed reluctant to follow us into. Perhaps they didn't understand or trust it, or were afraid that tainting the Ancients' machinery with their lowly hands would have reduced the chances of the Ancients ever coming back. Either way, once I had reactivated it and my phone began to charge, I looked back and saw the entire mob of them—about fifty individuals—clustered around the top of the stairwell like schoolchildren at assembly waiting to be dismissed.

"What pathetic creatures." Derby leaned against the charging station next to me with his arms folded. He was holding his newly reattached wristlet under one armpit so tightly that I could hear the leather in the straps creaking. "If Davisham Derby had not been so overcome with pity at the sight of them, I would not have stayed my Taser."

"What a relief," I said, staring at my phone as I held it against the side of the charging station unnecessarily. "I was starting to think Davisham Derby might have simply plied it up. Ah." The battery icon materialized in the center of my phone's screen, and the power bar began to swell. It'd need another minute before the operating system could reboot and I could call someone.

"And who, exactly, do you intend to call?" asked Derby archly, watching the power bar expand.

"Daniel Henderson."

"Excuse me?"

"Daniel. Henderson."

"Yes, I thought that was what you said." He clicked his tongue rhythmically for a few seconds, then said, "But I decided to harbor one last, desperate hope that anyone other than myself hadn't utterly lost their minds."

"Look, I've thought about it, and it's our best option. Who else is there? Warden? It's still safe to assume she sent those killers. Any other star pilot I know might be working for Salvation and therefore her, and even if they aren't, they're not going to want to get within a light year of plying Terrorgorn."

"Hm, yes, sound logic," said Derby, stroking his chin and nodding. "You've quite convinced me. The only remaining solution is to call up the victim of our recent heist, from which we barely escaped with our lives, and ask them nicely for a tow."

My phone lit up, my contact list obligingly spreading itself across the screen. "Trust me." I looked for the Ds, which was where Daniel Henderson's number could be found under the heading "Dangerous Doints." "Daniel's a Jacques McKeown fan. And, more importantly, he's an idiot. I can tell him what he wants to hear."

"Fine," said Derby, eyeballing the Biskottis with a disgusted sneer. "The ingenious cunning of Davisham Derby has yet to produce a more reasonable solution. Unless we can find a chunk of jagged glass with which to slit our own throats."

I had already punched the Call button and was holding the phone to my ear. The speaker purred gently as a revolutionary wonder technology virtually indistinguishable from divine miracles created a connection that would allow digital information to pass near instantly through a miniature pinhole in the fabric of reality itself, all so that I could hear Daniel Henderson say, "Yello?"

"Daniel," I said, heaving a little sigh to steel myself. "This is Jacques McKeown."

There was a moment's silence, during which I fancied I could hear the slow clicking of the cogs in his dozy brain, before I heard some hurried rustling and the sound of something heavy falling off a bedside table. "Jacques!"

"McKeown. Yes."

"Ja–cques?" he repeated, the tone of his voice shifting from excitement to hurt confusion when he remembered the manner in which I had left his hospitality.

It was performance time. I closed my eyes, flicked the imaginary switch in my head, and put on my best hero voice, with an overtone of stern mentor. "Daniel, I'm very disappointed in you."

"I'm really sorry!" he said automatically, before actually thinking about it. "Wait, er. Why?"

"I thought you believed in the true values of star piloting. I came to your convention because I believed you wanted to further the message of truth, justice, and fighting for the helpless peoples of the galaxy."

"I do! I do!" he protested.

"Then why did I find the frozen body of Terrorgorn inside your fridge?"

In the shocked silence that followed, I fancied I heard a penny drop. Daniel emitted a few phlegmy choking noises as he made a couple of abortive attempts at explanations. "It's cool! It was cool!" he finally said. "They said it wouldn't do anything as long as it stayed frozen! Wait, why were you in the fridge?"

"I had no choice," I said dramatically, nimbly sidestepping the question. "Terrorgorn was too dangerous to keep in the middle of Ritsuko City. Especially not at a convention full of kids and especially, especially not in the middle of your home." I shook my head and released an angry, tolerant sigh. "You don't know how close you came to a terrible fate."

He was soaking in the bulltrac like an expensive fur coat in a septic tank. "I thought . . . I thought it would be all right . . ."

"It's okay," I reassured him, magnanimously. "I'm sorry I had to leave the convention early, but I had to get Terrorgorn away from there, to somewhere he couldn't do harm. I could only hope that you would understand that I did it in the name of galactic peace." Derby gave a smirk and slowly flapped his hands in sarcastic, silent applause.

"So . . . why did you take Dad?"

I took another deep breath. This round of bulltracing was going to be trickier, because I expected Daniel would talk to Henderson Sr. at some point to get confirmation of everything I told him now, and the long-term situation was still a concern. "Your father decided to come with us," I began, double-checking my words carefully to ensure I was technically telling the truth. "Of his own free will."

"Dad's awake?!" Daniel's tone was somewhere between eager excitement and sudden fear.

"Yes," I said, stalling. "Because, when he noticed me moving Terrorgorn, he realized how dangerous the situation was. And how important it was to get back in action. For your sake."

"Wow!"

"But now he needs your help," I said, moving hastily on. "Jacques McKeown needs your help. Are you ready to step up, for the sake of the universe?"

I could practically hear his chest swelling up like a water balloon being squeezed in a tight fist. "You bet!"

"Do you have a ship?"

"Yeah! Totally."

I had a feeling he would. His last ship had been destroyed, thanks in no small part to me, but he'd started learning how to pilot it. After he gained free access to his father's seemingly limitless wealth, I knew he wouldn't have wasted time before squandering it on a new joy ride. "Great. I need you to pick us up from the Biskot system. It's pretty clearly marked on most old star charts. We're on a space station in orbit around the third moon of Biskot 2."

"Sure, sure! I can head out right now!" I heard the rustling of bed sheets and undergarments being thrown around.

"Great," I said. "You can pick us up just as soon as we've dealt with Terrorgorn."

"Sure!"

"You're a good kid, Dan." I infused my voice with a hot gallon of stoic pride. "The galaxy will never understand how much it owes you for this."

I ended the call. I fought the urge to blow on my phone as if blowing smoke from a gun barrel before returning it smoothly to my hip pocket.

"Masterful," said Derby, bored. "I notice you glossed over a couple of details. Such as the matter of how, exactly, you intend to 'deal' with Terrorgorn."

I winced. "You know he's awake?"

"I deduced it was inevitable, after power was lost." I had begun to slowly walk back toward the center of the concourse and the steps that led up to the landing pad, so Derby fell casually into step beside me. "Hence my decision to scout ahead."

I tongued the mic in my tooth and patted my ear. "Sturb, are you receiving? Make any kind of sound if you are."

The silence dragged itself out to a worrying length before the reply came, in the form of a long sigh that transitioned naturally into a tuneful hum about as casual as the sound made by someone with a toilet brush up their nose. "*HAAHHhhhmmmm-hmmmm-hm-hmm-hmmm.*"

"You're still there with Terrorgorn and Henderson?"

Another musical hum, this one with a note of impatience. "*Hm-hmm-HMMM! Hm.*"

"We'll be back soon. The good news is we have a ride. I called up Daniel Henderson."

"*HMMMM!*"

I suddenly noticed that we'd drifted close to the crowd of Biskottis, and as it became clear that I was subtly steering myself toward the central pillar, they collectively took on the appearance of a roomful of shelter dogs watching the departure of the last visitor of the day.

"O Ancient," said the high priest, who had given his name as Ho during the walk back up to the concourse, after much prevaricating and I'm-not-worthying. "Do you return, now, to the palace of the heavens?"

"Erm, not just yet," I said, caught off guard, before hastily adding, "Verily. I need to go back to my ship. For a bit."

"Then let us regale you with the traditional dance of temporary farewell!"

"Please Come Back Soon," chanted his daughter, whose name was Ic. I had formulated a theory that their names had to be short because they had limited time in which to introduce themselves.

The Biskottis spread out, surrounding us to a radius of several meters, and began swaying left and right with their arms held high in the air, as if they'd only gotten as far as the Y in "YMCA," before they started rhythmically rotating their elbows with rather amazingly good choreography. It took a moment for me to realize that they were vaguely imitating the motions of air traffic controllers giving the signal to take off.

I plastered a benevolent smile on my face and inched toward the base of the winding stairs, picking my way carefully around the minefield of plated offerings as the Biskottis whirled and danced around us, their tiny feet dodging the plates with no apparent conscious thought.

"Praise the Ancients!" cried Ic as she pirouetted past.

"Appreciate it," I muttered in reply, as one would quietly chant "excuse me" while sidling through a crowd. "Thanks. Bless you."

"Please Come Back Soon!" sang another Biskotti as they leapt across our path.

"Bless you, yep. Blessings on you."

"Hmph."

This was such an abrupt change of tone that I felt moved to stop dead, with one foot already on the bottom step of the access stairway. I found myself addressing a Biskotti I hadn't noticed before, who wasn't dancing, but was standing at the base of the stairs with little arms folded and eyes narrowed. He was wearing a T-shirt with a stylized image of a ship flying through stars, but the ship had been scribbled out with permanent marker.

"You haven't fooled everyone, creatures," he said, in a quiet nasal voice that only we could hear. "Some of us have turned their back on the ridiculous superstitions of the Ancients and embraced the true ways of science." He punctuated his statement with a little snorting noise that I think might have been a reflex action.

"Really am just trying to get back to my ship," I said, not making eye contact.

"Just answer this!" he pressed. "If the Ancients created the universe for us, why does observable space indicate that our home is a relatively young creation?"

"Ath!" Ic suddenly bulldozed her way into the conversation. "Stop bothering the Ancient with your nonsense."

"I'm just trying to ask questions!" ranted Ath, keeping his feet rooted to the spot as Ic pointedly tugged at his clothing. "Why are you all so willfully blind? Is it so absurd that our station could have simply been spontaneously created by the smashing together of random particles?"

"Yes, that is quite absurd, actually," said Ic, getting heated. Most of the dancers had awkwardly stopped to watch the debate, although a few individuals on the outskirts were too enraptured to notice.

"That's how it happened!" insisted Ath. "Smash together particles often enough over infinite time, it's bound to happen! Look at all the pieces in the sky, those were the failed attempts!"

At that point the Biskottis faded out of earshot, as I had taken the opportunity to hastily ascend the stairs while everyone was distracted. I heaved a sigh, and a few pints of the foul-smelling air created by the older food offerings on the higher steps made my eyes water.

"Another planet of grateful primitives saved by the age of star piloting," said Davisham Derby in a tone calculated to annoy. I'd barely been aware of him following closely behind, but that was cat burglars for you. "You're sure you wouldn't like to 'rescue' them? Seems like the sort of thing a star pilot would do."

"Are you sure you wouldn't rather take the job at the fish shop?" I snapped, turning on him with fists primed.

Instantly he endeavored to drop all expression from his facial features and freeze them in place. "How much do you know?" he said, barely moving his lips, although his mustache wobbled dramatically. "How much do you think you know?"

"I know that I might be a has-been, but at least I'm not living some kind of traccy plied-up midlife crisis that's gotten more out of hand than your left arm. Now shut your face, you bracket, I'm thinking."

Specifically, Derby's taunt had made me think about the last time I'd saved a primitive people, or rather, what I had taken for one. In the end, it had turned out to be nothing more than an elaborate, planet-wide piece of theater engineered by Robert Blaze and Malcolm Sturb. I remembered how angry I'd been when the truth was revealed, how stupid I'd felt for actually thinking I was liberating those adorable furry fakes.

But now the Biskottis had made it all clear: at the end of the day, star pilots had done very little overall good for the primitive races of the Black. How many of them were out there now, holding out for their alien liberators to return and solve whatever new problems had arisen? Not knowing that it would never happen, for no better reason than because liberating them was no longer fashionable.

I was so distracted by my thoughts that when I reached the airlock, I bitterly jabbed the section of hull plating just to the left of the access panel and sprained my finger. I shook myself. There was no sense dwelling on the past. After all, I was a villainous space pirate now, not a star pilot. I had to focus on fixing the Terrorgorn situation, so that I could get back to fixing the Henderson situation, so that I could be free to start terrorizing the galaxy or whatever.

The three individuals in the passenger cabin were basically where I had left them, looking like a roomful of future in-laws with whom a new girlfriend had left me alone. Terrorgorn hadn't moved from his seat, but was now wearing an ill-fitting hoodie and sweatpants, which did nothing to reduce the powerful aura of evil and hatred that radiated from his awkward smile. Sturb was sitting on the seat that was as far away from Terrorgorn as possible, with his hands clasped in his lap and head bowed.

Henderson, meanwhile, was sitting with his back straight and arms folded, his face set like a police barrier being used to hold back an angry mob. To continue the future in-laws analogy, he had the look of a furious dad who had already decided he was going to throw the interloper out on his ear if he so much as forgot to hold the door open for the family cat.

"So I think our ride will get here in about a day," I said as we walked in and everyone looked to me with varying levels of desperation.

"Wonderful. Davisham Derby could not stand for much longer being without the company of Daniel . . . Henderson," said Derby, his speech slowing when he noticed that I was urgently making a cutthroat gesture so hard that a violin placed in my hands at that moment would have been playing "Flight of the Bumblebee."

Just as I'd feared, Mr. Henderson's grin almost split his face in half. He leaned back in his chair and crossed his legs, suddenly relaxed. "Oh, what was that?" he said, dripping with satisfaction. "The person coming to save us is one Daniel Henderson, Esq.? Who will no doubt be bringing several employees of the noble Henderson organization? Well then, I suppose it becomes extra important that our rescuer should find his dear old dad here, doesn't it?"

Sturb turned his shoulders toward me, but kept his gaze fixed on his shoes. "Could you possibly tell him to hold off a little longer?" he quietly asked.

"Okay, new rule, nobody talks but me," announced Henderson, standing up and subtracting all levity from his voice. "I'm making the rules now. Second rule, I think the four of you are going to have a little knife fight to decide who gets to eat. And then maybe we'll have a loser's bracket to decide who gets to be the food."

A chill ran down my spine. Not because of Henderson, but because I was watching Terrorgorn's expression change. It was an expression that would have been familiar to anyone who'd grown up with someone of British descent like my mum. She'd always wear that kind of face when Dad was doing something she disapproved of, like putting his feet on the table, or speaking French at home, or maliciously eating loudly. That flat line of a mouth, eyebrows raised, gaze firmly pointed ceilingwards, the look of someone who is completely plying livid but far too polite or passive aggressive to say anything out loud.

"Erm, Terrorgorn, are you okay with this?" I asked.

"Hmmmmm," said Terrorgorn noncommittally, which was about the worst possible response.

"And another thing, I've been sitting here all evening watching you people bricking it over this Terrorgorn thing, and all it's done is sit there like a turd on a placemat." He stood in front of Terrorgorn with hands on hips. "Are you really what amounted to a supervillain to these idiots? What do you do for the final battle, pick your nose?"

Terrorgorn finally stopped staring at the ceiling and looked Henderson square in the eye. Then Henderson collapsed where he stood.

It wasn't like he had suddenly lost the strength in his body and keeled over. It was more like he'd been trodden on by an invisible elephant, instantly pinning his head to the floor. He thrashed his limbs and grunted, fighting to get back up, until the invisible force twisted his arm behind him and shoved his wrist up toward the back of his neck.

I looked at Terrorgorn, aghast. Two spherical objects beneath the skin of his brow appeared to be glowing bright orange. As he gently cocked his head and allowed a vacant smile to cross his face, the glow pulsated slightly and Henderson was dragged a few feet across the floor, which couldn't have been pleasant, given how infrequently I vacuumed.

Henderson's neck craned around. At first I thought he was trying to look at his attacker, but his eyes were screwed shut and his head trembled as he used every ounce of effort to fight against whatever was trying to rotate it.

"Erm, Terrorgorn," I said hastily. "I think you've made your point, perhaps you'd like to let Mr. Henderson go, now?"

The glow faded from Terrorgorn's brow, as did his smile. He looked down at Henderson's squirming form, then at me.

"No, I'm fine," he mumbled.

Henderson's eyes opened and caught my gaze. There's something quite disturbing about seeing someone who has never once in their entire life experienced fear suddenly having to learn it on the fly. It was almost as disturbing as the dull clicking sound Henderson's neck made as it snapped.

CHAPTER 21

I HAVE DIFFICULTY remembering what happened in the hour or two that followed. Probably because I was spending most of it writhing around with a splitting headache. I think I must have gotten overexcited about what Terrorgorn had done, and he had felt the need to calm me down. Whatever the case, when the raging tide of agony finally subsided and I could stand to unclutch my skull, Terrorgorn had Terror-gone.

Derby and Sturb were both writhing around on the floor with me, so they must also have offered token resistance. And there was the corpse of Mr. Henderson, still flat against the floor with limbs knotted at terrible angles. For a moment, as my senses struggled groggily to become fully operational, it seemed like his pale, twisted face was the only thing in the universe. The voids in his empty eyes were lifeless galaxies.

"Oh, trac. We are beyond calculus," I moaned, sitting up. "We are somewhere in the region of differential geometry right now."

"Perfect," said Derby. "So now we've got a day to figure out how to explain this to the Henderson clan in such a way that they don't murder us all. And if we survive that, then we get to explain to the rest of the universe that we set Terrorgorn loose. Wonderful. Marvelous. What a textbook operation this has been." By then, he was ranting, pacing irritably back and forth across Henderson's corpse.

"Mr. Derby, I really don't think that was a helpful thing to say," said Sturb hotly, sitting with his knees drawn up. "Now. What does everyone think we should do?"

"You're asking me?!" Derby stopped dead in front of him. "None of this was Davisham Derby's idea. None of it is my fault." He scowled at me, then yanked at the wristlet on his arm stump until the straps came loose and flung it into the corner. "Davisham Derby's going to have a nice private little midlife crisis somewhere." He stalked off in the direction of the head, slamming doors behind him.

"Okay," said Sturb, with moist frustration in his eyes. "We tell Daniel Henderson the truth. We apologize. He was the one who bought Terrorgorn's body in the first place. He has to realize that everyone has to share some of the blame for this situation."

By now I was on my feet, checking Henderson over. I nudged his rapidly graying face with my foot. His head flopped over to the side like the page of a very difficult and unpleasant book.

"It might work on Daniel," I said through a sigh. "Maybe. I've no idea where he'll go, mentally, over this. But then there's the rest of Henderson's people." I thought of Heller, with his body like an upright refrigerator and fists like flesh-covered toasters. "This is gonna leave a power vacuum like a plying black hole. Half of them will want to go to war on the spot."

"So what do you think we should do?!"

I had been squatting on my haunches, examining the body, but as I fully considered Sturb's question, I rocked back and let my posterior thump to the floor. I exhaled through pursed lips and let them flutter musically for a good few seconds before finally looking up. "Die?"

"Come on, seriously, now."

"I might be serious." Henderson's face was starting to bother me, so I positioned my knee between it and mine so I wouldn't have to look. "And we might not even live that long. Terrorgorn's probably mowing through the Biskottis as we speak, and then he'll realize this ship's the only way off the station."

"Listen, we mustn't stop believing in ourselves!" said Sturb, raising the pitch of his voice by an octave as he tried to be inspiring. "We're not completely helpless, are we? You're a star pilot . . ."

"Ex–star pilot."

"And Davisham Derby's the greatest thief in the galaxy . . ."

I looked up at him. "And you're a supervillain."

"Ex-supervillain," said Sturb, with remarkable speed, every muscle in his body visibly tensing before he forced himself to relax. "Come on, we're

Penelope Warden's handpicked heist crew! There's got to be something we can do about all this!" His words penetrated my fog of despair, and my neck slowly rolled around as I took in the contents of the room, feeling the little tentative roots of plans forming in my mind. I mentally cataloged the suite of skills we had available to us. I stared at Henderson's body, my eyes narrowing in thought, then looked to Sturb again.

"You're a . . . cyber . . . cyborginator?"

"Cyberneticist, I'd say," said Sturb, with a hint of reproach.

"Could you turn Henderson into one of your cyborgs?" I felt hope returning, like a cleansing rain through my limbs, as the sheer obviousness of the scheme hit me.

He was taken aback, the corners of his mouth twisting into a grimace like I was suggesting he use his fingernails to scrape the hardened brown bits off the side of a toilet bowl. "Uh. No. He's dead."

"That's a problem?" I was thinking back to my encounters with Malmind drones in the past, and they'd always been pale and vacant looking enough to be dead.

"Yes, because my tech was designed to redirect higher brain functions." He dug his hands into his pockets uncomfortably. "It wouldn't do anything if they were dead. Because they wouldn't have brain functions to redirect. That's what *dead* means."

"All right," I said, feeling stupid but not quite ready to be completely deflated. "But couldn't you rig something up? It wouldn't have to pass for long. Prop him up, make his head move around . . ." I patted my pockets. "I could find, like, a text-to-speech app and make it say something psychotic . . ."

"No," said Sturb firmly, drawing himself to his full height. His love handles were quivering and his face was turning very pink. "I can't do that."

"Serious?" I looked over the body again. "I'm pretty sure *I* could rig him up with some hydraulics from the cargo bay, worst comes to it."

"All right, well, let me be clearer." Sturb puffed his chest out even further. "I *won't* do that. I'm not going to do it because I don't want to."

I tapped my fingers rhythmically upon the metal floor while I waited for the punch line, but it didn't come. "You're an evil cyberneticist and you don't want to do it."

"Evil cybernetics was something that I *did*," he said insistently. "It is not something that I *am*."

That sounded suspiciously like a recitation. "Where did that come from?"
He lowered himself from tiptoe sheepishly. "I go to a support group."

"You go to a support group for former supervillains."

"Supervillains, career pirates, star pilots who can't let go." His eyes glazed
over in memory. "Penelope organized it on Salvation Station. She said we
could all help each other turn a page in our lives."

Warden had gone straight from the Henderson organization to Robert
Blaze's employ at Salvation, of course, but if she'd intended to move on from
her life as a manipulative criminal psycho-div, I would have thought that the
first step would have been to stop being a manipulative criminal psycho-div.
If she'd turned a page, she'd left a few bookmarks.

I kept these thoughts to myself, because talking about her had made Sturb
stare reverently into the middle distance. "Look," I said. "I'm not asking you
to set up a new cybergulag and start rounding up tourists again. We're just
going to temporarily make use of a body that the previous owner doesn't
need anymore."

He seemed to be considering it, but then he smacked his hands around
his ears. "No. No, no, no, no. That's the little voice."

"What?"

"It always starts with the little voice; we've talked about it at the group."
I could see tears glinting in his eyes. "The little voice that says it can't hurt
to do just a tiny bit of evil cybernetics when it's convenient. But you do it
and that sets a precedent, and the little voice gets louder every time, and the
next thing you know . . ."

"Sturb, this is, like, one million percent less evil than the kind of stuff you
used to do with the Malmind."

"That's the other thing the little voice says!" He pointed a shaking finger
at me like he'd just figured out who the last real human on a planet full of
evil alien clones was. "Always forward, never back! Clean slate! A supervillain
without villainy is just a super person!" He backed toward the door. "Stop
trying to bring me down to your level!"

Then he ran off. I heard his heavy footfalls rapidly ascend the steps,
and then the cockpit hatchway slammed shut like the bedroom door of a
teenager whose parents persistently fail to understand them. So that left me,
having successfully alienated everyone in the plying universe, sitting alone
on the floor of an unswept passenger cabin with a highly inconvenient
corpse. The thought occurred at that moment that I could always put my

gun to Sturb's head and *make* him raise Henderson to a nightmarish state of animatronic undeath.

I rubbed my eyes. No, I couldn't. It was a stupid idea. What was I proposing, dangle Henderson's body from the ceiling with tow cables and make his legs do a little happy Irish jig when Daniel walked in? It was insane. Monstrous. The sane solution was obviously to remove Henderson's skin and wear it.

I rubbed my eyes again. No, no, no. There was definitely something wrong with my thought processes. It was probably related to my recent identity crisis. In which case, it was about time I started reining that in.

So I looked at Henderson's corpse, at the unnatural stillness of his face, and tried not to think about all the ways it was going to make my life difficult. I didn't think about what clever lie I was going to spin to his grieving child, or even that I could at least take comfort that he could no longer force us to knife fight each other. I pushed these thoughts out of my head until I saw the body as what it was: the remains of a fellow human being who had wanted to live as much as I did, and who, whatever he might have done or been, hadn't deserved this.

I clung to that notion like it was my carry-on baggage and I was the world's most paranoid bracket in a crowded departure lounge. Then I slowly rose to my knees, found an old hoodie that Terrorgorn had elected not to wear, and covered Henderson's face with it.

"Rest in peace, you poor mad bracket," I muttered.

Right, I thought. That was a start. Now I could work on dealienating the universe.

I was heading for the door when I picked up a rhythmic tapping sound. The sound of knuckles tapping on a solid surface, the kind made by someone who is in two minds about whether they want to draw attention to themselves. I followed my ears, and found Derby's discarded wristlet lying in the debris in the corner.

"Uncle Dav?" came Nelly's nervous voice as I cracked the wristlet's lid open. "It's just me. I promise I'm not going to bring up the fish shop. Please don't slam the lid shut again."

I held it up to my face. "Hi."

"Oh." Nelly appeared to have propped her end of the tube up in front of her, and was sitting forward in a "let's have a serious conversation about this" kind of way—familiar to anyone who has had to attend an intervention, or inform a coworker that their body odor is affecting morale. "Did Uncle Dav get captured again?"

"No, he did it himself, this time."

She bit her lip and winced. "You didn't . . . tell him off, did you?"

In keeping with being in a walking-back kind of mood, I opted to be honest. "I might have said something about him living an insane midlife crisis."

She tutted. "Great. So he's probably going to blame me for telling you too much."

"Look, why do you . . . enable him?" I asked, only faintly aware that standing over Henderson's corpse with death closing in from multiple directions wasn't the best time to have this conversation.

Nelly dropped her gaze. "You wouldn't understand. We, me and the family, we kinda felt bad for him after he lost his job at the research facility."

A few small flags suddenly raised in my memory. "He's a scientist?"

"Chemical engineer," said Nelly. "He devoted, like, twenty years of his life trying to create a, a . . . more efficient kind of hydrogen fuel, and he was so close to having a commercial product, and Speedstar had seen the work and were really interested, and then . . ."

"And then Quantunneling happened," I said flatly.

"Um. Yeah. That's partly why he came up with the wristlet idea. He said it was, like, taking back what quantum tunnels took from him."

I had to admit, that was a much cleverer response than the one star pilots had come up with, which had been to sit around Ritsuko City Spaceport complaining and to start using mathematical terms as swear words. But more importantly, the revelation had stirred something up from the back of my memory, something that cut through all my confused thinking like a rigid anchor cable.

"If he's a scientist," I heard myself say, "do you think he'd have any interest in a new job opportunity?"

Again, I heard the sound of knuckles rapping against a solid surface. And this time I knew it wasn't coming from Nelly, because I could see that all of her knuckles were gathered worriedly beneath her chin. It was coming from behind me. Someone was knocking on the airlock.

Derby's wristlet still in hand, I went to answer. I wasn't exactly expecting a kissogram, but I knew that the situation had to develop in some hideous manner and I didn't see much point in putting it off. I arranged my face into a suitably deadpan expression and hit the Open controls.

It was Ic, the daughter of the Biskotti high priest. The lower half of her face was wreathed in the usual enraptured smiles, but her eyes were rather urgently wide, and her brow was furrowed enough to be about ready for a season's worth of potato seeds. "Um, all hail the Ancients, the Speed-star Cor-po-ra-tion wel-comes you," she chanted at lightning speed. "I beseech that you forgive my unworthy form trespassing upon your celestial vessel, but we were wondering if you wouldn't mind descending from on high one more time to, to, um . . ." She tapped her index fingertips together a few times. "Resolve an argument?"

She politely moved aside to let me see what was going on at the far side of the landing pad. A small throng of Biskottis was rising into view at the top of the stairs, headed by Ath, the argumentative one we had encountered just before leaving. He was marching with the kind of confidence in his step that sets out to make everyone else feel discouraged. It was certainly working on me.

"The Ancients are false deities!" he declared, waving a burning rolled-up magazine. "Throw off the shackles of outdated superstition! Embrace the true power of he who would stand against the lies of the Ancients!"

More Biskottis were surging up onto the landing pad, their eyes wide with bewilderment but nevertheless holding up their fists and making vaguely bellicose noises. As the last few stragglers arrived, I saw that Terrorgorn was, inevitably, among them. He was sitting in a plastic chair from the food court that four of the burlier Biskottis were holding aloft.

"The Ancients have abandoned us!" clarified Ath at full volume to be heard over the background grumbling. "Assemble beneath the banner of Tarragon!"

"Uh, hmmm," coughed Terrorgorn, somehow loud enough to be audible. Instantly, every single one of the assembled Biskottis flinched and fell into terrified silence.

"Not Tarragon?" asked Ath, looking back and sweating profusely. "What was it? Terragon?"

"Hmmmmm." Terrorgorn tilted his head slightly, pointing his eyes sideways.

"Terrorgorn," I suggested.

"Terror-gorn?"

"Mm," went Terrorgorn, nodding his head one fraction of a centimeter.

"Terrorgorn." Ath shook himself back into full enthusiasm and waved his fiery magazine. "Burn the pretenders!"

"Yes, so, um," said Ic, still fiddling with her fingers. "If you could just quickly explain to them why the Ancients are the true lords of the heavens, that would be super."

I watched the situation develop, the crowd of Biskottis spreading themselves across the landing pad toward us like a giant serving of hostile custard. Then I casually leaned back until I was fully inside the airlock again and smashed the Close button violently enough that the external door very nearly claimed the tip of my nose as it slammed shut. Then I pulled the mechanical locks into place.

After retreating through the internal door and locking that as well, I pressed my back against it and silently cursed myself. It would have been so easy to play up the god thing. There was no end of ways I could have faked up a miracle to enforce the position a bit. My gun, my phone, the graviton generator, trac, I was pretty sure I had a mechanical pencil lying around somewhere that would probably have turned heads. Not to mention Sturb's portable quantu—

The realization hit me at the exact same moment that a number of angry fists crashed upon the side of the *Neverdie*'s hull, enhancing the effect somewhat. Of course. The portable Quantunnel gate, still leaning against the wall of the passenger cabin, was our ticket out of here. With any luck, the other side was still intact in Henderson's meat freezer, and with Henderson's corpse and son both confirmed to be here in the Black, it was probably the safest place to be, short of burying ourselves alive under thick concrete.

Trac. Why hadn't I thought of it before? This was exactly why star pilots had been left behind by the Quantunnel revolution: we just didn't have the creativity to consider the applications.

I stumbled back into the cabin, tripping on the base of the door frame as another blow shook the entire ship. The Biskottis must have been coordinating their blows remarkably well, as a single Biskotti fist against the *Neverdie*'s hull would have been like hitting a leather shoe with a matchstick.

The portable Quantunnel frame was still leaning against the far wall, with Henderson's body sprawled between it and me as if he had only just hurled himself through it. I was midway through stepping carefully around his outspread limbs when I realized that the Quantunnel couldn't be activated without power, which the *Neverdie* was presently lacking. But there was plenty of perfectly good electricity in the station; I wondered if Terrorgorn and his new angry mob would be willing to let me borrow a cup.

As if in response to my thoughts, the entire ship shook and tilted slightly, sending an avalanche of crumbs and discarded Biros cascading across the floor like a herd of gazelle spotting an indiscreet cheetah. Henderson's broken neck lolled sickeningly again as his body rolled into the corner.

I could hear the moans and complaints of the Biskottis, recently abandoned by God, right through the hull. They made a collective huff sound and the ship tilted again, further this time, before rocking back and tilting even more the other way.

I'd seen enough riots to know where this was going. I grabbed the backrest of one of my fixed seats just as a particularly violent tilt threw my feet right off the ground and I was pelted with a fresh shower of lost coins and sweet wrappers.

Holding on to the furniture, I was able to stop myself from being thrown around as the tilt grew closer and closer to a full right angle, but there was nothing I could do about Henderson's body, which was rolling around like a wet sweater in a tumble dryer. I was trying to grab the Quantunnel gate as it spun by my head, so I was taken by surprise when Henderson bodychecked me from beyond the grave.

I lost my grip just as the ship rolled fully onto its side, and fell awkwardly into the section of wall behind the bench that was very swiftly becoming a floor. I heard the sound of plexiglass breaking and a cheer from the Biskottis. Deliriously, I searched my pockets for a mechanical pencil, before Henderson's flying leg smashed my head into an electrical cabinet, and everything went black.

CHAPTER 22

ONCE AGAIN I beat the odds by getting knocked unconscious without suffering crippling permanent brain damage. The trick is to have lived a life of adventure, and have so many memories from it that you can lose quite a few before you start feeling the loss. In this case, I was apparently out for less than a minute, so I was probably only going to have to ditch a few more months of high school.

It was long enough for the Biskottis to flood into the *Neverdie*'s interior, and things quickly became too confusing to keep track of. Multiple sets of matching hands covered my eyes and mouth and held me off the ground by all four limbs, ferrying me down staircases and along corridors, carelessly letting my head bang into multiple walls, railings, and door frames along the way, renewing the pain in my skull with each one.

Finally I was heaved up, flipped onto my front, then thrust backwards into what felt and sounded like a wheelchair, which rolled a few feet before slapping into a wall. My head made heavy impact with a piece of horizontal piping, and I lost touch with reality again for a reassuringly small handful of seconds.

When I regained awareness I was by myself, strapped to the wheelchair by my wrists and shins. A fifth strap held my waist, meaning I couldn't even pelvic thrust the chair into movement.

I was in a room that I took to be a small infirmary somewhere in the depths of the station. There were some empty cabinets directly in front of me, and an examination bench that looked like yet another perfectly functional object that the Biskottis had converted into an object of worship. This one was adorned with highly dribbled novelty candles that had originally been shaped like the Happiyaki Burger mascot.

I could hear raised voices in the corridor outside. Raised about as much as Biskotti voices could be raised, in that they sounded like a middle-school orchestra arguing through their recorders and tambourines. A few moments later, the door opened and Ath entered, carrying a loaded plastic shopping bag that jingled metallically as he set it down.

"Where are my . . . friends?" I demanded, hesitating as I sought a better word.

"Hm?" asked Ath, picking through the contents of his bag. "Sorry, I'm a little distracted. It's all happening so fast out there." He bobbed on his heels and made a little clenched-teeth grimace that was loitering somewhere on the outskirts of being a smile. "Slightly faster than I can keep track of, actually. But, you know, lots of really positive energy, and that's great."

He had produced a large butcher knife from his bag, which his small limbs held as if it were a two-handed bastard sword, and now laid it on the cold floor tiles with a loud click to punctuate his sentence. Then he returned to his bag and produced what looked like a pair of aluminium salad tongs.

"Are you going to sacrifice me?" I stared at the knife.

"No!" said Ath, offended. "This is the dawn of the Biskotti Renaissance. We are turning our back on the brutal and primitive superstitions of our past and dedicating ourselves to a new philosophy of reason, rationality, and science. We've already confiscated all the station's remaining supplies, for . . ." He waved a hand vaguely. "Science purposes."

"So what is this?"

"Thiiiiis . . ." He extended the word as he rummaged through his bag again, then triumphantly produced a school science textbook that must have come from an abandoned bookstore. "Is a 'dissection.' I think. I thought I could, in the name of science and learning, 'dissect' you and determine the secret of the Ancients' immortality." He hefted the blade and stared at it uncertainly. "Just let me know if you don't think I'm doing it right. This is all new to me."

I swallowed. "Terrorgorn will destroy you the moment you stop being useful to him. Let us go and we can help you."

Ath was struggling to hold up the knife in one hand as he leafed through the textbook. "Well, my rationality and reasoning skills are telling me that you're just saying that because you don't want to be killed. Therefore, in the name of science, I must refuse." He lowered his arms and looked me in the eye. "Terrorgorn has brought much-needed change to this community. Exactly the kind of change I have always wanted. I'm very happy with it."

He was nodding so quickly that I had to vibrate my entire head to maintain eye contact. I narrowed my eyes and waited for the nodding to slow to a stop. "Are you really?" I said.

He chewed on his lower lip for a second, then blinked. "Yes. Shut up. The Ancients will never drag the People's Enlightened Republic of Biskot back into the dark ages." He returned to his textbook, then frowned and examined his knife. "That can't be right, can it? Wouldn't it smell bad? Hang on, I'm going to look in the other book."

The door opened and the bustle outside began anew as Ath slipped out. I caught a glimpse of a number of other Biskottis arguing about the initial direction of the new world order, as well as another wheelchair waiting in the hall, into which Sturb was strapped. Derby couldn't have been far behind, judging by the slightly refined edge to some of the background shouting.

I desperately continued vibrating myself in an attempt to dislodge the straps, but it was pointless. They must have been used at one time for keeping cargo in place, and Speedstar were never ones to ply around when it came to keeping hold of their property.

I cast another look around the empty infirmary, and noticed that my blaster was lying on top of the row of cabinets directly opposite from me, as well as my phone, Sturb's phone, and Derby's wristlet.

"Nelly!" I whispered, leaning forward as far as the strap could allow. I decided there wasn't much point in keeping quiet; these Speedstar modules had sturdy walls. Also, there was a mad little bracket coming back soon who was going to slit me up in one of my smelly places. "NELLY!!!"

The wristlet opened from the other side. From where I sat, all I could see was a glimpse of slender hand, and a silhouette of half a head. "Captain? Is it safe?"

"What have you got that can cut these straps from over there?"

"Er . . ." The lid closed for a few seconds as she went over the inventory. "How important is it that it doesn't damage anything other than the straps?" A brief pause. "You know what, never mind, I think I know the answer to that one. I've got, like, this pen-laser thing, but it'll take about a minute to cut through."

I wasn't convinced that we had a minute. "All right, what kind of weapons have you got? The Taser?"

"I could push it out, but the trigger's on, you know, the bit that comes out," she said, flustered. "So I can't trigger it from in here and I can't aim it. Really sorry. Not my fault."

The wristlet was propped up against the wall rather than lying flat. I considered the geography of the situation. "What's the longest, heaviest thing you've got in there?"

"Er . . . probably the big wrench. I can barely lift it. So I don't know why we have it at all, but Uncle Dav said—"

The volume of shouting in the hallway outside was growing again and I could hear the pitter-patter of approaching tiny feet. "Hide!" I hissed.

The wristlet clapped closed just as I heard Ath's hand fumbling with the door handle, and then he came back in hurriedly, pausing a moment with his back to the door. "Whew! Everything's still. Er. Very exciting out there. Mr. Terrorgorn's just bringing the last few of the misguided Luddites of the old ways to, erm, their senses." He made an expression like something in his mouth didn't taste nice. "Very exciting time. Very happy with how things are going."

"Good," I muttered.

He hefted the knife again and began to approach slowly. "So. It turns out bad smells are one of the things you just have to deal with when you're doing science. So it's fine. I'll, er. I'll start dissecting now, then."

"Are you sure you're up to this?" I asked as he drew close. "Because it sounds like it might be a bit of a WRENCH!"

I had directed the last word over his shoulder, but the wristlet stayed shut. Ath looked behind him, following my gaze, and smiled nervously. "Um. Possibly."

"WRENCH!" I yelled, louder. "What a WRENCH it would be if a WRENCH came out and caused something to WRENCH!"

"Wrench?" He looked to his textbook for answers, finding none. "Look, you need to understand, we are living in a rational universe guided only by the principles of science. Wrench isn't going to answer your prayers. There probably never was a Wrench to begin with." He raised the knife.

The wristlet finally snapped open and two feet of industrial-grade, orange-painted metal were thrust into existence, neatly clocking Ath about the side of the head. His entire body toppled stiffly over like a bowling pin.

"Did I get him?" asked a breathless Nelly, after she had pulled the wrench back into the little world inside the wristlet. "Sorry it took so long, it's really heavy."

I looked down at Ath. He was still unconscious and didn't look to be coming out of it any time soon, not having had as much experience as me when it came to getting biffed on the head. I looked up. "Pen laser!"

"What?"

Derby and Nelly's blinking code was seeming like a smarter idea by the moment. "Pen laser! On the straps! Now!"

"Oh, right. You're welcome, by the way." She disappeared, then came back to the little porthole with what looked like a red whiteboard marker made of reflective steel. She awkwardly poked it through the hole, holding it with the tips of her fingers as she tried to aim without blocking too much of the view with her own hand.

A glowing line of energy scored through the dim artificial twilight and struck me in the chest. The heat was intense, but the dot was jiggling around too much to cause any sustained burn. After a few false starts, she was able to focus on the strap that held my left wrist in place, and the tough fabric began to fray and smoke. Shortly, enough had been burned away that it tore apart with a sharp yank, and I endeavored to snatch my arm away from the little glowing circle of pain.

"Is Uncle Dav all right?" asked Nelly. She had pressed her face right up to the Quantunnel hole, so without context I appeared to be talking to a brass disk with a human mouth.

"I saw him outside," I relayed, my tone turning thoughtful as I realized that the crowd outside the door was no longer making crowd-style noises, or indeed, any noises at all. Once I had freed myself from the wheelchair, I pressed my ear to the door, then pulled it open the tiniest crack, toying with the idea of talking our way past the Biskottis by holding up Ath's carcass and putting on a squeaky voice.

But the corridor outside was empty but for two occupied wheelchairs, some chocolate wrappers, and a dislodged poster advertising the merits of "coffee and Biskots." I drifted out, checked the corners, and went to release Sturb and Derby. I noticed Derby had been gagged again, this time with a handful of fast-food restaurant serviettes that his saliva had already started turning into a single solid lump.

"Where'd they go?" I asked Sturb, as Derby was still dislodging wet papier-mâché from his gums.

"I don't know." Sturb massaged his liberated wrists. "One minute they were all arguing over how to display our bodies in a way that best emphasized their commitment to scientific reason and progressive values, then some-one shouted something, and they all ran out. That way." He pointed up the corridor.

"I assumed Mr. Terrorgorn emitted a particularly passive-aggressive sound," said Derby in his usual dry tones.

"Do you think we can fix the ship now?" asked Sturb. "You can get at the damaged underbelly, so we can fix it now, right? If we work together I'm sure we can get it done in no time."

Exasperated, I made a passive-aggressive sound of my own. "I can fix the reactor and the engines, yes." I sighed. "Not sure about all the new issues it acquired from being turned upside down. And then we'd need to flip it back over, unless we're planning to take off through solid floor." I gave him a second to look pathetic, then came to the rescue. "I had a better idea. What about the portable Quantunnel?"

Realization and hope swept across his face in waves as he, too, remem-bered that we had that. "Yes! Assuming the other side is still intact, it should take us straight back to Ritsuko City! That's a really good idea, Captain. And I'm not sure how you escaped from your chair just now, but I'm sure that took some really top-rate thinking as well."

"*Assuming* we can power it," sneered Derby, brushing off his sleeves. "*Assuming* we can fight our way through an entire station full of crazed zealots plus the most dangerous entity in the universe."

"Look, we just need to distract the Biskottis, get the gateway off the ship, and take it to a power outlet." I looked around. "And the Biskottis seem to be pretty easily distracted."

Derby pointed to his arm stump like a stern father pointing to an incom-plete stack of homework. "Where's my wristlet?"

I ducked back into the infirmary to get it, and stopped when I saw that my phone was buzzing. The screen identified the incoming caller as Daniel Henderson. So as the phone intermittently attempted to vibrate its way off the shelf, I took a few moments to weigh the pros and cons of picking up.

What the hell, I thought. *Let's dig ourselves as deep as possible.* At the very least, it would deter grave robbers. I took the call. "Daniel?"

"Hi, Jacques!" he said. I could practically hear the relish leaking out of his mouth as he exercised his first-name privileges. "I'm at the station now. Sorry it took a while, I stopped at, like, three empty ones before this."

"You're here already?" I tried to sound impressed, rather than harassed. I had already hurried back to the corridor and chucked Derby his wristlet.

"Yeah, I think I got lucky with those catapult-gate things you have. Is that your ship? Did you know it's upside down?"

I cast a look around for the quickest way to the exit, swiftly concluding that it was probably the way indicated by the EXIT signs, and gestured to Sturb and Derby to follow before breaking into a jog. "I'm aware, Daniel, thanks. We're on our way up to the landing pad. Whatever you do, do not touch down."

"Oh," he said, before sucking noisily on his teeth to fill the awkward silence. "I might've already done that."

"Okay," I said, upgrading the jog to a run. "It should be fine. Just don't open the airlock until we get there." After a moment's thought, I added: "The galaxy is depending on you."

"Oh, sure! Cool! Right on!" He managed to wait in silence for all of eight seconds. "So, is my dad with you? Does he think my new ship looks cool?"

Of course Speedstar had apparently thought that the lowest plying level of the station was the ideal location for the plying infirmary. I swung around another flight of stairs, gripping the banister tightly. "He thinks it's cool, Daniel. He thinks it's very cool."

"Cool!" From Daniel's end of the line, I heard the faint sound of a businesslike knock. "Oh, that's probably you. See you in a bit!"

"Daniel, that's not me! Keep the door shut!" I yelled, but he'd already rung off. I upgraded my run to a sprint, taking the steps three at a time and grabbing and yanking on the banister as I went for the extra bursts of speed.

By the time I reached the top-level concourse, my knees were aching and my thighs felt like kippers that had been left on the grill for too long. I stumbled to a confused halt when I saw that the concourse was completely empty. Even the food offerings had been removed to reflect the Biskottis' rejection of the old faith, although some of the particularly old and whiffy plates were still there.

There was a high-pitched cry, and a Biskotti fell from above, hitting the concourse with an upsetting wet sound. I looked up, and saw the edge of the Biskotti mob, mumbling and squeaking indistinctly as it tried to stay on the landing platform.

"Up," I suggested, more to myself than anyone else; I wasn't about to stop and check that the others were following. I bolted for the steps that surrounded the central pillar, my knees complaining like rusty hinges.

When I reached the landing pad, the first thing I saw was Daniel's ship. His first ship had been the decadent and cumbersome Platinum God of Whale Sharks, and he had apparently learned from that experience and invested in a blood-red Hemingway EZ Cruise 9, the narcoleptic three-toed sloth to the God of Whale Sharks' overfed hippopotamus with bowel cancer. I think he may have customized it to an extent, but it was hard to tell, because most of it was covered in Biskottis.

Countless yellow bodies had packed together into a single anvil-shaped cluster that was wrapped around the Hemingway's nose cone, like a swarm of ants trying to bring down a giant wasp. The ship shuddered violently as it tried to lift off, but the thrusters were losing the battle against multiple hands and feet clinging to the landing pad with a death grip.

I managed to snap out of my gawp and fumbled at the phone that was still in my hand, trying to call Daniel back. No answer came. Going by the ship's bucking motion, he was probably having to use both hands to do something to his thrust controls that would probably violate the warranty.

The Biskotti swarm was spreading across the port side of the ship's hull. They were just feet away from the seam of the exterior airlock door, and that distance was closing one Biskotti hand span at a time.

I let instinct take over and darted forwards, shoulder charging a wall of struggling yellow bodies. Instantly, tiny wrists shot out of the churning mass and fastened around my arms and legs.

For a brief moment, I saw Terrorgorn through a gap between someone's armpit and the crook of someone's knee. He was sitting calmly in a hollow space in the middle of the Biskotti swarm like it was a sedan chair made of bodies. He met my gaze, and gave the sort of tightlipped apologetic smile you give when you notice someone you vaguely know in the street but hope they don't want to stop and talk because you really can't be bothered.

Then the hands that held me in place tensed, and I was hurled back onto my arse. Looking up, I saw that the barely visible seam around the Hemingway's airlock door had become a thick black line that six or seven Biskotti hands had worked fingers into. A moment later, it flew open with a *chunk*.

The next few things happened so fast, I had to take time later to piece them together in my head. First, the Biskottis, along with Terrorgorn, boarded the ship. Their entire mass seemed to be sucked into the airlock like a plate of ramen into the mouth of a Ritsuko salaryman with only two minutes left in his lunch break.

After the airlock slammed shut again, the ship froze, then quivered madly in midair like an insect fighting a takeover by some kind of brain-eating fungus, then stopped. It bobbed daintily, then shot upwards through the station's force field. Within seconds, they had slalomed clumsily around the nearest debris field and disappeared from sight.

I aborted my attempt to stand up and fell back again on my arse, defeated, staring straight upward at nothing. I was alone on the landing pad with Davisham Derby, Malcolm Sturb, and the upturned *Neverdie*.

It was Derby who spoke first. "Well, that's one way to distract them," he said, with insincere optimism. "On to phase two?"

CHAPTER 23

WE SUDDENLY HAD the run of the now-deserted Biskot Central, cold comfort as that was, so I wordlessly picked up the portable Quantunnel gate from the *Neverdie*'s passenger cabin—pretending not to notice Henderson's body, now arched over the ceiling light—and carried it down to the recharge station in the concourse, laying it reverently like a funeral wreath. Sturb, who had been following me like a lost puppy throughout, took the hint and stepped forward, digging out his phone to set up a connection.

He gave a little cough to break the mournful silence. "Jimi, do you think you can reestablish the tunnel to the other gate?"

"Assessing," reported Jimi. "Checking for secondary gate. Found. Secondary gate is intact. Approximate location: Ritsuko City, Luna, Sol system."

"All right, well," began Sturb, self-consciously keeping his voice low in the station's deafening quiet. "At least things could be worse."

"Do we have a plan?" asked Derby skeptically. He had also followed me like a lost puppy, but from a greater distance, taking every opportunity to fold his arms and lean on whatever items of furniture were convenient.

"A plan," I repeated flatly. "Yes. The plan is, we get back to Ritsuko City, and then we find a nice flat rock to hide under until we're sure nothing is coming back to us."

"An elegant scheme," he said, spitting his words. "Dare I admit I'm fully behind it."

"But there has to be something we can . . ." began Sturb.

"Do?" I said witheringly. "Do what? Save the Hendersons?"

"We should tell Penelope. I must say I'm still not one hundred percent convinced that she sent those killers after us."

I stared at him with tired eyes. "How about we have a big, long, fruitful debate about that while we're lying low."

He grimaced. "But . . . what am I supposed to do? My whole life is at Salvation Station now. Where else can I go?"

Until that moment, I hadn't had an answer to that question, but looking into his anxious eyes caused an idea to hit me that, like the idea to use the portable Quantunnel, was mind-meltingly obvious in retrospect. "Cybernetics," I said to myself. "That's kind of like being a scientist, isn't it?"

He gave the kind of obnoxious wince that overly educated people use when talking down to anyone normal. "Um. I suppose you could say that. It's all STEM."

I wasn't sure what he was driveling about, but I pressed on. "I have an in with the Oniris Venture Company. I happen to know they're desperate for scientists to fill out their new crew rosters. Probably desperate enough to skip a few stages on the background check."

"Deep space recon?" said Sturb distastefully, but then his expression changed and his gaze traced a complicated path as he gave the matter serious thought. "That's not a bad idea, actually."

I leaned in, encouraged. "You said something about a supervillain support group. Do you think any of them would be interested? Are any of them scientists?"

"Yes, actually, quite a lot of them."

I nodded, completely unsurprised. My lifelong distrust of university education was justified yet again. I looked back at Davisham Derby. "What about you?"

He thrust his shoulders back. "What about me?"

"Are you gonna sign up as well?"

He jerked his nose upwards and to the side dramatically. "Davisham Derby is no—"

"Yes, we're all fully aware of what Davisham Derby is and is not," I interjected wearily. "The question is, what are *you*?"

There was a truly pathetic look on his face for all of half a second before he erased it and looked away, tightening his folded arms even further as if manually reinflating his chest. "I suppose . . . it will suffice as a hideout. Until adventure calls for Davisham Derby once again."

Something told me he'd finally made a breakthrough. I turned back to Sturb, who was adjusting the contours of the Quantunnel in accordance with Jimi's instructions. "Is it ready?"

"Deviation: point two nine millimeters," reported Jimi.

"Yes," translated Sturb. He jabbed the screen of his phone a few times. "It's about ready to open. Um. I should mention that this will light up on Ritsuko City's Quantunnel monitoring system, so as soon as we confirm it's safe, we'll need to run before the police arrive."

"That is an issue for *there*," said Derby. "For now, the primary concern is no longer being *here*."

"What if the police redirect the tunnel?" I asked Sturb.

"I'm still not entirely convinced that that technology exists. But I'll have Jimi monitor the connection and confirm we're heading to the same exit tunnel we used before. Also, if we look through it and see a prison cell, we could just, er, not go in."

"Right," I muttered.

Sturb pressed another button on his phone. "Could you both look away, please?"

I promptly covered my eyes and turned away, after which the Quantunnel gate made the telltale clicks and clangs of the metal frame aligning itself metaphysically with a different point in the spacetime continuum. I had to admit, having very recently hit my lowest emotional point, I was feeling more and more buoyed. We may have liberated Terrorgorn and left him free to enslave half the universe, but that still left a good fifty-fifty chance that our Oniris job placement would be in the other half.

"Huh," said Sturb uncertainly, which I took as the signal that I could look again. The Quantunnel had connected, but the metal frame now contained a rectangle of complete darkness. The illuminated signs that looked down upon the concourse did very little to shine light on the situation.

"Is that the meat freezer?" I peered in. "Did they really not move it?"

"Well, there would have been no reason to think it was important, after it was turned off," hazarded Sturb.

I activated the flashlight on my phone and poked it into the black rectangle. It wasn't the freezer. It wasn't a prison cell, either. The room was blandly decorated in beige walls and uncarpeted concrete, more like a storage room, which I supposed made sense. Although storage rooms, in my experience, were usually used to store something, and this one was empty.

Keeping myself tensed for action, I fed one leg into the room, then the other. There were no windows and only one door in the far wall, painted a sensible, industrial gray. This didn't feel like Henderson Tower. It did create the same uncanny sensation that I was walking into the open mouth of a Fylerean worm, but the surroundings weren't nearly ostentatious enough.

I turned around and shone my light over the wall behind me. As well as the metal frame that I had just emerged from, through which I could still see the cocked heads of Sturb and Derby silhouetted against electric signs, there were a number of other metal frames stuck to the wall of varying size and shape. All of them were empty, like I'd stumbled into an unfinished display room in an art gallery.

And finally, I realized where I was. "Oh, trac on a tracksuit," I commented, before diving toward the open Quantunnel.

A shutter slammed down from above just before I reached it, covering the wall of Quantunnel frames with impenetrable sheet metal and very nearly shearing off my face. At the same time, the ceiling light snapped on, drilling my tired eyes with a whiteness so bright that I fell to my knees as if taking a blow to the head.

A beat later, with perfect coordination, the door flew open and the room was very swiftly filled with men in gray shirts and black ties, the uniform of the Ritsuko City Police Department. A truncheon swept at my legs, which was apparently a part of the procedure that didn't account for me already being on my knees, so all it did was bruise my thighs a bit. Several pairs of hands firmly pushed my face to the floor, and I felt handcuffs snap onto my wrists.

The man in front of me was familiar, and only became more so as my gaze tracked up his black trousers to his substantial waistband, rumpled dress shirt, and dense black mustache.

"So which would you prefer?" asked Inspector Honda, bored. " 'Jacques McKeown, you're under arrest' or 'Dashford Pierce, you're under arrest'?"

CHAPTER 24

WHAT WITH RITSUKO City being the modern, progressive shining jewel in the crown of humanity's development, the holding cells in the city's main police precinct were actually relatively nice. I had a room to myself with a plumbed-in toilet and washbasin, and the bed even had a pillow. I'd been on some planets where the prisons were considered liberal and wishy-washy if only one of the walls was covered in rotating saw blades.

My cell was, nevertheless, inescapable. There wasn't so much a door as a six-inch-thick sheet of plexiglass making up the entirety of one of the walls, which slid up into the ceiling to let things in or out and must have weighed about as much as Frobisher's mum.

The cell was part of a ring of cells going around the perimeter of a large circular chamber, with a round guard station in the middle that was always manned by at least two officers, ensuring that the entire room could be kept under constant surveillance. Nothing was getting out of this jail without a supremely skilled lawyer or a medium-sized tactical nuke.

Still, considering the number of different groups and individuals that I had been and was currently being hunted by, there was something very anticlimactic about the local police finally being the ones to succeed. It was like a veteran wild-animal trainer coming home after a long day and getting nibbled to death by the cat.

I had been in the cell for a night and about half a day, and had spent most of the time staring at the floor, thinking. Some kind of jammer was blocking the signal from my tooth mic and ear speaker, but all I had to do was get out of here, and I could talk to Sturb again. Presumably he'd been smart enough not to try to follow me, and to shut the tunnel down on his end before the cops could bring the shutter back up, because I hadn't seen him or Derby being brought in to furnish the other cells. He'd probably know how to get hold of another portable Quantunnel so I could get back to Biskot and recover the *Neverdie*. And as long as I was fantasizing, maybe there'd be a beautiful woman waiting for me with armfuls of money and cake.

I was stirred from my contemplation by an irritating grinding sound, and looked up to see Inspector Honda casually walking toward my cell, dragging a metal folding chair that was leaving a thin trail in the cement floor behind him. He stopped about ten feet from my cell door and slowly opened the chair, getting momentarily confused by how the folding action worked. Then, after testing the seat with his hands, he settled into it, releasing a sigh like the cloud that flies up when a dying horse collapses onto dusty ground.

He rested there for some time, mouth still hanging open from the sigh, staring at me as if trying to place me in his memory. Then he sat forward and turned his attention to the paper bag he had been carrying in his other hand. He examined the contents the way a sleepy bear investigates a hastily abandoned picnic basket.

It was only after he'd taken a bite of his sushi sandwich and chewed it slowly for half a minute, keeping his eyes fixed on me, that he finally spoke. "Did you like our trap room?"

His voice was quiet and low, without a hint of expression. His eyelids drooped heavily, and he permanently looked like he was about to fall asleep. I answered him with a frown.

"Every time we find a new portable Quantunnel going around, we add it to the wall," he continued. "Me and some of the boys built the shutter over a couple of weekends. Works pretty well, doesn't it?"

Honda was playing a game that I didn't have the rules for, so I decided to start laying some cards of my own. "What am I being charged with?"

He gave a slightly baffled smile. "Well. The use of illegal Quantunnels, for a start. That's the easy one. That's the gimme." He produced some crumpled papers from his lunch bag, brushed off the crumbs, and peered at the writing. "Beyond that, it's a lucky dip, really. Assault. Conspiracy to assault. Armed robbery. Conspiracy to commit armed robbery. Kidnapping. Conspiracy to— just assume all of these have conspiracy as well. Damage to civic property. Oh yes, and fraud. That's the big one. Got a big asterisk next to that." He brushed the paper again, as if making sure the asterisk wasn't a crumb of nori. "A lot of that one hinges on you not really being Jacques McKeown, though." He looked up. "Speaking of which, are you really Jacques McKeown?"

I kept quiet and expressionless. I wasn't falling for this one. My dad had exhaustively drummed into me his three most important rules for modern living: don't tell the police more than you have to, always assume the back of your ship is ten feet longer than you think it is, and never underestimate how much trouble can be avoided by complimenting your wife's appearance.

" 'Cos if you aren't," continued Honda, "and you've accepted money for being Jacques McKeown, then I have to add another asterisk."

I said nothing, staring at the ceiling, feeling his soft eyes bore into me.

"I don't think you are him," he said, dropping a small bath bomb of dead seriousness into the otherwise calm pond of his voice. "Any more than you're Dashford Pierce, or Claude Hart, or . . . any of these other names." He was consulting his paper again. "Word of advice. If you're going to keep changing your identity, consider changing your ship, as well."

"Maybe I bought the ship," I tried, since my silence didn't seem to be helping. "From Dashford Pierce."

Honda nodded. "That's what I said. I said, maybe he just bought it from someone who happens to look exactly like him. In one of those special ways that leave no sign of any money changing hands. But the chief inspector shot me down on that. You know how people are. In any case, we know that you were on the ship when the ship in question was used to carry out a heist on Henderson Tower."

Considering the various parties that had been involved in that heist on both sides that far more richly deserved to be arrested than me, this treatment didn't feel fair. "Why are you picking on me? There was—"

He put up his hands. "I know! I know! That's the other thing I said to the chief inspector. There were much bigger fish involved in that, I said. Plus, he's a star pilot. He fights for justice in the galaxy. Sure, he bends the rules now and then, but if we had to arrest every star pilot who's done that, we'd never see the end of the bastards. You hungry?"

"Y-yes," I said, caught off guard, as my empty stomach jumped up from its despairing doze and started wagging its tail.

Honda addressed one of the desk officers. "Mitch? Could you go out and get us a couple of currywursts from Gunther's cart?"

Mitch glanced around, waiting for the punch line. "Er. No."

"Oh?" said Honda, disappointed. "Why not?"

"Because . . . his cart got flipped over by a flying concrete block on a tether? When that ship was flying down the street?"

Honda snapped his fingers. "That's right. I forgot. Poor Gunther. Will he get it back on insurance?"

Mitch sat up, realizing the role he had been assigned in this delightful little performance. "No. The company rejected his claim. They said it was 'ridiculous.'"

"Oh dear," said Honda, clicking his tongue. "He'll have to shut his business down. And him with three kids to feed. Tragic."

"Tragic," emphasized Mitch, nodding.

The pair of them turned their heads slowly to look at me, nodding in unison, both wearing exaggerated pouts. I stood up, tired of the game. "Do you know who was in that plying cryopod?" I said. Maybe the same appeal that had worked on Daniel Henderson would work here.

"I think we eventually bumbled our way into figuring that out," said Honda, looking through more papers.

"Right," I said. "So you understand how important it was to get him away from Henderson. And out of Ritsuko City."

"Well, let me speak for all of Ritsuko City when I express my gratitude for your courageous act of heroism," said Honda, getting up and taking a few slow steps toward me. "After all, our humble, fully equipped police force were doomed to fail where only a middle-aged space bum could succeed."

"Look—"

"No, you look." He hurled his sushi sandwich to the floor and injected enough sudden venom into his voice to instantly render me silent. "We've done some digging on you, since you made yourself so public. You've got a history going back even before Quantunneling. Smuggling. People trafficking. Nuclear-waste dumping. Did you know there's an entire colony of sentient ferrets on Pushka 5-Beta that are sterile because of you?"

I knew I should've picked a moon with less-cute inhabitants. I shook my head.

"You're the worst kind of star pilot," he pressed on, stepping closer still like a hunter stalking a wounded gazelle. "Throwing out some bullshit self-righteous philosophy while you tread all over innocent people's lives because giving a shit about anybody else is slightly less important to you than looking cool and devil-may-care. Well." He slapped his paperwork. "We've got enough on you already to keep you in a cell just like this one until Jacques McKeown books come back around to being fashionable."

By now, he was right up to the plexiglass. I looked down, and noticed that I had unconsciously sagged back down onto the bed. When I looked up, Honda was holding out a smartphone.

"Sorry." He had regained his sleepy, expressionless voice. "That's for me. I collect pictures of bad guys in the moment when they realize they're the bad guy. So. You were thinking about how you're going to wriggle out of this one?"

"No," I said, probably too quickly.

"Yeah, you were. Don't exhaust yourself. I've got a convenient wriggling-out package all nice and prepared for you." He dangled his papers in front of me, attempting to clean off a smear of soy sauce with the back of his hand. "This can all go away. It'd save me having to type it up over the weekend. You'll just have to help me out with something."

I replied with a mildly intrigued silence. Encouraged, Honda turned about and went back for his chair. I had to sit and wait as he noisily dragged it the ten or so feet to my cell door and plopped back into it, exhausted from the effort.

"You're a little fish, Dashford Pierce," he said, once he had his breath back. "You're a little fish swimming in the wake of a very big shark. Called Henderson."

My silence became a few notches more intrigued, but not for the reason Honda probably thought. It occurred to me that his intelligence on the state of the Henderson organization was almost certainly out of date.

"You're in with the Hendersons. They think you're Jacques McKeown," he continued. "I don't know what that kidnapping business was about, but I know Henderson isn't the kind of person who just lets things happen to him. I don't care what the big scam was, I just know you're in it and that means we can help each other out."

I gave a little cough. "So just to clarify," I said, not daring to let myself believe it. "You'll drop all the charges against me if I promise to help . . ." I took a moment to choose my words carefully. "Remove the Henderson problem?"

Honda's ever sleepy eyes narrowed even further. "Don't try to slip me up with language. *After* he's removed as a problem. Then you get your pardon."

I pretended to think about it. "I'm going to need this in writing."

There was a crash as a distant door flew open, and I saw two new figures striding across the circular room toward me. Honda jumped to his feet and gathered his hands behind him, visibly gritting his teeth.

The first new arrival was a broad man in a dark suit far too expensive and well tailored to belong to a police officer. He also had Japanese features and a haircut that had clearly been carefully chosen to be completely inoffensive to most demographics and pressure groups, so I assumed he was some kind of politician. "All right, stop whatever this is," he demanded as soon as he was in conversational range. "We've got his lawyer here."

The second person was a stately woman in a blouse and skirt, who was holding some paperwork out in front of her the way a vampire hunter holds a crucifix. "I am the lawyer representing Blasé Books," she stated, for her manner of speech could only be described as *stating*, never *saying*. "And whatever this is needs to stop."

"Mayor Sanshiro," said Honda in greeting. "How nice of you to visit. I was just asking Mr. McKeown to sign a couple of books for my daughter."

Sanshiro shook a meaty finger under Honda's nose as Honda politely leaned away from it. "I don't know what you're up to, Honda, but you can forget about it. Whatever was said before we got here doesn't count."

"I am a lawyer and anything my client said before my arrival must be disregarded," said the lawyer.

"Do you know how much Jacques McKeown has done for this city, Inspector?" asked Sanshiro.

Honda ran his gaze sluggishly across the papers he still had with him before answering. "Yeah, I have a pretty complete list of things he did to the city right here. Extensive damage to the tarmac of four major streets. Extensive—"

"Jacques McKeown fans from all over the galaxy come to this city to see the star pilots lined up at the spaceport!" boomed the mayor. "The hotels on those streets are already booked out for months with tourists wanting to see the damage! And perhaps you could do your job as a police inspector and inspect what the contents of that cryopod were?"

Honda gave a little grimace. "I apologize, Your Grace, please inform me what was in the cryopod."

"Terrorgorn himself!"

"Oh my goodness." Honda was expressionless. "How shortsighted of me not to have investigated that."

"Well, you should have done," huffed Sanshiro. "Now, please explain to us why you are holding Mr. McKeown prisoner when you should be shaking his hand and thanking him for his service to the people of this city?"

"I am a lawyer and my clients are requesting an explanation along the aforesaid lines," said the lawyer.

Honda let his head fall forward and shake back and forth, looking more and more like he was going to collapse into a narcoleptic coma at any moment. He squinted at me, blinking rapidly as if the light of my being had begun to dazzle him. "The thing is, Your Grace, I'm not entirely convinced that we are holding Jacques McKeown. I have reason to suspect this gentleman may have infiltrated Henderson's convention under false pretenses."

Sanshiro scoffed. He was very good at scoffing, he had exactly the right build for effectively drawing himself back as his powerful lungs barked their entire contents in disbelief. "Preposterous! We've got a lawyer here and she would know!"

"I am a lawyer and I can confirm that records show royalties for Jacques McKeown book sales being paid to this individual's account," said the lawyer.

"Is that right." Honda produced a ballpoint from his stained shirt pocket.

"Yes, and believe me, Honda, Blasé Books has the kind of money that doesn't make mistakes," said Sanshiro.

Honda added the promised asterisk to my list of charges. "Unfortunately, the civic destruction is something we are certain about, and it is still a crime."

"You can let it slide, can't you?" said Sanshiro. He turned to the lawyer, who pointedly swiveled her gaze elsewhere, not wishing to join him on this shakier ground.

"I could, if I had some kind of official order from the city council," said Honda nonchalantly. "Which I'm assuming you have, because I'm sure you wouldn't storm in here trying to muscle over my jurisdiction if you didn't."

Sanshiro sagged as the lawyer maintained silence and continued sweeping her gaze around the rest of the room, stopping just short of breaking into a casual whistle. The mayor of Ritsuko City didn't hold much actual power, since all government action needed to be debated and voted on by the city council. The mayor's main duty was to cut ribbons at opening ceremonies, because it was a position elected by popular vote, and as such couldn't be trusted with any responsibility.

"The council are debating it," he admitted. "But don't make any long plans for Mr. McKeown's stay, Honda. The council understands his value."

"Debating it, are they?" Honda straightened up. "I've always wanted to see a council debate. Perhaps I'll pop over for a visit. I've been working on a file for this case, and I'd love to get their opinion on it."

Sanshiro and I watched him amble slowly across the room, like a delinquent who'd been ordered out of class but was determined to draw their performance out as long as possible.

"I'm so sorry about this, Mr. McKeown," said Sanshiro, turning to me and wringing his hands. "I hope you won't judge your city's government by the way one representative treats such an eminent personage as yourself. But don't worry, we'll have you out of here as soon as possible."

"I am a lawyer," explained the lawyer.

I was still keeping quiet and expressionless, because I had the feeling that events were still developing in ways I didn't necessarily want to interrupt, but my eye was drawn to Honda. He had been stopped on his way to the exit by one of the desk officers, who now appeared to be showing him a video on their tablet.

When the video was over, Honda shifted his weight backwards, clutching his sides with his hands, apparently contemplating some new development. Then he resumed his walk to the exit with a much more determined gait, and pushed the door open a crack without attempting to pass through it.

He slammed the door closed again after being greeted by an explosion of camera shutters and flashbulbs, then took a moment to put his hands on his hips and think for a while, shaking his head. Then he ambled back toward my cell, neatly grabbing the tablet from the central desk as he passed it by.

"Sorry to interrupt, ladies and gents," he said, elbowing his way back into Sanshiro's expanding cloud of platitudes. "Something here you should probably be aware of." He held the tablet out.

On the screen, accessorized with the idents of every news media company that had gotten hold of the video, was the face of Terrorgorn. The camera was zoomed closely in on his insincere nervous half smile, but I could tell he was still wearing the clothes I had given him. I also recognized the color scheme of the decor behind him. He was on the main concourse of Salvation Station.

He let his natural menace exude for a few moments before opening his mouth to speak, but then his cheeks reddened and his mouth clamped shut again. He took a deliberate step back, and a Biskotti came into frame, apparently pushed there by several pairs of small yellow hands. It blinked rapidly in the spotlight, before sheer panic made it start talking.

"Er, we, the followers of Terrorgorn, have been brought by our wonderful leader to this, the palace of the Ancients," it squeaked. Their eyes began to glaze over in rapture. "We, the forgotten people of Biskot, will avenge ourselves upon the Ancients and the false deities of Speedstar for the crime of abandoning—"

"Hmmm," went Terrorgorn uncertainly. The spokes-Biskotti flinched in terror and snapped out of it.

"Um, yes, okay, relevant details," it stammered. "Our wonderful master demands that the chief peddler of the Ancients' insidious lies submit himself to our judgment." It looked worriedly to their left, and then the several pairs of small yellow hands came back in shot to push a paperback book into their hands.

"Trac. On. Toast," I muttered.

Obviously it was a Jacques McKeown book. Specifically, it was *Jacques McKeown and the Terror of Terrorgorn*, the particularly uncreatively titled volume in which Jacques McKeown gave a heavily fictionalized version of Terrorgorn what for. Published, notably, only after Terrorgorn's confirmed cryonic imprisonment and disappearance.

"Jacques McKeown," announced the Biskotti, holding the book too close to the camera so that the image became unfocused, "our leader Terrorgorn commands you to come to the place you know as Salvation Station and submit yourself to public judgment for your blasphemy against his divine name. We remember your ship, and if we detect any other ship approaching, or if we detect your ship and that more than one person is onboard, we will—"

"Ah-hm," coughed Terrorgorn, who up until this point had been nodding along with the speech.

The Biskotti looked to him, eyes bulging with fear. "My lord, I meant no disrespect! I was given such a small time to memorize the *blek*—" The sentence ended with a violent squawk as Terrorgorn's left eyebrow twitched and the Biskotti's neck instantly bent ninety degrees to the right.

A second, female, Biskotti was hustled in front of the camera, tripping lightly on the newly created corpse. She held up three fingers and counted off them. "We detect any other ship, we detect your ship with more than one person aboard, *or* we detect your ship with any kind of shield up that stops us detecting anything, we will shoot it down with this station's defenses." She looked to Terrorgorn, who gave a tiny nod, appeased. "Um. If you do not come here within five days, we will exterminate every Ancient on this station."

The camera tracked shakily across, first over a small mob of worried Biskottis, and then to a makeshift cage constructed from benches and pedestrian traffic barriers. The space inside was packed with the residents of Salvation Station, mostly star pilots of my acquaintance. Warden was there, tightly hugging herself, trying not to look scared.

Next to her was Robert Blaze, looking conspicuously healthy and not suffering from Ecru Death. His eyebrows were set low in an expression of stoic anger, and as the view tracked by, he looked directly into the camera lens and mouthed "don't."

I wondered who he was addressing. Blaze had once told me that he knew who Jacques McKeown really was, but refused to say anything more, out of respect for McKeown's apparent goal to keep the legends alive, plying stupid as that now seemed.

The camera returned to Terrorgorn and his spokes-Biskotti. Terrorgorn was leaning forward and the Biskotti was flinching, so I assumed he'd lightly poked her in the back to remind her of something. "Five days!" she reiterated loudly, before the feed abruptly ended.

It was swiftly replaced by an image of a newsreader, wearing the raised eyebrows, slight head tilt, and serious mouth of someone about to explain something extremely grave and life threatening that they personally don't need to worry about for a plying nanosecond. "If you've just joined us, the galaxy has been rocked by the news that Terrorgorn, the most prolific and violent force for evil in the entire history of the universe, has returned. This video, released online earlier today, indicates that Terrorgorn and his followers have taken over the star pilot refuge of Salvation Station and are calling for a final battle with his oldest nemesis, Jacques McKeown."

I wasn't sure I liked the way they referred to Salvation Station as a refuge. It made star pilots sound like a rare species of giraffe in need of conservation efforts.

"With Jacques McKeown himself also having recently revealed himself, and currently being held at Ritsuko City's police precinct facing charges of criminal damage committed during his recent daring heist, the universe asks one question." The newsreader leaned forward to give the camera the full force of their blazing eyes. "Will the greatest star pilot of them all take up the mantle once again?"

Honda turned off the tablet and let it drop to his side, then jerked a thumb behind him. "Not that I want to hurry anything, but there's about two hundred reporters outside who all have questions along basically the same lines."

Mayor Sanshiro looked to me with grave seriousness. "You let Terrorgorn get out?"

"No," I said through my teeth. "It was more like, he let himself get out."

Sanshiro bowed his head and planted his feet, clenched fists shaking with subdued emotion. "Mr. McKeown. Please. Don't go to that station. It's too risky."

"Um, okay," I said.

He didn't move. "I understand you must be feeling responsible for Terrorgorn getting loose again, but you're just one man. It'd be suicide. None of those people on Salvation Station would blame you. They knew the risks of living in unregulated space."

"Yeah, I agree."

His squared shoulders wobbled as he choked back an angry sob. He smashed the door controls next to my cell with a fist, and the plexiglass slid upwards. "Damn it, I won't be part of this madness! Ignore every warning and go play the hero, but you'll do it alone. Just remember this." He pointed a dramatic finger at my face. "Come back to us, Jacques McKeown. The universe will never forgive you if you don't."

"You are formally requested to come back to us," said the lawyer, choking back tears of her own. "I am a lawyer."

The two of them turned about and marched solemnly away without a backward glance. I watched Sanshiro open the exit door and put up his hands to abate the immediate barrage of camera flashes. I could just about see him beginning his spiel as the door closed behind them.

I looked to Honda, who was standing with his documents dangling loosely by his side, his head tilted, and his lips mashed together into a bemused pout.

"Aren't you going to close this door?" I suggested.

He chewed it over for a few moments, flicking his gaze around. "I could. Don't see the point. As we speak, you are executing your incredibly devious and heroic escape plan. I imagine any moment now you'll reach the trap room and use the portable Quantunnel to beam to an unknown destination, and there's nothing I or my officers can do about it." He pointed behind him. "In there. Follow the hall, second door on the left."

I gave him an exhausted look. "You can't make me. They can't make me do this. I'm not even Jacques McKeown."

"No, neither I nor they can make you do it," he said, nodding reasonably. "So your other option is to go to those people out there, tell them the opposite of whatever Mayor Sanshiro is telling them, that you're not Jacques McKeown and you're going to have to come back in here and start your lengthy jail sentence."

I hung my head, and raised one foot to step over the cell's threshold. "Second on the left?"

"Second on the left."

When I was ten yards away, I hesitated and looked back. "I don't suppose, during my daring escape, I was forced to tragically gun you down?"

"I think not," said Honda. "But I'm negotiable. I'm willing to go as high as being rendered unconscious from a blow to the head."

CHAPTER 25

FOUR DAYS LATER, the *Neverdie* completed the trebuchet jump to Salvation sector—knocking another handful of months off her operational lifespan, but I'd resolved to stop counting—and resumed occupying actual physical space. I leaned all my weight into the sticks until the stars stopped spinning madly around me like insects gathering to feed on a corpse.

I turned on the local scanner and it went through its usual routine of reporting everything from an incoming supernova to an entire battle fleet of rampaging Colossadroids before calming down and reporting actual reality. Salvation Station appeared as a little gray ring on the edge of detectable range, about half an hour's flight away. There were no other ships around.

I wasn't surprised. The pirate clans and hostile alien races of the Black had been effectively driven out of the area around Salvation thanks to the efforts of the station's residents, and those residents themselves were presently concerned with a hostage situation. Still, the loneliness did nothing to improve my mood as I closed the distance between the station and me. It would have been gratifying to at least draw a little crowd as I made the journey to my public execution.

The atmosphere became a lot more energetic as I entered Salvation Station's defensive range and my control bank lit up with warning readouts. In her new role as station administrator, Warden had done an excellent job of calling in old favors with weapon manufacturers, and all the results of her hard work were powering up and pointing directly at me.

I hurriedly slapped the communication system into life, scattering old coffee cups and crumbs with my flailing arm. "This is . . . Jacques McKeown,"

I declared, with faltering confidence. "There's no one else with me. Scan my ship."

I fancied I could feel the invisible probes running invasively across my ship. My skin felt hot and prickly where they passed through my body. Eventually, a high-pitched voice came through the speaker. "Are you armed?"

"No," I said, truthfully, as the empty space in my shoulder holster made my armpit itch.

"We'll scan you when you get here, so you had better not be," promised the speaker.

I let out a long sigh. By now, the giant broken bicycle bell of Salvation Station was filling the view screen, its cargo bay sneering open for me like the mouth of a Scalion chimpsnake. It had been a long time since I'd had to negotiate a ship through Salvation's contours, and I took it as slowly as I could, putting all my focus into each maneuver. Even so, the operation was over all too quickly.

There were numerous Biskottis waiting for me in the cargo bay, carpeting the surface with quivering yellow. It would have been the easiest thing in the universe to land a bit too quickly and pancake a good six or seven at once, but I didn't see it ultimately helping matters. I touched down slowly, giving them the chance to get out of the way.

After a few peaceful seconds, which was apparently the length of time it took to run a close-range scan over my ship and cockpit to confirm that I was unarmed, I heard hands scrabbling at the outside of my airlock door. I pulled the lever to remotely open it. Letting them force it open was another thing that I couldn't see ultimately helping matters.

I remained exactly where I was as I listened to the pitter-patter of little yellow feet, then closed my eyes and held out my arms as they burst into the cockpit.

That was my last chance for any dignity. Both my arms were seized and yanked in opposite directions, and I was pulled back and forth like a disputed rag doll until some wordless communication took place and both parties agreed to pull me backwards instead, hauling me over the backrest of the chair onto the floor.

My shoulder hit the metal grille with a jarring impact, but the Biskottis yanking on my arms weren't in the mood to let me stop for a quick massage. I tried to get my legs under me before they could pull me down the metal steps, but they really were in a hurry and shortly my back gained a new appreciation for the plight of laundry being pulled up and down a washboard. My ankle got caught on the external airlock door as I was being hauled through it, and the Biskottis collectively thought that the best approach would be to keep pulling until my ankle became twisted enough to fit.

At that point, I went with my usual instinct when caught in a losing brawl: I let my entire body go limp and waited for a chance to flee, unlikely as it seemed that any would come soon. The Biskottis seemed to have a natural gift for coordination, and the five tiny, fragile hands clutching my left arm were just as impossible to remove as the jaws of a Tinarian fangsheep.

I let them pull me along and took in the whirlwind sightseeing tour of the station. I noticed Daniel's ship in the landing bay, parked without landing legs at the end of a long skid mark. The hull was marked with circular scorches and bullet holes, so the station must have made some last-minute attempt to shoot it down as it landed.

I wondered why Warden hadn't ordered the station to blow it out of the sky the instant it came into range. It seemed unlikely that she wouldn't realize it was Daniel Henderson's ship. Then again, Daniel Henderson wasn't his father, and Warden's relationship with him was slightly more complex than immediate attempted murder. She acquired complex relationships with even greater ease than she did weaponry.

My pondering had to take a break after that, because a ringing blow to the head on the side of a door frame indicated to me that we had left the cargo bay. I admired the cheerful sight of spinning stars for a few moments before they drifted away and I discovered we were already on Salvation's main concourse.

A lot of the infrastructure had been stripped out, probably to be used as part of the makeshift cage that Blaze and the others were being held in, but the Biskottis hadn't had enough time to add much of their trademark religious graffiti. Most of the shops and stalls that lined both sides of the wide walkway were relatively unmolested, if deserted and sporting the occasional smashed window.

The exception was the souvenir shop that was directly across from the big Quantunnel gate, placed to immediately sucker in fresh tourists. Blaze's open-minded policy toward Jacques McKeown meant that it had been a veritable cathedral to his books and merchandise. It was completely sacked. Windows broken, stands smashed, the words DEATH TO THE ANCIENTS daubed across the front in multiple hands, and I could just about see a couple of Jacques McKeown cardboard cutouts in there hanging from the ceiling by their necks.

The mob of Biskottis slowed, and I felt myself being conveyed across their heads like a crowd surfer. Shortly the hands went away and I was unceremoniously dumped onto the floor, making my forehead crack ringingly against the tiles.

I lay there for a moment, enjoying the cool sensation of the floor against my face and acknowledging the little pains being registered by every part of my body. I slowly pushed myself up onto my hands and knees with all the haste of an overloaded cargo transporter trying to escape high-gravity orbit, but a sharp blow to the ear arrested my attempt to stand. I looked back and saw a row of five Biskottis, pointing spears made from Salvation Station–branded steak knives taped to the ends of mop handles. Any escape to the rear had been cut off.

In front of me was Terrorgorn's throne. In a prime example of panicky Biskotti logic, every chair, stool, and bench on the concourse had been thrown into a gigantic pile that reached halfway to the lofty ceiling. They'd even thrown in a few things that were only tangentially related to sitting, like the piles of discount underpants from the clothing stores being used to cushion the actual seat of the throne.

Terrorgorn was sitting on it, his knees held tightly together and his spindly fingers drumming on them. He offered me one of his uncomfortable half smiles.

In front of his throne was a row of Biskottis, all pointing guns straight at me. They were projectile guns, the kind that fired actual bullets, not blasters or stun beams. The kind of thing that's less concerned about cleanup and cauterization and more about making little unfeeling balls of blunt metal rip through the flesh and arteries of a thinking, feeling life form. Warden must have kitted out the station's security team on the cheap.

Warden herself was in the giant impromptu cage I'd seen before, a huge rounded shape just behind Terrorgorn's impromptu throne, like the shell to a trodden-on snail. She was at the front of the crowd of star pilots that had, until recently, been the station's entire staff and population, so she was still looking as out of place as a sex toy in a cucumber patch.

I followed the occasional worried glance she was making, and saw Daniel Henderson sitting on the floor just in front of her, staring at me through eyes as wide and frightened as his puffy bruises would allow. He was beaten up, but still in possession of all his parts, so Terrorgorn must still have been psyching himself up for the main atrocity.

After sitting on my calves for a few moments, taking in the scene, I saw some clamor rise up among the Biskottis, who had now more or less encircled the space. I saw Ic, the female Biskotti, take up position halfway up Terrorgorn's throne, puff out her chest, and prepare to speak. From the haggard look in her eyes, I could see that Terrorgorn had fully brainwashed her through his usual method of horrendous violence combined with his paralytically boring company.

Through her fear, I saw the disgust in the corners of her mouth when she looked at me. The devotion she had reserved for worshiping the Ancients had been efficiently turned the other way.

"Jacques McKeown," she announced, her small voice carrying well in the terrified silence of the hall. "As foremost representative of the Ancients and chief chronicler of their lies, you have been brought here to answer for their crimes against the divine adversary Terrorgorn, as well as the abandonment of their people. That is all right, isn't it?" She looked back at Terrorgorn worriedly.

"Yeah, it's fine," mumbled Terrorgorn.

"Yes." Ic turned back around and leveled a fiery glare at me. "It is fine."

I met Terrorgorn's gaze, which he almost immediately broke with an embarrassed smile. In that moment, bad at communicating as he was, I understood his angle. He wanted his revenge on Jacques McKeown for the book and on star pilots as a community for the whole cryonic-imprisonment thing, and he was going to get it through the Biskottis. I couldn't imagine the Biskottis having a terribly long life expectancy after that revenge was complete, even by their standards, but trying to talk down angry fanatics with rational argument is like trying to put out a fire by whipping it with dry straw.

"The Ancients," said Ic, her mouth curling with disgust around the words as if she were chewing a couple of rabbit turds. "Terrorgorn has enlightened us to their true nature. We are descended from their slaves, stolen from our ancestral homeland to serve in the Ancients' temple to themselves."

I had to wonder how long it had taken for Terrorgorn to communicate all of that to the Biskottis. I suspected it would have been the most lethal game of twenty questions ever played in the history of the universe.

Ic's pause for effect drew on until her lips started quivering too much to be kept closed any longer. "Do you deny this charge?"

"Look, the Ancients . . . star pilots never intended to be taken for gods," I said, settling back on my heels and putting my hands on my knees, as if I were dining at a traditional Japanese restaurant. "They didn't ask to be worshiped. They were just people. Like you. With longer lives and better technology. You all just . . . got them wrong."

From the grumbling all around me, I sensed I wasn't exactly getting the audience on my side. It was high-pitched Biskotti grumbling reminiscent of a cageful of puppies just before feeding time at the pet shop, but hostile nonetheless.

"*We* got them wrong. Immortal giants descend from the heavens and carry our people up to their glittering sky cities. They introduce them to their miraculous machines that convey them between the stars and produce food from thin air. And yet our ancestors were at fault for mistaking them for gods."

I opened my mouth and held up a finger, then I put the finger back down and closed my mouth.

"And then to abandon them," continued Ic, standing on tiptoe and staring madly into the middle distance as she worked herself into a proper religious froth. "To elevate them to your level, corrupt them with technology and lies, only to leave them to fend for themselves?! Is this how the Ancients treat all their subjects?"

"They weren't trying to elevate you! And you weren't their subjects!"

"Then we were slaves!"

"W—"

"*Confession!*" announced Ic, as one of the Biskottis behind me hit me across the side of the head with the flat of their steak knife. "The Ancients admit to the crime of slavery! We are the voices of the stolen generation! The Ancients are the adversary! Death to the Ancients! Praise Terrorgorn! Oh, praise him!" She interlaced her hands beside her face, eyes shining. The gathered Biskottis squealed and hopped up and down in excitement as a thin red line of pain throbbed across my ear and jaw.

"Look . . ." I said, composing myself.

"Silence!" cried Ic, still in something of a trance. Another spear swatted the other side of my face to give me a nice matching pair of red lines.

I pushed the spear away irritably and got to my feet before anyone could stop me. "Star pilots were heroes!" I declared loud enough to silence the raised voices of the Biskottis, which didn't actually take much; they all had lungs the size of ketchup packets. "Star pilots were the ones willing to risk everything to come out here and fight injustice when nobody else would. Sure, something went wrong here, but there are peoples like you all over the galaxy who are better off because of something a star pilot did!"

Terrorgorn recrossed his legs uncomfortably as he scrutinized Ic's reaction. Her eyes unglazed and focused on me through a curious frown, and she lowered her arms. "Other peoples like us? On other worlds?"

I considered clarifying that some of them were different colors and different sizes and that there was quite a broad range of limb arrangements, but I could only sense a small opening and it didn't have room for a biology lesson. "Yes! People like you. If they were being oppressed, or hunted, or hit by some natural disaster, and had nowhere else to turn, it was star pilots who came to help them."

"And what did the Ancients . . . the star pilots . . . get in return?"

"Nothing!" I said, taking a dynamic step forward to press the point. "They did it because it was the right thing to do."

Ic cast her gaze down, picking thoughtfully at the skin on the back of her wrist. "And they just wanted to do the right thing . . . because it felt good to do it?"

"Pretty much!"

Her gaze snapped back up to meet mine, and she rose back into her preacher stance. "Confession!" she yelled in triumph. "The Ancients confess to the crime of spreading their corruption to the innocent peoples of the universe for no reason other than their own sick gratification! May the executions commence! May the mighty seed of Terrorgorn rupture the hearts of the Ancients and germinate his offspring on a thousand worlds!"

A sharp swipe across the back of my legs sent me onto my knees again, and another blunt edge of a steak knife hit me across the back of the head, completing a continuous line of pain that wrapped my entire skull like a laurel wreath. Biskottis rushed to my sides and seized my arms, holding my torso perfectly vertical as the Biskottis with guns took aim for my heart.

I looked around. The Biskottis were in uproar. Robert Blaze and some of the star pilots were yanking at the "bars" of the cage, but Terrorgorn had built it too firmly. Terrorgorn himself was sitting forward, still drumming his fingers on his knees in anticipation.

In other words, I was the only one who was getting myself out of this. I opened my mouth, flicked the switch in my head, and let my subconscious figure this out on the fly.

"All right!" I shouted, again easily louder than the Biskotti mob. "You win! You want the truth? I'll tell you the truth."

The uproar died down, although my arms weren't released. Ic looked fearfully up at Terrorgorn, who replied with an unconcerned shrug. "Go on," she said.

"Star pilots . . . star pilots were people who went out into the Black because there was no one there to tell them what to do. They did some helping out. They were even important to the human race, because no one else could transport things through the Black, but they didn't do it to be helpful. If they did, they'd have stopped doing it the moment it was easier to do with Quantunnels. They did it to look good. I stopped. I stopped because I remembered . . . I couldn't remember why it was so important to me. So you can't execute me as a representative of star pilots because I'm not one. Not anymore."

Over the course of my statement my body sagged and the tone and volume of my voice slipped down from "defiant speech" to "reluctant admission of guilt." In the corner of my eye, I could see Robert Blaze clutching the bars of the cage, no longer pulling, and I didn't have the bottle to look directly at his face.

"For a while, recently," I continued, staring at the floor, "I thought I'd become one of the space villains, because if I wasn't a star pilot that's what I had to be, right? But that wasn't it. Space villains and star pilots . . . they're the same thing. They're all kids who got let out on the playground. Some of them wanted to be goodies and some of them wanted to be baddies, but none of them cared who got trodden on as long as they were having fun. And looking good."

Ic's brow was furrowed, genuinely thrown for a loop this time. "You . . . denounce your own kind?"

"I'm sick of it," I muttered. I'd let my entire body go limp, and now hung from my elbows like wet laundry on a line. "I was trying to get a real job."

Ic leaned forward. "But do you denounce the Ancients?"

"Yes, fine, I denounce them!" I snapped. "If that's what it takes."

She and Terrorgorn both narrowed their eyes in confused suspicion. "Then why are you still dressed like them?"

I looked down. Rather, I was already looking down, so I just refocused from the floor to my flight jacket. I'd zipped it up to the neck, as I tended to do during flight to ward off the cold created by a combination of the dreadful void of infinity and the *Neverdie's* dodgy air conditioning, so my view was the usual kaleidoscope of patches and stains. Each one carried its own story from the Golden Age of star piloting. I'd had to refresh some of the stains more than once, and incidentally, cyberserker hydraulic fluid is a real pain in the doints to import.

"It's just . . . a jacket. It's just a jacket for flying in." I swallowed. "It's a flight jacket."

"You are adorned in symbols of the Ancients' oppression," clarified Ic loftily. "Take it off."

The Biskottis holding my right arm suddenly released it, almost sending me flying into the Biskottis on my left like an elastic band. I brought my hand up to my jacket's zip, and held it there as it began to tremble. I looked to the star pilots in the cage, all wearing similar jackets. They were crowding against the bars, packed closely enough to resemble a patchwork quilt.

"What are you going to do with it?"

"Burn it," said Ic, as if this were the most obvious thing in the world.

I looked at my shaking hand. "But it's my jacket. I mean, it's just a jacket."

"Then you should have no trouble giving it to us," cooed Ic. "If you want us to believe that you truly denounce the Ancients and their ways."

I held the tag of the zip between my thumb and forefinger and squeezed until my knuckles turned white, but I couldn't bring myself to pull it down. I sensed the unhappy murmur of the Biskottis starting to build up again. "Hang on," I suggested.

Ic ascended to tiptoe again. "The corruption of the Ancients runs too deep," she announced. "The execution will begin."

The Biskottis grabbed my free arm and pulled it away, stretching my chest taut. The ones with guns straightened their rifle barrels again, and I felt a hot sting of anticipation in my chest where their sights had lined up.

"What if I ripped the sleeves up a bit?!" I cried.

The Biskottis opened fire. With their trademark excellent coordination, all of them hit the center of my chest with such accuracy that I thought I saw sparks from bullets bouncing off each other. A cry of outrage went up among the star pilots, and they hurled themselves against the bars of their cage with renewed vigor, but all of that seemed to fade away as I stared at the smoking ruin that was the front of my torso.

The Biskottis relaxed their grip on my arms, and I fell to my knees, then onto my face. One of the spear carriers behind me stepped forward, and as he thrust his weapon into my back and I heard the sound of fabric ripping, all I could think of was Frobisher, and how much he'd probably charge me for the repair job.

CHAPTER 26

FOUR DAYS PREVIOUSLY, I passed back through the portable Quantunnel gate by which I'd entered the Ritsuko police force's trap room, and found myself in the passenger cabin of the *Neverdie*. The dingy atmosphere was unmistakable, as was the increasingly potent stench of decomposing crime lord.

The first thing I detected after that was Malcolm Sturb, standing nearby with his hands over his eyes. This didn't surprise me, as I'd been talking to him through our miniature speakers for the last ten minutes. "Are you through?" he asked in stereo.

"Yeah."

"All right, just cover your eyes so I can close the link."

I did so, and a moment later the voice of Jimi piped up. "Quantunnel closed."

I looked back, and the only thing I could see through the Quantunnel frame was a section of bulkhead in dire need of polishing, just as any sensible person would expect. "Where's Derby?"

"He's in the cockpit, keeping watch."

"On what? Are there any Biskottis left on the station?"

"Um."

Something about that *um* gave me a sinking feeling. I cocked an ear, and noticed the telltale hum of the onboard air cyclers, which weren't necessary inside a station atmosphere.

"Oh, you brackets," I muttered. I reached for the shutter control, and discovered that there was nothing outside but space. Black, infinite, and as indifferent as ever to my feelings. "Did you steal my plying ship?"

"Well, I wouldn't say steal," Sturb said, standing beside me and examining the blackness as if trying to understand what I saw in it.

"Where are you taking her? What are you trying to do?"

"Ritsuko City." Sturb glanced about in a slightly overdone effort to avoid eye contact. "To answer the first question. And . . . to rescue you. To answer the second."

"Oh, sure," I snarked. "I'll bet you were gonna get right on top of that."

Sturb let out an exasperated huff and he took a tone that seemed unfamiliar to him. "Look, I really think you're being unreasonable, Captain. There was no other way off the station and the last we saw of you, you were being hauled off by police. What were we supposed to do?"

I glared at him and made some disgusted throat noises to put off having to actually answer his question. Finally, I said, "Did you sit in my chair?"

"Somebody may have sat in the chair, yes."

I darted up the steps two at a time and almost ran straight into Derby, who was standing in the cockpit hatchway. I shoved past him and took my seat, and the angle of my limbs and back instantly felt wrong. "Urgh. It's all plied up. I don't like it anymore."

"We know," said Derby dryly. "That's why we're signing up with Oniris, isn't it." When I gave his remark the silence it deserved, he gave a little harrumph. "All right. How did you escape? In the trade, getting away from Ritsuko police is known as 'easy mode,' but I'm professionally curious."

"I cut a deal," I said, checking the navigation computer to determine exactly where we were.

"Ah." He folded his arms and leaned on the rear wall. "Cheating on easy mode. Foolish of me to expect anything else, I suppose. Where are you taking us?"

I had keyed Salvation Station's coordinates into the navigation computer, and it was flashing up a short flight time. Evidently Derby and Sturb hadn't gotten too far from the Biskot system. "We're going to Salvation Station to confront Terrorgorn. That was the deal."

"What?" Derby asked. His tone was flat and abrupt, but there was a kernel of well-disguised terror hidden in the little dot of the question mark. "First you need to cheat to get through easy mode, now you want to go all the way up to hard mode?"

"As I said, it's part of the deal."

"Here's an interesting little fact that many people don't seem to realize," said Derby condescendingly. "Criminals don't have to do what the police tell them they have to do. Astounding as it sounds, it is actually the definition of the word *criminal*."

I finally looked at him, wishing as I did so that I could spit blood out of my eyes like a lizard. "Some of us want to go home at the end of all this. We're not all trying to run away from something. This is the deal. We sort out Terrorgorn, we're in the clear."

"I think we should do it, actually," said Sturb, who had quietly snuck into the background. "If Terrorgorn is at Salvation Station, I need to help bring him down. Salvation's all I have left."

Derby snorted. "Star pilots, space villains, you're all the same. Kids let out on a playground. You think you can all just stop and go home because Mummy called you in for dinner."

"Look, we probably couldn't have joined Oniris anyway with the police hunting for us," I said distractedly as I set the ship's new course. "Don't worry. It'll be easy. It's just one amoral, psychotic superbeing with an army of followers and powers none of us truly understand, how hard could it be."

The pointed silence that followed my rhetorical question eventually made the hairs on the back of my neck stick up. I slowed and stopped my labors at the console, then turned my chair around, not moving a muscle in my upper body. Shortly, I found myself staring right down the barrel of Derby's arm stump.

The lid was closed, but he was gripping his wrist with his other hand like a crazed gorilla, his thumb primed and ready to flip the lid open at any moment. "I do not recall signing a suicide pact."

"Mr. Derby . . ." said Sturb. Derby briefly trained his wrist on him and he threw his hands up in surrender.

"Both of you, stay where you are!" he commanded, taking a step back to keep a bead on both of us, although in the cramped cockpit he could only manage about six inches. "Hands off the controls."

"All right." I showed him my hands. "I've already set the course, so I don't actually need—"

"Hands on the controls! Stop this ship!"

I kept my hands where they were, with my thumbs almost going into my ears, but far enough away to create deniability. "What are you going to do,

Derby? Saw our heads off? Fly this ship to the nearest planet, maroon your-self, dress up in leaves, and eat pineapples for the rest of your life?"

"I am instructing you to stop the ship."

"I'm not going to do that."

He flicked his thumb, and the lid of his wrist device flew open. Sturb and I both flinched and recoiled, but nothing came out. I peered into the hole, and saw Nelly, sitting with her hands clasped together in front of her like a mournful newsreader.

"Hi," she offered.

Derby glared up his own wrist. "Nelly. I did left wink, right wink, blink. Don't tell me that doesn't mean—"

"It means the mini Taser, Uncle Dav, I know. I didn't bring it out because I don't think you should tase them."

He gave us an apologetic look, then turned away, bringing his wrist right up to his mouth, although he couldn't move nearly far enough away to prevent us hearing him. "Nelly, this operation hinges on your trusting my judgment on very short notice," he said in his normal voice, minus his upper-class affectation.

"I know, Uncle Dav, but I really think Oniris is a good opportunity for you, and I don't think you want to spoil that now."

"Nelly . . ."

"Also I already told everyone you're going to join Oniris. Uncle Ted's finding someone else to take the job at the fish shop."

Some of the color drained from his face. He looked at us—we both still had our hands up—as if wanting support from his audience, then turned back to his wrist. "You told Ted?"

"Yeah. He was really impressed."

Derby frowned. "He was?"

"Yeah. And Auntie Pru says she's really proud of you."

The color had come back to his face, leaving him with a little more than his usual level. "Prudence said that?" His gaze drifted off into a little reverie, until he accidentally caught my eye and shook himself out of his happy place. "Damn it, Nelly, it's Terrorgorn! We don't even have a plan!"

"I have a plan," I interjected casually.

He let his arms drop to his sides, and I heard his wrist tut in annoyance as Nelly was unexpectedly dropped from the conversation. "Do you indeed. Well. Why was I ever worried. The star pilot who planned to stop being a star pilot has a new plan for defeating the all-powerful avatar of galactic evil. By all means, tell. No, wait, let me guess: it ends with the phrase 'and then figure out the rest on the fly.'"

"He's not all-powerful. He's just . . . willing and able to kill us from across the room with barely any effort. But!" I added hastily as he opened his mouth. "But, we have one advantage, and it's a big one. All we have to do is press it as hard as we can before we lose the element of surprise."

"What advantage?" asked Sturb.

I managed to give him a knowing smile and a raised eyebrow through my ever draining supply of confidence. "He's invited Jacques McKeown, that is, me, to Salvation Station. Probably wants to put on a big satisfying show of defeating star pilots."

"Sounds plausible," conceded Derby, standing with arms folded again.

"He told me to get there within five days, and to come alone. Said that he'd shoot down any other ship that turns up. What does that tell you?"

My two colleagues exchanged glances. "That you're completely screwed?" said Derby.

"It means," I said patiently, emphasizing my words by making little gestures with my pinched fingers as if moving imaginary chess pieces into place, "that Terrorgorn believes that the only way to get to Salvation Station is by ship."

I watched Sturb's furrowed brow twitch as his eyes rolled back and he put the pieces together, then the penny dropped and his face unfurled like a window blind. "Oh. Oh! I see! It's so obvious, isn't it!"

"Of course it's obvious," said Derby quickly. "So obvious that it's hardly worth mentioning. So how do you propose we press the advantage that this obviously gets us?"

I came to his rescue. "Terrorgorn doesn't know about quantum tunnels."

"You see, he was frozen during the Golden Age, before they were invented," added Sturb. "And he's only been hanging around with Biskottis since then. Of course he doesn't know about Quantunneling."

"And if the crew of Salvation have any sense, they probably haven't clued him in, either," I said.

"Yes, as I said, it's obvious!" Derby pouted thoughtfully and his gaze tracked all across the ceiling as he considered it. "Hm. It certainly does present a significant surprise advantage, but how exactly do we use it?"

"We get close, we let him think he's won, then we hit him with as much as we can, from every angle he doesn't expect," I said, clenching a fist.

Derby raised an eyebrow. "And then?"

"And then . . . figure out the rest on the fly," I finished, throwing up my hands loosely in a weak little "ta-da" gesture.

Sturb loudly cleared his throat as Derby's eyes threatened to roll a full one hundred and eighty degrees. "Erm. How about this? We prioritize blinding him, the first chance we get. I'm pretty sure he can only use his powers on specific things if he can see them. See, I've read some of the reports they put together from going through surveillance footage . . ."

"Perfect," said Derby brightly. "So, we blindfold him, and then all he can do is snap the necks of every person in a two-mile radius."

"No, you see, a neck's not actually very big, and he'd need to be very precise to snap it," said Sturb, scratching the top of his head. "I suppose he'd still be able to . . . throw everyone around a bit."

Derby made a show of thinking, slowly letting his head rotate from one shoulder to the other, like the needle on a fuel indicator. "I feel I must say, gentlemen, that even with our obvious advantage in mind, I still wouldn't place our odds of surviving this plan on the optimistic side of suicidal."

"Then it's a good thing we have three or four days for you to figure out the fine details, isn't it," I said. "Sturb. Can you make a new portable Quantunnel gate?" I nodded my head vaguely in the direction of the stairs, down which lay the passenger cabin, inside which was one end of his hobbyist's Quantunnel set.

"Not legally . . ."

"Yeah, trust me, the cops are letting this slide from now on. Can you do it?"

"Yes, I can do it. I just need two frames with the same dimensions, made from the same material."

I bit my lip. "Can you make more? Different shapes and sizes? Assuming we might need to have more than one running at a time?"

He winced. Like the true tech specialist he was, he needed to take a moment to weigh the difficulty of the task against how much he could charge for it. "Prrrrobably." He drew out the word like a bout of constipation. "I'd need some more parts."

I switched on the local area scanner, and the debris field running through the Biskot system appeared as a symbolic sprinkling of pixie dust on the screen. "We salvage, we plan, we build what we need," I summarized. "Four days. Four days, and then we bite the floor tiles."

CHAPTER 27

FOUR DAYS LATER, I was biting the floor tiles in front of Terrorgorn and his mob, as the spear carrier behind me thrust his spear into the back of my jacket again and again, yodeling with delirious religious glee as he did so. After seventeen or eighteen stabs, he began to slow down when a couple of odd details apparently dawned on him. Firstly, there wasn't any blood leaking from the holes in my jacket. Secondly, the spear was passing through both my body and the floor with suspicious ease.

The crowd, which had been split between the triumphant cries of the Biskottis and the angry yelling from the star pilots, gradually began to quiet down as the same two revelations washed lazily across the assembly. Terrorgorn gave a little baffled frown, as one would when an aging, oft-used appliance refuses to turn on.

The Biskotti with the spear finally stopped stabbing, and decided to simply push his spear experimentally into my back as far as he could. Subsequently its entire length disappeared into the frayed hole in my flight jacket, followed by his hands and wrists.

I pushed my tongue against my teeth to reactivate the mic. "Phase two," I whispered.

The Biskotti was yanked off his feet as something grabbed his spear and pulled. He disappeared into my lower spinal region, and his terrified wail was cut off by the faint sound of something fleshy being clouted with a leather cosh.

The other spear carriers were clearly unsure what to make of all this, but a few of them were slowly advancing in short hops, waiting for someone else to take the lead and charge forward. Before any of them could, three small spherical objects were burped out of the hole in my back, all clattering to the floor and rolling in different directions.

Even from the floor I could feel the entire room instinctively tensing up with anticipation in the moment before the smoke grenades exploded.

Trac knows how Derby was able to squeeze so much smoke into such a small grenade, but it was certainly in a hurry to get out and stretch its legs. Within seconds, I, the crowd, and, most importantly, Terrorgorn were engulfed in a blanket of blinding white smoke. The Biskotti firing squad swiftly panicked and unloaded what remained of their bullets at the place where they had last seen me, but I had already scrambled to my feet and darted to the side so the bullets only hit walls, floor, and Biskottis.

I pulled off my shredded flight jacket. So far, things were going well. It was only sheer blind luck that the Biskottis had all aimed for my chest, where I was wearing a harness with an activated Quantunnel on both sides. Each about fourteen inches wide and a foot and a half tall, protecting as much of the torso as possible before it would've been obvious under the jacket. Still, it had left quite a few heart-achingly vulnerable spots. I had suggested another, smaller, triangular one to put down my jeans, but my two partners had vetoed that one.

"You guys all right?" I said quietly as I kept low and attempted to get my bearings in the smoke.

"A little more warning before the gunfire would have been appreciated," came Derby's reproachful voice, simultaneously coming from my chest and from a rented storage unit on the other side of the galaxy. "With what they did to these walls, I fear we've already lost the deposit."

"You ready for your part?"

His voice moved to the Quantunnel on my back. "Yes, let's decant a little professionalism into the situation."

It's a strange experience, having a full-grown man climb out of your back, even if that isn't technically what was happening. I can't say I recommend it. I could feel the straps of the harness shifting around like a backpack full of monkeys, and then I was almost bent over backwards when Derby briefly rested his entire weight on the Quantunnel's bottom edge, but the moment it lifted I heard the sound of sensible shoes slapping onto the tile floor as Derby scooted off about his own mission.

This done, I turned my attention to the wall of opaque smoke in front of me, currently containing one armed mob and one galactic scourge, both unaccounted for. Without warning, a Biskotti with an assault rifle stumbled into my two-foot visual range, coughing squeakily, and peered up at me. Its gaze focused, and its face looked like it was turning hostile in the brief moment before my foot got in the way and I kicked it back into the fog.

"Thermal goggles," I requested. I heard the sounds of panicky rummaging and items falling off shelves, then I recoiled in distaste as Sturb's pudgy hand emerged from my chest, clutching a pair of black goggles on a rubber strap. This was turning into the kind of experience that could give a guy body issues.

With the goggles on, my vision went from uniform gray to uniform blue decorated with red and yellow sprites panicking and fighting each other over whether they were fighting to get me or to get out. In contrast, there was a cooler, yellow-green figure sitting on a higher position just ahead. Terrorgorn didn't seem too animated, but I could see he was tapping the ends of his fingers together anxiously, not happy with events but not wanting to cause a fuss.

I was creeping up on his flank when I took a step forward and, to my alarm, the smoke disappeared instantly, exposing me to Terrorgorn and what members of his Biskotti security team had had the presence of mind to stay around him. I hopped back into the wall of smoke before I could be noticed by anyone with the will to pursue.

It was turning into a good day for the ongoing process of researching and fully divining the extent of Terrorgorn's abilities. He had pushed the smoke away from himself, creating a clear bubble about thirty feet across, which gave a pretty blatant indication of the maximum range at which his telekinetic powers worked. Fifteen feet didn't sound like much, but it was a tall order to sprint across it in the fraction of a second it would take for him to focus on my spine and snap it like a fast-food chopstick.

I edged carefully around the perimeter of Terrorgorn's circle of influence until the vague, featureless yellow-green blob reported by my goggles looked like it had its back to me. That was the obvious approach, but some of the armed Biskottis were here as well, protecting their new god. It would only take a second to alert Terrorgorn to my position, and the smoke looked like it was starting to dissipate. I silently cursed the efficiency of Salvation's air cyclers. I whispered "Derby" so quietly, I was practically just mouthing it, but it was enough for the tooth mic to pick up. "Status?"

The high-pitched whine in my ears, that I had, up to this point, been attributing to some nearby Biskotti in a state of weirdly continuous torment, suddenly stopped. "Status is, pausing briefly in the middle of my crucial task to acknowledge a dolt." The whine started up again.

"When you're done, I need some covering fire directed at Terrorgorn. Think you can manage that?"

"But of course," said Derby over the whine, which I had by now deduced was the sound of his largest power saw working against the metal bars of the giant cage. "I don't suppose any of you heroic star pilot types managed to secrete blasters about your persons, which you were planning to use the instant you saw an opening?" There was a faint rustling of flight jackets, and Derby clicked his tongue. "Ah. Only most of you, then."

The smoke had lifted enough that I could see the outlines of Terrorgorn and his protectors without the goggles, but before they could register my presence, a barrage of blaster shots from the opposite direction peppered Terrorgorn's position, stunning two Biskottis and sending them spinning through the air like fainting goats. The remaining guards bunched together into a protective wall between Terrorgorn and the newly liberated star pilot assault force. This had the additional effect of removing all obstacles between Terrorgorn and me.

My flight jacket was still in my hands. I wound the sleeves around my wrists and bobbed on my toes to psych myself up. This was the moment. I had to act before I had time to think about it and produce several compelling reasons to not do it. I sprinted forward, scaled the back side of Terrorgorn's throne with three nimble hops, then brought my flight jacket down on Terrorgorn's head.

The zip was facing me and the sleeves were either side of his skull, so when I pulled back, it was like I was trying to use the jacket to garrote his entire face. His skinny arms came up, index fingers upraised as if wanting to politely interrupt me to raise a small point, but I kept pulling the fabric taut, so eventually he gave a little sigh and began to use telekinesis.

I should have realized that covering his eyes with the jacket didn't so much prevent him from using his powers as prevent him from using his powers on anything but one specific thing—meaning, the jacket. A ball of force ballooned the fabric outwards, almost yanking my arms out of their sockets before I could plant my feet on Terrorgorn's shoulder blades and pull back with all of my strength. A second burst of kinetic force exploded from his head, nearly giving me whiplash.

I kicked myself forward and was able to get my arms around his skull, my legs around his chest. Different parts of my body shook as he tried to throw me off, but without vision he could only blast in random directions. "Sturb, now!" I said through gritted teeth, when Terrorgorn's head was practically halfway into my chest Quantunnel.

"Um. Right," said Sturb from the speaker, although I could faintly hear it coming from my chest, as well. "Look. I know I agreed to do this, but I think a lot of that was me being swept along in the enthusiasm everyone had for the plan, and I'm really actually not very comfortable with doing this at all."

One of Terrorgorn's eyes was briefly exposed as the hole in the back of my jacket shifted over it, and the ceiling light directly above us promptly exploded. I slammed one of my arms around the hole and redoubled my grip. "Sturb, for plying out loud!" I yelled as Terrorgorn managed to escape from my legs and send my entire body swinging like a loose pendulum.

The smoke had all but completely drifted away now, and the Biskottis could see Terrorgorn's plight, but most of them were too busy trying not to be outflanked by Robert Blaze and his star pilot crew as more and more of them escaped the hole Derby had made in the cage. One Biskotti made a token effort to come to Terrorgorn's rescue, but a random telekinetic blast knocked them over like a bowling pin.

"I just need you to promise me that you'll sign some kind of statement I can present at my next support group meeting."

"Yes! Fine!" I was being flung from one of Terrorgorn's shoulders to the other like a sack of laundry.

My arms came away from his head, but I managed to keep my grip on the sleeves of my jacket. At that moment, Terrorgorn's head managed to find the tear in the jacket's back, and with a terrible rending sound, the hole widened. The jacket plopped down around his shoulders as if I were merely helping him put on a sweater.

Now wearing my ruined jacket like a poncho, Terrorgorn slowly rotated around, then tilted his head down to examine me. He gave a confused little smile, as if I'd merely bumped into him on a packed monorail.

Sturb's hands emerged from the hole in my chest, followed by his arms, his head, and his shoulders. He reached up and plopped a curvy metal crown onto Terrorgorn's head, snatching his hands away as if from a hot stove as soon as it was in place. "Sorry," he whined, before falling back into my chest as if yanked by a bungee cord.

Terrorgorn continued smiling, rolling his eyes back to examine his new accessory. I stumbled back, missed my footing on Terrorgorn's pile of chairs, and fell all the way to the floor. The Quantunnel on my back hit the tiles with a metallic clang that sent painful echoes running through my shoulder blades.

I made to get up on my elbows, but was interrupted by a force like an invisible giant's foot pinning my entire upper torso to the ground. My arms were locked into place, outstretched either side of me in a crucifixion pose I hoped wasn't about to become appropriate. Above me, Terrorgorn cocked his head, admiring his own work.

"Strb," I managed, through a face that felt like it was pressed against an invisible window. "T's nt wrkng . . ."

"Yes, I, um . . . I haven't turned it on yet."

My attempt at a frustrated sigh turned into more of a squawking premature death rattle as further pressure pinned my head to one side. From this angle, I could see the small skirmish unfolding in the concourse. Robert Blaze's crew were gradually advancing along the concourse ring, taking cover in stalls and doorways, while the Biskottis were still trying to hold the line in front of Terrorgorn's throne. Their projectile weapons were more vicious, and they had the better accuracy and coordination, but they didn't have the cover, and the star pilots would have them outflanked soon enough.

All of which I put together after the fact. At the time, the only observations going through my head were that none of those selfish brackets were coming to help, and I was going to die any moment, and oh trac, oh God, I didn't want to die.

"Strrrrb . . ." I grunted as my nose was being ground into the tiles.

"All right! Yes, I know! I know I said I'd turn the slave crown on now, but I really don't think either of you properly appreciate what a massive cause of anxiety this is for me."

Derby, who was probably out in the concourse helping the star pilots, spat out a frustrated grunt. "Do you need me to come back in there and turn it on for you?"

"Nnngh," I offered.

"No, you don't need to do that, I just . . ." A few abortive squeaks emerged from the back of Sturb's throat before he found new words. "I signed a pledge that I'd never touch slave crowns again. Slave crowning people is evil."

My head was pulled an inch off the ground, and my neck, already turned to the side, began to rotate further. I caught a glimpse of Terrorgorn's dreamy smile before he directed my attention forcibly at the floor. I felt a crick in my neck that didn't seem like it was going to get any better.

"Sturb, would you consider it evil to smash someone's teeth in?" said Derby.

"Well . . . yes, I wouldn't want someone to do that to me."

"But what if your teeth had been glued together and your mouth was full of poison? Surely you would appreciate someone smashing your teeth in before the poison went down your throat."

"R's grt r prrnt," I added, as my field of view shifted another inch to the left.

"All I'm saying is, context matters more than following a strict interpretation of the law," said Derby. I would have been plying grateful if he'd made his point with shorter words.

I heard the sound of an expensive piece of electronics clattering onto a work surface. "Oh God, I pressed it," wailed Sturb. "I can't believe I pressed it. That was so bad of me."

The pressure that had been holding my entire body down instantly disappeared, giving me the wonderful sensation of floating on a cushion of air for a moment, unless it was the dopamine. I sat up and gripped my chin in both hands to make sure my neck was in order. Actually, Terrorgorn had done wonders for my usual stiffness.

Terrorgorn himself was still wearing the dreamy smile, but his eyes were wide and staring, the pupils wobbling in time with the flashing lights on the slave crown. He extended a shaking hand toward me, another index finger upraised to indicate that he wanted to politely interject something. "I . . . hm," he began. "Could you . . . hmm."

Two completely unprompted statements probably meant he was taking this very seriously. With his smile now frozen humorlessly in place, he lifted one foot into the air, lazily turned his body to face the crowd below him, then swung his entire torso like a sledgehammer, smashing his head on a nearby metal backrest with enough force to make every orifice in my body wince.

The clang of slave crown against seating device was loud enough to silence the skirmish taking place a short distance away. The stricken Biskottis, low on ammo and pinned down by blaster fire—nonlethal, of course, star pilots being what they were, but they didn't know that—looked back at their leader, and their already demoralized faces drooped another few inches.

Now with a full audience, Terrorgorn tried to right himself, or perhaps wind up for another blow, and ended up toppling right off his makeshift throne. His head struck the floor of the concourse like the clapper of a giant bell. I hurried around the pile of chairs and held him down before he could do any more damage to the slave crown.

It wasn't a fully functional slave crown, and couldn't force the wearer to follow instructions. It was a simple nerve dampener, designed to severely restrict the speed and extent of the subject's movements, along with Terrorgorn's psychokinetic abilities. The kind of thing Sturb was probably making in his high-school tech lab as a measure against the bullies he no doubt attracted.

Derby and I had spent several hours persuading Sturb to compromise on this, punctuated by the occasional long sulk in the bathroom. But now, holding Terrorgorn's limbs in place with my face six inches from his, I gained a full understanding of Sturb's reluctance to use the technology he had invented. Something about Terrorgorn's bloodshot eyes, and the way his muscles quivered as they fought the signals overpowering his nervous system, made me very queasy.

Finally, Terrorgorn gave in. A final burst of psychic energy did little more than make my ears pop, and he let his skinny limbs flop to the ground, exhausted, like overboiled frankfurters.

"Send a supervillain to catch a supervillain." I breathed heavily as I slowly released my grip and rose to a crouch.

"Can I just say, I resent that," said Sturb, like anyone cared.

Once I was satisfied that Terrorgorn wasn't about to jump up and shish kebab my doints with a single pointed finger, I surveyed the room, and the first person I saw was Ic. She was at the front of the battered mob of Biskottis, who had all ceased to fight their defensive battle, for the obvious reason that the subject of that defense was now lying stricken at my feet.

Ic looked at me. Then she looked at Terrorgorn. Then her gaze traveled back up to me.

"The Ancients have won the battle of the heavens," she reported, voice quavering with revelation. She threw out her arms wide. "Praise the Ancients! Oh, praise them!" Then she broke into a ceremonial dance of worship that seemed reminiscent of a waiter with two armloads of plates swaying their hips left and right as they attempted to navigate a packed canteen. The few Biskottis that joined in didn't really put their hearts into it.

Then Derby materialized from the misty atmosphere of relief that had descended upon the station. "I believe everyone is accounted for," he relayed. Securing the concourse had been the large part of his role in the plan. "Biskottis and star pilots alike."

"And plan B?"

"I believe we agreed to call it plan AB," Derby replied with a dry look. I refused to take the bait, and he quickly surrendered with a click of his tongue. "It's in place."

I nodded, briefly grinding my teeth in preparation for my next question. "What about Warden?"

"She's over there, with Blaze," he said, before hopping back out of my path, as one would after lighting a firework.

Warden was, indeed, talking to Blaze, as well as Daniel Henderson, the three of them surrounded by a crescent of victorious star pilots puffing their chests out at each other like a group of rival frogs. Warden appeared to be dressed identically to when I'd last seen her in the flesh, although she was exactly the kind of person who would own multiple versions of the same outfit, and with a single brush of the hand she was back to not having a hair out of place. This only made me angrier as I bore down like a yeti emerging from the woods.

"Oh, you!" exclaimed Robert Blaze when he saw me approach, a grin bisecting his leathery, careworn face like a zip fastener on a handbag. "Masterful. The way you pretended to denounce star pilots until you could take the upper hand? Masterful. You almost had me believing that was really how you felt!"

"Yeah," I said, not really listening, but keeping my eyes on Warden.

Daniel's face was still red and puffy from whatever treatment he'd received from the Biskottis, but now he was additionally colored with the blush of the truly in love. "Mr. McKeown, you . . . are . . . amazing . . ." he said, getting out words like blasts of air from a briefly released balloon.

I gave him a brief nod of acknowledgment, then smoothly transitioned it into a jerk of the head toward Warden. "You need to arrest her. She sent killers after us."

The numerous star pilots had been creating an excited bustle around us, but it faltered and drifted away to silence as my statement spoiled the party atmosphere. Warden gave me a scowl that could have stopped a charging Cantratic bonesaurus, while a little incredulous laugh puffed from Robert Blaze's lips. "What did you say?"

"We were attacked off the Biskot system as soon as we arrived by two star pilots," I elaborated. "And I think she sent them. Because she—"

Warden shifted a single inch to the left. A subtle movement, but its intended purpose was clear. It drew my attention to several of the star pilots in the group behind her, who were all wearing scowls identical to hers. "Did any of you go on an attack mission to Biskot recently?" she asked, not looking away from me.

"No, Miss Warden," said several of them, not quite in unison.

"None of us have, and therefore logic suggests that another explanation must exist," said one, coming right to Warden's side. I recognized him as the slightly older henchman of Warden's who had kidnapped me from Ritsuko City at the start of all this. His younger friend was noticeably absent.

"There, I'm sure it was all a misunderstanding," said Blaze, twinkling with charm. "You haven't spent as much time in the Black as the rest of us; it is still quite hard to tell the difference between pirates and true star pilots at first glance."

I was scrutinizing his face and tone for the slightest hint of insincerity, and found none. Robert Blaze at least was still entirely on the level, but it was clear that he wasn't holding the keys to power on Salvation Station anymore. I looked slowly and deliberately over Warden's goons before I replied. "I'm certainly getting that impression."

"I think the more important matter," said Warden, "is that of how Terrorgorn was released in the first place."

Blaze's face darkened. "Yes. Someone has a lot to answer for there." He noticed me and my carefully maintained lack of expression, and set to twinkling anew. "Don't you worry. We'll get to the bottom of whatever caused this. As long as Mr. Sturb's technology holds out, of . . . course . . ."

As his sentence faltered I followed his increasingly white-faced gaze, which had been directed at the part of the floor where Terrorgorn had been lying in a cybernetic stupor. It was, of course, now missing one Terrorgorn.

I jabbed two fingers to my earpiece so fast that it left dents in my earlobe. "Sturb! Turn the plying crown back on!"

"It *is* on."

A second look yielded no additional Terrorgorns. I stepped into the place where he was supposed to be in case he had an invisibility cloak, which I wouldn't have put past the bracket. Nothing. "Then why has Terrorgorn plying wandered off?!"

There was a moment of silence before Sturb spoke. "I thought we were clear on this?"

"Clear on what?!" I was already jogging along the concourse. Blaze, Warden, Daniel, and a small trail of followers were coming with me.

"It's not designed to totally paralyze him," said Sturb, with some reproach. "A massive electric shock could've done that. This was a little bit more sophisticated. It dampens psychic ability and higher thinking, but he can still move around in case he needs to feed himself or go to the toilet. It's inhumane, otherwise."

Under the circumstances, I was doing a very good job at staying calm. "You are the worst plying supervillain."

"Well good, actually. Good."

Daniel Henderson suddenly gave a little cry and pointed ahead of us. I caught a glimpse of Terrorgorn pink, topped with a flash of Malmind steel blue, disappearing through the archway that led to the hangar bay. "He's trying to get a ship," I realized.

"Well, there are plenty to choose from," said Blaze, panting. "Will he be able to take one without keys, or access codes?"

"He won't have to," I said, upgrading my jog to a run. There was only one ship in the hangar whose airlock was still open, there not having been an opportune moment to close it while I was being dragged to my trial by the Biskotti horde.

I rounded the archway just in time to see Terrorgorn pass through the airlock door of the *Neverdie* and disappear into the shadows within. I slowed to a stop, panting.

Daniel Henderson rushed up beside me, red faced. "Mr. McKeown! Terrorgorn's on your ship!"

"Yeah," I said, wincing.

"Aren't you going to go after him?!"

"Nah." I put my hands on my hips and shook my head, getting my breath back. "It's over."

"Don't give up now! There's still time!" He was getting overexcited. Flecks of spit were flying from his mouth and his feet were in constant motion, shifting through several inappropriate combat stances.

"You can't just let him take your ship, not while there's still a chance," said Blaze, running up in third place. "Terrorgorn with a ship is the entire galaxy's problem."

"Come on, Mr. McKeown!" cried Daniel. To my surprise and alarm, he pulled a blaster pistol out of his expensive imitation flight jacket. It didn't escape my notice that it was exactly the same model as mine, albeit brand new and with some added cosmetic chrome plating. The sort of thing that gun shops tend to upsell to naive buyers, and which don't do much more than reduce stability. "You're not past it, no matter what anyone says! Let's take down Terrorgorn!"

"Daniel, NO!" I shouted as he ran toward the open airlock.

"It's because of me that Terrorgorn escaped!" he cried over his shoulder. "I have to set things right! That's what star pilots doooooo . . ."

He kept the "ooo" going right up until he entered the airlock, and it faded rapidly after he disappeared from sight.

"Plying out loud." I ran after them before the second thoughts could set in.

CHAPTER 28

TWO DAYS PREVIOUSLY, the three of us were scouring the Biskotti debris field for the parts Sturb needed to manufacture new Quantunnel frames. With the autopilot and the external grapple controls, this was a task that Sturb could complete by himself, while Derby and I sat in the cabin, going over the fine details of the plan. Or rather, as Derby was persistently remind ing us, the lack of same.

"Forgive me if it seems like I'm belaboring this point," said Derby, in his bored, condescending tone that drove me up the plying wall. "But I still feel there are a few gaps in our plan."

I called toward the stairs. "Sturb, how are we doing? Need me to course correct?"

"No, the autopilot's handling things really well, actually," called Sturb from the cockpit. "Just need a few more organic transistors. Prostidroids are a good source. I'm checking the massage parlors."

"Great." I sighed. In other words, I had no excuse to stop talking to Derby. "Look. Of course there are gaps. We don't fully know what we're going to be dealing with on the station. So the gaps are the bits where we, you know, figure things out on the fly."

"We hide quantum tunnels under your jacket and use them as our trump card," summarized Derby. "What if someone shoots your legs? Or your head? How will you 'figure things out on the fly' with a hole in your skull?"

"I work well under pressure," I said patiently. "It's served me all right so far."

"We don't even know that Sturb's mind control technology will work on a being like Terrorgorn."

254   WILL DESTROY THE GALAXY FOR CASH

"Uh, yeah," interjected Sturb from upstairs. "That's something I've been meaning to talk to you guys about, actually."

"So what are you going to do if the crown doesn't work? Throw your shoes at him?" Derby clicked his tongue. "This is what I find so contemptible about star pilots. It's always figuring things out on the fly, making it up as you go. Then presenting that attitude as some kind of virtue, rather than the pure laziness that it is."

I chewed the inside of my mouth for a second, smarting from the dig. "All right. How would you suggest we plan for the things we can't plan for?"

Derby's wrist emitted a delicate cough. "I think what Uncle Dav means, is, maybe we could also think about a plan B?"

"We would need to complete plan A before we can add a plan B," said Derby. "What we need is a plan AB, if anything. We should at least consider what we're going to do if the slave crown isn't enough."

"Oh, are we going over the plan again?" said Sturb, descending the steps. "Great. I've got a few minutes while the grappler's bringing something in. So, just to go over the main points, the captain goes in there with Quantunnels under his jacket, and the moment he's close enough to Terrorgorn . . ."

"Assuming his head remains entirely unperforated at that point," added Derby, arms folded.

". . . we throw out a bunch of smoke bombs, and then the captain concentrates on keeping Terrorgorn blinded while Mr. Derby jumps out and secures the area."

"Then you slave crown Terrorgorn," I added, wishing to underline the point that much of the previous two days had been spent arguing over.

Sturb made a sickened grimace that I had lately become extremely familiar with. "Right. That thing."

"You're sure it'll work?" I asked.

He swallowed back a little wave of nausea, and slipped into the professional tone he used when he didn't want to dwell on his own thoughts. "It'll work. The fundamentals of synapses differ very little in sentient beings. It's one of the areas of least biological variance, alongside neck structure and eyebrows . . ."

"We were just saying," said Nelly, "maybe we should think about a backup plan?"

"Oh, do you think we need one?" Sturb dug his smartphone out. "Jimi, do you see any problems with the plan?"

"I have identified eight thousand four hundred and twelve potential scenarios in which unaccounted-for factors result in the failure of the plan and total fatalities," said Jimi cheerfully. "I have identified an additional one hundred and seventy-one thousand six hundred and fifty-eight scenarios in which only partial fatalities are suffered."

"But it *just might work*," muttered Derby, giving me a faintly accusing look.

"Okay, well," said Sturb hurriedly. "No reason to be discouraged."

"Would you like to hear my suggestion?" continued Jimi.

That gave me pause. It was the first time I had ever heard an AI actively prompt a response, rather than reply passively to requests. Then again, my experience with AIs was limited to basic autopilots and occasionally getting my smartphone to read aloud the lyrics to racy drinking songs, which somehow never ceased to be funny. "Okay?" I said.

"Terrorgorn fully or partially overpowering the effect of the slave crown is a potential factor occurring in approximately fifty-seven percent of my projections. Further projections indicate that Terrorgorn will either attempt to escape the station or kill all present. Creating a trap around an obvious point of escape would significantly increase the chances of success in the former case. In the latter case, death is certain, and no further amendments are necessary."

While Jimi was discussing our upcoming hideous violent deaths with less than what I would call a sympathetic tone, its intelligence was unsettling, and from the way Derby was exchanging slightly creeped-out looks with the inside of his wrist, I wasn't the only one feeling that way. Jimi was sounding less like a computer voice and more like a sentient being putting on a bad impression of a computer voice.

"And what's the obvious point of escape?" asked Derby guardedly.

"This ship. With the airlock facing the hangar door, open, and the engine on standby. Considering Terrorgorn's known psychological profile, he will take the obvious bait under stress. A quantum tunnel placed secretly just inside the airlock can be used to place Terrorgorn in a location that will pacify him. Davisham Derby can activate it while securing the concourse of Salvation Station."

"Okay, I'm onboard," I said, no pun intended. "So we use another Quantunnel in the *Neverdie*'s airlock to play the old 'cling film on the toilet seat' trick. And then we put the exit tunnel, where, in the middle of a sun?"

"Oh, it wouldn't survive in a sun," said Sturb, whose various extruding flab zones were vibrating with nervous excitement. "The alloy I'm using only has a melting point of around—"

"Yes, all right, I know; it's called thinking aloud, you doint," I said rapidly.

"No data exists on the effect of heat upon Terrorgorn," said Jimi, in the voice of a humorless primary school teacher explaining to me why it's a bad idea to stick crayons up my nose. "Data does exist on the effect of cold. Terrorgorn has previously been neutralized by cryonic suspension."

A brain wave occurred. Actually it had occurred some way into Jimi's statement, but only now could I get a word in edgeways. "There's an ice planet in this system. Biskot 9. Rudimentary atmosphere, so we won't depressurize the station. We drop the exit tunnel on there, Terrorgorn goes through, gets frozen. There we go. Plan B."

"Reassessing projected outcome. New most likely projected outcome: every person on Salvation Station dying of exposure."

I chewed on the inside of my mouth a bit more. "It was your plying idea."

"Furthermore, Terrorgorn would not enter the quantum tunnel if it obviously led to icy wasteland," continued Jimi patiently. "The tunnel must lead to a location sufficiently resembling the interior of this ship that Terrorgorn will be fooled for at least a short time."

Sturb thoughtfully reached over to the cabin shutters and parted them with two chubby fingers. "There're all kinds of old Speedstar station modules out there. One of the industrial outposts would look enough like a ship. We could tow it over to Biskot 9 and leave it on the surface."

"Measures would also be required to prevent the flash freezing of the station's interior the moment the planet's surface is exposed," said Jimi.

Sturb eyed the debris field. "Well, that's easy enough. The outpost'll have a force field generator for holding the atmosphere in. We could activate it before we crash it on the moon to keep most of the cold out, and then deactivate it remotely once Terrorgorn enters and we've shut the door behind him."

"This is turning plying complicated for a plan B," I complained, to the acknowledgment of no one.

"Reassessing projected outcome," said Jimi. "Likelihood of mission meeting parameters of success has increased by a significant percentage."

I gave Sturb's phone another suspicious look. As someone who still refused to use autopilot during takeoff or landing because it felt too much like cheating, taking Jimi's advice to this level wasn't sitting well with me.

"Of twenty-four percent," added Jimi, possibly sensing my unease.

I looked to Sturb. "You . . . created this AI, did you?"

"Yes. Well. Bits of it."

"Bits of it."

"It's open source." He waved his phone. "I am the only person with a smartphone that can run it. I modified it myself. See, the same micro-Quantunnels that allow the ansible function can also be used to create theoretically limitless processing power from—"

"Thank you, that clears everything up," I said loudly.

CHAPTER 29

TWO DAYS LATER, I passed through the Quantunnel frame that had been secretly placed just inside the *Neverdie's* external airlock door and into a Speedstar manufacturing facility on the surface of Biskot 9. I could hear the constant tinkling roar of Biskot 9's winds smashing shards of razor-sharp ice into the force field, but it seemed to be holding, even if it wasn't keeping all the warmth in.

We had been quite chuffed to find an industrial facility almost completely intact in the debris field. It was an old manufacturing unit set up to support multiple commercial stations by keeping them supplied with a constant flow of disposable plastic cutlery, napkins, and miniature shampoo bottles in a display of energy wastage that would have shamed a black hole.

It was also designed to be arranged confusingly, with several large factory modules connected by a somewhat labyrinthine network of corridors and miscellaneous infrastructure, partly to confuse OSHA inspectors. It would certainly pass for the interior of a ship for at least a minute or so, until Terrorgorn realized that he'd turned more corners than should reasonably exist.

That time was running out. I turned and made to close the *Neverdie's* external airlock, but paused when I saw Blaze and a small throng of star pilots standing around in Salvation Station's hangar like a pack of deck chairs waiting for arses.

"You don't have to do this alone . . ." began Robert Blaze.

"Oh, save the plying doint-waving-hero trac," I snarled, one hand on the airlock door handle. I noticed a figure to the side who, in contrast to the others, was standing with feet together and hands behind his back, wanting to look as uninvolved as possible. "Derby. Great. Fill these guys in on the plan, would you? I've got a doint to rescue."

"Very well," said Derby, as I resumed pulling the airlock door closed behind me. "Gentlemen. Allow me to explain the premise of what we eventually agreed to call 'plan AB' . . ."

The door clanged into place, and I turned my back on it to contemplate the corridor again. A strange feeling washed over me as I digested the preceding few moments and realized that I'd been infinitely happier to see Davisham Derby than Robert Blaze. Maybe I really had finally grown out of star piloting. Although the fact that I was presently risking my life to save another might have undermined that.

Something crunched under my foot as I took a step forward. A moment's examination revealed it to be a couple of mangled components from Terrorgorn's slave crown.

"Sturb," I said, addressing my chest. "Some bits came off the slave crown. Will it still be working?"

"Which bits?"

It was a fair-enough question, I just couldn't think how to answer it verbally. I knelt, gathered a few of the larger pieces, and held them in front of my torso as if offering a handful of food to a horse. Sturb leaned his pudgy head out of my chest to look. "Hm. I don't suppose you remember what that looked like before you stepped on it?"

We were wasting time. I shook the fragments out of my hand and let them tinkle back to the floor. "Never mind. Just pass me my gun."

"Oh, right." There was some clattering as Sturb fumbled around the various items scattered about the floor of the storage unit, and not for the first time, I wondered why we hadn't enlisted Nelly for this part of the job. Eventually, Sturb's hand and my blaster extruded as off-puttingly as ever from the center of my chest. "Here you go."

"Thanks." I took it by the grip, but Sturb didn't let go as I gently tugged.

"Not that I want to add on to the pressure you're under, but the generator powering the force field isn't going to hold out for very long."

"Are you going to tell me how long?"

"Twelve minutes, at most. When we were setting this up I was expecting we'd shut it off right after Terrorgorn went into it—"

"Great," I said, to cut him off. It was by now clear to me that his need to take every opportunity to have his voice be heard was probably some lingering habit from his supervillain days. I gave my gun another tug, but he was still holding on. "What else?"

"Do you mind if I get out of here?"

He finally let go of the gun, and turned his end of the Quantunnel upside down so we could talk face to face as I looked down at my chest. I think he thought it would make the conversation less awkward, which goes to show how overrated he was, as geniuses went.

"You what?"

"It's just, I feel like I can probably be most useful back on Salvation now. I can leave this Quantunnel on the floor so you can just reach in if you need any of this stuff . . ."

"You mean, you don't want to have to face Terrorgorn again, or be around if the force field goes down and this entire facility flash-freezes, including me and everything my Quantunnels are connected to."

"Well, let me just say, I would completely understand your position if you wanted me to—"

I cut him off by waving a hand. I didn't have the right to endanger him for the sake of whatever the hell I thought I was doing. "Yes, all right, just go."

"Thank you. Sorry. I, er. I think I'll go out your back."

An enormous weight was suddenly added to my harness and nearly gave me a back spasm before I sat down where I was and waited for Sturb to finish squeezing himself out like a bag of custard from a dog kennel. He scampered to the airlock door and returned to Salvation Station, offering me an encouraging thumbs-up before he slammed the door behind him.

I headed around the corner to a section of corridor with a porthole, through which I could see a small part of the facility ahead and a great deal of blank whiteness. We had activated the force field just before we had finished towing the facility into Biskot 9's gravitational pull, so it had survived reentry and planetfall largely unscathed, and was now sitting at the bottom of a gigantic, perfectly spherical crater in Biskot's frozen surface. Judging by the power of the blizzard that was still pounding on the force field, both the facility and the crater would be completely erased about half a minute after the power went out. I shivered.

I peered down the perfectly square corridor module to the next turn in the path, then looked out of the porthole again as the force field wavered with a brief brownout. It was entirely possible that it was already too late to rescue Daniel Henderson. If Terrorgorn had shaken off the effect of the slave crown, Daniel could already have been reduced to the thickness of a piece of paper and used to decorate one of the walls.

After a quick look back to gauge how long it would take to sprint to the exit, I decided to risk calling out. "DANIEL?" I shouted in the general direction of forward. "CAN YOU HEAR ME?"

Three seconds of silence, but for the distant ominous howling of wind. Then four. Then five. It couldn't be helped. There was no way to—

"Mr. McKeown?" came a worried, reedy voice from up ahead. "Your ship's really different to mine . . ."

Trac. There was still hope. "Daniel! You need to come here! Follow my voice!"

"Erm, I think I should maybe go," said Daniel, more quietly, addressing someone nearby. "Would it be all right if I . . . no? Okay. I think I'd better stay here, actually, Mr. McKeown!"

Double trac and calculus to boot. Terrorgorn was with him. I looked down and checked the readout on my blaster: fully charged. I suspected this meant it would in some way be taken off me very soon, but that was no reason to give up.

Daniel's voice was coming from a doorway in the next section of corridor marked with a knife-and-fork icon, which on this facility could equally mean a break room or one of the manufacturing centers. I took up position beside the doorway and peered around it.

Beyond was a large, perfectly square room filled with industrial machines for stamping out, cutting, and trimming molded plastic, all connected by conveyor belts and thick overhead pipes for housing cables and transporting raw materials, but there was an open space in the middle of the machine maze where Terrorgorn had made himself comfortable. He was sitting calmly on a bench intended for production line workers to lie on for their mandatory five-minute break, with hands by his sides and legs crossed. He was still wearing the slave crown, although it had been mangled by several more blunt impacts, and now resembled a shiny aluminium flat cap.

Daniel was sitting on the bench at right angles to Terrorgorn's, looking distinctly less comfortable. He was hunched forward with his arms wrapped around his stomach, and he grimaced sickly at me as I approached, gun drawn.

I stopped as the ceiling lights flickered ominously, and the wind became a notch louder. "Jimi's monitoring the power cell we used to get the force fields back up," said Sturb in my ear. "We're estimating about eight more minutes. Well. Probably closer to seven, now."

"Okay," I said, both in answer and to declare the final confrontation officially started. I waggled my blaster so that everyone could see and appreciate that the power dial was set to Solve All Immediate Problems. Terrorgorn gave me a pained smile, then looked away before he could accidentally make eye contact. "Daniel. Are you all right?"

"Erm." Daniel looked to Terrorgorn. "Am I all right?"

"Mm," said Terrorgorn.

"Yes, I'm all right."

"Okay," I repeated. There was no way of knowing what power level Terrorgorn was operating on, but the fact that I hadn't yet been divided into strips and fed through the nearest air vent was encouraging. I waggled my gun again. "Don't move, and this doesn't have to get nasty. I'm taking Daniel out of here, and you're staying exactly where you are."

"Hmmm." Terrorgorn winced and wrinkled his nose to indicate that he didn't entirely agree with my version of upcoming events.

Then I dropped my gun. I hadn't consciously wanted to do so, but the fingers of my right hand uncurled nevertheless, pulled by invisible telekinetic force. The trigger guard swung off my extended index finger, then fell off, and the blaster clattered to the metal floor. It was tough, always having to be right.

It felt like a tiny, slender hand had gripped each of my fingers individually and pulled them apart. They were still pulling, and I could feel them straining to snap the bones in my hand, but they couldn't muster the strength. I tried to crouch, to snatch the gun back with my other hand, but it was like moving through treacle, and shortly Terrorgorn had stretched out the rest of my fingers.

At the same time, my blaster crawled across the floor as if being conveyed by a helpful platoon of Tyrellian worker ants. It stopped at Terrorgorn's foot, and he bent down to pick it up, skinny arms shaking as he held it up in both hands. Apparently he didn't have enough telekinetic power to lift it, but that was small comfort.

"Five minutes left," said Sturb.

"You really think you can get away with this?" I blurted out, it being the first line of the usual script.

"Yeah," said Terrorgorn, nodding.

An awkward pause later, I tried again. "It's over, Terrorgorn. Your little game with the Biskottis is done. Salvation's safe. There's nothing you can get from holding us here, you might as well just let us go."

"Nah, I'm fine."

Another long pause. I coughed. "So that's it? At the end of all this, petty revenge? We both know you won't pull that trigger. It'd never be enough for someone like you."

"Nah, I'm fine."

I released a sigh, letting my arms flop down in defeat. This was unbearable. It was like being trapped in conversation at a wedding reception with a teenage cousin you've never plying met.

"Dude, come on," whined Daniel miserably. "You could just let us go. You don't have to be uncool about it. You can't do much with that thingy on your head, anyway."

Terrorgorn's power was reduced, but had apparently been diffused. I could feel every part of my body being lightly probed, seeking a weakness. I felt ill as my organs were jiggled experimentally, and lightheaded as my brain was pressed against the sides of my skull.

Terrorgorn's head was cocked to one side, considering Daniel's words. "Nah," he said finally. "I'm fine." Then he opened fire.

I saw it coming, from the way the veins in his arms bulged with the effort of squeezing the trigger, but moving out of the way was like pulling my legs out of a waist-high vat of half-melted marshmallow. I fell to my left as a white-hot ball of plasma roared past, banging my head ringingly on the edge of the nearest conveyor belt, which was a welcome distraction from the sensation of my right elbow getting caught by the edge of the blaster shot.

The moment I hit the floor, several ends of my body registered urgent complaints, overwhelming the command center in my mind. I inspected my elbow, and wished I hadn't. The sleeve of my T-shirt was burnt, and the straps holding my Quantunnels in place were a little warped, although the frames themselves were safe. I wondered briefly what would happen if you broke or reshaped the frame of an active Quantunnel, and concluded I probably didn't want to be between two of them when it happened.

All of which was distracting me nicely from the state of the flesh on my arm. I could just about see through the smoke that it looked like it would be more at home rotating slowly behind the counter of a kebab shop.

I forced myself to focus on Terrorgorn again, who had just about recovered from the heavy recoil and was about to fire a second shot. Instinctively I rolled to the side, passing under the conveyor belt into the maze of machinery surrounding the room's perimeter. I scrambled to my feet, almost brained myself on a low-hanging pipe, and leapt into cover behind an empty vat just as a second plasma ball utterly ruined the section of conveyor belt I'd recently disappeared under.

Now that I had broken Terrorgorn's line of sight, my body was fully under my control again, with the exception of my right arm, which dangled uselessly from the shoulder like a red vinyl stocking full of angry plums. It felt like I'd dunked the entire thing in a vat of liniment cream.

"Just under three minutes." Sturb's placid tone of voice was really starting to annoy.

Hugging my chosen piece of cover, I clenched every sphincter I had available and waited for the blaster to fire again, but it didn't. Instead, I heard what sounded like an altercation between two teenage girls slap fighting over their favorite boy band.

I risked a look around the empty vat, and saw that Daniel Henderson had grabbed both of Terrorgorn's wrists and was trying to wrestle the gun away from him. Terrorgorn was physically somewhat atrophied, but Daniel had the build of someone who got most of their exercise hammering out exclamation marks on their computer keyboard, and he was sweating copiously with the effort as Terrorgorn's uncomfortable face was pushed to the limits of passive aggression.

"Daniel?" I said, not entirely sure if I needed to intervene.

"It's cool, Mr. McKeown!" He gasped, digging in his heels and pulling harder. "I've got this!"

It was then that I realized, with instant foreboding, that Daniel was trying to get the barrel of the blaster under Terrorgorn's chin. I considered breaking cover and dashing over to stop him, but the gun was still a little too close to pointing at me for my liking. "No! Daniel, no!"

"It's cool! It's cool!" he grunted, like a mantra. Then he made a final burst of effort, pulled the barrel inwards a good six inches, and clumsily dragged the trigger down.

There was a fiery boom, a flash of pyrotechnics, and Terrorgorn, Daniel, and my smoking blaster all fell to the floor from different angles. I craned my neck out of cover, and saw that Terrorgorn's entire head had been reduced to an ugly streak of blood, brains, and leathery skin fragments that was still spreading from his burnt neck stump, and the slave crown was little more than a cloud of metal shards.

But only one of those two things was about to regenerate.

"Daniel, run!"

Daniel was sitting on the floor with knees drawn up and head bowed in the classic "thank God it's over" pose. He looked up. "What?"

"RUN!!"

"No, it's cool." He picked up one of Terrorgorn's arms and held up his limp form. "I shot his head off. Look."

It was too late. Terrorgorn's new head burst out from the narrow space between his shoulders like a parsnip being yanked from the ground. It was almost completely white, still greasy with mysterious bodily fluids, and as smooth as a billiard ball, lacking all the wrinkles and weathering of his previous head. It also had two pure black eyes, in each of which glittered a spark of befuddled annoyance.

In the next instant, Daniel was thrown off his feet by the full force of Terrorgorn's telekinetic power, and was stopped abruptly at the top of his arc, floating in midair in the center of the machine room. Then Terrorgorn flung him left, then right, creating musical *clong*s from his head making impact with hollow ceiling pipes, before slamming him to the ground and pinning his entire body down, flattening his legs and arms until he couldn't even twitch his fingers.

I had one foot on the nearest section of conveyor belt and was peering over the top of the empty vat. Terrorgorn had his back to me, but I could see Daniel over his shoulder, spread across the floor like so much AstroTurf. Terrorgorn slowly cocked his head to one side, and Daniel's neck began to mimic the motion, albeit in a much more exaggerated and considerably less survivable way.

"Erm, you've got one minute left before the flash freeze," said Sturb. "If you haven't started your climactic battle yet, it might be too late."

Thinking about this rationally, not to mention thinking about this in a stark terrified panic, clearly wasn't working out. I decided to let instinct take over. And no one could have been more surprised than I when instinct decided I was going to clamber on top of the vat and fling myself bodily at Terrorgorn. I had just enough air time to briefly touch base with every poor decision I'd ever made in life, and then my eyes instinctively closed the instant before impact.

I'd been shooting for something in the "wrestle them to the ground to buy Daniel enough time to escape" sort of area, but the next thing I felt was my chin making sharp, painful impact with the metal floor. I'd missed. Perfect. I can shoot down enemy star pilot ships easily enough whenever I'm specifically trying not to, but when it comes to bodychecking one stationary bracket from two feet away, that's just asking too much. I kept my eyes screwed shut as I waited for Terrorgorn to spin my neck like a merry-go-round.

When an entire two seconds passed without it happening, I risked opening one eye. Then two. All I could see was Daniel, picking himself off the floor in front of me and trying to manually uncrick his neck with both hands. Terrorgorn was nowhere to be seen.

"Where'd Terrorgorn go?" I hissed.

Daniel pointed a crooked index finger at me. "Um. He was right under there."

I looked down. The Quantunnel on the front of my chest was flush against the ground. I hadn't missed. I'd been dead on. Terrorgorn had passed straight through the Quantunnel like a winning basketball shot. The very moment I realized this, I felt something jog the edge of the Quantunnel on my back.

Instinct had been working out pretty well so far, so I let it take over again. I grabbed the back of my harness with my good hand and tore the damaged straps apart, almost dislocating my shoulder in the process, before slamming the rear Quantunnel face down on the floor next to the other, like a pair of recently buttered slices of toast. Then I pulled on the rest of the straps until I could detach myself from the front one.

"Twenty seconds!" said Sturb, his voice breaking slightly.

I gathered my feet under me and launched myself upright, smoothly grabbing my blaster with one hand and Daniel's shoulder with the other. "Now, we run."

He nodded, and after a tense moment when I had to manually rotate him when he started going the wrong way, we ran. Him first, me pushing him on with an arm outstretched. Behind us, I thought I heard something light and metallic moving, but it could just as easily have been the echoes of our feet slapping desperately against the metal floor.

We turned the first corner, then the second. The *Neverdie*'s airlock door was in sight, although the corridor leading to it suddenly seemed a lot plying longer than I remembered.

"Sturb, open the plying door!" I yelled to be heard over the clanking floor and Daniel's moist gibbering. "How long has the force field got?"

Ten yards to the door, I heard a sound rather like the short buzz a Vengarlian honeywasp makes as it gets squashed against a supersonic wind-screen, and the distant sound of howling wind became a lot less so. The temperature in the hallway started dropping instantly.

"That was it. I'm actually impressed I got as much as I did out of that generator. I had to replace parts of the coil transducers with scrunched-up chocolate wrappers—"

"SHUT UP!!" I roared, it feeling immensely satisfying to do so.

The floor was literally freezing beneath my feet. The Speedstar-branded tiles were turning blue white with a building crescendo of metallic crackles and pops. For the last few yards I felt my shoes losing traction, so I opted to use Daniel for balance and skidded the rest of the way.

A cold blast powerful enough to blow Frobisher's mum away from a buffet table went right up the back of my T-shirt, down all my extremities, and around my internal organs. Just as they started to lose function, I shoved Daniel with all my might, sending him flying into the airlock door with enough force to make his entire face two-dimensional. Fortunately, Sturb opened it just in time, and I fell straight through it onto Daniel, who it seems had opted to lie right where he was until someone explained what was going on.

The storm burst out into Salvation Station's hangar like the furious bellow of a caged beast. It took my entire body weight, combined with the body weight of Robert Blaze and several of his cronies, to get the door closed, and it still took long enough that everyone and everything in the room acquired a thin layer of frost.

"Jimi—" said Sturb, addressing his phone the instant the door mechanism clicked home.

"Decoupling quantum link," said Jimi, before any command could be issued. "Quantum link decoupled." Ice immediately stopped forming around the edges of the *Neverdie*'s airlock door.

"Wait, hang on." Daniel sat up. "What just . . . this is what?"

"There was a quantum tunnel over the ship entrance," I explained. "It was a trap for Terrorgorn."

"Yeah, yeah, I understand that, that's cool," said Daniel irritably. "But how was your ship on, like, an ice planet?"

I stared up at the *Neverdie* in silence for a few moments, listening to the calming sound of adrenaline still fizzing in my ears. "It wasn't. We went through a Quantunnel." I pulled the airlock open an inch and then, when I decisively wasn't being flash-frozen, the rest of the way. Beyond was the main hallway running through the center of my ship, just as it was supposed to be. I waved my hand at it like a magician gesturing over a seemingly ordinary hat.

"Oh, wow, it's different now." Daniel stepped into the airlock to look for the trick.

Robert Blaze stepped forward. "Is Terrorgorn . . ."

"Frozen solid on the surface of Biskot 9," I assured him. "Either that or frozen solid inside a storage unit that's currently connected to the surface of Biskot 9." I thought about this, then caught Derby's eye. "Should probably talk to the storage-unit people before they try to open that one up again."

"Indeed," said Derby grimly.

I checked around for Sturb, and saw him removing the pieces of Quantunnel frame from around the airlock door. He caught my gaze. "So . . . are we prepared to call this over? I'm thinking about it, and I'm pretty sure there aren't any individuals or organizations currently trying to kill us."

"No-o, there aren't," I said tentatively as I searched my memory. I noticed Warden standing in the hangar doorway, flanked by her henchmen. "Nor any with an obvious reason to start."

From inside my ship came an odd strangled noise, like a parrot trying to imitate the sound of a bicycle horn being trodden on. Sturb backed out of the *Neverdie*'s doorway, clutching the pieces of Quantunnel to his chest.

Daniel emerged from the airlock, staggering under the weight of his father's stiffened corpse. His jaw hung open in midsob, wobbling like a malfunctioning flush handle. He looked around the room, bewildered, his gaze pausing briefly on Warden, on Robert Blaze, and finally on me.

"Ah," I said, as several members of the congregation looked to me for something to say. "Forgot about that one."

CHAPTER 30

OVER THE COURSE of the next twenty-four hours, a strange atmosphere hung over Salvation Station. Everyone seemed to want to keep busy, while interacting with each other as little as possible.

This was largely because of Daniel, who spent most of the time standing in the hangar on his own, mouth set, eyes staring like two large-caliber bullets mounted on either side of his nose, watching a team from the station's engineering staff complete the repairs to his ship. There was something about the look in his eyes that made any conversation in his presence impossible. He wasn't just staring into space. Somewhere in the depths of his mind, intensive notes were being taken.

Mr. Henderson's body had been left alongside the small pile of fuel and supplies that were destined for Daniel's ship. Blaze had had the corpse wrapped in cloth Salvation Station banners out of respect, but after the smell had worsened he'd conceded to the whispered complaints of the workers and wrapped him in bin bags as well.

There had been plenty of work to chip in with. As well as repairing the damage Terrorgorn had done to the ships and to the station, there were the now extremely apologetic Biskottis to deal with. Several pilots were enlisted to ferry them back to their home planet, but not before they had been subjected to a series of informative seminars on space travel history and the importance of critical thinking.

That had been Warden's main responsibility, while I had concentrated on helping out with the ship repair . . . until the time came that Daniel's ship was ready to go, and when he didn't immediately move from his spot, some meaningful looks from the other pilots implied that it was my job to see him off.

I walked carefully up to his side, hands clasped behind my back. He blinked precisely once, which I decided to take as a gesture of acknowledgment.

"Well," I said. "I expect there are a lot of things you need to be getting on with back home." No response. "And I just want to say again how incredibly sorry I am, we all are, for what Terrorgorn did to your father." Still nothing. I rocked on my heels a few times. "It was a terrible thing to happen and I hope you don't feel responsible."

He blinked again, extremely slowly this time. It was like watching two portholes slowly closing and opening over a view of a catastrophic supernova. "It's all right," he said, without expression.

"Oh. Good."

"I understand now."

"Great! Understanding is important."

"I understand what you meant back there. Star pilots were never heroes like in your books."

"Er . . ."

"Real star pilots were just . . . people let out on the playground who didn't care whose lives they stepped all over." He finally met my gaze, and I leaned away, disturbed. "I'm going to change things, Mr. McKeown. I'm going to bring your vision back. I'm going to make star pilots into heroes again."

As he walked stiffly to the boarding ramp of his ship, I watched him go with a sense of unease. I wasn't about to shoot him in the back with my blaster just because of an odd hunch, but something told me that it wouldn't be long before I regretted not doing so.

When his ship took off, and no bits broke away as he passed through the one-way force field, I concluded that the repairs I'd assisted with were holding together, and turned to the hangar exit. At that moment, Warden stepped forward.

She was alone, and without her usual tablet, and had the look of a wallflower finally summoning the courage to sidle over and introduce themselves to their crush in the last five minutes of the dance. "Pierce."

For the second time in as many minutes, I was feeling a strange urge to spontaneously shoot someone. But the oddly vulnerable appearance she was presenting made me pause. I opted to merely give her a questioning look as my hand hovered near my holster, like a cowboy standing in the doorway of a pharmacy that he had mistaken for a saloon.

"I wish to apologize," she admitted, looking at her toes.

"Do you," I said, warily.

"As you may recall, I don't consider myself a good decision maker under extreme pressures. It was wrong of me to bring you into this situation the way I did, and I wish to apologize."

I sighed. It was difficult to maintain the energy for hatred, especially with a full stomach, my burns slowly recovering, and Daniel no longer bringing the mood of the place down. "I won't say 'no harm done.' I'm just happy we sorted it out before I had to kill more than one of your henchmen."

"I didn't specifically order anyone to shoot you down."

"I'm sure whatever you said was very legally airtight."

By now I had walked all the way onto the concourse in a none-too-subtle effort to indicate that I wasn't in the mood to talk, but she remained insistently by my side. "You know, I noticed you were assisting with the repairs. Have you rethought your decision not to join Salvation Station? It seems like a place where you fit in quite naturally."

I didn't slow my walking pace. "So I take it you're worried Henderson's death is going to bite you in the div."

Her walk became a notch stiffer. "Not just mine. All our divs. Robert Blaze's as well."

By now I was within visual range of the large Quantunnel that was the centerpiece of Salvation Station's concourse, around which a small crowd had gathered to prepare for the next scheduled connection to Ritsuko City. I slowed my pace and stopped, casting a gaze over the star pilots present. Some tall and wiry, some short and stocky, some in flight jackets, some in silvery jumpsuits, some human, some not so much, but all with one thing in common: I didn't feel kinship with any of them.

"No," I concluded, drawing the word out satisfyingly. "No, that's not going to work anymore. I don't belong here."

"Then where do you belong?"

On cue, I noticed Malcolm Sturb in the crowd, accompanied by Davisham Derby, and waved. Sturb hurried over eagerly, with Derby following in his usual manner, hands clasped behind his back and eyes directed elsewhere lest he fail to appear indifferent.

"Made the calls yet?" I asked, after glancing at Warden to make sure she was sticking around to eavesdrop.

"Oh yes," said Sturb. "The Mind Master's up for it. So is Doctor Kaos and Doctor Supernova. Professor Civious said he'd think about it, but right after he said that he put his necrolab up for public auction. I noticed because—"

I winced. "Just the four?"

"Well actually, Derby—"

"I have some paltry contacts in the fields of archaic engine-system research among my vast intergalactic network," interrupted Derby, taking a large stride forward and brushing imaginary dirt from his lapel. "I have enlisted a few individuals to ensure the success of our scheme to lie low amid the Oniris Venture Company."

"Yeah, it's a . . . great scheme, Uncle Dav," commented Derby's wrist.

"And also, I've already spoken to that lady from the recruitment office in Ritsuko," said Sturb, bobbing on his heels with excitement.

My face fell. "Loretta?"

He read my expression. "Oh, don't worry, I made sure she knew we were coming through you. She's really keen about all this and she said you'll have your pick of bridge crew positions."

"Okay," I said through a sigh of relief.

"Also, also," added Sturb testily, ever focused on getting to say everything he wanted to say. "She also said to tell you that she's going to blame you if the next ship ends up building doomsday machines on the edge of known space."

"O-kay," I repeated, with less confidence.

"Attention," came the voice of the bored star pilot in the hidden control booth who was operating the Quantunnels that day. "The Quantunnel to Ritsuko City will be opening shortly. All travelers to Ritsuko City, just, you know, get ready for it."

I took up the classic waiting-for-the-elevator pose, feet planted, hands behind back, gazing up at the Quantunnel's closed shutters like a baby bird waiting for a worm.

Behind my placid smile, my mind was racing, thinking about which bridge position to take. Captain was right out. I'd probably go with the helm, since it was closest to my main skill set, but the navigator might be the more relaxing, less responsible position. Then again, the navigator would have to take the helm in emergency situations, so there'd still be responsibility, and only when things were at their tracciest.

The Quantunnel shutter began to make the telltale signs of getting ready to open—vibrating, rattling, and occasionally halfheartedly clanging like the springs in a hotel mattress during a disappointing second honeymoon.

And then there was the *Neverdie*. It was safe for now in the hangar of Salvation Station; in fact, that was probably the place it was most likely to find a buyer. I was going to put it up for auction right alongside Professor Civious's necrolab. And even I was surprised by how undisturbed I was by the thought. The destruction of my flight jacket was already feeling like a great weight had been lifted from my shoulders.

Which reminded me: I had to invest in a new wardrobe once I had the proceeds from the *Neverdie*. Maybe a nice pea coat for those long, dull explorations of newly discovered ice moons . . .

The shutters rattled upwards, revealing the central concourse of Ritsuko City, and absolute bedlam, in that order.

The usual sampling of interstellar travelers and out-of-work star pilots trying to attract tourists had been shoved up against the far walls to allow for a thick mob of journalists and Jacques McKeown fans who were just barely being held back by a ring of riot officers armed with plexiglass shields and nightsticks. That was all I was able to make out before I was forced to shield my eyes from the flashbulbs. It was like being attacked by a swarm of radioactive fireflies from the swamps of Theda 8.

"Mr. McKeown!" cried a reporter.

"Over here, Captain McKeown!"

"Mr. McKeown, were you victorious in your final battle with Terrorgorn?"

"What?" I slurred, disoriented.

A figure emerged from the flashing lights to my right, a series of silhouetted blobs that gradually coalesced into Inspector Honda, tottering forward like he could just barely be bothered to do so. "Terrorgorn. How did it go?"

"Oh yeah. That's been sorted out." The flashbulbs paused momentarily. They were clearly expecting more. "He's back on ice."

I was deluged by a fresh outburst of questions, too loud and overlapping to be understood, so I just blinked repeatedly and kept my mouth shut.

As the pause between flashbulbs gradually expanded, I saw the integrity of the police barricade begin to break down. A couple of reporters had almost slipped through and gotten close before being grabbed and dragged back by their greasy ponytails. A few other, savvier, ones had escaped into

Salvation Station to point microphones at Robert Blaze and anyone else who happened to be around.

A small woman appeared before me, with her hair pulled back so tightly that she seemed to be physically incapable of blinking. "Mr. McKeown, I'm Emily, from Blasé Books? We've talked on the phone." She gave me approximately two nanoseconds to consult my memory. "We have some logistics that are really very important to discuss. You're due for another royalty payment and some really very interesting opportunities have—"

A very physically fit man wearing an expensive suit and a smile almost as wide as his shoulder pads materialized next, thrusting out a hand to shake. "Mr. McKeown! Tudge Burdinson. I represent Dreamweaver Pictures and, wow, we are just keen as hell to talk about a nineteen-film cinematic universe based on your books. We can set up a meeting just as soon as we get a signature on a few—"

"Out of the way!" commanded a voice louder and more experienced in public speaking than all the others. I saw Mayor Sanshiro violently shouldering his way through the crowd while it was still debating on whether it was going to part for him or not.

Eventually it spat him out like a cherry stone, and he staggered forward into the inner circle, where he suddenly remembered to pull his flushed features into a big smile to greet me. "Jacques McKeown. I would like to read a prepared statement from the Ritsuko City Council."

The hubbub grew silent, but for a few people asking if anyone knew what was going on and the subsequent shushing. Sanshiro grandly produced a rolled-up piece of expensive notepaper and held it vertically before him like a medieval herald bringing news of the battle.

"Jacques McKeown," he repeated needlessly. "We, as the elected representatives of the people of Ritsuko City, acknowledge your act of selfless courage and heroism that was the removal of Terrorgorn's body from our midst, and . . ." He read ahead a few lines, then switched to a whisper. "Did he defeat Terrorgorn?"

"Apparently," said Honda, bored.

"And defeating him once and for all," resumed Sanshiro in his announcing voice. "As enforcers of Ritsuko City's laws, we hereby issue a full and complete pardon for any crimes you may have committed during or related to the abovementioned act of heroism."

"Oh," I said as the flashbulbs started up again. "Um. Thanks."

Honda had sidled close and was squinting at the text of the document as Sanshiro proudly displayed it for all the cameras to see. "So that's the official pardon, is it?" he asked, with the tone of an uninterested tourist inspecting a museum piece.

"Yes, Honda, this is the one," hissed Sanshiro through his photogenic smile.

"I notice it's made out for someone called Jacques McKeown."

"What are you blithering about now? Of course it is!"

Honda produced a piece of paper of his own from his back pocket, this one sweaty, crumpled, and from a printer that was probably due for a new cartridge. "It's just, while we're in the mood, I've got a little prepared statement of my own." He mimicked Sanshiro's grand posture halfheartedly. " 'Frobisher. After I send this, I have to pretend to be Jacques McKeown . . . I'm sending you this to let you know that I'm totally, totally not really Jacques McKeown, and I'm just pretending to be to get one over on some of his stupid bracket fans.' Sent from the cockpit of the private vessel *Neverdie*, as registered by its owner, at that time known as Dashford Pierce."

"What?" barked Sanshiro, his expensive piece of notepaper crumpling in his two fists. "He didn't write that. You didn't write that, did you?"

"Do you deny that you authored this statement?" droned Honda, as if he were reading aloud an instruction manual for a new appliance.

Plying, plying Frobisher. I was willing to bet that he had thought showing that email to Honda had been doing me a favor; he was exactly that kind of inconveniently reliable. I subtly leaned into Honda's space, and tried to talk as quietly as possible without moving my lips. "How plausible would it be if I did?"

"Not very," he whispered in reply. "We can tie this email to your ID chip in . . . I stopped counting at forty-seven ways."

"Right." I leaned back, took a breath, flicked the little switch in my head, and spoke at full volume. "Yes, I wrote that. Of course I wrote that." I rolled my eyes like it was the most obvious thing in the world. "I was about to make a huge public appearance, and the last time I went public, all the star pilots, er, overreacted. A bit," I finished lamely, because I was only becoming more conscious of the dead silence, and the lack of flash photography. "I was nipping it in the bud."

The moment hung by a thread as Sanshiro stared with mouth agape and shoulders slouched, before he promptly straightened his posture and closed his mouth with a pop. "Of course! Nipping it in the bud. That just makes sense. Doesn't it make sense, Honda?"

"Perfectly," said Honda, disappointment writ large across his reasonable face. "Forethought is important. I often have to remind myself to think very hard and take a good long look around before continuing with what I'm doing."

I took a look around. Not surprisingly, a hostile atmosphere was brewing around the cluster of star pilots back in Salvation Station, with Robert Blaze at the head, his arms folded and head tilted forward like a disapproving nanny. Warden, meanwhile, was standing with the interested pose of someone watching a friend pick a fight in a crowded bar, body tensed and ready to flee at the first sign of danger to themselves.

Sturb had vanished, presumably because the presence of the police didn't mesh well with his whole "intergalactic fugitive" thing, but Derby was still there. He was wearing a very similar expression to Honda's: skeptical eyebrow up, mouth tight, wordlessly recommending caution.

"So just to confirm, just for the official record," said Honda with agonizing slowness. "You, the individual also known as Dashford Pierce, are Jacques McKeown, the author?"

Half an hour. All I had to do was not get arrested or lynched for half an hour, which was how long it would take to get to the Oniris recruitment office and sign up. After that it wouldn't matter how many doints thought I was Jacques McKeown unless the company filled the new ship's entire complement with autograph hunters. "Yes," I said, decisively.

Honda shifted his weight. "No take-backsies?"

"Yes, I think we've all heard quite enough of your conspiracy theories, Inspector." Sanshiro moved to my side and slapped a hand around my shoulder like an insecure boyfriend at a crowded party. He gestured to the assembled press. "All right, you lot, Jacques and I will be holding a proper conference in the spaceport convention room and you can get all your pictures and questions there. Move aside, please."

"Um, only if it doesn't take too long," I said as he began to propel me forwards. "I need to—"

"Yes, we have a really very important lunch meeting planned with Mr. Burdinson's people," said Emily from Blasé Books, appearing at my other side. "And after that, we need to sit down and go over some opportunities that are really very worth considering . . ."

Soon I was being carried inexorably along on a wave of human traffic. I tried to look back, to shout a message to Derby or Sturb, but I didn't see them amid the sea of faces, and respectful hands swiftly steered my shoulders back on track.

CHAPTER 31

THE NEWEST RECONNAISSANCE vessel of the Oniris Venture fleet, loaded with a full complement of former star pilots and evil scientists, was launched three months later. After being constructed in the sky directly above Ritsuko City, its hydrogen engines—boosted by a little something Davisham Derby had cooked up—flashed a brilliant blue as it sped off toward the nearest trebuchet gate, bound for the very edge of known space.

I watched them go from the balcony of my luxury penthouse apartment, propping my chin up with one hand. In the end, there hadn't been time to go to the recruitment office after the press conference, the lunch meeting, the afternoon-tea meeting, the dinner meeting, and the drinks that my publisher had decided were needed to celebrate the previous three meetings. And then, before the recruitment office could even open the following day, I was informed that the three-week signing tour of all Luna's colonies was about to start.

The Oniris ship was already nothing more than a twinkle amid a star field full of the brackets, but I was determined not to let it get me down. After all, a bunk on a deep space recon ship wouldn't have been as nice as this apartment. It was only the second-tallest building in Ritsuko City after Henderson Tower, but that just meant it was on the classier side of excessive.

I cast a look at the Henderson Tower, it being a prominent fixture of my new million-euroyen view. The spaceport on its roof had been lit up constantly for the last few days with a steady stream of ships coming and going. This was another thing I was determined not to think about.

I turned away, passing through the balcony doors back into the apartment. I grabbed a glass from the kitchenette to make myself another cocktail. It was still warm from the dishwasher and its contents would taste faintly of chemical cleaner, but I found that this gave me a pleasantly nostalgic feeling.

On the whole, things could certainly have been worse. This "living a lie" business had been easier than expected, so far. All I had to do was field the daily phone calls, agree to whatever the publisher thought was a good idea, and be as cagey and taciturn as possible while people wrote it off as the antisocial attitude of the auteur genius. Remembering of course to always be completely vague when asked about future works.

And the rewards were staggering. The lap of luxury, good eating, and a constant stream of money. As I sat on my crushed-leather couch in my fur-lined dressing gown, dug my toes into my thick-pile carpet, and sipped aged whiskey with subtle notes of bleach, I could feel that I was probably mere days away from starting to enjoy it.

My phone rang. I tilted my head back, let my mouthful of drink slide all the way down my throat to my gut, counted three more rings, then answered.

"Hi, Mr. McKeown, it's Emily. We've got New Dubai Radio on the line, are you up for an interview?"

"Sure," I said, without even token enthusiasm, but my other plans for the evening had consisted of mainly sitting around drinking myself numb. "What about?"

"The new book, of course! It came out this morning; didn't you get the comp copies?"

I glanced at the door. A rectangular box had indeed been delivered a couple of days ago and was still sitting on the welcome mat, but I had assumed it to be yet another round of reprint editions. Normally I'd want to read through it before I tried to bluff my way through an interview, but on this occasion, I was in the mood to be even more cagey and uninformative than usual. "Right. Put me through."

After some clicks, thumps, and a brief snatch of light jazz, I heard the voice of an aggressively energetic young person. "Hi, Jacques, I'm Raj, I'm producing the weekly review show on New Dubai Radio. In a moment the host, Phara, she'll introduce your book and we'll cue you in, okay?"

"Okay," I said flatly.

"Can I just say, big fan. Really liking the new direction."

"Okay," I repeated, wondering what he meant.

Another few moments of clicks and nondescript sounds and his voice was replaced by that of another aggressively energetic young person. ". . . And now, bit of a treat for all you highbrow-literature fans, we have the man himself on the line, Jacques McKeown. Jacques, welcome."

"Hi," I said, injecting what I felt was the right amount of self-important contempt.

Phara pressed on, unconcerned. "So, let's start with a brief summary of the plot. Interestingly, it's set in a more contemporary era, after the invention of Quantunneling, and our hero Jacques McKeown has fallen on hard times, selling day trips to tourists from Ritsuko City Spaceport."

"Yeah," I said, not really listening, but then my subconscious sounded the alarm. "What?"

"From there, he's enlisted by a mysterious femme fatale–like figure to chauffeur the son of a dangerous crime lord, and, well, I won't spoil the rest, but they end up going through all kinds of scrapes together. So, first of all, what was it that made you want to take such a dramatic change of tone?"

By now I was on my knees on the welcome mat, trying to rip the tape off the rectangular box. "Um, you know," I replied, flustered. "You've got to, er, grow up sooner or later, and all that . . . trac."

I finally opened the box, releasing the sharp odor of freshly printed books, and pulled out a copy of Jacques McKeown's latest. In contrast to his previous works, this one wasn't called *Jacques McKeown and the Div Disaster* or anything along those lines, but was simply entitled *I Know Who You Were*.

The cover depicted a star pilot, but instead of standing with legs wide enough apart to admit a Parchalian buffalo, hotties clinging to each leg, he was standing with his back to the viewer, gazing up at a huge, colorful star field that seemed to envelop him with its cosmic vastness. I couldn't help noticing that his cap and flight jacket were of types and colors very similar to the ones I used to wear.

"And many fans are already divided over the, er, tone of the ending," continued Phara. "It's certainly more downbeat than usual. Grimmer, maybe. Gorier, certainly. Are you at liberty to tell us if this really is the canonical death of Jacques McKeown? Spoiler warning."

I flicked through the pages, and after noticing a couple of standout references to the planet Cantrabargid and to Zoobs, I realized what the book's title meant. *I Know Who You Were*. It wasn't an avant-garde new direction for mainstream star pilot lit. It was the real Jacques McKeown finally making contact with the outside world.

He was sending a message. One that would be seen by billions, but was intended for the only person who understood it. Jacques McKeown knew who I was. And by the sound of it, he had an unpleasant fate in mind for me.

It eventually penetrated my thick coating of cold dread that the voice on the phone was waiting for a reply. "Uh, maybe," I stammered out. "I hope not."

"We all hope not," said Phara. "Now, a lot of readers have suggested you may have taken some inspiration from *Flowers Dying in Electric Lights* by Geranium Pleasant, arguably the original progenitor of star pilot literature. I believe we have her on the other line right now. Miss Pleasant?"

I braced myself. I had a feeling it was going to be a long publishing cycle.

ABOUT THE AUTHOR

Ben "Yahtzee" Croshaw is the sole creator of Zero Punctuation™, a popular weekly game review on the Webby Award–winning *Escapist* online magazine, for which he also earned the 2009 IT Journalism Award for Best Gaming Journalist. He was born and raised in the UK, emigrated to Australia, and then emigrated again to California. In his spare time he designs video games and emigrates.